A CHILD OF
FORTUNE

A CHILD OF FORTUNE

Caroline Gray

This first world edition published in Great Britain 1995 by
SEVERN HOUSE PUBLISHERS LTD of
9–15 High Street, Sutton, Surrey SM1 1DF.
First published in the USA 1996 by
SEVERN HOUSE PUBLISHERS INC of
595 Madison Avenue, New York, NY 10022.

British Library Cataloguing in Publication Data
Gray, Caroline
  Child of Fortune
  I. Title
  823.914 [F]

  ISBN 0-7278-4861-5

Typeset by Hewer Text Composition Services, Edinburgh.
Printed and bound in Great Britain by
T. J. Press (Padstow) Ltd, Padstow, Cornwall.

Author's Note:

I did not meet Cynthia Haslar until after the death of Alexandra Mayne, Countess d'Eboli. This was when I had received Alexandra's papers, and commenced work on her biography, as told in my book, A WOMAN OF HER TIME. Of course I knew that the Countess, in the years down to 1945, had been the most successful madame in Europe, and probably the world. As an aspiring writer, this did not make her any the less attractive to me.

I also knew that, having married the millionaire Spanish aristocrat Pedro d'Eboli, and inherited all of his wealth, she had largely retired from the purely commercial side of her business. However, retirement was never something to appeal to Alexandra, and thus she found it amusing to recruit various young women, as she had done during her more active life, and place them on the sexual market, at the very highest level. That this was also an extremely lucrative occupation was irrelevant, although Alexandra, never forgetting her own poverty-stricken early years, always required payment for her services, and those of her protégées.

When, in the course of my research into the book, I visited Eboli after Alexandra's death, I met several of these young women, and found them quite the most fascinating creatures it is possible to imagine. With one exception, they were totally loyal to their new mistress,

Alexandra'sdaughter Mayne, and would, and indeed did, carry out the most remarkable, and occasionally dangerous, assignments for her. The exception was Cynthia Haslar.

It is possible that Cynthia was a natural rebel; she was certainly a young woman who liked to do things her own way. Alexandra had undoubtedly recognised in her a kindred spirit, and had forgiven her a hundred transgressions of what might be called house rules. It helped, of course, that Cynthia was the most beautiful of all her women as well as the strongest personality.

Alexandra's daughter and successor was less tolerant, and Cynthia's life became more difficult following the old lady's death. I found the girl a delight to talk with, and now that she has emerged triumphant, as it were, I have managed to persuade her to tell me *her* story.

In some ways it is a sordid tale; a life of vice is hardly uplifting. Yet it is also an intensely exciting tale, and Cynthia invariably seems to have risen above her often horrendous circumstances. It is also a shocking story; Cynthia has lived the sort of life of which we only get glimpses in television newscasts or tabloid revelations.

In talking to me, Cynthia has left out nothing. And I have put down everything she has said.

Chapter One

Cynthia says: *"From quite an early age, perhaps as early as nine, I was certain I would one day find the means to leave my mother's house. I was definite about wanting to leave her. Any self-confidence I possessed arose not from the security of my relationship with her and my stepfather but from the comments and compliments other people paid me, and there were many of them. I grew up knowing I was different . . . special, attractive in a heart-stopping way, and while it made me fearful at times it also gave me courage."*

"What are you doing here?" James asked.

Cynthia turned a face streaked with blotchy red and her tear-filled, swollen eyes on her friend.

"You should be in school," James pointed out. He sat beside her, moved by her evident distress, and tugged playfully at her long golden plaits. "What's up then?"

"Billy beat me," Cynthia managed. "Really hard this time. I hate him! Why aren't you in school?"

"I'm poorly," replied James. "Mum said I could stay off." He looked hard at Cynthia. She was so beautiful, his beautiful friend, whom he was one day going to marry. Today she looked awful. "Why'd he do it?"

"A man I didn't know gave me chocolate. Mum saw him kiss me on the mouth. He asked me to thank

1

him properly, so I did. Billy was angry. He said I was a slut."

James put a consoling arm around Cynthia's shoulders. She untied the ribbons from her hair and removed her school blazer. "I'm not going to go to school today. I'll just sit here with you in the sun and rest. I'm glad he's not my real father because I . . . I wish he was dead!"

James could see her slender golden body through the thin white cotton of her school blouse. He took her hand protectively. When they were married, he would see to it that nobody ever hurt Cynthia again.

"When I grow up," Cynthia said, "I will kill somebody before I will allow them to hurt me."

Cynthia Haslar was eleven years old. She hardly remembered her father but she recalled vividly the day Billy had moved into the semi she and mum shared in the village above the Cornish seaport of Looe. Billy's coming had changed everything. There were nightly visits to her room for good-night cuddles that she despised; Billy's beery breath appalled her and the stubble on his chin grazed her cheeks. She had tried to love him as a father, as he obviously loved her, but she had failed. And then the beatings had started. Cynthia's mother, bound as she was by her gratitude to Billy, who was handsome and had money, refused to interfere – and Cynthia had begun to hate her too.

"I've got some money," James said. "Fancy an ice-cream cone?"

Cynthia smiled her enchanting smile at James and took his hand.

"You," she told him, "are my only friend."

Cynthia struggled into adolescence, fending off the blows from an increasingly possessive Billy. She had few friends

2

– the girls at school made fun of her burgeoning figure and teased her about her height – and no one in whom she could confide. She put her faith in James, her loyal companion, now a fifth former and a prefect.

Miriam Haslar encouraged James to visit her daughter at home. She provided cool drinks and biscuits and allowed them to play records in the lounge. One evening, Miriam had been called next door to a neighbour who had had a fall. James and Cynthia were left alone in the house. James had kissed her – properly – for the first time, and she had responded with evident pleasure. When Cynthia had broken away to giggle and smooth her hair from her face, James had lunged at her, breathing hard, a strange expression on his face. He had struggled with her, his hands beneath her skirt. Cynthia had not wanted to lose her virginity in this way; she was horrified.

"Stop it," she protested. "Get off! "James!" Cynthia had pummelled his chest with her fists, and had failed to hear the front door open and shut. When she looked up from the carpet where she had been pushed onto her back, it was into the furious face of an outraged Billy, whose roar of anger made her fear of James' determination pale into insignificance.

"I've been looking for an excuse to get my hands on you for a while now, girlie," shouted Billie, as James leapt to his feet and Cynthia tried to adjust her clothing. "I'm going to thrash you within an inch of your life, you filthy slut!"

An icy fury settled deep in Cynthia's soul. She looked at her stepfather, as if for the first time. Billy, she saw, was smiling. "Go to your room," Billy told her, rubbing his palms in anticipation and ignoring James, who had left quietly through the French window. "I'll deal with you later."

*   *   *

3

There was a main road only a mile from the village. Cynthia, with the folded notes from Mummy's wallet in her jeans pocket, pulled her duffel coat closer around her and made for this, across the fields. In her sports bag she had hastily packed some changes of clothing and her teddy bear, so it was relatively light to carry – and her heart sang. She had little idea of what she was going to do, but London, and its myriad possibilities, beckoned. She would find a job, a small apartment . . . a new life.

Women drivers scowled at her as she stood on the roadside with her thumb out. She knew it would be a man that would eventually pick her up; she was prepared for that, having grown accustomed to the appreciative stares of men wherever she went these days.

"Where are you going?" The man peered up at her face from the driver's seat window. He was, she estimated, in his mid-thirties; nice looking, balding, with friendly brown eyes. "I'm Robert," he told her, as she climbed into the car. "You want to be careful hitching alone these days. Not afraid?"

"A little," Cynthia admitted. "But I need to get to London."

"You running away?"

"Yes," she said. "From my boyfriend."

"Ah." He digested this. "Friends in London, eh?"

"Yes, but I'm not sure they'll be in. I couldn't let them know I was coming."

"Quite. Roughed you up did he? Your boyfriend?"

"He, um, threatened to."

"Bastard. How old are you?"

Cynthia lied. "Eighteen," she said, knowing that she easily looked it.

"We have quite a drive ahead of us. Just settle back and enjoy, OK?"

*　　*　　*

4

Cynthia did enjoy her drive with Robert. She was growing excited as the prospect of being in London on her own became more of a mental reality.

"Know the city well do you?" Robert asked, after he had bought her a Coke and a packet of crisps.

"Oh, yes."

"That's good. My route is around Marble Arch, across Charing Cross Bridge and then on south of the river to Hammersmith. That suit you?"

"You could drop me at the bridge."

"I could," he said thoughtfully, and suddenly pulled off the road into a layby. An empty layby.

"What are you doing?" she said nervously. "I should warn you that I do karate."

"Is that a fact? I figure you know as much about karate as you do about London. Tell me, how did Hammersmith get south of the river and how did Charing Cross suddenly develop a bridge and why on earth should I wish to make a detour round Marble Arch to get south of the Thames?"

Cynthia reached for the door handle. "Don't be a fool. I'm not going to hurt you. But I might be able to help you, if you would try telling the truth."

She was close to tears. Her heart pounded in her ears. "OK. The truth? I'm running away. I don't know London. I don't know anyone there. But I have no money and I am not going back home. I need to find a job."

Robert moved towards her on the seat of the car and put an arm around her shoulders. She allowed the tears to fall and rested her head on his broad shoulder. He smelled nice and reassuring.

"You come with me, huh? I'll take care of you tonight. Come to my flat. You'll be alright with me. Just until you get settled."

*　　*　　*

5

Inside Robert's apartment in central London his attitude towards her swiftly changed. He couldn't believe his luck. He had captive a truly beautiful girl of eighteen; she was calm and smiling and didn't appear to mind what was coming either. In fact, he was willing to bet she was as eager for it as he was.

Cynthia says: "*I suppose I went into business in a kind of defiant anger against the world. I wouldn't have chosen Robert as my first lover but, suddenly being in an intimate situation with an older man, sex seemed inevitable and, instinctively, it appeared to me a kind of passport to where I wanted to be in life. Besides, he'd taken me to where I wanted to be and I was grateful.*"

Robert gave her a whisky sour and suggested she have a shower. When she emerged, glowing from the warmth of the water and fragrant with his wife's talcum powder, he thought her the most exquisitely lovely creature he had ever laid eyes on. The way he looked at her, his sudden intake of breath, the way his eyes glazed over and he reached for her with evident loss of control, imbued Cynthia with a sense of power she had never before experienced. She was, instantly, heady with it.

"Do you," she asked, "want me?"

"This has got to be the luckiest day of my life," Robert said.

But not necessarily of mine, Cynthia reflected. She stood beside the bed and his hand moved up her thighs and over her buttocks, then up to caress her breasts, then down to stroke her pubic hair. To her relief his touch was gentle. "What do you want me to do?"

"Undress me."

Cynthia crawled on to the bed and lay down beside

6

him. He turned on his side to caress her and kiss her. "Just relax," he said. "You're going to love every minute of it."

It wasn't half as painful as Mummy had said it would be, and it was over before she remembered that he hadn't worn anything to protect her from pregnancy. If she was now pregnant on top of everything else . . .

"Good, eh?" he asked.

"Terrific," she said, faintly.

He got up. "Can you cook?"

"Yes."

"Then cook." He went into the lounge, still naked, and still unwashed. Cynthia certainly wanted to wash, and as there was no bidet, she was forced to sit in the basin. Then she opened her sports bag . . . but she hadn't packed a dressing gown. It hadn't seemed to go with running away.

"You got a problem?" He was standing in the doorway, a glass in each hand.

"Just wondering what to wear."

"You don't wear anything. I want to look at you. Drink."

It was another whisky sour. The first one hadn't had all that effect, but this one seemed to hit the spot at the first sip. "I'm going to be out in a moment," she told him. "I've nothing in my stomach."

"So cook us something." Cynthia went into the kitchen and scrambled eggs. There was a toaster, so that was no problem. "Shit!" Robert commented. "I was looking for something exotic."

"Aren't I exotic enough?" Cynthia asked. The whisky was definitely getting to her.

"You are that, darling," Robert agreed. "Have some wine."

7

She supposed she might as well; she didn't see them discussing the state of the economy after dinner, and she didn't want him switching on the box, just in case she was on it, although logic convinced her that the disappearance of a provincial schoolgirl would hardly have made London televison by now, if it was going to at all. "Shall I wash up?" she asked.

"Forget it. Let's go back to bed." Looking at her had apparently done the trick, for him. Looking at him had done nothing for her, and she fell asleep before he was finished with her. Thanks to the alcohol she slept heavily, and awoke not knowing quite where she was, aware of severe pain between her legs. She rolled on to her back, and blinked . . . at two men standing above her. One was Robert. The other was a black man. Cynthia gave a startled gurgle and reached for the sheet. "Get up," Robert said. She goggled at him. "This is Cuthbert," Robert explained. "You're to go with him."

Chapter Two

Cynthia writes: '*I was terrified. I'd never even met a black man before, much less been exposed naked to one. And to be told to go with him . . . I couldn't believe it.*'

Cynthia pulled the sheet to her throat; for the moment she couldn't speak. "Get up, you silly girl," Robert said. "We haven't got all day."

"You said I could stay here till Sunday."

"You have that wrong. I said my wife wasn't coming home till Sunday. Now listen, don't start playing silly buggers. You're on the run, right? You have no money, right? You have no job, right? You have no friends, right? And you have no place to live, right? Cuthbert will take care of all that. I can't. I'm a respectable married man."

That was a claim Cynthia thought she could argue, but now was not the time. She looked at Cuthbert more closely. He was very obviously a good deal younger than Robert, and in fact was quite startlingly handsome. He was also very well dressed, in a three-piece suit with a quiet tie, and there was an expensive-looking watch on his left wrist. "What do you want with me?" she muttered.

"Man, you are something. When Rob here called me, I said to myself, shit, he's day-dreaming again, but I was wrong. You get up and dress, eh?"

Cynthia looked at Robert. "You called him?"

"You can't stay here, girl. Surely you understand that."

"All right, I'll go. But not with him."

Robert looked at Cuthbert, who merely grinned. "What you going to do, girl? Walk the street? That ain't no place for a chick like you. Come with me and it'll all be good times."

"Doing what?"

"Well, wearing nice things. You like this?" Cynthia stared at the necklace he had taken from his pocket. It was made of thin gold, and suspended from it was a pendant, with . . . "They're real," Cuthbert said, and extended his hand. "Take it. It's yours."

Cynthia licked her lips. Her instincts told her that if she took the diamond necklace she was damned forever. But then, was she not damned forever anyway? She had never seen anything more beautiful in her life. Cynthia got out of bed to pack and dress.

Cuthbert drove an American car, a huge thing with so many dials and lights on the dashboard it might have been an aircraft flight deck. Cynthia could not help but feel that everyone would stare at them on the street, but those that did were more interested in the car than in the white girl riding with the black man. "You really eighteen?" Cuthbert asked.

"I'm sixteen," Cynthia said. She didn't think it would matter any more than if she was twelve, but she decided to play it safe.

"I figured that," Cuthbert agreed.

"Are you and Robert friends?" Cynthia asked.

Cuthbert grinned. "He owes me bread. Everyone owes me bread. Bobby more than most."

"You mean he gave me to you to pay a debt? Listen, mister: I am nobody's to give away."

"You're here, ain't you?"

"Right," she said. "Stop the car. Right now. I'll walk." She reached up and unclipped the necklace. "You can have this back."

Cuthbert continued to grin. "You ain't going to cause trouble, I hope, darling? Because if you do, I am going to bust your ass so hard you won't ever sit down again." He spoke so quietly, watching the street, that he took her breath away. Now he glanced at her and gave one of his grins. "But I'll tell you how it'll be," Cuthbert went on. "You be nice to me, and you'll enjoy life. You like to travel?"

"I've never travelled," Cynthia muttered, trying to think.

"OK, so we'll travel. Where'd you like to go? Spain? We'll go to Spain, tomorrow morning."

She turned her head. "Just like that?"

"No problem."

"Don't you have work to do?"

"Sure, baby. But it's a special kind of work."

"Lending money."

Cuthbert grinned. "In a manner of speaking."

Whatever he did for a living, he was certainly successful at it Cynthia realised, as she took in the Chelsea flat, with its plush carpets and designer furnishings, its hidden lighting and its general air of opulence. But before she could really appreciate these new surroundings she was pinned against the wall by a mountain of white fur. "Aaagh!" she screamed. "For God's sake, get him off me."

"Down, Hannibal," Cuthbert said, and the dog sank to the floor.

"What in the name of God is it?" They had never had a dog at home – Billy was afraid of them – and she had

11

no idea dogs ever grew quite this big, while looking quite this ferocious.

"It's a he, named Hannibal," Cuthbert explained. "He's a Dogo. That is an Argentinian hunting dog. These are the most intelligent as well as the most ferocious dogs in the world. Hold out your hand."

"You joke."

"Do it." Cautiously Cynthia extended her hand. "This is Cynthia, Hannibal," Cuthbert said. Hannibal stretched forward, teeth bared. "Don't move," Cuthbert warned, as Cynthia involuntarily took a step backwards. She made herself stand still, while Hannibal sniffed her fingers. "Cynthia is our friend," Cuthbert explained. Hannibal stopped baring his teeth and produced a tongue instead, with which he licked Cynthia's hand. "Now you're friends for life," Cuthbert said.

"Well, that's a relief."

"There's just one thing," Cuthbert explained. "Hannibal don't let anyone in who isn't a friend. Once you're in this flat you don't have to be afraid of anything. However, he don't let *anyone* out either, without my say-so. For God's sake remember that. You try opening that door without an OK from me, and he'll tear your throat out."

Cynthia swallowed. "You mean I'm a prisoner?"

"I mean you're a guest. You had breakfast?"

"No." And now she came to think about it, she was starving.

"Sit yourself down. I'll do it. Put the necklace on again. I like to see it on you."

Cynthia obeyed. "Makes you think I'm yours, eh?"

Cuthbert grinned as he broke eggs in the kitchen, with some expertise. "That's the idea." It was amazing to think that he had not yet actually touched her. Maybe pimps never touched their women. Because he had to be

12

a pimp. On the other hand, from everything she had read, pimps operated by making sexual slaves of their whores. Not that she intended to be anyone's whore. "Grub up," Cuthbert said.

Cynthia got up, and Hannibal got up too. "Remember we're friends," she said. "And I'm not going near that door." She went into the kitchen, the dog at her heels, looked at the laden table in astonishment. "Where'd you learn to cook like that?"

"Tha's how I began life, cooking," Cuthbert explained. "But I got bored with it. Tuck in."

Cynthia helped herself to eggs and bacon, mushrooms and tomatoes, fried bread and a huge glass of orange juice. "If I eat a breakfast like this every day, I'll get as fat as a pig."

"Some guys like them fat," he said. But he himself ate little, she observed. The phone jangled, and Cuthbert picked it up. "Yeah," he said. "Yeah. Yeah. Tomorrow. I'll need another ticket. Yeah. One of those too. I'll complete it here. Man, you got it. Yeah. Sure, I'll bring it. Don't I always? Send your stuff over by courier, right? Yeah." He replaced the receiver.

"You mean, you were going to Spain anyway?" Cynthia said.

He grinned. "That bother you? You're still invited."

"I suppose all men are liars. Is there coffee?"

He poured. "You know what I liked about you, right off? You're cool, babe. No hysterics. No wanting to rush home to mummy. Or even to telephone mummy. Mind you, I'm sure I'm going to find out a whole lot of other things about you to like. Finish your coffee and come to bed."

Cynthia drank some coffee. "Don't I have any say in this?"

13

"Don't spoil my illusions, darling." He leaned across the table. "You have to face the facts of life. Everyone has to, some time. Now's your time. You're on the run. I don't know, and I don't care, whether it's from your husband, your lover, your parents, the police, or the devil, but you're running. And you ain't got no place to go, save here. You have no proper clothes, and you have no money. I'll give you proper clothes and pocket money. Your only assets are your ass and your tits, and that hair. Oh, and you have quite a face as well. You look like an angel. Only you ain't no angel. All of that is marketable. But beautiful girls are a dime a dozen in big cities, and they don't come bigger than London."

"I won't be a whore," Cynthia muttered.

"It would be a shame, surely. I think we can do better than that. But you need someone to help you, and take care of you until you make it. Right now, I'm the only one in sight, right? So what am I asking in return? To teach you the nitty gritty of your trade? Now come to bed."

The girls at school had always said that black men were bigger and better than most. Well, Cynthia thought, she had absolutely no way of comparing. And Cuthbert was certainly frightening, to look at. And, initially, to feel. He wanted her sitting on him while he lay on his back, and she thought he was going in so far he'd split something open, especially as she was still sore from her session with Robert. But from then on it was tremendous. She broke through every barrier and kept on going for several seconds after he'd subsided. When she fell off him he sat up to look at her. "That was really something. You were howling like a banshee."

Cynthia opened her eyes. "Was I? I'm sorry."

14

"I enjoyed it."

"But the neighbours . . ."

"Hearing that noise at nine o'clock in the morning, they'll think I'm skinning the cat."

"Do you have a cat?"

"No. Hannibal would eat it. Now listen, we'll have a bath, then we'll go shopping. We want you looking good, eh?"

It was terribly exciting. It was late that afternoon, when Cuthbert was watching television, before Cynthia had the chance to think about what was happening, what she was doing. But she didn't have a clue on either count. She felt she was whirling through space without a map or a compass. Without even any controls for her to hang on to. But for the moment it was simply heavenly, no constant recriminations from Mummy, growling comments from Billy, no recurrent desires which had to be suppressed . . . all her desires had been stripped bare and then satisfied. She felt utterly, lazily, content.

Of course there had to be a down side. There always was. She was the mistress of a black playboy, who, when he got tired of her, would probably throw her out. And before that, probably beat her up. Although she was beginning to feel he wasn't into that, for all his threat. He was certainly big enough and strong enough to beat up anyone he chose, but his lovemaking was deliciously gentle. Maybe he'd set the dog on her.

And meanwhile, she could survey the clothes he had bought her, in Harrods, of all places. She had only ever read about Harrods before. She had asked him if he'd like her to wear make-up, and he had said, "Sure, baby, but we'll buy the cosmetics in Spain. They're better there." That was news to her, but she assumed he knew best. And it had all happened in twenty-four hours. "You're not on the telly, anyway," he called out from the lounge.

She went to the door. "What would you do if I were. Would you turn me in?"

"Depends what they want you for." He looked at her over his shoulder. "You haven't done anyone in, have you?"

"It was arsenic," she said. "Oh, he suffered dreadfully."

"Good thing I do the cooking around here. But I reckon a few days out of the country is a good idea."

"But they'll stop me at the airport," she gasped. She hadn't thought of that. And then slapped herself on the back of the head. "I don't have a passport!" She hadn't thought about that either.

"It came half an hour ago," he said, gesturing at the packet on the table. "With your ticket."

Cynthia ran to the table and opened the packet, took out the little blue booklet. "Charmaine Butts?"

"Well, you couldn't travel under your own name, baby. Come to think of it, I don't even know what that is."

"This doesn't have a photograph, and my description and place of birth isn't filled in."

"We'll do that now, if you'll give me the gen. As for the photo, we'll nip out to one of those booths."

"But . . . it has to be stamped."

Cuthbert got up and opened a drawer in his desk, took out the stamp machine. "No problem."

Cynthia sat down. "Are you a crook?"

"Sure. We're all crooks. You have a problem with that?"

Cynthia considered. Presumably travelling on a forged passport meant she was breaking the law. But perhaps she was breaking the law by just being here. "No," she said. "But I don't much care for the name Charmaine Butts!"

She was scared stiff at the airport, but they sailed through Immigration, the man on the desk giving only a cursory glance at the two passports. "When we're a United States of Europe," Cuthbert explained. "You won't need a passport at all."

Cynthia had never flown before either, but she had watched sufficient movies not to be scared of that, whatever her stomach was doing as they took off. Once again she felt like pinching herself. In forty-eight hours she had crammed in more firsts than in all the rest of her life, beginning with James. James! They were supposed to meet tomorrow, in the wood, and she was supposed to yield him her virginity. What would he say if he could see her now?

But then, whatever was happening at home? Mummy would have reported her missing to the police, of course, but probably not until yesterday morning; they'd have assumed that she had gone out to avoid the confrontation with Billy, and would be coming back when she reckoned the heat was off. And then, when they did start looking, the fact that she'd taken clothes and a bag, and money, would have indicated that she hadn't been raped and murdered. On the other hand, she *was* a runaway, aged only fifteen. They'd be looking, all right.

She felt not the slightest remorse for what she had done. She could not remember anyone making her feel loved and wanted, save for James. And James would soon get over her. Would she ever go back? When she was rich and famous. That would be the day. But it could happen. Maybe in Spain.

* * *

17

Spain was in fact everything she had expected it to be. They flew to Marbella and magnificent beaches and sunshine. They stayed in a first-class hotel, and she was treated like royalty. They watched flamenco dancing and ate paella and drank sangria, and she wore the new swimsuit Cuthbert had bought her.

She had expected some problems because of Cuthbert's colour, but there were none, because of Cuthbert's money. Was he really a crook? But anyone who made a habit of forging passports had to be a crook. "Do you know," he remarked. "There's no extradition treaty between England and Spain. Worth remembering."

"You plan to stay here?" she asked.

He grinned. "I'm not wanted for anything."

He took her down to Algeciras. Cynthia found this even more exciting. They went by plane to Tangier, and then crossed in a boat to Gibraltar. Cuthbert appeared to know a great many people, in both places, and spent a lot of time conferring in a low voice. Cynthia didn't mind in the least. She was too busy enjoying herself, from watching the belly dancers shaking their stomachs at her to sampling exotic dishes like couscous. She could also tell that she was a tremendous turn-on to the various locals to whom she was introduced. That was also exciting, as long as she had Cuthbert to protect her. Gibraltar was more of the same, except that everyone spoke English and after one very long meeting with his friends, from which she had as usual been excluded, Cynthia awoke from her afternoon nap to find him standing by the bed, grinning at her. "Bought you some presents," he said.

She sat up in delight, then scrambled out of bed to look into the huge box on the table. It was absolutely filled with make-up, from lipsticks and perfumes to huge jars of

18

face and body creams. "Can't risk having that complexion spoiled, can we?" Cuthbert asked.

"They're gorgeous!" Cynthia cried. "But I thought you said we'd get these in Spain?"

"I meant Gibraltar. They're cheaper here. No tax, you see," Cuthbert explained, and took her back to bed.

Cynthia says: *"Of course, looking back, I realise what an innocent twit I was. I can only claim that I was only fifteen, and knew absolutely nothing about anything, while feeling all the while that I was the hottest property on earth. I don't think I was too far out in that judgement, but it was meaningless in the plans of Cuthbert and his friends. I was a good lay – I was terribly enthusiastic – and they had those plans, into which I fitted very well. And I didn't have a clue."*

"That was great," she said, leaning back in her seat as the aircraft soared into the sky above Marbella. "But I guess there's no place like home. Do you think they'll still be looking for me?"

"After a week? They'll have forgotten all about you," Cuthbert said reassuringly. She supposed he was right; he was right about most things. "Hungry?" he asked, as they pushed their trolleys through Customs.

"Ravenous."

"Well, I think we'll go out tonight. To a Spanish bistro, right? You have to come back down to earth, slowly. You got a problem, man?" This was addressed to a customs officer, who was beckoning them over. "This is the green channel, man," Cuthbert said.

"We run a spot check in this channel, sir," the officer said, and now he had been joined by a female colleague. "Back from Spain, are you, sir? Miss?" He looked at Cynthia.

19

"Why," she said. "Yes. However did you know?"

"Someone told them," Cuthbert said. "This is harrass-ment, man."

"Just a spot check, sir," the official repeated. "We'd like to look at your bags."

Cynthia looked at Cuthbert, who shrugged. "They got the right. Just because I'm black."

I'm not black, Cynthia thought, beginning to get fright-ened, as she placed her suitcase – brand new and bought at Harrods at the same time as her new clothes – on the counter and flipped open the locks. Beside her, Cuthbert was doing the same. It was the woman who delved into Cynthia's bag. She was quite a young woman, good-looking in her uniform, although with a somewhat stern face. But a pleasant manner. "Nice things," she remarked. She examined a label. "Are they all from Harrods?"

"Every last one," Cuthbert said.

"What a lot of cosmetics," the woman remarked. "Are they from Harrods, too?"

Cynthia opened her mouth but again Cuthbert beat her to it. "Sure they are. Can't you see the labels?"

Cynthia looked down in dismay as the woman actually took the lid off one of the jars of cream. But there, inside the lid, was a Harrod's lable. She glanced at her companion. Who did not look pleased. "The whole hog," he grunted.

The woman smiled at Cynthia. "Will you come with me, please?"

Cynthia looked at Cuthbert, now she was definitely scared. "You can't do nothing with her," Cuthbert pro-tested. "She ain't done nothing."

"She's with you," the officer pointed out.

"This way, please, miss," the woman said.

20

"Ah, let them get on with it," Cuthbert recommended. "They only want to feel your ass."

"Feel my . . ."

"In here, miss."

Cynthia followed the woman through a door into a corridor. Now she wished she hadn't drunk all that champagne on the flight. "What's going to happen to me?" she asked.

"I'm afraid we are going to have to search you," the woman explained.

Cynthia nearly collapsed when they got into the taxi. "Do you know what they did?"

"Yes," Cuthbert said. "Did you enjoy it?"

Cynthia hugged herself. "I have never felt so *dirty*."

"If it's any consolation, they did the same to me."

Cynthia glanced at him. "You serious?"

"Sure I'm serious."

"Didn't you have a doctor present? I did."

"Sure I had a doctor."

Cynthia hugged herself. "What were they looking for?"

"Those bastards don't have to be looking for anything. They're a law unto themselves. All because of the colour of my skin, mind. They were probably looking for drugs."

"Oh!" She stared out of the window.

He squeezed her hand. "So forget it. You travel a lot, you're bound to get turned over by Customs every so often."

Yes, she wanted to say, but this is the first time I've *ever* travelled. And there was something else on her mind. "When did you stick those Harrods' labels on those jars?"

"Last night, while you were sleeping."

"Why?"

21

He grinned. "It's a game, right? They try to catch me out, so I catch them out."

She considered this. "Are you smuggling something?"

"You bet. I'm smuggling you, darling. You're the biggest bit of contraband in the world, right now. And the most valuable."

Cynthia wasn't sure how to take that. Her doubts about Cuthbert were quickly submerged in the excitement of getting home and bathing and dressing to hurry out to dinner. By then Hannibal had been returned by the friend who had been minding him in their absence – and who seemed to get on with him – and so there were hugs and kisses all over again. It wasn't until she was lying awake in the dark with Cuthbert gently snoring beside her that she found herself reappraising the entire situation. She had jumped, inadavertently but with both feet, into a *demi-monde* she'd only ever seen represented on the screen. There could be no denying that Cuthbert was a crook. She didn't know what at, although drugs seemed the most likely thing, but there didn't seem any doubt that the authorities knew he was a crook, and were just waiting to catch him out. When they did that, they would catch her out as well, if she was at his side.

Therefore she should get out, as quickly as possible, before she wound up in deep trouble. When she really started to think about it, she was horrified at what she had done, had allowed to happen to herself. She was having frequent sex. It was surely wrong, in all the circumstances, especially the sex. And Cuthbert never wore anything to protect her; she could very well be pregnant, and not know it. Well, she was due next week. She'd sure as hell know then. And if she was . . . she didn't dare even think about it. There was so much else. She was travelling on a false passport and living a false identity. Whatever he had been doing in Spain and Morocco and Gibraltar, she had been there, and was therefore an accomplice by association.

Go, girl, go, she told herself. But if he caught her trying to sneak off . . . On the other hand, if she went home, he wouldn't dare attempt to follow her. In fact, she suddenly had the strongest urge to go home. She had had her adventure, now a return to the quiet life seemed attractive. Of course, it wouldn't be a quiet life, in the beginning. There would be shouts and screams and interviews with the police. But at least she had *lived*. She even thought she could deal with Billy. While if she stayed here . . . where was she going? Cuthbert had said, upwards. But up to now all her progress had been horizontal.

She decided to try him out on that first and raised the subject at breakfast.

"When are we going to make a move?" she asked.

"What kind of move? You don't like the flat?"

"I love the flat. I was talking about me. About finding me a career."

He put down the *Financial Times*. "You in a hurry? Baby, you have all the time in the world."

"Nobody ever has that much time."

"I felt like that when I was sixteen, too," he said. "You get over it. Give me a break, Cyn. I don't want to lose you right now. And when those big boys get a load of you, I'm going to be squeezed right out. I know it."

"I'm not that ungrateful," she protested.

"You won't have any say in the matter. Now, get dressed and let's go shopping. There's something I want to buy you."

That come-on was irresistible; no one had ever bought her anything but the bare essentials before. Cynthia hurried into the bathroom to shower, hurried back into the bedroom to dress, and found herself looking at the cosmetic selection Cuthbert had bought for her in Gibraltar. She hadn't really tried any of them yet, had intended to sample them at her leisure, but . . . she frowned: she was sure they were not as she had left them before going out last night. And on coming in she hadn't even looked at them. She unscrewed the lid of one of the jars of cream, and her frown deepened. The surface of the cream had been smoothed with something, perhaps even a finger, but it had definitely been disturbed. Someone had been using her face cream!

She opened the other jars. All had been disturbed. Someone had had a real go at them. "Cuthbert?" she called. He came in, knotting his tie. "Someone's been in the flat."

"Who?"

"I don't know. It must've been last night while we were out."

"You mean, burglars? No way."

"Well, look." She showed him the jars of cream.

"You mean someone stole your make-up?"

"No, no, they're all here. But someone has been using it. The cream."

Cuthbert grinned. "You telling me some guy broke in here to use your face cream? Shit, I know a lot of the guys are gay, but not that gay. They know I'd bust their asses. Anyway, Hannibal was here. There's no way anyone could get into this flat without my being here; Hannibal wouldn't let them. And if they did manage to get in, he sure as hell wouldn't let them back out. We'd have burglar splattered all over the floor. You're hallucinating, babe. All that excitement yesterday has been too much for you. Let's go shopping."

*　　*　　*

She wasn't going to argue with him; she was even less inclined to when he took her to a jewellers and bought her a gold Omega, and then a furriers and bought her a pastel mink, although she was a bit anxious about wearing it on the street. "Don't you like it?" he asked.

"It's the most beautiful thing I've ever owned. But suppose someone throws paint over it?"

"They'll only do it once, with me around," he assured her.

She believed him.

He now apparently felt that she could be seen in public, and began taking her to discos. Like the bistro, these were apparently all owned, or at least managed, by friends of his, and the drinking and the dancing was fast and furious. Everyone wanted to dance with her, and quite a few, men and women, wanted to do more than that. But Cuthbert merely smiled indulgently, even when he saw someone fondling her breasts or putting his hand under her skirt. He was confident she wouldn't let anyone go further than that.

Cynthia was having the time of her life.

This was the sort of life of which she had always dreamed: drinking and dancing every night until the small hours, then sleeping in until about ten, then brunch, always accompanied by champagne just to set them up again, then either watching television or shopping before it was time to bathe and dress for the evening. Not even the consumption of so much alcohol caused her any trouble. She relaxed further when she discovered she was not pregnant. One evening, just after her sixteenth birthday, although she didn't tell anyone about that, she was sitting with some friends while Cuthbert was at the bar using the phone, and one of the girls produced a little box filled with white powder. "Try some."

"That's drugs," Cynthia said. "I don't use them."

"That's what's wrong with you," the girl said. "You're too stiff. You want to relax a bit."

"I am relaxed," Cynthia said. "If you want to relax me some more, get me another G and T."

"Alcohol is for the birds," said the boy on her other side. "This stuff sends you higher and you don't have a hangover." He poured a little on to the back of his hand and sniffed it.

"Well?" Cynthia asked. "Where's the turn-on?" He blinked at her, then took her face between his hands and kissed her on the mouth, using his tongue like a battering ram. "Hey," she said, pushing him away. "You want to lose your knock-knacks?" To her relief Cuthbert had his back to her.

"That's what it does to you," the girl said, and she also sniffed off the back of her hand. "Come on, Cyn darling. Have a go at paradise." She put some more on the back of her hand and raised it to Cynthia's nose.

Cynthia gave a cautious sniff and thought she had burned herself. "Ugh!"

"Give it a chance," her friend said. "Give it . . . hey!" Her face twisted in pain as Cuthbert held her wrist and squeezed it. "What the fuck . . .!"

"Just forget it," Cuthbert said. "And you, baby doll, out of there."

Cynthia made to rise and overbalanced and sat down again. Her head was spinning. "Now look here, nigger," said the man who had first offered her the drug, also getting to his feet.

"Listen, lad," Cuthbert said. "Those teeth real?"

"Well, of course they are."

"They're all going to need replacing if you don't get out of my way."

The man sat down again, and Cuthbert grasped Cynthia's arm and jerked her to her feet. Several people had gathered round now, and they were shouting at her, or certainly at Cuthbert – although no one attempted to stop him – but she hardly heard what they were saying as she was dragged out into the very welcome fresh air and thrust into the front seat of his car. The door was slammed and he went round the other side, while she hugged herself. She had never seen him really angry before. She didn't dare look at him until the car was actually moving so that he had to watch the road. "I'm sorry," she said.

"I thought you had some brains."

"Everyone was doing it."

"Sure. And did you ever meet such a bunch of shit-heads? There's those who use drugs, and there those who supply them. Don't ever get that mixed up."

The import of what he had just said slowly sank into her brain. "You mean you're a pusher?"

"No, I am not a pusher. That's for little guys."

"But . . . you deal in them?"

"Listen, baby, when I decide to tell you what I do, I'll tell you. Until then keep your nose out of my affairs. And don't ever, as long as you live, take a sniff of coke again. Or anything else."

"Is it dangerous?"

"It can be. Its real danger is that it's addictive, and that it leads you to wanting bigger flights, so you move to something like heroin. Now that kills." He half turned his head, and grinned at her. "But people pay to have it. The world, they say, is full of subnormals. Lucky for us, eh?"

*   *   *

27

Yet again Cynthia found herself lying awake and considering her situation. Cuthbert was into drugs. He might not push them himself, or use them himself, but he was obviously involved in the supply side. That was the dangerous side. If he got caught he'd go to jail for twenty years. And if she got caught with him, then she'd go down as well. But even worse, according to all the movies on the subject she'd seen, he would eventually get turned over by some rival dealer, and wind up at the bottom of some river with his feet in concrete. With her beside him.

She almost got out of bed there and then, to run away. But of course Hannibal wouldn't let her leave, and Cuthbert was already annoyed with her. They'd had sex as usual before he had gone to sleep, and for the first time he had been rough with her. He hadn't actually hurt her but he had squeezed her, a buttock in each hand, as if he wanted to tear her in two. What he'd do if he found her trying to sneak out . . . She'd have to plan. But she had to leave, while she could. He usually accompanied her whenever he went out, but he often left her alone in the flat. With the goddamned dog! "What's eating you?" he asked over breakfast.

"I'm just sorry about last night," she said, as contritely as she could.

"So forget it. They had to try it on you sometime. Now you know. Go and pack. We're flying out this afternoon."

"Where to?"

"Istanbul." She thought it was a swear word. "Turkey, baby. You'll love it there. Istanbul is hot and sexy."

Istanbul was shrouded in a thin drizzle. Cuthbert took Cynthia on a ferry ride across the Golden Horn, the inlet of the Bosphorus, and on another ferry ride across the

Bosphorus itself, so that she could say she had been to Asia. When they returned they explored Istanbul, visiting the Topkapi Palace where the sultans had lived and which was now a museum containing the most fabulous jewels, and the Blue Mosque, and then the Hagia Mosque, which had once been the Cathedral of St Sophia, in the days before the Turkish conquest. Cynthia was enthralled by it all, and as in Morocco and Gibraltar, was not the least concerned at the numbers of people Cuthbert seemed to know, and with whom he wanted to have little chats.

And of course they went shopping. Turkish clothes weren't very fashionable by Western standards, so Cuthbert insisted on buying souvenirs instead, including a set of Russian dolls which were in varying sizes and which fitted one into the other until the largest, some nine inches tall, contained them all. As usual, Cuthbert seemed to know the shopkeeper, and there was much chatter between them. "I didn't know you could speak Turkish," Cynthia remarked when the dolls had been removed to be wrapped.

"I'm a man of hidden talents," Cuthbert asserted. "Aren't you impressed?" She was exhausted as well as soaking wet by the time they got back to the hotel. "Why don't you have a hot shower and a lie down before dinner?" Cuthbert suggested.

"While you do what?"

"I have someone I need to see. But I'll be back in time for dinner," he assured her.

Cynthia had her shower and went to bed. She was deliciously tired, and had the comforting feeling that when she woke up there would be nothing but more entertainment for the rest of the evening. She slept heavily, and awoke with a start just as it was getting dark, to the sound of the

29

muezzin's tape blaring across the city. And to an empty bedroom. What on earth was Cuthbert doing?

She had another shower, then got dressed. Still no Cuthbert. She stood on the balcony, looked out over the houses and then down at the street below. Then she rang room service and ordered a drink. The waiter arrived a few minutes later with a tray, and a note. "Your man left this for you," he explained.

Cynthia signed the chit and snatched at the envelope. The boy backed from the room, grinning at her. Then she locked the door and opened the envelope, her fingers trembling.

'*Dearest Cyn*,' Cuthbert had written. '*Something has come up, and I have had to leave Istanbul immediately. Now baby, there is nothing at all for you to worry about. You are booked out on the eight o'clock flight tomorrow morning. The ticket is in your suitcase, I have paid the hotel bill, including your dinner tonight, the show in the night-club, and over the top for drinks. So have a good time but don't fuck any of these Turks. There is also money for taxi fares. When you get to London, go to Edgar and pick up both Hannibal and the keys to the flat. I'll be there soon.*'

It wasn't signed, but it was most certainly Cuthbert's writing.

She opened her suitcase, and then the envelope that lay in the bottom. As with Spain, she had left all of their travel arrangements to him, and there was a plane ticket, for tomorrow morning as he had said. They had come to Istanbul for two nights? There was also the copy of a credit card slip, signed by Cuthbert and made out to the hotel for an indecipherable amount of dinars, and there were fifty pounds as well as an equivalent sum in dinars. Exactly as he had said there would be. She sat on the bed and scratched her head. She supposed she should be scared, suddenly being abandoned like this, but actually

30

she felt pleasantly excited. Suppose someone *did* try to pick her up? A Turk? Cuthbert could never know. Unless, of course, he had some of his pals staked out in the hotel. She wouldn't put it past him.

But where on earth had he gone off to? Something to do with drugs, of course; that was obviously why they had come here for such a brief visit, just to pick up a consignment. Well, thank God he hadn't involved her this time; no doubt he could tell that she had been really upset by the incident at Heathrow the last time. But suppose he got caught? He had to get caught some time. Well, this time she wouldn't be around. And tomorrow afternoon she'd be back in London, safe and sound.

She went downstairs, had dinner, and again saw the show. "My husband has had to leave," she told the *maître d'*, "but I understand he has paid the account."

"Oh, yes, madame."

"He also said I could have anything I liked to drink."

"Of course, madame."

"Champagne?"

"Certainly."

"French champagne?"

"But of course."

A bottle of Mumms was produced and she sipped and watched the dancers, aware that every man in the room was watching her. It gave her a tremendous feeling of power, which was increased when one of a group of three men seated on the far side of the room got up and came over. She reckoned he was definitely a Turk, but very good-looking, with a pencil moustache and chiselled features. "Are you not lonely, mademoiselle?" he asked.

"Not in the least."

"But you would like someone to sit with you, would you not? My name is Samih."

31

Definitely one of Cuthbert's associates, placed there not only to keep an eye on her, but to try her out. "I might like it, Sammy," she said. "But my husband wouldn't."

"Do you always do what your husband wishes, mademoiselle?"

Cynthia smiled at him. "Always."

He gazed at her for several seconds, then got up, and bowed, clicking his heels as he did so. "Perhaps we will meet again, in more propitious circumstances."

"Perhaps," Cynthia agreed.

She finished her bottle and went to bed, feeling distinctly woozy. But she remembered to book a five-thirty call at the desk, and was duly awakened, just after dawn. She showered and put on a light-weight linen dress and then packed, squeezing the wrapped-up packet of dolls into her suitcase with some difficulty. Then she thrust her feet into a pair of sandals and called the bellboy and went down. She had booked her taxi the previous night as well, and it was waiting for her. There was no one around save for the hotel staff, who saw her off most obsequiously.

She was at the airport by seven, and her taxi-driver summoned a porter to take her bag through the throng to the check-in desk. "You may go through Immigration now, Miss Butts," the clerk told her. "Your flight will be called in ten minutes."

Cynthia smiled at him, clutched her handbag into herself as she joined the queue before the Immigration desk. When she reached the desk the man glanced at her passport, then at her. She gave him her best smile as well, but he didn't seem impressed. "Your ticket," he grunted.

Cynthia opened her handbag and took out the ticket. The man flipped it open and looked at it. "This is not right."

32

"How do you mean, it's not right? The clerk said it was all right. Look, he's given me a seat allocation."

"It is not right," the man said again, and gave her a slow, lazy smile. "But it will soon be all right. You go with this man."

He must have pressed a button hidden under his desk, because another man had appeared, also wearing uniform, and what he no doubt intended to be a reassuring expression. "You come with me," he said.

"If there's something wrong with the ticket," Cynthia argued, "I should go back to the check-in desk."

"You come with me, now," the man said, seizing her wrist and jerking her forward.

Cynthia looked over her shoulder to see if any of the other people in the queue were going to help her, but they were all unaware of the commotion. She found herself stumbling forward and being turned into a side corridor which took her out of sight of anyone else. "Listen!" she said. "I'm a British citizen."

The man opened a door and thrust her through the aperture, releasing her wrist as he did so. Cynthia did some more stumbling before coming up against a table. Oh, God, she thought: not again! But I am leaving, not arriving. On the table was her suitcase. She straightened, and attempted to turn, but had her arms seized, so that she was thrust forward against the table, forced over it. She wanted to protest but had run out of breath. She watched one of the men walk round the table to stand in front of her, beyond the suitcase. He smiled at her. "I told you we would meet again, Miss Butts. My name is Samih. Do you remember?"

Chapter Three

Cynthia says: *"I have had quite a few heart-stopping moments in my life, but I think this was the very worst. I suppose because I had really never suffered anything before. But I knew then that I was in for a very unpleasant experience."*

Again Cynthia tried to push herself up, and again she was forced down, even further this time, so that her face banged into the suitcase. Samih said something in Turkish, and she felt hands on her thighs, pushing her skirt up. "You can't *do* this," she shouted. "I am a British citizen!"

Samih spoke again, and the hands became still. But they were still holding her arms to keep her bent over the table, and they were still grasping her thighs. There were three men, at least, behind her, holding her motionless in the most humiliating of positions. Samih smiled at her, moved the suitcase away from her face, and opened it. He took out the parcel containing the Russian doll and unwrapped it. "If it's illegal to export that, then you can have it," Cynthia panted, trying not to burst into tears. "I didn't know."

Samih unscrewed the head of the doll, turned the doll upside down. Instead of the four smaller dolls falling out, there was a cascade of white powder. "This has a street value of perhaps a million pounds," Samih told her. "You would have been a very wealthy woman, had you got away

34

with it. But it is a crude way to attempt to smuggle drugs."
Cynthia could only goggle at him. "So you see, you have
not a leg to stand on," Samih told her. "Or perhaps I
should say, not an ass to sit on." He spoke in Turkish,
and her skirt was thrown up on to her back while someone
pulled down her knickers. Now her buttocks were pulled
so far apart so thought she would be split in two while the
fingers probed her.

Breathless with a mixture of terror and outrage, she
hardly realised it when she was released. No longer
sustained by the clutching hands she slid off the table
on to her knees, her face against the edge of the wood.
"Get up, Charmaine," Samih said. "Charmaine. It is a nice
name, Charmaine. Stand up." Cynthia held on to the table
and dragged herself up. To her surprise she was not crying.
She was too angry. And too afraid. But she was not going
to show her fear. "Strip," Samih commanded.

"Have you not already searched me?" she protested.

"I wish to look at you. Strip."

"I wish to have a doctor present, and a woman," Cynthia
said, speaking as evenly as she could. She felt the one thing
she could do wrong would be to let these thugs know how
near she was to having hysterics. "And I wish to be allowed
to telephone the British ambassador."

Samih came round the desk to stand beside her. She
made herself continue staring straight in front of her,
while he rested his hand on her shoulder, then slid it
down her back to caress her bottom. Then she started;
she was so confused and distraught she had forgotten
they had taken off her knickers. "If you do not do as I
say," Samih said into her ear, "I am going to hurt you very
badly."

Cynthia heard herself inhaling, slowly and carefully. But
she knew she had to make herself maintain some control

35

over her situation. "I will undress for you, if you wish," she said. "But not in front of them."

"But you will, little Charmaine," he said. "They wish to look at you too." Cynthia had to bite her lip to stop herself hitting him. That would undoubtedly earn her a beating, and there seemed little point in that. She had simply to get through the coming ordeal. Survive, and then see what she could do about her situation. She unzipped her dress. She was wearing nothing else save her shoes, and she stepped out of these. Then she turned to face him. "You are exquisite," he said. "It would be a shame to disfigure such beauty." His men came to stand around her, squeeze her buttocks and finger her breasts, run their hands through her hair. Samih unfastened his breeches. "Bend over the table," he said. Cynthia glanced down at him, then turned away. At least she would not have to look at him.

She hardly felt Samih, although from the noise he was making he seemed to be enjoying himself, urged on as he was by his three henchmen. And when he was finished it was their turn, one after the other. Cynthia found that by stretching her arms to their fullest extent she could reach the far side of the table, and she wrapped her fingers around the edge while she gasped for breath as her stomach was driven into the wood again and again, and her face also banged on the hard surface. She was taken by surprise when someone suddenly slapped her hard on her right buttock. "All right," Samih said. "You can get up now." Slowly, painfully, Cynthia straightened. She didn't want to look at any of them. "In there," Samih said. Instinctively she looked at her clothes, thrown into a heap in the corner; they couldn't mean to take her out of here naked! "You douche," Samih said. "You need to douche."

One of his men had opened a door on the far side of the

room, and she saw that it led to a toilet compartment. She walked across the room, feeling as if she was in a dream. A very bad dream. The very worst nightmare she had ever had. There was a shower stall at the far side of the room. And even soap. She stepped into this and turned the water full on. It was cold and took her breath away, but it also made her feel clean, and she became cleaner yet as she soaped, again and again. But she was never going to be truly clean again.

The men gathered in the doorway to watch her, commenting to each other in Turkish. "You've wet your hair, you silly cow," Samih told her. Cynthia wet her hair again and again and again. She thought she could stand beneath the shower forever. "All right," Samih said. "Come out."

She looked at him through the cascading water, and one of his men reached past her and turned off the shower. Another offered her a towel. Clearly they were going to watch her drying herself as well, so she merely got on with it. Even nightmares had to end. "Now dress," Samih commanded.

Cynthia pulled on her clothes, realising that one of the men had left the interrogation room. But now he returned, carrying a bandanna. "Cover your hair," Samih said. Cynthia obeyed, and Samih put a pair of dark glasses on her nose. "Now you listen to me," he said. "You make any trouble when we leave here, and I am going to beat you till you bleed. You understand me?"

"Where are you taking me?" Cynthia asked. "I demand to be allowed to see the British ambassador."

Samih grinned. "You must make that request to the magistrate."

"You are taking me to a magistrate?"

"Right now."

Cynthia sighed in relief, and looked for her handbag. "Where's my bag?"

"It is evidence," Samih said. From his belt he took a pair of handcuffs, pulled her wrists forward to clip them on.

"Hey, wait a minute," she protested. "I'm not a criminal."

"You are a drug smuggler," he told her.

The courtroom was crowded with people, all talking at once. No one took the slightest notice of Cynthia, with her hair concealed and wearing the dark glasses, and she took no notice of them. She was interested only in finding herself before a magistrate. There were actually several magistrates, seated in a row behind a long, high desk, and each involved in trying or hearing a case at the same time, which accounted for the noise. Three of them were women. Oh, please let me be taken before a woman, Cynthia thought. She was. The woman was small, had neat, greying dark hair, neat features, and was neatly dressed; in front of her on the desk was Cynthia's handbag. Samih spoke to her in Turkish, and then turned to Cynthia. "Her Honour speaks English. Take off the glasses so she can see you."

Cynthia obeyed. "Thank God for that. Your Honour . . ."

"These officers say that five hundred grams of heroin were found in your suitcase. Is this true?"

"I know they found something. But I didn't put it there. My boyfriend did." What the hell, she thought – she owed Cuthbert nothing, now.

The magistrate made a note. "You admit the heroin was in your suitcase?"

"Yes, but . . ."

"Your boyfriend put it there without your knowledge."

38

"That's exactly it," Cynthia said, feeling waves of relief starting to seep through her body.

"And where is this boyfriend now?"

"I don't know. He went off last night, and didn't come back. He left me a note telling me to take the plane out this morning."

"You do realise, Miss . . ." The magistrate looked at the passport on the desk beside the handbag, "Butts, that everyone who is arrested smuggling drugs always says that his or her boyfriend planted them on her and then disappeared?"

"But it's true. Listen . . . look in my handbag. You'll find his note."

The magistrate opened the handbag and emptied the contents, sifted through them, and found Cuthbert's note, which she read. "You could have written this yourself, Miss Butts."

"But I didn't. Please believe me. I didn't."

"What is the name of this boyfriend?"

"Cuthbert Lucas."

The magistrate wrote it down. "Very good. A search will be made for this Cuthbert Lucas. However, in his absence, I am afraid you will have to be committed for trial." She looked down and began writing, as if her part in the affair was over.

"Hey," Cynthia said. "What do you mean, committed? And there's a lot more." To avoid hassle, she hadn't been going to mention the rape, if they'd just let her go. But if they weren't going to do that . . .

The magistrate looked up. "By committed I mean that you will be taken to a remand home where you will remain until your case comes up."

"Remand home? For how long?"

"I am afraid our courts are very crowded right now. I

would estimate it will take about six months for your case to be heard."

"Six months?" Cynthia shouted.

"You may of course apply for bail, but I must warn you that in the case of heroin smuggling it will have to be a considerable sum."

Cynthia swallowed. This cannot be happening, she told herself. I have got to be dreaming. "Listen," she said. "This man raped me. He and his friends. They each raped me."

The magistrate looked tired. "That is what everyone says, Miss Butts."

"Everyone?" Tears began to fall rapidly.

"Can you prove this assault?"

Cynthia gulped. "I need a lawyer. Don't I get a lawyer?"

"The Court will provide you with a lawyer, certainly."

"And I need to see the British Ambassador. I must see the British Ambassador."

"The embassy will be informed, Miss Butts. Now I cannot give you any more time."

Cynthia opened her mouth and then closed it again. If she attempted to speak again she knew she was going to scream. And if she was going to see someone from the embassy surely this mess would be sorted out. She turned, and found that Samih had been replaced by two women police officers.

"Do either of you speak English?" she asked. "Please, help me!"

Apparently they didn't, although they talked a lot, as they escorted Cynthia outside and into a police wagon. People stared at her but she was past caring about people. "I need someone who speaks English," she said, urgently.

One of the woman snapped at her, and she decided to

keep quiet for the time being. But keeping quiet meant thinking, realising what had happened to her. She had been held across a table and raped. By four men. Nothing in her wildest nightmares had ever been like that. She still didn't want to think about what had happened, because she could still feel . . . she gave an involuntary shudder, and both women looked at her. She clenched her teeth and made herself keep still. Because this was going to end. It had to end, somehow.

She was driven out of the city and to a building set by itself and surrounded by a high wall. There were armed policemen on the gate. Inside there were several other walls, leading away from a high, square building with masses of windows, all barred. Cynthia was made to get down at the door, and escorted into a front hall where there was a counter and several other people. One of the policewomen produced a document which a man behind the desk inspected and then signed. I've been delivered and signed for, Cynthia thought, just as if I were a shipment of meat. Then she realised that to these people she *was* just a shipment of meat.

The man at the desk spoke in Turkish, and one of the women came forward. She was quite young and her face could have been attractive had it not been quite so cold. She wore her black hair long and in a pony tail, beneath a little sidecap. "You are English," she announced.

"Oh, thank God," Cynthia said.

"I will take these off," the jailer said, unlocking the handcuffs. "But if you make trouble, I will put them on again."

"I'm not going to make trouble," Cynthia assured her, rubbing her hands together and massaging her wrists. Not until I can get out of here, she promised herself.

"That is wise," the woman said, and pulled the scarf from Cynthia's head. Damp yellow hair tumbled past her shoulders, and the woman stranded some of it through her fingers. "Such hair . . . You will come with me, please."

She led the way to a flight of stairs. Cynthia hurried behind her. "May I ask you a question?"

"You may."

They climbed the stairs together. "My suitcase, and passport . . . my handbag. They kept them all."

"They are evidence," the woman said.

"You mean I am not going to get them back?"

"You will get them back when you are acquitted." She gave a brief smile. "If you are acquitted."

"But . . . the magistrate said I might be here for six months. I can't wear these same clothes for six months!"

"You will not." They had reached the first floor and turned along a corridor, halting before a door which had a nameplate on it, although Cynthia had no idea what it said. Her companion knocked, and then opened the door. "Go in," she commanded. Cynthia stepped inside, and found herself gazing at a man. She didn't like the look of him at all. He was very big, about as big as Cuthbert, but much older and heavier, with jowls and a blue chin. He wore uniform but not very neatly. He was seated behind a desk, his eyes sleepily shrouding her, and then suddenly becoming very awake as he took her in. "Butts, sir," the woman said in English. "Found in possession of heroin, remanded for trial."

The man continued to gaze at Cynthia for several seconds. Then he asked, also in good English, "What is your first name?"

"Cynthia. I mean, Charmaine."

"Which?"

"Charmaine," Cynthia said.

42

The man's eyes seemed to shroud her. She knew he was stripping her in his mind. But she had a suspicion he was going to want to do that in more than his mind, very shortly. But if any man was to touch her now, she'd go mad. "We get all sorts in here," he said. "Mostly prostitutes and drug addicts. Hold out your arms." Cynthia obeyed; she wasn't going to argue with this man, about anything – unless he tried something. The commandant held her wrists and twisted her arms to and fro. "You do not use heroin yourself?"

"I don't use any drugs," Cynthia said. "I was framed."

The man smiled, briefly. "That is a hackneyed defence, Charmaine. Sir. You must call me sir."

"Yes, sir," Charmaine agreed.

"This prison is full of drugs," the commandant said. "If I put you in with addicts they will have you mainlining in five minutes. If I put you in with prostitutes, they will wish to have sex with you. Do you like having sex with women?"

Cynthia gave the guard a hasty glance, unable to deter-mine the safest answer. "I've never tried it."

The commandant grinned. "You are an all-English heterosexual female. I like that. I cannot give you a cell to yourself; we are very crowded." He spoke Turkish to the guard, who replied, also in Turkish, not apparently agreeing with him. But he ignored her opinion. "I will put you in with a woman called Natasha," he said. "She is Russian, but she speaks English."

Cynthia didn't know whether to thank him or not. "The magistrate said I would be provided with a lawyer, and that someone from the British Embassy would come to see me. Sir."

The commandant shrugged. "When someone comes to see you, you will be informed." His tone indicated that the operative word was actually if, rather than when.

43

"Then I would like to renew the request, to you, now. Sir. I would also like to complain that I was raped by the customs officers who searched me. By all of them."

The commandant rose, and came round his desk to stand in front of her. Now he took her chin between his fingers and moved her head to and fro. "In here, I make the rules, and I decide what shall be done and what shall not be done. And my first rule is, no complaints. Remember this, and you may be quite happy here. Forget it, and you will be very unhappy. Do you understand me?" He released Cynthia's chin, and her head bobbed up and down as she nodded. Never in her life, not even when Cuthbert had threatened her, had she felt quite so menaced. "Good." The commandant returned behind his desk and sat down. "Now, this woman Natasha. Be careful what you say to her. She is awaiting trial for murder."

"For . . .?" Cynthia hastily clamped her mouth shut. He couldn't be serious.

"She is a psycho," the commandant said. "But she is not dangerous as long as you do not upset her. In anything. Do you understand me?"

"Yes, sir," Cynthia said faintly. She had supposed all nightmares had to end, but this one was just getting worse and worse.

"Very good. I will see you later." The guard touched Cynthia on the arm.

"What did he mean when he said he'd see me later?" Cynthia asked, and they walked along the corridor.

"He will send for you, later, to have sex with him."

"To have . . ." Cynthia stopped walking. "And suppose I refuse? I have already been raped four times today."

"How interesting for you. You're bearing up very well.

44

But you cannot refuse the commandant. If you do, he will have you caned."

"You can't be serious. This is 1983, isn't it?"

"What has that got to do with it? In Turkey we believe in corporal punishments. Your English way of treating criminals is childish."

"And flogging people is an Arab custom, right?"

"We are not Arabs," the woman said coldly. "Come along."

Cynthia hurried beside her. "But I haven't been convicted of anything. When my case comes to trial, and I'm acquitted . . ."

"You were found carrying a suitcase full of heroin, Butts. There is not the slightest possibility of your being acquitted. As for why you are being put in with Natasha Rykova, Major Izantsi wishes you to be so anxious to get out again that you will make him very happy. I advised against it, because anyone can see that you have a headstrong personality, and that you and Rykova may well clash. But he is right when he said that she is not dangerous, providing you do not attempt to argue with her. You should remember this. In here."

She opened a door, and Cynthia, after a brief hesitation while she braced herself, as she had no idea what she was going to face, stepped through. But instead of a cell containing a deranged murderess she found herself in a storeroom. Behind the counter there was another woman, also in uniform, overweight and ugly but full of smiles. "Strip," the guard commanded.

Cynthia sighed and obeyed; it was at least better than having her clothes torn off her. While she undressed the two guards chattered at each other in Turkish, and now, to Cynthia's alarm, the fat one came round the counter, still talking and smiling. Before Cynthia realised what she was going to do, the woman had taken a nipple between her thumb and finger, and given it a little pinch. "Ouch!" Cynthia jumped backwards, and cannoned into the English-speaking guard.

"She says you are very beautiful."

"Well, tell her if she touches me again I'll kick her in the crotch."

"I would not like to tell her that because if I do she will beat you up. Do you want to be beaten up?"

Cynthia panted. She was terrified, confused and her heart pounded. She did not want to be beaten up. But she did not want to be raped by a woman either. But now she discovered that the other guard was holding both her arms, and she was very strong. She was helpless as the storekeeper stroked her all over. She more than once raised a leg to aim a kick, but each time decided against it; she could not possibly fight them both, and as with the customs officers, there seemed no point in being beaten to no purpose. The two women continued to chatter away, but now the storekeeper's face fell, and she went back behind the counter. "She wishes to have you, now," the guard said. "But I have told her she cannot, now, because Major Isantsi wishes you first."

"Thank God. And thank you."

The guard released her arms. "Why are you thanking me? She will have you, eventually."

Cynthia licked her lips. "And you?"

The guard smiled. "Oh, yes. Me too."

"Don't you people think of anything but sex in here?"

The guard shrugged her shapely shoulders. "It passes the time. There is nothing else *to* think about, unless you are into drugs. Then you think about your next fix. But you are not into drugs, so you may as well think about sex. There is no point in thinking about food, because

46

the food is very bad, or in thinking about getting out of here, because that is not going to happen."

"I am thinking about sex, believe me," Cynthia muttered. "And hating my every thought."

The guard squeezed her buttock. "You are going to make a lot of people very happy during your stay here. You *are* very beautiful." Oh, Jesus, Cynthia thought. I am going to go stark raving mad during my stay here. To think that not four hours ago she had been lying in her warm bed in the hotel, without a care in the world, and a few hours before that she had been drinking champagne and watching a belly dancer perform . . . and snubbing Samih. My God, she thought; they must have known about the heroin even then, and been just waiting for me to attempt to leave the country!

The storekeper had been hunting through various cupboards and shelves, and now she lay on the counter two shapeless pale blue dresses, two pairs of pale blue drawers, and one pair of ankle-laced thongs. To this she added a ragged towel and a bar of soap. "Make the soap last," the guard recommended. "Dress."

Cynthia pulled on one set of the clothes and felt distinctly safer. "You will attend the laundry once a week to wash your clothes," the guard told her. "You will bathe every day."

"Where?"

"There are communal showers. You will be shown."

"There's no toothpaste or brush."

"You will use water and your finger."

The storekeeper was speaking again. "Take off your watch," the guard said.

Cynthia took off her Omega. "That's an expensive watch. Do I get it back when I leave?"

"Of course. If you leave. Come."

*   *   *

47

Cynthia was led to another flight of steps. Now they entered a world of sound. She realised the sound had been there all the time, but distant, muted. Now it was all around them, people talking, moving. This was reassuring, but occasionally there would be a shout or a scream, or a volley of loud words which had to be abuse, although she couldn't understand any of it. "It is the addicts who make the most noise," the guard commented.

"Can't you stop drugs entering the prison?"

"We could," the woman agreed. "But it would be more trouble than it is worth. Then the addicts would make even more noise, and probably riot. It is better to let them get on with it." She glanced at Cynthia. "You are very sensible, for one so young, never to have used drugs."

Now they were walking down a corridor between cells, and the noises were louder and more frightening. The peep-windows were all closed, and two male guards walked up and down, truncheons hanging from their belts, occasionally opening one of the windows, invariably to be met by a volley of abuse. They greeted Cynthia's guard warmly, and regarded Cynthia as a hungry man might have regarded a fillet steak. She felt quite breathless. "This is the woman's floor, isn't it?" she asked. "But you have male guards. Is that right?"

"Why not?" her escort said, simply.

They turned a corner, and were in a quieter corridor. Cynthia realised she had to make a decision, and quickly. "Please," she said. Her guard glanced at her. "May I ask your name?"

"My name is Carol."

"Carol?! But that's an English name."

"My mother was English."

"Oh, how splendid. But . . . you said was? She's not dead, is she?"

"She ran off with a sailor," Carol explained. "I do not like Englishwomen."

"Oh!" Cynthia bit her lip. But she had to persevere. "We're not all bad. Carol . . ." Another deep breath. "If . . . if you wished, I would be very nice to you."

There were less peep-windows in this corridor, and a single guard, seated at the far end and smoking a cigarette. Carol stopped walking and turned to face Cynthia.

"What do you mean by that?"

Oh, help Cynthia thought, if she's not a lesbian I've dug my own grave. "You said I'd make a lot of people happy while I'm here. I'd rather make just you happy."

"In return for what?"

"For just being yours."

"I cannot stop Major Isantsi having you. He is the boss."

"I understand that. But . . . anyone else. Please."

Carol smiled. "We will have to see. In here." She had beckoned the seated guard, and he came forward, shaking the bunch of keys hanging from his wrist. He also spoke to Carol, quiet vehemently. Carol shrugged, and replied. Cynthia had a pretty good idea what the conversation was about. But she could only brace herself for whatever lay ahead; she would aim just to survive in this place, and until something more promising turned up, Carol was her best bet. The door swung outwards, and the guard stood in the opening, speaking Turkish. A voice replied and did not sound harsh or vicious. The guard stepped aside and jerked his head. "Go in," Carol said. "And remember what I told you. Do not upset her, and she will not be violent."

Cynthia stepped into the cell and the door clanged shut behind her, actually banging into her back, causing her to stagger forward. The cell was about ten feet long and five feet wide. At the far end there was a barred window, and beneath the window there was a plain table and one chair. Beside the table there was a bucket with a lid. She regained her balance, gazed at the woman seated on the lower of the double-tiered bunks; as the bunks were perhaps three feet wide, the entire floor space amounted to a corridor two feet across. "Hi." The woman glanced at her; she had been reading a book. She was a small woman, shrouded in long black hair. Her face was actually quite beautiful in the symmetry of its features, allied to their perfect calm. "I'm to share your cell," Cynthia explained nervously. "I hope you don't mind."

"You will be company," Natasha Rykova said.

"Yes. That will be nice." Cynthia looked at the bunks.

"You have the lower one," Natasha said, getting up, and reseating herself in the one chair.

"Oh. Right." Cynthia placed her spare clothes on the bed, tried to stop inhaling the stench of stale urine arising from the bucket.

"You get used to it," Natasha said.

"Oh. Right."

"Hang your clothes in the cupboard."

Cynthia opened the cupboard, hung her spare dress beside the other spare dress that was in there. There was a shelf for her spare knickers, alongside another pair. She closed the cupboard, and looked at Natasha. Natasha had put down her book and was leaning back in the chair, looking at her. "I'm Cynthia. I mean, Charmaine."

"I'm Natasha, but they will have told you that. Why are you using a false name?"

"Well, it's the name on my passport. Charmaine. It was my boyfriend's idea." She bit her lip; she had not yet discovered Natasha's sexual habits. "I'm in for drugs," she added hastily.

50

"That is stupid," Natasha said. "You are very beautiful. You should be in Hollywood. Why ruin your beauty?"

Cynthia sat on her bunk, feeling relief slowly seeping through her. This woman seemed more rational and kinder than she had been led to believe. "I don't use them, myself. I had some in my suitcase. My boyfriend put them there."

"If you are smuggling drugs, you deserve to be hanged," Natasha said.

"I didn't know he'd done it. He's run off and left me carrying the can."

"Then *he* deserves to be hanged. Or castrated." Natasha's voice became dreamy. "I castrated mine."

Relaxation drained from Cynthia's mind as if someone had turned on a tap in her brain. "You *what*?"

"I tied him up when he was sleeping," Natasha said. "Then I cut them off. Slowly. You should have heard him scream."

"Oh, good God," Cynthia muttered. "You mean he was awake?"

"Of course. He had to understand what was happening to him."

Cynthia swallowed. "They said you'd committed murder," she said, without thinking.

"Oh, yes," Natasha said. "When I'd cut them off, I stuffed them into his mouth. He was a sight. Then he choked to death. Well, he would have bled to death, anyway."

Insensibly Cynthia found that she had drawn up her legs and was pressing her back against the wall. "What had he done?"

"I found him with another woman."

"That's a bit extreme, isn't it?"

"Listen," Natasha said. "When anyone goes with me, it's for keeps."

51

Cynthia swallowed. "Was . . . was he a Russian?"

"No, no, he was a Turk. A bastard in every sense." Natasha got up and stretched, while Cynthia watched her in fascinated horror. Then she stood at the window, looking out. "They are going to hang me."

"Oh, surely not," Cynthia protested.

"I am guilty," Natasha said. "He was there, dead. I was there, covered in blood. The knife had my finger-prints on it."

"But . . . a good lawyer . . ."

"There is no such thing, in Turkey. What you need is lots and lots of money. And I have no money. They recognise *crime passionnel*, you know. But only when it's committed by a man. So . . ." She sat down again.

"But Natasha, this is a remand centre, isn't it? You haven't even been tried yet. There's a long way to go. You should not despair."

"Do I look as if I am despairing? What is there to despair about in being hanged? It will be an experience. Do you have any cigarettes?"

"I don't smoke."

"Well, then, tell me about yourself. We have nothing else to do until dinner call at one o'clock."

At least she hadn't suggested having sex. "When do we have exercise?"

"This afternoon. Then we have to shower, then we are returned to our cells."

Cynthia licked her lips. "These showers . . . well . . ."

"Oh, yes. They will take one look at you and want to have you. Would you like me to protect you?"

"Would you? Can you?"

"Oh, yes," Natasha said. "They are all afraid of me. Even the guards are afraid of me. But I cannot protect you against them."

52

"I understand that," Cynthia said. "What . . . what would you require, in payment, if you protected me from the other prisoners?"

"The pleasure of your company," Natasha replied, enigmatically. So that you can cut off my breasts if you ever found me with another woman, Cynthia thought. Natasha cocked her head. "They are coming for you."

Cynthia stood up so violently she banged her head on the upper bunk; her ears weren't as sharp as the Russian's. "Ow! They can't be coming for me. Not so soon."

"Well," Natasha said. "They are certainly not coming for me."

The footsteps reached the door, and the key rasped in the lock. "Come along, Butts," said the female guard, and this was a different guard, not Carol. "There is someone to see you."

"My name is Trubshawe," said the self-important little man in the white suit. "I am from the Embassy."

"Thank God!" Cynthia instinctively reached across the table for his hands, and he hastily withdrew them.

"You are not allowed to touch me, Miss Butts."

"Oh! I'm sorry." Cynthia, glanced at the guard, staring at her, and sat down. "Can you get me out of here?"

"I'm afraid that would be rather a tall order." Trubshawe stroked his small ginger moustache. "You *are* aware of your situation?"

"Listen, I didn't know anything about those drugs. My boyfriend . . ."

"I have read your deposition," Trubshawe said. "You realise that it reads exactly like every other deposition in a case like this?"

Cynthia's shoulders hunched. "You mean you don't believe me."

"It is not my business either to believe you, or disbelieve you, Miss Butts." Although he obviously didn't. "The Embassy is here to help, if it can, British citizens who may get into trouble in Turkey. In your case, however, I really do not see what we can do. You have broken the laws of the land, Miss Butts."

"God Almighty!" Cynthia cried. "Do you know what has happened to me? I have been raped. Not once, but four times. And when I go back to my cell I am going to be raped again, and again and again and again. You can't allow that. I am innocent!"

Cynthia sobbed and her head sagged onto her arms. "You can't leave me here, Mr Trubshawe. You can't. Isn't it possible to obtain bail?"

"Bail has been set, in the sum of ten thousand English pounds."

"Ten . . .?"

"To be accompanied by confiscation of passport until the trial. Have you got ten thousand English pounds, Miss Butts? Or a place to stay in Turkey until the trial?"

"No," Cynthia whispered.

"So, do you know of anyone who could help you? Surely your parents?"

Cuthbert had ten thousand pounds, she had no doubt at all. But Cuthbert wasn't likely to come forward. That left . . . "My mother might be able to raise the money."

"Ah." Trubshawe managed to convey his surprise at the possibility that she had a mother. "Do your parents know you are here?"

What he meant was, she knew: do they know what you have been up to? "No," Cynthia said.

"Do they know about this friend of yours, Cuthbert Lucas?"

"No."

54

"You mean he's not your regular boyfriend?"

"Well, he is," Cynthia explained. "But you see . . . he's black."

Trubshawe might have been clearing his throat. "And you felt they might not approve. I see. Well, I suppose they'll be prepared to come to your rescue. Give me your father's name, and I'll get in touch with him."

"It would be better to get in touch with my mother. My father is . . . well, I don't know. He ran off. A very long time ago. I don't remember him. I think he's dead."

"I see. So your mother lives alone."

"Well, not exactly."

"I see," Trubshawe remarked. "Well, give me the name of your stepfather."

"Billy Hemp."

Trubshawe raised his eyebrows. "I wouldn't write him, though," she said. "He doesn't like me. Mum's the one you should get in touch with."

Trubshawe had been writing down the name anyway. Now he looked up. "Well, give me your mother's name."

"Haslar. Miriam Haslar."

Trubshawe laid down his pen and looked at his notes. Then he looked up again. "Forgive me for prying into your personal affairs," he said as sarcastically as he could. "But you have a stepfather named Hemp, a mother named Haslar, and you are travelling on a passport bearing the names of Butts. Would you care to explain that?"

Cytnthia licked her lips. "Well . . . Mummy and Billy aren't really married, you see, and . . ."

Trubshawe sighed, very loudly. "Explain about the passport."

"Well, Cuthbert thought it would be best for me to have another name, you see. He was afraid Mum might be having a look-out kept for me, at airports and things."

55

"I see." As usual there was a wealth of feeling in the two words. "But merely deciding to use a false name does not entitle you to a passport. Who is this woman Butts?"

"Me."

"My dear girl, you have to have a birth certificate to obtain a passport."

"Well . . . Cuthbert did all of that."

"Are you telling me that this passport is forged? My God! Do you realise that is a most serious offence? You could go to jail."

"I am going to jail," Cynthia pointed out. "If you won't help me. I am *in* jail."

Trubshawe gathered his papers into his briefcase and stood up. "I will contact your mother. However, I will also have to make a full report on your situation to the proper authorities, and I must warn you that even if we succeed in getting you out of Turkey, you will face criminal charges in England. However, as it is extremely unlikely that we will be able to get you out of Turkey, I suppose that is a minor matter. Good-day to you, Miss Butts, or Miss Haslar, or whatever is your name."

Cynthia stood up too. "You mean you're just abandoning me?"

"I can do nothing to help you, at this moment."

"But . . . can't you at least speak to Colonel Isantsi? Tell him not to let his goons touch me?"

Trubshawe went to the door.

"What about a lawyer?" Cynthia shouted. "They promised me a lawyer!"

"I believe one has been appointed. Good-day."

Cynthia looked at the guard, and the guard looked at Cynthia. When she went to the door, which Trubshawe had closed behind himself, he shook his head and began unzipping his pants. Cynthia exploded. She leapt across the room, picked up the chair, and hit the man across the head as hard as she could. He gave a yell of pain and sank to his knees. Cynthia hit him again, and this time the chair disintegrated into a mass of flying bits of wood. The guard yelled again. Cynthia turned back to the door as it opened, and two men came in, followed by two women. Cynthia stooped beside the guard to draw his gun, even if she had no idea how to use it. All the hours of careful self-restraint were gone: she wanted only to hurt someone, anyone, or everyone, as much as she could, before she died.

But before she could draw the gun the guard had thrown both arms round her legs and brought her heavily to the floor. Then the others descended upon her, grabbing any bit of her they could. She screamed as loudly as she could; Trubshawe had to be still in the building, but he did not return, and she was lifted bodily from the floor, kicking and writhing, trying to scratch at them with her nails.

Then she was in the corridor, temporarily dazed as she had banged her head on the door as they carried her out. Now she was too out of breath to fight and just sagged in the arms carrying her. So they put her on the ground and kicked her to her feet. Then she was dragged forward by her arms, sometimes stumbling to her knees but immediately being kicked in the backside again to drive her back to her feet. Dimly she was aware that she was falling down some steps instead of going up. Then there was another corridor, and then she was being thrust through a barred doorway, to collapse on her hands and knees. A man knelt to either side of her, stripping away her clothing. So what was new? she thought with looming hysteria. But she was not to be raped, at this moment. She was made to sit against the wall, her wrists were carried above her head and secured to manacles in the wall, and the men stood up and surveyed her. There were quite a few people beyond the bars as well, looking at her. The men made some remarks in Turkish, and there was movement beyond the bars. Cynthia turned her head with dazed indifference, and gazed at the nozzle of a hose. The men stepped away from her and the hose was switched on.

The water struck her in the face with a force which drove her back against the wall. Manacled as she was there was no way she could escape the jet. Then it played on her stomach, driving the breath from her lungs. Then mercifully it was switched off, leaving her panting, water dripping from her hair. "You scream," said one of the men in English. "More water." He and his companion left the punishment cell, and the door was banged shut and locked.

I'm alone, she thought. Oh, blessed thought. Then she realised that she wasn't alone; there was a rat on the far side of the cell, staring at her, nose twitching. And she was naked and couldn't use her arms. She drew up her legs, ready to kick if the rodent approached, but it did not, and after a few moments it scuttled off into the gloom. Cynthia realised she had been holding her breath, and very slowly allowed it to escape. She was in solitary confinement for attacking the guard. That figured. And inspite of her manacles she was just happy to be alone. Anyway, they couldn't mean to leave her here, manacled to the wall, for any length of time. Then it occurred to her that, judging by everything else she had endured today – was it still only today? – they might very well intend to leave her here, unable to move more than a couple of inches, wallowing in her own filth. They could always wash her clean with the hose.

But what was she to do? She could not endure much more of this. She was nearly out of her mind as it was.

58

And now she discovered that although she was sitting in a pool of water, she was terribly thirsty. She was almost tempted to start screaming, so that they would again flood her with the hose; some of the water might get into her mouth. But perhaps they would not stop at the hose. Better to hold on.

What wouldn't she give to be back in her cosy attic, even if it had meant a beating from Billy. Billy was a knight in shining armour compared with this lot. She wondered if Natasha knew what had happened to her. And if she would ever be returned to her cell. Even sharing a tiny cell with a self-confessed murderess was starting to seem like heaven. As for ever getting out of this prison, unless something dramatic had happened to the family finances in the past few months there would be no hope of Mummy raising ten thousand pounds. And even if she could, there was no chance that Billy would let her spend the money on getting her errant daughter out of jail.

She was here for six months! And then, as they would certainly find her guilty, she'd be sent some place worse for the next twenty-five years. She felt physically sick with despair. And then she heard footsteps. Oh, God, she thought. They're coming to torment me again. Carol stood at the bars. "You are a foolish girl," she remarked. "Why did you behave like that?"

"I lost my temper," Cynthia said.

"You realise there is nothing I can do for you now. That is a pity. I was looking forward to your company."

"They're going to let me out, aren't they?"

"Eventually."

"What's that supposed to mean."

"You will be let out when the commandant decides you have suffered enough. There is no limit to the term of solitary confinement."

Carol gazed at her for several more seconds. Then she said, "Such a waste," and left.

While Cynthia fought back the waves of panic that were creeping over her. Now she realised that she had lost all feeling in her arms, while her bottom was starting to feel sore. She *was* going to go mad.

Cynthia didn't know how long she sat there, alternately dosing off and waking up with surging horror. From time to time the rat emerged and looked at her, and then went away again. He clearly had an agenda, and she wasn't quite ready yet. God, if he attacked her . . .

She had no idea what time it was, down in the bowels of the prison. She had been thrown in here just before lunch, she thought, and realised that she was very hungry. But she felt too sick with the horror of her situation really to wish to eat, or even think about food. Her thirst was overwhelming. She listened to distant noises, but couldn't identify any of them. She thought how wonderful it would be if some other prisoner could attack a guard and be thrown in here, just for the company. But she'd probably be put in another cell.

She slept, head drooping between her shoulders. She kept waking, both because of her fear of the rat and because of the steadily growing numbness in her arms and shoulders. She was sure she had no blood left in her fingers. She'd get gangrene and have to have her arms amputated!

Footsteps. She tried to sit straight. But now there was no feeling in her bottom either, and her legs had also gone to sleep. But the feet were coming closer. Maybe they were going to feed her. They couldn't just leave her to starve to death.

She looked up, blinking in the electric light, and gasped,

as she saw Colonel Isantsi looking at her through the bars. He was accompanied by two women jailers. And amazingly, one of the women carried a bundle of clothing, and even a hairbrush, while the other had a thermos. Isantsi unlocked the door and stood above her. "Stupid girl," he said in English.

Cynthia didn't argue. If he was taking her out of here to rape her, that was all right by her, as long as he took her out of here. He reached past her to unlock the manacles. Her arms just dropped, her fingers thudding into the floor. She never felt a thing. Isantsi spoke in Turkish, and the other guard came in to kneel beside her, regardless of the water that still lay there. She filled a plastic cup with Turkish coffee and held it to Cynthia's lips. The liquid burned and she gave a little yelp of pain. It burned even more as it dribbled down her throat, but nothing had ever tasted so good.

The other guard also knelt, took Cynthia's arms and began massaging them. Cynthia still didn't feel able to move, so she just submitted, and submitted too as Isantsi also knelt beside her and started peering at her, feeling her legs and then her stomach and breasts. "You are not marked," he said. "This is good."

Sensation started to return to Cynthia's arms in the form of a thousand red hot needles being driven into her flesh. "Oh," she gasped. "Ow! Ouch!" Tears of pain rolled down her cheeks.

"It will soon wear off," Isantsi said. "Stand up."

Cynthia was pushed and pulled to her feet. Her legs gave way and she fell, but was caught by Isantsi himself; to her amazement he held her as tenderly as if he were her lover. Then he set her on her feet again and went behind her, examining her back with as much care as he had just examined her front. Now the pain in her arms

61

was beginning to wear off. She could feel again and she could move. "I am so thirsty," she said. "May I have some more coffee?"

The guard refilled the cup and gave it to her; the liquid had cooled a little by now and tasted even better. From his tunic pocket Isantsi took a flask, uncorked it, and handed it to her. "Brandy," he said.

She took a swig. The alcohol made her choke and her head spin. "Now you dress," Isantsi said.

The two women helped her to stand on one leg after the other as she was inserted into the drawers, then the dress was dropped over her shoulders and settled into place. The other woman knelt to fit the sandals on her feet and tie the ankle thongs. Cynthia, her head still spinning from the brandy, didn't know whether she was standing on her head or her heels, and became even more confused when one of the women used the brush to untangle her hair, with great care separating the golden strands and making sure they lay in perfection past her shoulders.

"Now you are beautiful again," Isantsi said. "You come." Cynthia went without protest. She was out of that dreadful cell. "Your lawyer is here to see you," Isantsi explained, as they climbed the stone steps to the ground floor.

So that's why they had tarted her up; they couldn't let a lawyer know how they really treated their prisoners. But would the lawyer be able to help? At least he might be more interested than that dreadful man from the embassy.

She was shown into a different interview room; presumably they hadn't had the time to put the other one back together yet. What was surprising was that she was accompanied into the room by Isantsi himself, but not the two guards, and there were no other guards present.

62

Equally to her surprise, Cynthia saw that her suitcase and handbag were on the floor next to the table. She gazed at the woman who sat at the table. She was middle-aged, neatly but conservatively dressed in a grey suit, with her glossy black hair in a bun. Her companion, on the other hand – for there was another woman in the room – wore a white linen suit with a matching straw hat, from which there descended a veil so that it was impossible to see her face or her hair. But she was tall and well built, and wore three quite magnificent rings. She stood against the far wall.

"Sit down," the woman at the table said.

"I'll stand," Cynthia said.

The woman looked at Isantsi. "She has not been harmed," the Colonel protested. "I have personally examined her. There is not a blemish."

"But my bottom is sore," Cynthia explained. "I've been sitting naked on a stone floor for the past twelve hours. At least."

The woman looked at Isantsi again. "Why has she been in solitary?"

"Because she attacked one of my guards and all but killed him. It would have been suspicious had she not been put in solitary."

Cynthia frowned. Something was going on, of which she knew nothing. The lawyer was looking at the standing woman, questioningly. "It shows she has spirit," the woman said. "I do not object to that. As long as she has not been harmed."

Cynthia's head jerked. Never had she heard such a voice, pure liquid gold, soft and husky yet perfectly clear.

"Then you are prepared to complete the transaction?"

"Come here, girl," the woman said. Cynthia glanced at

both the lawyer and Isantsi, but neither seemed to be objecting. She moved towards the woman. "Stop there," she was commanded, when she was within arm's length. "Tilt your head." Cynthia obeyed. She didn't know what was going on, but she felt it had to be to her advantage. "Now lift your dress." Cynthia gazed at her. "I wish to see if you are as beautiful as they claim," the woman said. Cynthia lifted the dress to her shoulders. "Turn around." Cynthia obeyed. "Slip down that abomination."

Cynthia hesitated but a moment, then slipped the drawers down to her knees. "Bend over." Again she obeyed, tensing herself, but the woman never touched her, never moved, so far as she could tell.

"Thank you," the woman said. "You may pull them up again. And drop your dress." Cynthia did so, cheeks glowing. As if I were a slave girl, she thought. "I think she will do very well," the woman said.

"As you wish," the lawyer said, and opened the briefcase which lay on the desk before her. From inside the case she took two thick manila envelopes, which she held out to Isantsi. "There is ten thousand in each." Isantsi stretched out his hand, but the lawyer pulled hers back. "You have destroyed the evidence?"

"Of course. Have I ever failed you?"

"See that you never do." The lawyer allowed him to take the money. Then she reached into the briefcase and took out the Russian doll. While Cynthia stared at it in consternation, she unscrewed the head, and from within took out the other four dolls, one after the other, unscrewing each head to reveal the next. "These are yours, I believe, Miss Butts?"

"But . . ." Cynthia licked her lips, and glanced at Isantsi.

"The charges against you are being dropped," the lawyer

64

said. "It has been discovered that the substance was not, after all, heroin."

Cynthia drew a deep bewildered breath. "Is that so. Well, then . . ."

"There are of course other charges against you," the lawyer went on. "Travelling on a false passport, and now, assaulting a prison officer, it appears."

"And what about my having been raped?"

"You would find that impossible to prove. These other charges I have mentioned will be held in abeyance, providing you leave Turkey immediately. This lady has kindly agree to assist you in this, and provide you with transportation. You will go with her now, please."

Cynthia gazed at her, then at Isantsi. "Just like that? It's all over and done with, after all I've been through?"

"It is all over and done with," the lawyer agreed. "You would be very foolish not to accept the situation. Do you wish to be returned to solitary? How long were you contemplating keeping her in there, Colonel?"

Isantsi grinned. "I was thinking of two weeks. At the end of that time she would not have an arse at all."

"That would be very foolish," the woman said. "Come along, girl. I have a car waiting."

Cynthia hesitated a last time, but only for a few seconds. She could not avenge herself from inside this prison. But once she got out . . . "Bring your suitcase and bag, dear," the woman said.

Cynthia picked up her belongings. Isantsi opened the door for her. "You'll be hearing from me," she said.

He merely bowed, and then she was following the woman down an empty corridor, and through a side door, into a private courtyard. A liveried chauffeur opened the back door of an American limousine for her, and she got in, found herself sitting beside another woman, this one obviously much younger than her rescuer, but also beautifully dressed and heavily veiled. The older woman sat opposite them, and the car moved away.

"Would somebody please tell me what the hell is going on?" Cynthia enquired. "Who are you? And why have you got me out of that hell hole?"

"My name is Mayne Mayne," the woman said.

"Mayne Mayne? That's a name?"

"Anything can be a name," the woman pointed out. "As for why I got you out of prison, why, I bought you, my dear. You now belong to me."

Chapter Four

Cynthia says: "*To be told that you have just been purchased is a considerable shock to the system. One's first reaction, of course, is disbelief. That sort of thing simply does not happen, in the modern world. How little we really know of what goes on in the modern world.*"

Cynthia's head turned, sharply. "You what?"

"I have just bought you," Mayne Mayne said with perfect composure.

"You can't be serious. You can't just buy people."

"It has its problems, in Europe or North America," Mayne Mayne agreed. "But elsewhere, it is simply a matter of money."

"Well, I'd say you have thrown yours down the drain. Suppose I don't want to be owned, by anyone? Suppose I just told you to stop the car now, and let me out. If you refuse, you could be up on a charge of kidnapping. OK, so you've paid my bail. I'm grateful, believe me. I'll pay you back, just as soon as I can. But you can't own me as if I were a car or something."

Mayne Mayne smiled. "You are far more beautiful, and valuable, than any motor car, Cynthia. Let me fill you in on a few facts. I did not pay your bail. I bribed Colonel Isantsi. I've done this before, whenever he has an especially good-looking young woman available. In return

67

for my bribe, he has seen that the evidence against you has somehow been mislaid. It happens all the time. You will remain on his books for a few weeks, at the end of which time, his friend and mine, Lawyer Gomih, will appear in court on your behalf and submit that as the evidence has disappeared, you should be released. The court will agree to this, after censuring the Customs for their negligence, with the recommendation that you be deported. Lawyer Gomih will agree to this in turn, and will volunteer to see to the matter. Thus the case will be closed, and forgotten. All we are doing is anticipating that deportation by a few weeks. You see?"

Cynthia's brain was in a spin. "Why have you done this?"

"Because you are a most beautiful woman, my dear, and I adore beautiful things. We have arrived."

Cynthia had been so caught up in trying to understand what had been happening to her that she hadn't been looking out of the window.

They had driven through Istanbul and were at one of the docks on the Golden Horn. And alongside the dock was a breathtaking ocean-going motor yacht, some hundred feet long, and festooned with navigational equipment. She squinted at the name: *Eboli*. The chauffeur was opening the doors, and the woman Denise was already out and waiting for them. "Come along," Mayne Mayne said. "We want to be away as rapidly as possible."

Cynthia got out, suddenly aware she was still wearing prison uniform, and that people were staring at her; that put the kibosh on her immediate, terrified thought that she might make a run for it. "Do you think the owner will let me on board?" she asked.

Mayne Mayne gave one of her smiles. "Of course she will. The owner is my mother."

"Your . . ."

"The Countess of Eboli," Mayne explained. "Do not worry, she is not on board herself, at the moment. She seldom travels much nowadays. So to all intents and purposes, I am the owner. After you."

Cynthia drew a deep breath. For the second time in her life she was jumping with both feet into a world of which she had simply no concept outside of films. But this impressive and obviously wealthy woman appeared kind and completely in command of the situation. She did not look the least bit vicious. And there would surely be many more promising times to think of escape; after all, no one could be kept as a slave in this day and age. Until a good opportunity presented itself, there didn't seem any point in trying to oppose her – even if she had truly wanted to. She was being taken out of a Turkish prison, away from a possible life sentence. That was all she wanted to happen, at this moment.

Denise was already on board, assisted by a sailor waiting at the head of the gangplank. Now he was joined by an officer, who ignored Cynthia as she followed Denise, but stood to attention and saluted Mayne. "Are we cleared?" Mayne asked.

"Of course, Miss Mayne."

"Then I wish to put to sea immediately," Mayne said. The officer, who was clearly the captain, saluted again, and went up to the wheelhouse, which was on the upper deck. "You may go up also," Mayne invited. "Take a last look at Istanbul. I do not think you will be returning, for a while."

Cynthia climbed the ladder, various crew members watching appreciatively as her skirt flew in the breeze. Mayne was behind her. She has bought me, Cynthia thought in disbelief. For what purpose? There was an

69

immense rumble from beneath them. The captain pressed various buttons, and the seaman on the wheel made some adjustments. The *Eboli* moved away from the dock.

Cynthia stood and gazed out at the mosques and houses of Istanbul slipping by. Was it really only the day before yesterday that she had been walking those streets with Cuthbert? Buying little Russian dolls? "Are you hungry?" Mayne asked.

"Hungry! I could eat a horse."

"I am sure we can do better than that. Go down those steps." The woman's manner was friendly; Cynthia began to relax.

The companionway was at the rear of the wheelhouse. She went down the ladder, a trifle unsteadily as the yacht trembled slightly on entering the currents of the Bosphorus. Through the huge window half way down the steps she saw a large open upper deck, on which there was a motor launch as well as various items of navigational equipment, but also two deck chairs. Then she was entering a huge, beautifully appointed saloon. At the forward end was a dining table and chairs; forward another companionway led down to what she guessed was the kitchen; delightful smells wafted upwards. Cynthia saw there was a curtain which could be drawn to shut off the dining room when required.

At one side of the lounge there was a bar, behind which stood Denise, pouring champagne. Cynthia had been so caught up in her surroundings before that she had not paid enough attention to the two women. Now she saw that Denise, having removed her hat and veil, was an extremely attractive woman of about thirty; she wore her red-brown hair relatively short, cut just below the ears, but it made a perfect frame for her classical features, straight nose, wide mouth, pointed chin. Her

70

complexion was technically marred by a dusting of freckles on the otherwise pale skin, but this rather added to the attractiveness of her features, while she clearly had a voluptuous figure, at least from the waist up; her legs were surprisingly thin.

Cynthia turned to look at Mayne, who had taken off her hat and veil as well. She guessed her 'owner' was about twice Denise's age, which did not mean that she was not still a most handsome woman, with unusually strong and distinctive features and a perfect figure. Her hair was a very dark brown with streaks of lighter brown; there did not appear to be any grey. Her complexion was unusual too, in that she seemed to have a very heavy tan. "Have a glass of champagne, dear," Mayne said. Cynthia took the glass, although she felt she might fall down when that hit her empty stomach. "Here is to us." Mayne raised her glass. "I am sure it is going to be great fun."

"What is?" Cynthia asked. "I wish you'd explain it to me."

"Time enough for that when you have had a square meal, and a lie down," Mayne said. "But first, I think you'd enjoy a bath. Denise will show you."

Cynthia knew that she did need a bath. She willingly followed Denise down another companionway, set in the after bulkhead of the saloon, and descended to the cabin level. Here there was a corridor, the thick pile carpet of which helped to dull the sound of the engines. There were three doors leading off, one on the left hand side. "That is the master cabin," Denise explained. "Mayne sleeps there." The other two were on the right. Denise opened the second door, and showed Cynthia into a double cabin. It had a small double bed, rather than bunks. Cynthia saw her suitcase resting on the covers. "Your bathroom

71

is through there." Denise indicated an inner door, leading forward.

"Thank you." Cynthia waited, and Denise smiled at her, and then left. Cynthia followed her to the door, but there was no means of locking it – and all the furniture was bolted down. Well, she thought, there wouldn't be much point in attempting to keep them out, anyway.

She dropped her prison clothes on the floor, added her thongs, and went into the bathroom. Here all was sweetly scented soap and soft pale blue towels. There was a tub as well as a shower, and she opted for the tub, dumping in a generous helping of foam; it was going to feel so good. While it was filling she cleaned her teeth with one of the cellophane wrapped toothbrushes, using an eqully new tube of toothpaste, slowly and carefully; she had not expected to be able to do that for a long time.

The water was ready. She stepped in and sank beneath the bubbles. Her bottom was still sore, and stung in the heat, but she could stand that. To be clean. To feel all that hell was behind her . . . even if she didn't know if there was another hell in front of her. But no hell conjured up by Mayne Mayne's lusts – or even those of her mother – could possibly compare with Colonel Isantsi's prison. Oddly, the only regret she had was not seeing Natasha again. She had felt that within that tormented mind there was a human being trying to get out. Instead of which that mind was going to be closed forever.

As she soaped herself, slowly and luxuriously, she heard the cabin door open. Well, she reflected, it had to happen. The bathroom door opened as well, and Mayne came in. "That smells good," she remarked.

Cynthia opened her eyes. Mayne had undressed and wore a towelling robe which did not quite reach her knees. When she sat down on the toilet seat it was easy to see that she was naked beneath it. It was also easy to determine that although she might be in her sixties, she still possessed a very good figure. "Does that feel better?" she asked.

"It feels glorious," Cynthia said, suddenly certain of why she was here. "So now it's collect time, is it?"

Mayne smiled. "You must not be in a hurry. Tell me about yourself. I know your real name is Cynthia Haslar. Tell me everything."

Cynthia resumed soaping while she considered. Any shyness she might one have felt was absent. There did not seem to be any mileage to be gained from lying. So she told Mayne everything. While she did so, she finished soaping, soaked for a few minutes, and got up. The ship was now moving at some speed through some quite choppy seas; they were in the Sea of Marmara. Cynthia found herself overbalancing and slipping at the same time and gave a little shriek. Mayne was on her feet in an instant, catching her before she could fall. For a moment she held her in her arms, their faces only inches apart. Then Mayne kissed her on the lips, very gently, and released her. "You'll soon get your sea legs," she said. "You don't get seasick, do you?"

"I don't know," Cynthia said, her face colouring from the kiss. "I've never actually been at sea before."

"You have so many pleasures in front of you," Mayne said, handing her a towel. "And you have already experienced more than most people in an entire lifetime. You are a treasure."

Cynthia dried herself, slowly and carefully, aware that the older woman was watching her all the time. The presence of her gaze, almost tangible, made her feel surprisingly hot. Cynthia felt that if it was going to happen, it should happen now. But Mayne was clearly in no hurry. Well, why should she be? "Where are you taking me?" she asked.

73

"Spain."

"Just like that? We're still in Turkey, aren't we?"

"Technically, yes."

"Well, don't we have to stop some place, for food or fuel?"

"This ship has a range of seven thousand miles, and all the food we need is in the deep freezes, save for what was bought fresh today."

"Heck," Cynthia commented. "You live like this all the time?"

"I live like this whenever I wish to travel, yes," Mayne agreed.

Cynthia hung the towel on its hook, and wrapped her wet hair in a clean one. "Do I get dressed now?"

"There is a robe in your stateroom. That will be sufficient. Then we'll eat; lunch is just about ready."

"Oh. Right." Cynthia went into the stateroom, put on the robe. "I thought you were . . . well . . ."

"About to rape you? I imagine you have had enough of that for the time being. If you have just been telling me the truth, you have never been with a woman?"

"Well . . . no," Cynthia said.

"And now you are impatient."

"I am trying to face facts."

"And you have naturally assumed I have bought you to have sex with you. Would you like that?"

"Like I said," Cynthia repeated. "I am trying to adopt to the new and strange reality that has become my life."

"And as I said, my dear, you must never be impatient, or fearful. Everything in its proper place. And now, food."

Cynthia was not going to argue with that. And the meal was a sumptuous one, containing just enough Turkish delicacies, such as egg-plant and kebabs, to remind them

74

where they were, but with a main dish of mouth-watering pork.

There were only the three woman at the table, and Cynthia gathered that they were the only passengers on board. There was wine to drink as well as deliciously fresh water, and they were served by a somewhat swarthy young man who Cynthia reckoned was probably Spanish, as that was the language Mayne and Denise used when speaking to him, but who showed no great interest in his three mistresses, not one of whom was wearing more than a single garment. Denise had changed her shore clothes for a wraparound, and Cynthia realised that her initial judgement had been entirely correct: if Denise's legs were a little thin, she compensated with a thirty-eight inch bust; her breasts were astonishingly heavy. "It may interest you to know," Mayne said, "that I purchased Denise, oh, twelve years ago. Isn't that right, Denise?"

"Twelve years and three months," Denise said, helping herself to salad.

"And are you not the happiest woman on earth, Denise?"

"In many ways, certainly," Denise said equably.

Mayne smiled. "She is sometimes unhappy because she has never had a child. But children are not acceptable, in our profession."

"Whatever the Countess may say," Denise remarked in a low voice.

Mayne made a *moue*, but Cynthia missed the by-play. "You have a profession?" she asked.

"Well, of course, my dear. It is not one I practice often, nowadays, but Denise is still active. While you, you are our newest recruit. And I think you will be very successful."

"You will have to explain that to me," Cynthia said.

"Finish your lunch," Mayne told her.

"I am going to sunbathe," Denise said when they had drunk their coffee.

"Oh, that sounds brilliant," Cynthia said without thinking; despite her bath, she was still feeling chilled from the prison.

Mayne considered. "Very well. You may. You could do with some colour. But only for fifteen minutes. We do not want you getting burned; you have a very fair complexion."

They went up to the sun deck via the wheelhouse, where three mattresses had already been spread on the deck, while another deckchair had been added. One of the crew was waiting with an assortment of accessories. Mayne chose an enormous floppy sun hat and sat in one of the chairs, after removing her wraparound. Denise also stripped but lay on one of the mattresses, on her face, declining a hat. The crew member looked at Cynthia. "Definitely a hat," Mayne said.

He held one out and Cynthia took it, then drew a deep breath – she was still not used to casual, and public, nudity – shrugged off her wraparound, and lay on the mattress next to Denise, on her stomach. She heard the sailor descending the ladder to the wheelhouse. Mayne knelt beside her and began applying sun tan oil to her shoulders and back with gentle hands. "We are actually going to make a stop before returning home," she remarked. "We are going to pick my mother up, in Malta. She has been visiting friends. Have you ever been to Malta, Cynthia?"

"No," Cynthia said. "I have been to Spain, though. Briefly."

"As you told me, with your boyfriend. Yes. Would you like to see him again?"

76

Now she was coating Cynthia's buttocks, and it was difficult to concentrate.

"Only to kick him in the balls."

"Well, perhaps that could be arranged. But there is a great deal to do first. Let me tell you about my mother. She has had a very unusual life. She was born in a place called British Guiana. Does that mean anything to you?"

She had moved down to the thighs and calves, which was a great relief. Cynthia had been quite good at geography, at school. "It's a country in South America which is now called Guyana. It used to be a British colony."

"Absolutely. You are a bright girl. When Mummy was born it was still a British colony. Mummy was the daughter of an Indian princess."

Cynthia rolled over and sat up. She hadn't expected that. But it would account for Mayne's slightly unusual features and colouring. "I am speaking of an Amerindian, of course," Mayne went on. "An American Indian. A redskin, you might say, only of the South American branch. I never knew my grandmother. She was bitten by a snake and died young. But by then she had become the mistress of an Englishman named Mayne, a cattle rancher. Mummy named me after him."

"Wasn't that rather an unusual thing to do?"

"Lie down, on your back," Mayne commanded, and Cynthia obeyed. This time Mayne began with her feet and shins. "My mother is an unusual woman. On the other hand, when I was born, she thought she was naming me Mayne Lowndes. That was the name of her first husband."

"Your father?"

Mayne moved up to Cynthia's thighs. "Open them a little," she suggested. Cynthia obeyed. The gentle massage was enormously pleasing. "He was my father, yes. But he also died before I was born. And then, some time later,

Mummy decided to revert to her maiden name. So I became Mayne Mayne. I have never found the name a handicap. Rather, is it a conversation piece."

She skipped Cynthia's groin, poured some of the oil on to her stomach, and resumed her massage. "The point is that Mummy was left absolutely destitute. She had to earn some money or starve. I would have starved as well. So . . ."

"She became a prostitute?"

Mayne allowed her nails to score Cynthia's flesh, ever so gently. "Mummy always thought of herself as a courtesan. She only ever dealt with the best. She became the most famous courtesan in Europe, perhaps in the world. Alexandra Mayne. Did you never hear of her?"

"I'm afraid not."

"Well, I don't suppose you have had much to do with the real world, until now," Mayne said, condescendingly, and began to massage Cynthia's breasts. Cynthia closed her eyes. "It was not all easy going, of course," Mayne went on. "Mummy's adventures and experiences would fill a book. In fact, I think she does mean to have her life story written, one day. And during the Second World War she was captured by the Gestapo. She was a heroine of the Resistance."

"She must be quite old," Cynthia muttered. Now it was even more difficult to concentrate, as Mayne was showing no hurry to move on to her neck.

"She is eighty-three. Now, of course, she is a very wealthy woman. Her second husband, the Count of Eboli, made her so when he died. But I suppose, all those years of endeavour, of sexual endeavour, had a psychological effect. It is her only source of excitement, and she craves excitement, activity. I know how she feels. I feel the same way myself."

78

Cynthia opened her eyes. "You mean you're a prostitute too? I mean, courtesan."

"I'm sure you do, dear. And I would remember to choose your words carefully, when you meet Mummy; she can be very strict. But yes, I worked for her. I still do, although nowadays I am more on the executive side than in the field." To Cynthia's enormous relief and yet vague disappointment, she ceased her massaging and got up to seat herself in her deck chair. "So, as I was saying, Mummy maintains her activity. She does what she has always done, provide a service for those men, or women for that matter, who need such a service and are prepared to pay well for it. As always, Mummy only operates at the highest level. But to do this, of course, she needs a coterie of young women. These young women must possess three characteristics. They must be beautiful, and they must find sex interesting and stimulating, in all its forms, and be willing to accept it in all its forms, too. I am sure you qualify on both those first two counts. And thirdly, and most importantly, they must at all times conform and come up to Mummy's standards, which are very high, just as they must at all times obey Mummy in everything and be utterly faithful to her. You will have to receive some training in that, but I do not imagine you will find it difficult."

Cynthia sat up again. "You mean you bought me to turn me into a whore? Well, forget it. Just get me out of Turkey and put me ashore some place. OK, so I owe you twenty thousand pounds. I'll raise the money somehow, and pay you back. But, please, just let me go home!"

"You are the sweetest child," Mayne said. "My dear girl, you have absolutely no choice in the matter."

Cynthia says: "*She was of course quite right, and I think I*

79

understood that even then. I had slipped into sex with some enthusiasm but I had never actually chosen the man I would have sex with, nor had I exactly been a willing partner with any of them, even with Cuthbert the first time. But the idea of being paid for it, and even more that someone else should be paid for handing me over, as it were, was repulsive to my still essentially innocent, and dare I say it, moral, mind.

But I was, as Mayne had pointed out, absolutely helpless – certainly at that moment."

Denise was now also sitting up, gazing at her. There was no hostility in the gaze, but Cynthia could not doubt that she would do whatever her mistress commanded. And in any event, what was *she* going to do, in the middle of a sea? Jump overboard? Land was only just in sight. She hadn't the courage for suicide. But anyone who thought they could keep her a prisoner was wrong. "So I have been kidnapped, after all," she remarked, and lay down again.

"Only until you come to accept your situation, dear," Mayne said. "I cannot imagine what you are so upset about. How many men have you slept with?"

"Just two."

"The famous Cuthbert being one. I suppose the other had your virginity. But you have had sex with more?"

"I was raped by four thugs masquerading as customs officers, if that's what you mean."

"We will have you examined by a doctor as soon as we reach Eboli," Mayne said ressuringly. "The point is, you cannot pretend you do not have a working knowledge of men. And as you say, four of them were thugs, one was no doubt a chance encounter, and the other was a drug-smuggling bastard who left you in appalling trouble. I can guarantee you that the men Mummy will rent you

80

to are all perfect gentlemen and very well bred. They will treat you like the beautiful creature you are."

"But they'll still want sex," Cynthia said.

"Of course. That's what they are paying their money for. I should mention that they will be paying a great deal of money, because they are all very rich. And that a percentage of the fee is yours."

Cynthia raised herself on her elbow. "What percentage?"

"You are a new girl. Twenty-five per cent."

"So you and your mother collect seventy-five per cent of what I can earn for you."

"My dear, it is the principal of the thing. Money as such means nothing to Mummy. But she enjoys making men pay. When you become established, you will receive thirty-three per cent of each fee. And of course, if you please the men, you will receive tips. Some of these can be extremely large. And those are entirely yours. Now, is that such a dreadful prospect? All for doing what comes naturally?"

Cynthia lay down again. It actually wasn't an unpleasant prospect at all. Especially when considered as an alternative to what she had gone through, and if she could make some serious money. But she wasn't going to let Mayne know that.

"Our clients are most carefully screened," Mayne went on. "You will be in no danger." Mayne was smiling at her. "Now I think you have had enough sun. Come below, and wash off that oil, and then, I think you and I should become better acquainted."

"Well," Cynthia says, *"if you can't beat them, join them, I decided. At least on a temporary basis. Actually making love with Mayne Mayne was a most exciting experience.*

This was, I suppose, at least partly because I had anticipated it for several hours, and was almost relieved that we had at last arrived at the crunch, as it were. You must also remember that I was still only sixteen, and if in some ways I felt a lot older, my sexual experiences had all been of the violent variety. Even Cuthbert had never been exactly gentle. With Mayne it was entirely a matter of kisses and caresses, even if some of the kisses were in places not even Cuthbert had been before. She was certainly passionate, and I gained the impression that she could be as violent as any man if she was crossed or upset in any way. But I wasn't going to do that. I just lay there and let her play with me until I made the biggest jump of my life. Shocking? Well, decadent, perhaps.

When she had satisfied herself, Mayne kissed me some more, and said, 'Mummy will adore you.'"

Cynthia had already shelved any immediate plans for escape. Perhaps in her heart she knew those plans had been shelved indefinitely. But it was easy to remind herself that escaping the *Eboli* while the yacht was at sea was impossible, and the yacht spent the next two days at sea, as it slipped through the Dardanelles, down the Aegean, round Cape Malea, and then west across the open Mediterranean for Malta, maintaining a steady fifteen knots. It was the most delightful experience of her life to that moment, especially when she realised she was not going to be seasick. She had nothing to do but eat, sleep, lie in the sun for carefully timed periods, watch videos . . . and make love. And after what had happened to her in Turkey, the fact that both her lovers were women and utterly gentle was the most relaxing thing about the whole situation. Denise was just as passionate as Mayne, but in a different way, in that she preferred to receive than to give. But Cynthia discovered that being in the driving seat, with a most exciting body at her disposal, was even more of a challenge than submitting herself.

So, she wondered, am I in heaven or in hell? Which did not solve the problem of her future. But with every hour she spent on the yacht she was realising that her future had solved itself. She had only two alternatives. One was to jump ship whenever the opportuntity presented itself. That would undoubtedly be the morally correct thing to do. But what would happen then? Whether it was in Malta or after they got back to Spain, she would be destitute, and far from home. Presumably she could go to a British consulate, and she might just be repatriated, but to what? Trubshawe would have contacted Mummy, and the whole world at home would know that she was the drug-smuggling mistress of a black man. There would be no one who would wish to know her. As Trubshawe had no doubt also been active with his superiors, she would also be on a forged passport charge.

So she'd run away again, and either walk the streets or become somebody else's mistress, and be let down and abandoned again as soon as he felt like it. Her alternative was to go to work for these people, and become a whore. And make lots of money, according to Mayne. Was there really a choice?

On the third day they motored past Gozo, with the island of Malta immediately in front of them. It had so far been a perfect voyage, with not a hint of bad weather. "I'd like you to go to your cabin, and stay there," Mayne told Cynthia, as the castle of the Knights of St John loomed high on the horizon, dominating the City of Valletta.

"I'm not going to try anything," Cynthia protested. "And I'd so like to see Malta."

"None of us are going to see Malta on this trip," Mayne told her. "We are putting in, picking up Mummy, and leaving again. Unfortunately, even to do that we need to clear Customs. That means your presence would have to be explained, and you don't even have a false passport; the Turks kept that one. I really don't want any trouble. So you'll please do as I wish."

Cynthia went below, accompanied by Denise. "Don't you have a passport, either?" she asked.

"I am to see you do not make trouble." Denise locked the door on them. "Please do not make trouble."

Cynthia considered the situation. She was as tall as the Frenchwoman, and as strongly built. But then there was the crew to be considered. Besides, she had already just about accepted her situation, even if Mayne didn't recognise that. "I'm not going to make trouble," she promised. "What shall we do to pass the time?"

It was difficult to concentrate on the matter in hand, even when the matter was as attractive as Denise. Cynthia found herself listening as the engines reduced speed to a low grumble, and the ship's movement slowed through the water. There was less lateral motion as well, as the hull entered the calm waters of Valetta Harbour. Denise, sated, was lying on her back, but when Cynthia made to get out of bed she held her arm. "Do not go to the port."

"I want to look at the place."

"You must not," Denise insisted. "Someone may see you. Do not worry, you will come here again, legitimately." Cynthia lay down again, listened to the rasp of the anchor chain, and then the engines changing pitch. "Captain Olivares has dropped a bow anchor," Denise explained, "and will put our stern up to the

84

dock. This is one of the visitors' berths. Well out of town."

Even lying on the bed Cynthia could see the green of overhanging trees as the *Eboli* backed into position. A few moments later the yacht came to rest, and the engines stopped. For the first time in more than two days it was absolutely quiet, but almost immediately the hum of the generator took over, maintaining the air-conditioning in the cabins. "How long do we wait?" she asked.

"Not long. Captain Olivares will have radioed ahead to let them know when we were coming. *Eboli* is well known here."

Cynthia rolled on her side. "Tell me about it."

"About what?"

"The life I'm going to lead."

Denise's lips twisted. "Providing you always obey the rules, it is a very good life."

"Then what are the rules? Oh, I know the bit about always obeying the Countess and being utterly loyal to her. But there have to be others."

"The others are dictated by logic. They are three, mainly. One is to remember always that while you belong to the Countess, within that you belong utterly to the client to whom you are rented, for the entire period of the rental."

"You make me feel more and more like a car," Cynthia pointed out. "You mean these aren't just one night stands we're talking about?"

"Oh, no. Sometimes they are for quite lengthy periods. I was once rented to a man for a month. I became quite fond of him."

"Despite the fact that he could beat you and belt you as it took his fancy?"

"Our clients are not allowed to harm us."

"What I don't get is what the Countess can do about it once this client has carried you off to his tent?"

"There is no client would dare go against the Countess," Denise said fervently. "She is very powerful. She has a network of agents and friends all over the world. It would be very dangerous to cross her. Besides . . . she is the Countess."

Cynthia lay down again. "I'm not quite sure whether you love her or are scared of her."

"A bit of both," Denise confessed. "You'll understand when you meet her."

Cynthia listened to sounds from aft, on deck. Heavy boots. She couldn't hear any conversation, but she presumed those were the Customs officers. They were not in any event her favourite kind of people. Then she listened to a car on the dockside, and the banging of doors. "That'll be the Countess," Denise said.

It was quite an effort to remain lying on the bed, listening, and waiting. But then she heard the boots clumping again, and fading aft. As they did so, the engines started, a low rumble which took over the entire ship. A few minutes later *Eboli* began to move. "That has to be the shortest stop ever." Cynthia swung her legs off the bed and put on her wraparound.

"It would be better to wait for the Countess to summon you," Denise suggested.

"I've waited long enough," Cynthia said. She opened the cabin door and stepped into the corridor. There was no sound from above her. She went up the companionway into the saloon, and gazed at Alexandra Mayne.

The Countess was seated on the settee, beside her daughter, with whom she was deep in conversation, but she turned her head as Cynthia emerged, and Cynthia caught her breath in surprise. Alexandra Mayne might be eighty-three years old, but she looked hardly more than half that. Her features had the boldness of her daughter's, but were somehow more harmoniously composed. Her eyes were huge and black and deep. Her hair was also jet black, and was clearly dyed, but still worn long, even though at the moment it was confined beneath a headscarf. She was obviously as tall as Mayne, and although it was impossible to determine her figure, as she was wearing a white trouser suit and was sitting down, the ankles and feet revealed by her white leather sandals were at once smooth and brown and perfectly shaped. "Cynthia," Mayne snapped. "Don't you realise we are still in the harbour? If someone was watching us through binoculars and saw you, when have declared that I am alone on board save for the crew . . ."

She checked, because her mother had laid her hand on her arm. "Come here, child," Alexandra Mayne said. Slowly Cynthia crossed the carpeted floor to stand before her. "Oh, indeed," Alexandra said. "For once, Mayne, you have not exaggerated." She reached forward and released the tie at Cynthia's waist, pushing the material back to either side. "Yes, indeed," she said again.

"So you are Cynthia. And you are going to work for me." Her voice was like liquid gold. It caressed.

But Cynthia was determined to establish her position as quickly as possible. "So I'm told, Countess," she said.

"I warned you, Mummy, she is a bit of a rough diamond," Mayne said.

"An uncut diamond," Alexandra said, as softly as ever. "But still a diamond. I am impatient to work on her. Are we out of the harbour yet?"

Mayne looked through the huge windows. "Just."

"Well, tell Olivares to increase speed. Let's be away

87

from land as quickly as possible." Mayne reached up for the intercom behind the settee and gave the necessary instructions. Immediately the engine noise increased and the ship surged forward. "Now it does not matter if anyone sees you or not," Alexandra said. "Or hears you. Did my daughter tell you to stay in your cabin until summoned?"

"Well, yes, she did. But I'm really not used to being locked up."

"Of course not," Alexandra said sympathetically. "But on the other hand, you are on a ship, and you have disobeyed the orders of your superior. That makes you guilty of mutiny. Do you understand that?"

"So what do you mean to do to me?" Cynthia enquired, frostily, suspiciously.

Alexandra smiled. "Having so far invested twenty thousand pounds in you I should hate to throw it all away, so you will not be harmed. But you will have to be punished, if only so you will learn not to disobey again."

"You must be nuts."

Alexandra looked at her diamond-encrusted wristwatch. "I intend to have you spanked," she said. "I will not use a whip or a cane because I do not wish to mark your skin. Ah, Denise!" She looked at the Frenchwoman, who had just emerged from the companionway.

"It is good to see you again, madame."

"It is good to see *you*, Denise. And this charming young girl we have accumulated. But she sadly lacks discipline. Bring me the ferrula."

Denise opened a drawer in the bureau set against the bulkhead and took out a thick leather strap, some eighteen inches long, and fitted with a handle. Cynthia watched her in disbelief. "You dare not touch me with that thing . . . I'm not a child."

88

"I operate," Alexandra said, "on a system of complete mutual trust and understanding. The sooner you understand that, Cynthia, the happier you will be. Now, you have disobeyed Mayne, and thus you will have to be punished. If you will do as I ask, and lie on the dining room table, you will receive six strokes of the ferrula. This will be painful, but you will soon recover. If you refuse to do as I ask, I will call in some of my crew to place you on the table and hold you there. That will be very humiliating for you, and the punishment will be doubled. You will find this *extremely* painful, and your bottom will remain sore for several hours. The choice is yours."

"You . . ."

Alexandra held up her hand. "I should warn you that if you curse me or any of my people, the punishment will again be doubled. It would be better of you did not speak at all." She smiled. "I have no objection to a few yelps. But do try not to scream; it is so undignified."

Cynthia stared at her. This can't be happening, she thought. She looked at Denise, but as always the French-woman's features were immobile. Only half an hour ago they had panted to orgasm in each other's arms. But now she was going to obey her mistress. Alexandra looked at her watch again. "Your time is up, Cynthia. May I have a decision, please?" Cynthia shrugged the wraparound from her shoulders, and went into the dining saloon.

Chapter Five

Cynthia says: "*I knew I was on a hiding to nothing, quite literally. So I climbed on the table, lay on my stomach, and took what was coming. It wasn't so bad: the leather strap stung rather than cut, as a cane would have done. Which is not to say I didn't hate the guts of all three of them when I had taken my six strokes and I could rub my bottom. I think it was the humiliation – Mayne held my wrists and Denise my ankles while Alexandra applied the strap with surprising strength – of it more than the actual pain. But I still had no doubt that the Maynes were my only hope of emerging from this whole ghastly business with even the slightest profit. In that context to be beaten with a leather strap as if I were an errant schoolgirl was hardly relevant.*" She gave one of her glorious smiles. "*And actually, of course, I suppose I was just an errant schoolgirl.*"

"How is your bottom today?" Alexandra asked.

Cynthia blinked as she awoke. "Sore."

"It will soon feel better. Let me look at it." Cynthia had been lying on her face anyway – it had been too painful to sleep on her back – and so she merely lay still while Alexandra pulled down the sheet. "Oh, that's not bad at all. The last mark will have faded in a few hours." She stroked the softly rounded flesh, while Cynthia made her muscles relax; there was no point in getting uptight now. "Have you never been spanked before?" Alexandra asked, slipping her hand down to caress the back of Cynthia's thigh, and then drifting between.

"My stepfather beat me once. Ten years ago."

"Did he interfere with you?"

"He wanted to. But he couldn't, with Mummy there."

"Of course. And so you hated him."

Her fingers were causing the most delicious sensations, and Cynthia couldn't speak for some seconds. "Yes," she muttered into her pillow. "I hated him."

Alexandra released her, left the bed, and sat in a chair. "Go and shower," she commanded. Cynthia slid off the bed and went into the bathroom. She left the door open. "So do you now hate me?" Alexandra asked. Cynthia turned on the water. Alexandra waited until the flow had ceased. Then she said. "It would be very stupid of you to be that childish. How old are you, truly?"

Cynthia stood in the doorway while she dried herself. "Sixteen."

"And so well built," Alexandra said. She reached into the pocket of her dressing gown and produced a tape measure. "Stand still, with your hands at your sides." Cynthia obeyed, while Alexandra took her measurements. "Thirty-five, twenty-six, thirty-five," she said. "Oh, perfect. How tall are you, dear?"

"Five eight, when last I measured."

"Perfect. Now, show me what you have to wear." Cynthia opened her wardrobe. "Hm," Alexandra said. "Not at all good. We shall have to do some shopping for you." Cynthia rather liked the sound of that. "What jewellery do you have?" Alexandra asked.

"None at all. I had a good watch, but the Turks took it away from me, and didn't give it back,"

"We'll get you another watch," Alexandra said. "And

91

some accessories." Cynthia liked the sound of that even more. "Take out that dress," Alexandra commanded. Cynthia obeyed. It was a black and gold sheath Cuthbert had bought her, especially for the Turkish trip, and was the best thing she had with her. Now for the first time she remembered that she had a wardrobe full of quite good clothes in the London flat, including her fur coat. But Cuthbert had probably already given them all to her replacement. Not to mention her teddy bear! "Put it on," Alexandra said. "Don't worry about underclothes," she added, as Cynthia instinctively reached for a pair of knickers. "Life is so much more exciting without them." Cynthia put on the dress. "Now brush your hair." Cynthia brushed her hair, while Alexandra continued to gaze at her.

"I'm sorry, I don't have any lipstick," Cynthia said.

"I'm not really sure you need it. We'll think about that. Come into the saloon." She led the way up the companionway. Mayne and Denise were waiting for her. "We'll begin by sitting," Alexandra said, and did so. "Opposite me." Cynthia sat down in one of the armchairs, knees pressed together. "You are not about to be interviewed." Alexandra beckoned her daughter and Denise to sit either side of her on the settee. "Sitting is the most important preliminary move a woman makes, when she wishes to attract a man. Forget all the twaddle about walking with a book on your head; I'm not trying to make you into a mannequin. You walk with a natural, athletic grace. If you bob a bit, well, you have the breasts for it. But sitting is an art. I want you to consider me a man. Forget Mayne and Denise. I need their eyes, but they are not here, as far as you are concerned. Now, I may be thinking to myself, what a looker. Now, I do not know you have nothing on under that skirt. It is your business to inform me of that fact, without in any way being lewd or lascivious or

92

downright vulgar. If you are any of those things, you may put me off. You will certainly put off any men who are *my* clients. So, stand up." Cynthia stood up. "Now, sit, and as your bottom touches the cushion, cross your legs." Cynthia sat down, winced at the sudden pain, and crossed her legs. "Well?" Alexandra enquired.

"Too much," Mayne commented. Denise nodded.

"My opinion exactly," Alexandra agreed. "The leg was raised far too high and crossed far too slowly. I may say, Cynthia, that the technique of revealing everything up to your hip for the briefest of moments works even when you have knickers on, but it is a matter of timing. When you have nothing on, the movement must be so rapid that the man should be left wondering what he did see, or if he saw anything. Thus he will become even more interested than he was in the beginning. Now, do it again. And remember, your skirt rises as you cross your knees, and then settles again. The crossing of the knee must take only a split second, and the skirt must come down, just as quickly. Assist it with your hands if necessary. So after half a second the man is left looking at your knees and calves and feet, and remembering." Cynthia did it again. "I think you're a quick learner," Alexandra remarked.

Cynthia was actually fascinated by every aspect of learning to project her sexuality, so much so that her still simmering resentment at the way she had been treated soon became submerged beneath her enthusiasm. Walking was a part of the business, although as Alexandra had indicated, she was not bothered by a certain amount of bobbing. Bending was equally important. So was stooping to pick something up. "And remember," Alexandra told her. "There is always something to be picked up when you feel it necessary to show a bit of thigh, or to give a man

93

a good view of your bum under a tight skirt. Even if it is only your handkerchief."

Then there was eating and drinking. Cynthia actually had quite a good education in table manners, thanks to Mummy's ideas above her station, but she yet had to become familiar with a full dinner set of cutlery, and she was still inclined to drink too quickly. "For some reason," Alexandra explained, "women are considered vulgar if they gulp their drinks. In any event, it pays to drink slowly in order to let the man get tight in front of you. That way you always retain control of the situation."

Cynthia had done no more than skim the surface of all of these subjects when only two days after leaving Malta, they motored into Alicante Harbour. Nor had she had undiluted training during that period. Just west of Sardinia, as they had turned up for the Balearics, they had run into a mistral. It was Cynthia's first storm at sea, and she was terrified, even if the other three women were unconcerned. But with *Eboli* pointing into the weather, and thus slowly climbing up great white-topped green mountains before commencing a terrifying lurch down the other side into an apparently bottomless pit, all ideas of walking or sitting correctly, much less sitting down to a seven-course dinner, had to be abandoned, while the constant howling of the wind, which drowned out even the sound of the engines, made conversation at a normal level impossible.

It was this night, their second out of Malta, that Alexandra took Cynthia to bed.

As Alexandra only ever slept in the master cabin, this meant that Mayne had to move out for the night, but she did not seem disconcerted; she was going to sleep with

94

Denise. And Alexandra's intentions were less sexual than a desire to allay Cynthia's obvious fear, although they both quickly became mutually aroused as Alexandra went into her gentle stroking routine, and required Cynthia to do the same, to an amazingly firm and attractive body. "There really is nothing to be afraid about," she murmured into Cynthia's ear. "I have been on board *Eboli* when Olivares has driven her through a hurricane, and compared with that, a mistral is a breeze." Cynthia wallowed in the stimulating warmth of the older woman's arms, and almost felt reassured. "There is actually nothing in life that one need ever be afraid of," Alexandra told her. "And that is a very important consideration in our profession. Mayne tells me you were raped by some Turkish men?"

"Yes," Cynthia said.

"How many men?"

"Four."

"I was raped, by three men, when I was even younger than you," Alexandra said. "And I was a virgin. Mayne says you were not a virgin when you had this experience."

"No," Cynthia muttered, and raised her head in astonishment, peering at Alexandra's face in the gloom. "And then you were tortured by the Gestapo," she said.

"Well, I was taken prisoner, yes. Briefly. But the two incidents were a few years apart."

"What a life you must have had," Cynthia said. "And you can speak of such things as incidents?"

"I have a few memories," Alexandra said. "But that is the key to life, don't you see? To regard whatever happens to you as an incident, rather than an accident, and never as a misfortune, or heaven forbid, a calamity."

Cynthia thought Alicante a beautiful city, but she was not

95

allowed to see much of it. Alexandra was, apparently, well known and treated like royalty. Customs formalities were kept to a minmimum, and no one seemed interested whether Cynthia had a passport or not. A limousine was driven on to the visitors' dock, where *Eboli* was moored, and Cynthia, dressed in her best black and gold dress with her matching shoes, and with a black head scarf to conceal her hair and enormous, very dark glasses to conceal most of her face, was hurried ashore and behind the tinted windows of the back seats, where she was joined by the other women. "I feel like royalty," she muttered.

"Who knows, one day you may be royalty," Alexandra said. "But for the moment, we don't want anyone seeing you."

So my kidnapping goes on, Cynthia reflected. "Does the yacht stay here all the time?" she asked.

"No. It will leave in an hour and go on down to Gibraltar."

"I thought the Spanish weren't having any dealings with Gibraltar? Cuthbert told me."

"Things are better now. It is lack of mooring space that is the problem. One day there may be marinas in Spain capable of holding *Eboli*. But it is no great nuisance. Should we decide to go anywhere, the ship can be in Alicante in twenty-four hours, or Barcelona in forty-eight."

"Isn't that a marina?" Cynthia asked.

They had turned off the dock and on to the main street, which ran between the ramblas and the waterfront, and to their left was an imposing building, beyond which was a mass of pontoons and moored yachts.

"Indeed it is," Alexandra said. "That is the Alicante Yacht Club. But they will not have me as a member. Me, the Countess of Eboli."

"Why not?"

"Because I am a whore, my darling. Or was a whore, once. It is dear Pedro's family who has done this. There was a great scandal when he chose to marry me, and an even greater scandal when he left me all his money and land. They tried to have the will set aside on the grounds that he was incompetent. Well, they failed at that, but they have done their best to make themselves a nuisance ever since. But then, what is a yacht club?" It was interesting, and somewhat salutary, Cynthia reflected, that even Alexandra Mayne did not have the *entire* world at her fingertips.

By midday they were high in the mountains behind Granada, and that night they stopped at a parador, one of the government-owned hotels, north of the Tagus. "Now, Cynthia," Alexandra said, as the limo pulled into the courtyard of the converted castle. "I do hope you are going to behave yourself."

"Me?" Cynthia asked, sounding as surprised as she could.

Alexandra smiled at her. "Do please remember that none of us was born yesterday. This will be the first time since leaving Turkey that you will actually be in the midst of people who do not work for me. However, I should warn you that I use this parador regularly. The management and staff are old friends. It follows therefore that long before you could convince them that you are being held against your will, if you do feel that way, I shall have regained control of the situation, and of you. And I promise you, if you put me through that embarrassment, I will put my twenty thousand pounds at risk in order to punish you most severely. I do wish you to remember this."

Cynthia looked into her eyes, which had suddenly become as hard as flint. "I will remember it," she said.

Alexandra's eyes softened, and she smiled. "I am sure you will. Remember always what I am offering you: a life of great splendour, great wealth and great pleasure."

Cynthia reflected, when they went down to dinner, that making a scene would be quite simple; the hotel was full, and there was not a diner of either sex who could resist gazing with great interest at the four exceptionally beautiful women dining together, no doubt speculating as to whether they were actresses or aristocracy.

The thought of what they might say, or do, were it to be revealed to them that they were actually looking at three prostitutes in the act of kidnapping a fourth for their profit and amusement, was almost amusing. But there was no point in it. She believed Alexandra when she claimed that she could ride a scene, and the thought of what might then be done to her . . . besides, she still had not made a penny out of her situation, was actually more destitute than when she had run away from home with twenty pounds in her pocket. Patience, she told herself.

The next day they were on their way again, driving north, into country which was at once hilly and wooded. They climbed a fairly steep hill and arrived before a pair of huge wrought-iron gates. These opened to a coded flick of the lights from the limo, and they drove in, still climbing, but now through a pine wood. Half a mile further on they came upon the house, which had clearly once been a wrecked castle, on to which a modern mansion had been cleverly built. "When I first came here, with dear Pedro, oh, more than fifty years ago," Alexandra said, "the castle was intact. It was so romantic. But then in the

Civil War the Communists virtually tore it down. It was a great pity."

"Gosh!" Cynthia said, lost in the beauty of the place. "Aren't you glad you weren't inside it when that happened?"

Alexandra smiled. "But I was." Cynthia stared at her in consternation, and Alexandra's smile widened. "Did you suppose that being gang-raped as a girl and then captured by the Gestapo as a woman are the limits of my experience, my dear? One day you will have to read the story of my life. This is Madeleine."

Cynthia gulped as she watched a woman approaching from the front doorway. One had to describe Alexandra Mayne as beautiful; there was no other word that could be used. How then, she wondered, could this woman be described? Madeleine was also in her eighties, Cynthia estimated, and yet . . . she supposed exquisite was the word. She was as tall as Alexandra, and retained as good a figure, but she was fair – there were still traces of gold in her white hair – where Alexandra was dark. No American Indian ancestry here, Cynthia deduced. It turned out that like Denise, Madeleine was French, and had been Alexandra's confidante and lover for some sixty years; she had, in fact, been married to the man who had set Alexandra up as his mistress and thereby inadvertently launched her on her career. What a time they must have had in the roaring Twenties, Cynthia thought.

But she was lost in wonder at everything with which she was now surrounded. At the stupendous views from her window, over vine-covered slopes . . . "Pedro earned his fortune from rioja," Alexandra explained. "But when I returned here after the war I decided to lease the vines out to other bodegas. Part of the rent is two cases of wine every week. I have a well-stocked cellar."

99

Just visible in the next valley was a ruined village. "Those houses were occupied by Pedro's tenants and servants, before the Civil War," Alexandra explained. "But they sided with the Communists. It was they who lynched Pedro, tore down this building, murdered my servants, and raped Madeleine and myself."

Cynthia looked at Madeleine, who smiled. "They would have lynched us as well," she said. "Had not a regiment of soldiers arrived. Then we had to service their commander. My God, the *stamina* we had in those days." Cynthia was open-mouthed.

"So when I returned after the war," Alexandra said, "I would not have any of them back. Most of them had been killed, anyway, by the Fascists. Now I employ only handpicked servants, whom I know will never let me down. But it is time for you to meet the girls." Cynthia was escorted to a terrace overlooking a swimming pool set in a courtyard situated within the very heart of the building. The pool was enormous, and in or around it were six stunningly built young women, all naked.

"Girls!" Alexandra clapped her hands. "This is Cynthia." They left the water or their deck chairs to greet her. "Angela," Alexandra introduced. Tall and slim and dark-haired, with flashing black eyes. To Cynthia's surprise she turned out to be English rather than Spanish.

"Maureen." Shorter, plumpish, and red-haired, with a wide smile. Her pale complexion was dotted with freckles and even her pubic hair was reddish-brown. She was definitely Irish, Cynthia knew, even before she spoke.

"Rona." Dark, but with curly rather than straight hair, worn very long; short, with a slight but elegant figure. Rona was Spanish.

"Carmen." Not tall, but strongly built and voluptuous,

with golden brown skin and flowing black hair. "Carmen is Afro-English, from Jamaica," Alexandra explained.

"Ingrid." Ingrid was Swedish, as blonde as Cynthia herself, but taller and more powerfully built. Her hair was pale yellow, like Cynthia's, and as dead straight. She was the only member of the group who regarded the newcomer with the least hostility. Cynthia suspected that in their similarity of appearance she sensed a rival. But she also moved with some difficulty.

"Ingrid is recuperating," Alexandra explained.

"And Irina." Another blonde, but this woman was shorter than Cynthia, more voluptuous even than Maureen, with curling yellow hair drooping past her elbows. She came from the Ukraine, and had had to be smuggled out of the USSR.

The women surrounded Cynthia as she was delivered into their midst, and a few minutes later she was as naked as they, and being thrown into the pool amidst shrieks of laughter. "You are going to be very happy here," Alexandra assured her.

Cynthia was called upon to submit to a very detailed medical examination by Alexandra's personal physician, Dr Cardona. This included a blood test, after which the doctor was able to declare that she was free of HIV, or anything else.

"What would you have done if the test was positive?" Cynthia asked Alexandra.

"I would have had to accept a loss on my investment," Alexandra said, disturbingly. "But all is well that ends well. Now, to work."

Cynthia didn't doubt that she could be happy on Eboli, providing she followed the golden rule: obey Alexandra's

101

every whim. And her women seemed happy to do so. Life on Eboli was lived on a high level, with the best of food and drink, but also with a serious amount of daily work to be done. Alexandra had given a great deal of thought to the pleasing of men, or women, and had drawn certain very definite conclusions from her years of experience. One of her most firmly held opinions was that clients did not appreciate companions who had any hang-ups. "Nothing," she told her women time and again, "annoys a man so much as to take a woman out for a meal at a top-class restaurant, and have her refuse all the tastiest dishes because she is on some kind of a diet. But this applies even at the breakfast table."

They were thus required to become familiar with, and fond of, every possible variety of unusual food, from caviar to truffles, not excluding pigs' trotters and goats' testicles – Cynthia gathered that a large proportion of Alexandra's clientele was Arab. They could eat to their stomachs' content – but they were not allowed to get fat. The answer lay in exercise, and the women indeed exercised for several hours every morning. Cynthia thought she would never forget the expressions on the faces of the bodega workers as they watched six women – Ingrid was excused for the time being – wearing only catsuits darkened with sweat jogging by. Alexandra and Mayne, and either Madeleine or Denise, accompanied them in the estate Land Rover and saw to it that nobody flagged.

The business of consuming as much as one was offered without noticeable effect extended even more importantly to alcohol. "Men do not like women who refuse drinks," Alexandra told them. "But even less do they like women who become drunk and make a spectacle of themselves. Unless, of course, they are deliberately setting out to make you drunk, in which case it is in your interest to realise

102

this and decide whether to go along or not. That must depend on circumstance. But usually, the idea should be resisted."

That meant that they had drinking sessions at which they had to consume a great deal, of either wine or spirits or both, while retaining their mental alertness. "The secret is liquid," Mayne explained. "Non-alcoholic liquid, taken in advance. Some recommend milk, but if this isn't available, then plain water or squash will do. A litre of non-alcoholic liquid, taken as close as possible to when the actual drinking commences, will double the amount of alcohol you can consume before getting drunk."

The jogging was varied by horseback riding, which Alexandra in any event considered an important part of a young woman's accomplishments. For Cynthia, this meant beginning at the beginning. Denise, a superb equestrian, took charge of this aspect of her education, and the pair of them spent at least two hours a day, beginning with the most basic principles and gradually progressing to low jumps. Again Cynthia proved a quick learner, and after only two months she was galloping across country with the rest of them. But by then a great deal else had happened.

There were a good many other accomplishments Alexandra required of her women. One was ballroom dancing. Cynthia, who had only ever jiggled to rock, found this almost as difficult to master as learning to ride. For these lessons her tutor was Madeleine, who played the part of the man, waltzed her around the dance floor at the castle.

They were also required to learn both French and Spanish.

Then there were more masculine pursuits. Mayne and Denise drove her down to the coast for a week, for her to be instructed not only in water-skiing, something else at which she had never tried her hand, but also in handling a speedboat. "A woman who can do that always excites men," Mayne told her.

As usual, Alexandra was pleased with her progress. "This winter," she said, "we will go into the Sierra Nevadas and you will learn snow-skiing."

Even more surprising was her tutelage in karate. "This is an insurance policy," Alexandra told her. "Under no circumstances must it be used save in the most extreme circumstances. Any man to whom I rent you will have been most carefully vetted by myself, and Mayne and Madeleine. And any man, having rented you, is entitled to indulge to the full the terms set out in his contract, however repulsive they may be to you personally. You will refuse a man nothing, save grievous bodily harm. That includes spanking, or even whipping, if it has been paid for. However, it can happen that a man goes right over the top because of his lust. In this case, and only if it is undertaken to save yourself from actual physical and lasting damage, you will be entitled to use what you are about to learn to extricate yourself from your situation."

Cynthia was taught by Denise the secrets of both ju-jitsu and karate. "Of course," Denise pointed it, "if you use any of these methods, you must carry it through to the end, and leave the man unconscious, or certainly incapable. If you hurt him and allow him to recover, he will be very difficult to cope with, and you will have lost the element of surprise."

"I'm glad you and I didn't fall out on the yacht," Cynthia said. Denise merely smiled.

"Always bear in mind that if you ever do have to lay a

104

client out," Alexandra told her, "while I, if it is humanly possible, will extricate you from the hands of the local law, you will have to give a full and sufficient explanation of your actions and the reasons for them, to me." She gave one of her terrifying smiles. "At the end of which, if I consider what you did was unjustifiable, you may well wish you had remained in the local prison." But Cynthia nonetheless felt much more in control of herself and her surroundings. And, indeed, of her future.

Best of all were the clothes she was given. Alexandra did not take her women into Madrid or Barcelona, or even Saragossa, the nearest big town, certainly while they were at Cynthia's stage of learning loyalty, but she had couturiers come out to Eboli, and Cynthia very rapidly found herself the possessor of a more beautiful wardrobe than she had imagined possible. "Of course no man is going to want you to wear any of these nightdresses to bed," Alexandra pointed out. "But it is so enjoyable for them to take them off."

As for jewellery, she did not need to buy any. When Alexandra unlocked her safe and took out the various trays, Cynthia was quite breathless. "What is that stuff *worth*?" she asked. "Or are they fakes?"

"Everything I possess is genuine," Alexandra said, not taking offence. "And this collection is worth millions."

"But, aren't you afraid you'll be burgled?"

"There is no chance of that," Alexandra explained. "Let me show you our security system."

Cynthia had not paid a great deal of attention to such matters; she had been too busy and her head had been in too continual a whirl since her arrival at Eboli. She knew there were quite a few men on the premises, most of them large, muscular and young – the cook and all the butlers were men – but none of them was ever allowed into the pool area or the sleeping quarters, the women being required to attend to their own laundry and keep their own rooms neat and clean. Now she discovered that there were a score of men servants, all apparently devoted to Alexandra. A couple were always on duty, twenty-four hours a day in the house itself, and a couple more men were on the walls, while there were actually three fences inside the outer wall, and each of these was electrified as well as linked to an alarm system in the house itself. "Suppose someone came in by helicopter?" Cynthia asked. That was what James Bond would have done.

"My people are armed," Alexandra told her. "And are quite prepared to shoot. And there are always two men on the roof, as well."

"But if *they* were to turn against you . . ."

"There is no chance of that," Alexandra told her.

There was of course a negative side to life at Eboli. Cynthia didn't need the other girls to tell her that the guards were there just as much to stop anyone getting in as to stop anyone getting out; she was in as secure a prison as she had been in Istanbul. More secure, indeed, as she did not suppose there was anyone knocking around with twenty thousand pounds to buy her out of Eboli – or that Alexandra would now accept twenty thousand pounds for her! But for the time being that did not seem to be a problem. She was living on a scale she had never supposed possible. So what if at the end of it she would be required to pander to some man's perversions? It had to be worth it. Besides, she still had nowhere to run – and no money to run with!

*   *   *

106

There was another reason for the presence of the masculine contingent in the castle, and it soon occurred to Cynthia that this was as compelling a cause of their loyalty to Alexandra as any salary she might be paying them: they were required for practice. In her brief relations with the men she had known Cynthia had always done whatever came naturally, and her skill was limited in the extreme. Alexandra explained: "Sadly, few of my clients are young. Young men, except in rare instances, do not have the money to pay my prices, and those who do have the money are usually very capable of collecting beautiful and willing women without needing to come to me. The men you will be dealing with are nearly all in middle age or older. They will have been married, perhaps several times, and be sexually experienced.

"Sadly, as they pass fifty or so – it varies – while their appetite for youth and beauty grows, as does their appetite for the unusual or the perverse, their performance declines. This leads them into a 'catch-22' situation. As they are uniformly wealthy, they have the financial ability either to marry for the umpteenth time, or set someone up as a mistress. But either of these steps is filled with potential disaster. There is the matter of alimony or palimony, which they are probably paying already to previous companions; there is the matter of a woman's scorn, or the risk that, unsatisfied at home, she may wander; and most important of all, in this day and age, there is the matter of what happens when they fall out, as they must eventually – people always do.

"Then she is as likely as not to rush to whichever tabloid is prepared to pay her most to reveal all, including his shortcomings, and these may be literal. In all of these there is, above all, the feeling that he is not in control of the situation. And men do like to be in control. Now,

107

compare that unhappy scenario with spending somewhat less – in the long run – to obtain the services, for a specified period, of a beautiful and willing woman, who will never laugh at him, or wish to do anything but please him and satisfy him, no matter what he wishes her to do, and who, when the contract is terminated, will simply fade away into the sunset and never trouble him again."

"Do none of your clients ever fall in love with one of us?" Cynthia asked.

"Indeed, some do. In which case we may well negotiate a long term contract, if both parties wish it. But it remains a contract, which can never be disputed in a court of law."

"But there is nothing to prevent one of . . . of your women from still going to a newspaper with her story," Cynthia argued.

Alexandra smiled. "There is, darling. Because she knows I would crucify her. And I mean that, quite literally." Cynthia believed her. "So it follows," Alexandra went on, "that it is necessary for my girls to know every possible way of satisfying a man, of arousing him, of sating him. And then, more important yet, of re-arousing him. You will begin with Miguel."

Miguel was Spanish, in his early twenties, and very eager. His session with Cynthia was carefully monitored, by both Alexandra and Madeleine, which created unwelcome tension. But she was soon lost in her work, as the other women showed her how to arouse him again and again. "One has to use one's common sense, of course," Alexandra told her. "Miguel is now quite exhausted. But a good's night sleep will restore him to as good as new, even if he may be a bit sore. But he is only twenty-two. Again, as I have said, I endeavour to monitor our clients most carefully, and this includes their health. This is where observation and understanding come in. If your client can't make it, by all means encourage him as far as is sensible, but it is most certainly *not* sensible to encourage him to the state where he has a heart attack on you. That can be most embarrassing and indeed dangerous. I had an old and favoured client drop dead on me during my early days, and it was a most unpleasant business."

Cynthia began to wonder if there was *any* experience this formidable old woman had not had. Anticipation of the future began to be mixed with apprehension.

But she could not help but be excited, as were all the girls, when, after she had been at Eboli three months and the summer was well advanced, Alexandra informed them that they were to entertain. "I wonder who it will be," Maureen said, brushing her hair.

"A film star," Irina mused, lying on Cynthia's bed and kicking her legs in the air. "Someone from Hollywood. I've never been to Hollywood."

"What makes you suppose a Hollywood film star would choose you?" Carmen enquired.

"Because all American men are crazy about Russian women," Irina suggested.

"Ah," Angela said. "But how many Hollywood film stars are actually American?"

In the event, their guest turned out to be an Arab. "That figures," Rona whispered to Cynthia. "They have all the money."

"Girls, I wish you to meet Sheikh Abdullah el-Mehmet," Alexandra said. "Sheikh Abdullah is the cousin of the Emir of Karnah, and controller of Karnah's oil revenues." She paused to allow this important fact to sink in, and then introduced them in turn.

Cynthia, as the youngest and most junior, was the last, and was dismayed to observe that however much

109

he had been taken with the others, Sheikh Abdullah's eyes widened in surprise when he saw her. But she didn't take to him at all. He was shorter than she was, extremely stout, and had an unpleasant twist to his lips. He was by no means old, which actually made him even less attractive, as it suggested that he would be able to maintain his activity longer, whatever his favourite activity might be – she had no doubt that it would be something unpleasant. On the other hand, he was impeccably dressed in white tie, and was obviously tremendously wealthy. "By Allah," he remarked. "But you have some beauties here, Countess."

"I offer only the best," Alexandra told him. "But there is no need for you to make a decision now, Abdullah. You have all evening."

"I have made my decision," Abdullah said, continuing to gaze at Cynthia. Her knees felt quite weak.

"You mean, Cynthia? Alas, Abdullah, she is not yet ready."

"Not ready?" He turned his head.

"Not ready," Alexandra said firmly. "She is still learning her trade, as it were. You will have to take one of the others, this time."

"Now that is a shame," Abdullah said. He took Cynthia's hand and raised it to his lips. "You must tell me when she is ready." Cynthia felt like kissing Alexandra in sheer gratitude.

Abdullah was wined and dined, somewhat to Cynthia's surprise, as she had not supposed he should be drinking, and finally chose Carmen. Apparently he was hiring her for a week, to be his companion on a trip to the Caribbean. As for Carmen this meant she was going home, she was delighted, and hurried off to pack, as Abdullah wanted her

110

to accompany him that night. The fee was not mentioned; Cynthia gathered it was astronomical, as Abdullah liked 'extras'. This did not seem to concern Carmen, but it left the other girls in a state of high excitement. It was nearly dawn before they waved Carmen and Abdullah's Rolls-Royce out of sight, and could get to bed. "I'll bet he has her right there in the car," Rona said. "I mean, wouldn't you?"

"It's big enough," Maureen giggled.

Cynthia had a shower in the hopes of dulling her senses. She was more exhausted than any of the others, but she was also more excited, because he had, in the first instance, chosen her. She could be in the back seat of that car now, being . . . what? She wondered what the 'extras' were? She flopped across her bed, and did not turn her head when her door opened; it could only be one of the other girls. Angela flopped on the bed beside her. "How do you feel?" she asked.

Cynthia raised her head. "On a high, I guess. Delayed reaction."

"That's it." Angela rolled on to her back; she was wearing a pyjama top with deep pockets. "I get so turned on by these things." Angela felt in her pyjama pocket and produced a folded envelope. "Do you take this stuff?"

Cynthia sat up. "You must be out of your mind. The Countess will do her nut if she catches us with coke. Where did you get that stuff, anyway?"

Angela rose to her knees. "Miguel got it for me."

"Miguel? The idiot. What did you pay him with?"

Angela giggled. "Me."

"Idiot," Cynthia muttered.

Angela opened the envelope and poured a little of the white powder on to the back of her hand. "Don't be scared," she said.

111

"I am scared," Cynthia said. "Look, go sniff in your own room. Go . . ." The bedroom door opened.

"Damn it," Angela said, hastily trying to get the powder back into the envelope and the envelope back into her pocket, but instead spilling cocaine all over the bedspread.

"You are an incredibly foolish young woman," Alexandra remarked. She was, as always, accompanied by Mayne, Madeleine, and Denise. "As for you . . ." She turned her gaze on Cynthia.

Cynthia pushed herself up the bed until her back was against the headboard. "I haven't touched it," she gasped. "I swear. I didn't even . . ." She looked at Angela, biting her lip. She didn't want to let her down. But she didn't want to be punished, either.

Angela shrugged. "She didn't want any," she said sulkily.

"Well," Alexandra said. "I am glad of that, Cynthia. I am really relieved. But you will witness Angela's punishment. It will do you good. Madeleine, will you summon the other girls, please. And bring that material."

Madeleine left the room. "So, get out your stupid old strap and get on with it," Angela said.

Alexandra gave one of her cold smiles. "I think you need more than the strap, Angela. Especially as you seem to be looking forward to it. Come to your room."

Angela looked from her to Mayne and then to Denise. "What are you going to do to me?" Her breathing had quickened. So had Cynthia's.

"I am going to make an example of you," Alexandra said. "An example neither you nor any of the girls will ever forget."

"Now look here," Angela began.

"Come," Alexandra said. Angela looked at Cynthia, as if

wondering if she could expect any support from that quarter. But Cynthia remained pressed against the headboard, too scared to move. "Denise," Alexandra said. Denise stepped forward.

"All right," Angela said. "I'm coming." She obviously knew all about Denise's ability at karate. Now she got off the bed and went to the door.

Cynthia found that she had been holding her breath, and slowly released it. "You too," Mayne commanded.

Cynthia eased herself off the bed, pulled her dressing gown from the hook on the door, put it on. Denise had followed Alexandra and Angela, but Mayne waited patiently. "I never touched the stuff," Cynthia muttered.

"We believe you," Mayne said. "But it would be best for you not to be tempted, at any time in the future." In the corridor they were joined by the other girls, all clearly very frightened by what had happened. None of them dared speak to each other, or question Cynthia, but she reckoned they must know that Angela had a habit: this couldn't be the first time.

They went into Angela's room, and lined up along the wall without any instructions from Alexandra. "Take off your jacket and lie on the bed," Alexandra told Angela.

Angela attempted a smile. "What am I going to get? A gang rape?"

"Do it," Alexandra snapped. Angela shrugged the jacket from her shoulders, and crawled on to the bed. "On your back," Alexandra commanded. Angela obeyed.

Alexandra nodded to Mayne and Denise, and they each carried one of Angela's arms above her head and secured the wrists to the bed posts. "I've seen movies like this," Angela said, still attempting to be light-hearted about her situation.

"I'm sure you have," Alexandra agreed. "Ah, Madeleine." Madeleine stood in the doorway, carrying a plate, on which there were four small red peppers and a kitchen knife. "Wirri-wirris, from South America," Alexandra explained.

Angela caught her breath and tried to push herself up the bed with her heels. But Mayne and Denise caught an ankle each and stretched her legs out again. Angela started to pant. Madeleine had also brought a pair of rubber gloves, and these Alexandra pulled on. "Wirri-wirries are probably the hottest peppers known," she remarked, picking up the knife and delicately slicing one of the peppers in half. Alexandra sat on the bed beside Angela, holding one of the half peppers in her gloved fingers.

Angela gasped. "Don't touch me with that thing . . ."

"The first touch is quite pleasant," Alexandra said, and stroked the cut piece of pepper across Angela's left nipple. Angela gave a little jerk, and stared at her tormentress. Alexandra stroked the second nipple, and then did so again to each, but more firmly this time. "I imagine it is starting to burn," she suggested. Angela gasped again, and gave a little shudder. "The nipples will swell, of course," Alexandra said, adding some more to each breast. "They will swell until you will feel they are going to burst. I read once of an Indian rani who was so displeased with one of her maids that she rubbed hot red pepper between the girl's legs. The case became widely known because the rani was charged with murder. The girl swelled up to such an extent, you see, that she died. Do you know, I cannot remember if the rani was convicted or not. How are you feeling, dear?"

Angela had been biting her lip in an endeavour to stop herself from crying out. But now she suddenly shrieked,

114

and began to writhe, kicking her legs as she twisted to and fro, trying to bring her knees up far enough to touch her breasts and perhaps remove some of the pepper. "You won't die," Alexandra told her. "Not from swollen breasts. But you will feel, my dear, and for some time."

Angela shrieked again. "You bitch!" she screamed. "You horrible old woman. You . . ."

"I could put some on your tongue," Alexandra reminded her. "You wouldn't enjoy that."

Angela screamed, again and again, as the tremendous burning sensation took hold of her entire chest. Sweat poured from her hair and she tossed and kicked. Alexandra stood up. "We will leave her now," she said. "She is unlikely to sleep tonight, but there is no reason why we should stay awake." She went to the door, watched by the petrified girls. "You know the rules," she told them. "No drugs. And by the way, I know who supplied them," she said. "Miguel is also screaming away. I put pepper on penis."

The girls returned to their beds, but not to sleep. Cynthia certainly did not sleep a wink. The thought of what Angela was suffering . . . she continued to scream for some time, making herself heard even through the closed doors. Next morning there was a very subdued gathering for breakfast, and no horseplay about the pool. Angela was not in evidence. While Cynthia found herself shaking when Alexandra appeared, and beckoned her. The other girls watched her go, silently. "Come into the study, Cynthia," Alexandra invited. "And do stop shaking. I'm not going to punish you." Cynthia sat down before the huge oak desk. "Were you on the pill?" Alexandra asked. Cynthia shook her head. "What, never? How long did you live with your boyfriend?"

"About a month."

"And you never got pregnant? Hm. Do you know, a whore who cannot become pregnant is worth her weight in gold. Although it would be a shame for you to be quite unable to have a child. Mayne and I often disagree on this. But I always say, if I had not had a child, she would not be here. However, whether to become pregnant or not must be a decision, not an accident."

"I don't think anything is the matter with me," Cynthia muttered.

"Starting tomorrow, you will go on the pill. Dr Cardona will bring a first set up for you. From then on you will stay on the pill."

"Does that mean . . .?" Cynthia bit her lip. She was not in the mood even for thinking about sex, today.

"Why, yes. It means you are ready to go to work. And I have a man who is very interested in you. However, there are a couple of formalities necessary before I can put you out." Cynthia waited, with some apprehension. "Firstly . . ." Alexandra opened one of the drawers of her desk and produced a passport. "This is for you to keep."

She held it out, and Cynthia took it, gazing at the name in astonishment. "You mean you're using my real name?"

"That is a genuine passport, Cynthia. I obtained your birth certificate, and sent off for it."

"But . . . didn't anyone question you?"

"I didn't do it personally, silly. I had one of my agents do it. And it was sent to a convenience address in London. It may well be that your family will wish to follow it up, but it will get them nowhere. Unless you attempt to return to England, but you shall not be doing that for a while. On the continent, with this Common Market thing, they very seldom look at passports anyway, so long as you have one.

116

And outside the continent they are even less interested. Now the second thing that is required, is your brand."

"My what?" Cynthia leapt to her feet, and realised that Mayne and Denise had come into the room and were standing behind her.

"I consider it very necessary to be able to prove, at all times, that my girls belong to me," Alexandra explained. "And the simplest way to do this is to have you wear a mark which is unique to my establishment. Mayne?"

Cynthia turned, and saw that Mayne was holding a small iron rod, at the end of which there was a tiny iron butterfly, at right angles to the rod. Extending from the rear of the rod was an electric cable. Cynthia gasped, and Alexandra smiled. "Denise?" Denise was wearing a skirt. She now raised her leg and rested her foot on the desk, while pulling the skirt above her waist. "There, you see," Alexandra said.

At the very top of the inside of Denise's right thigh, where it was more often than not hidden by her pubic hair, was the mark of the butterfly. "Oh, my God," Cynthia muttered.

"It is painful, but only for a little while," Alexandra explained. "Lie on the floor." Cynthia licked her lips and wondered if she could make a run for it. But she knew that was not on. She lay down. "On your back," Alexandra commanded. "Now, as I said, the pain will be sharp, but brief. You must not move. If you move, it will all have to be done again. Do you understand that?"

Cynthia gritted her teeth as she watched Mayne pull on a pair of thick gloves and plug the electric cord into a wall socket; within seconds the branding iron was glowing red hot, and then turning white. Meanwhile Denise was holding her arms in a vice-like grip, and Madeleine was holding her left leg. Alexandra herself pulled her right leg away and then pushed it up so that the knee was bent. She held it in that position while Mayne carefully parted the pubic hair with one hand, and then, almost without warning, thrust the glowing butterfly against Cynthia's flesh. For a moment the agony took Cynthia's breath away. Then she uttered the most piercing scream of her life. She tried to move, but the women were holding her too tightly. Dimly she realised that the iron had been withdrawn, and that Mayne was sprinkling the mark with powder. Alexandra smiled at her, and kissed her sweat-wet forehead. "Now you are one of us," she said.

Chapter Six

Cynthia says: *"Oddly enough, I did have a sense of belonging, and this was in fact reassuring, rather, I suppose, like being given a key to the director's washroom. But at the same time I understood that my apprenticeship was over."*

Three weeks later Alexandra, Denise and Cynthia drove north from Eboli. Cynthia deduced that she was now regarded as being impregnable. She also gathered that this was a very special client, in that he had not come to Eboli, but had been sought out by Alexandra, who apparently knew his requirements. She had also been decked out with new clothes, a gold necklace, and a gold Omega which was even more valuable than the one Cuthbert had given her. She carried her passport, suggesting that she was going to be leaving Spain, at least for the duration of her rental. "Jacques will teach you a great deal," Alexandra said as the Pyrenees loomed in front of them. "More than I can, in certain directions. He will be an experience for you. Just remember, always, that you belong to me."

Cynthia glanced at Denise, for whom she had cultivated a distinct apprehension. Denise smiled at her. "Sadly," Alexandra said. "He is no longer in his first youth. But he is still very eager. You will have the time of your life."

Cynthia hoped she was right. She found herself in a very uncertain mood. On the one hand there was a very real fear of this man to whom she was being delivered like a slave girl after an Arabian auction – because she was just a slave girl, she reflected bitterly – but on the other there was a certain wish to get up and go, at what she had been so carefully trained to do. Even more confusing was the feeling of freedom, that she was leaving Eboli and the Maynes. Would she ever go back? But would she ever dare not go back? Angela had reappeared after two days, but she had obviously still been very tender. The thought of what might be done to *her* if she tried to escape and was caught and brought back . . . she fully intended to escape but she was determined to wait for the right moment, when she had the funds and the experience, and the situation, to do so successfully.

So, first, Jacques. They stopped for lunch on the Spanish side of the mountains, Alexandra at her brilliant best, full of conversation and anecdotes. Denise was an attentive listener, Cynthia less so; she was too aware of a man seated on the far side of the restaurant, watching them. Or more particularly, her. He was quite a good-looking man, tall and well built, with soft, straight black hair, graying at the temples. She put his age down to between forty and fifty. His expression was off-putting, however. He looked terribly bitter and aggressive, and she gained the impression that the aggression was directed at her, so much so that she could not help wondering if he had seen her before. But she certainly could not remember him.

Their meal ended and Alexandra paid by credit card. Then she got up and led her two women to the door, where they were joined by the tall man. Cynthia's knees suddenly touched as she realised who he had to be. "Are you pleased?" Alexandra asked, as they walked to the limo.

"Very," Jacques replied. "Is she as willing as you claimed?"

120

"Absolutely," Alexandra assured him. "If she disappoints you in any way you know you have but to say, and you will get your money back. Now, please, if you would like to settle the matter." Jacques took a cheque from his inside breast pocket and gave it to her. Cynthia would have loved to have known what the amount was, but she couldn't see. "I will meet you for lunch, here, a week today," Alexandra said, and got into the back of the limo, Denise behind her. The limo drove away, and Cynthia was left standing in the heat of the car-park, her bag by her side.

"Put it in the boot," Jacques recommended, pointing at a big Citroën.

So he intends to treat me as dirt, Cynthia thought. She picked up her bag and placed it in the boot. Jacques was already seated behind the wheel. Cynthia sat beside him, and he drove out of the park. "You are very beautiful," he commented.

"Thank you."

"But also very young."

"I am sixteen," Cynthia said.

"Younger than I thought. But the Countess tells me you are very experienced."

"I really don't know about that," Cynthia said. "You will have to judge for yourself."

He glanced at her. "I like them young." She didn't reply; she didn't really like being referred to as 'them'. "You are English," he said chattily. "I wish to get to know you better. Take off your dress." Cynthia's head jerked. While talking, she had been admiring the scenery, which was growing more rugged by the second as they climbed into the hills. But at least there was no one around. She unzipped her dress, eased it out from beneath her, and lifted it over her head. "Throw it in the back seat," he

121

recommended. Cynthia obeyed. He glanced at her. As usual she was not wearing a bra, only a pair of nylon briefs and high-heeled shoes.

"The rest?" she asked. He nodded. She kicked off her shoes, then slipped the briefs down past her ankles and threw them also into the back seat.

"Exquisite," he commented. "Now uncover me."

Cynthia gulped. "While you're driving?" The road was becoming narrower by the moment, and every so often there was a sheer drop.

He grinned. "I like to live dangerously." Cynthia reached and unbuckled his belt, then released the zip. He raised himself from the seat to allow her to slide the trousers down past his knees. "Take them right off. I might have to use the brake." I should think you will, Cynthia thought; she had to kneel on the floor of the car to get the trousers right off. She added them to the collection in the back seat. "Now the underwear," he said.

"You don't feel we may be arrested?" she asked.

"Not up here."

She wrestled with his briefs, discovering that he had quite the largest penis she had ever seen – it could not be less than eight inches, and it was only half erected. My God, she thought, when he's up straight he'll measure a foot. And he means to put that inside me? He'll be an experience for you, Alexandra had said.

Once again she had to kneel to undress him. "Now play with yourself," Jacques said. "And do it for real. I will be able to tell." Cynthia leaned back in her seat and obliged. She closed her eyes, grateful not to have to look at him. He was a complete stranger. But as he had said, he wanted to get to know her better, and she didn't suppose one could know a woman better than watching this kind of performance. She shuddered quickly to orgasm

122

and opened her eyes to look at him. "I liked that," he said. "Now try me."

"And you're still going to drive?"

"Yes."

She turned on her knees to get at him, realised he had not changed in the slightest over the five minutes he had watched her; he was neither any harder nor had he dwindled at all. Presumably he had seen it all before. Yet he had to have been turned on, surely. She took him into her mouth, but found not the slightest response. So she used her hand as well, and began to experience a certain panic. There was still no response. She didn't know what else to do; this was certainly an experience she had never had before – the mere touch of her hand had always had Cuthbert hard as a rock.

Jacques' hand closed on her neck in a grip like a vice, and her head was lifted. She couldn't speak, so tight was the grip, and before she could make up her mind what to do he had thrown her away from him, across the car. She banged her head on the far door, and remained a crumpled heap for some seconds, while the car, momentarily out of control, swayed to and fro across the road before settling. Cynthia had got her breath back. "That was a silly thing to do," she remarked. "I might have bitten you."

"Do you think that would help?"

"Do I . . .?" She pushed her hair out of her eyes and lowered her feet to the floor. She wasn't at all sure what to reply.

"I get so angry," he said. "Sometimes I want to hurt, and hurt, and hurt." Cynthia considered this while she withdrew right across the seat against the door. Jacques glanced at her, and grinned. "Oh, I must not hurt you. Much as I would like to. Alexandra has refused to put that in our contract." He sighed. "I had a beating clause

123

in my last. But I suppose I got carried away. The girl reacted badly. She actually tried to defend herself with some unarmed combat, would you believe? So I beat her some more."

Cynthia found she was pressed against the door. She wondered if there was any chance of jumping out: he had to take some of the corners very slowly. But how could she jump out into the middle of the Pyrenees with no clothes on? Even if she didn't break something she'd certainly be arrested, and what Alexandra would say . . . or do! "Alexandra was very angry," Jacques said. "She made me pay a hefty fine. And I still couldn't get it up."

"The girl was Ingrid," Cynthia said.

He glanced at her. "Why, yes. So it was."

"And you mean you can never get it up?"

"There are ways," he said, half to himself.

"But you'd never go against Alexandra," she reminded him, anxiously.

"Only if I thought it would work. I keep hoping, a new girl, someone like you, young and delicious . . . do you have any idea what kind of hell I'm in?"

"Of course I do," Cynthia lied. She didn't have a clue. "You mean you can't reach orgasm?"

"A dribble, sometimes."

"Well," she said, hopefully. "As I'm clearly a complete failure, I guess you'll want to call the whole thing off. I know Alexandra will refund you. Well, most of it." She had stripped for him and had masturbated for him and had a go at him. Presumably those were all chargeable items, although she didn't know what Alexandra's scale of fees were.

"Early days," he pointed out, to her disappointment. "You'd better get dressed. We're coming to a town."

*   *   *

124

Cynthia was very happy to obey. She asked him if he wanted his trousers back on, but he didn't, just drove with them draped across his lap. They dipped down into a valley and drove through a village, where Jacques was apparently known, because more than one person waved or hooted a horn. Then they turned down another valley, the road again lonely, and came to a large farmhouse, but with no animals to be seen. "This is where I bring my women," Jacques explained.

"You mean you don't live here all the time?"

"Of course not. I have my business to run, from my office and my home in Paris."

"Oh. Yes."

"Nobody in Paris knows of my sexual problems, of course. That is why I keep this place."

"And use Alexandra."

"Exactly." He pulled the car to a stop in the yard before the house, and got out. "Bring your bag." Presumably he also stopped being a gentleman when he left Paris, Cynthia thought. Or maybe he just wasn't a gentleman. She collected her bag and followed him. He had already unlocked the front door, and she entered a large and rather attractive if untidy room, comfortably furnished, with a huge fireplace in the far corner in which a log fire was just dwindling. "I'm afraid the place needs dusting and sweeping," he said. "And the fire needs a log or two on it. You want to do that first, or it may go out, and then you'll have to riddle it and reset the whole thing." He went to the stairs.

"May I see the terms of your agreement with Alexandra?" she asked.

"There's nothing to see. She hired you to me for a week. And I mustn't beat you," he repeated regretfully.

"What I would like to know," Cynthia said, "is whether

125

she hired me as domestic help or a sexual companion?"

"She hired you to me to do whatever I wanted," he said. "Your room is downstairs, on the right," Jacques said, and continued up the stairs.

Cynthia carried her bag to the right, and found a comfortable but very ordinary bedroom; at least it had an *en suite* bathroom. She peered at herself in the mirror, took off her dress, and drew a brush through her hair. In for a penny, she told herself, and reminded herself that there had been talk of substantial tips if she pleased her client. Well, it didn't look as if she was going to have any great success sexually, so the least she could do was please him in every other possible way. Wearing only her briefs she went into the back yard where there was a substantial wood store, selected half a dozen small logs, and carried these into the lounge; holding them as she had to in her arms she became smothered in odd splinters and pieces of bark. These she brushed into the fireplace, and when she had à blaze, added a log.

By now she was aware that she was being watched, so she got to work with enthusiasm, dusting and sweeping the ground floor before climbing the stairs with her various tools tucked under her arms. When she opened the upper bedroom door, he was lying on the bed, but she reckoned he had only just got there. He was naked, but in the same half-erected situation as before. "Shall I do you now, sir?" she asked.

He turned his head, saw her approaching him with the vacuum cleaner. "What the hell do you mean?"

"Well," she said. "I reckon it's a case of all hands to the pump, if you'll pardon the expression. This might just do the trick."

He moved with alarming speed, was out of bed and

126

holding the nape of her neck before she had adjusted her thinking, was making her kneel and pressing her face into the bedclothes. "Are you taking the mickey?"

Cynthia fell on the mattress and tried to reach him with either her hands or her legs, but couldn't. When he released her, she sank to the floor by the bed, panting. "You're going to break my neck," she gasped. "If you keep that up."

He sat on the bed above her. "I wonder if you have an erection as the guillotine comes down."

"Jesus," she muttered, and sat beside him. "Wouldn't do you much good. What you want is to commit murder in a country which hangs you."

"Eh?"

"Well, don't they say that a man has an erection when he's strangled?" He stared at her, so intently she was startled. "They don't hang you in France," she pointed out.

He threw her across the bed. When he started to pull down her briefs she helped him. Oh, dear God, she thought, please let him succeed. But although he squirmed all over her, squeezed her breasts and her buttocks, drove his fingers between so that she was left gasping for breath, after some minutes he collapsed beside her, exhausted and breathing as heavily as she was. But not angry, this time. Yet, at any rate. She lay very still, not knowing what was going to happen next, and after a while he rose on his elbow. "You are a treasure," he told her.

"Am I?"

"Go and shower and join me for the evening. Wear something slinky. No underclothes."

"Right." She ran down the stairs and into her room. When she got into the shower she found a trace of semen on her thigh. Presumably that was quite a triumph. And he was pleased. She began to wonder what size tip he had in mind.

She wore a pale green sheath and nothing else except her high-heeled shoes. Jacques was already in the lounge. Two more logs had been added to the fire, and he was mixing champagne cocktails. "You look good enough to eat," he said.

"Thank you," she said, keeping her distance. He was so unpredictable it was impossible to tell when he was speaking literally.

"I have been thinking about what you said." He came across the room towards her and gave her a glass. "I am a fool not to have tried it before. I have read about it, often enough."

"Tried what?" Cynthia sipped.

"This neck constriction thing." Cynthia put down her glass. "So here's what we do," Jacques said. "I have been taking some measurements. Those beams are eight feet from the floor. That stool . . ." he pointed, "is eighteen inches high. I will stand on the stool, with the rope round my neck and thrown over that beam. It will be secured to this hook." He indicated the hook set in the next upright by the bar. "When I am ready, you will take away the stool. The moment I come erect, you will cut the rope. Here is the knife; it is very sharp, so you should have no problem. And then, as I fall to the floor, you will mount me. Right?"

"You have got to be stark raving mad," Cynthia told him.

"The terms of your contract state that you will do anything I require, so long as I cause you no bodily harm," Jacques reminded her.

"I'm sure Alexandra did not have in mind that I should help you commit suicide."

128

"You are here to see that I do not, you silly girl."

"But . . . supposing it doesn't work? Supposing you don't have an erection?"

"Then you will cut me down anyway. But I am sure I will have an erection. And then you will have me inside you. Is that not an exciting thought?" In the circumstances, Cynthia did not find it the least exciting. "We'll do it now, before supper," he said. "When I have had you, I will take you out to supper, eh? You'll like that."

She wished he would stop telling her what she would like and not like, watched in fascinated horror as he produced a length of strong nylon rope from behind the bar, threw it over the beam, and secured the end. "May I use your telephone?" she asked.

"No, you may not. Who do you wish to telephone?" He was busily knotting the loop.

"I thought I'd call the Countess and make sure I wasn't exceeding the terms of the contract."

"She would tell you that you are not," Jacques assured her. "But in any event, I do not have a telephone on the farm. The whole point in having the farm is that people should not be able to bother me." The knot was ready, and now he undressed. "You too," he told her. "We may not have a moment to spare at the other end." Cynthia took off her dress. "Now come and stand beside me," he said. "You must be very close. Don't forget the knife."

Cynthia grasped the knife and stood beside him as he placed the stool beneath the loop, and then adjusted the length of the rope. I have got to be mad myself, she thought. I am going to wind up in jail. I just know it. My God! I could be guillotined myself. She wondered if Alexandra would be able to get her out of that. "Right," Jacques said. "All set. Now, are you sure you are in top gear, Cynthia?"

129

"Oh, yes," she lied.

"You realise I am placing my life in your hands?"

"Yes. I wish you wouldn't."

He ruffled her hair. "It is going to be the time of your life," he promised. Cynthia did some deep breathing. Jacques stood on the stool, placed the noose round his neck, adjusted it. "The point is to strangle, not snap the neck as they do in a judicial hanging," he said.

"Aren't you scared?" Cynthia asked.

"Of course not. I am relying upon you."

"Well, get on with it, or I am going to wet myself," Cynthia told him.

He rested his hand on her shoulder. "Now," he said.

Cynthia took another deep breath, stooped, and pulled the stool out from under his feet. He made a strangled sound, literally, and she straightened, watched his face begin to turn blue, but, incredibly, she also watched his penis begin to rise. She slashed the rope with the knife – it was indeed sharp and went through it like butter, then threw the weapon away. Jacques had fallen to the floor and lay in a heap. He certainly had an erection, but he also had the noose still tight round his neck. That had to be attended to first. It took her several seconds to free it, and to her enormous relief he was breathing. But by then he had dwindled again. She sat on the floor for several seconds, gazing at him, panting as hard as if she had just been hanged herself. Then she knelt beside him, and shook him. "Jacques!"

There was no response. But he *was* breathing, and some of the colour was returning to his face. Heck, she thought; he could have suffered brain damage. She shook him again, without success, so she went to the bar and got the open bottle of champagne. She took a swig herself – she needed it – and then poured some on to his face. He

130

stirred and moved. "Thank God for that," she muttered. He opened his eyes, and licked his lips, slowly. "I know you must be thirsty. Drink this."

She held the bottle to his lips, and he took a few sips, then made a face – his throat had to be very sore – and lay back with a sigh. "Did we make it?"

She considered lying. But he would realise that soon enough, and in any event, if she pretended they had he might want to try it again some time. "No."

"Damn," he said.

"I'm sure you don't feel like going out," she said. "I'll cook dinner, shall I?"

She had learned quite a bit about cooking from Cuthbert, and of course she had been taught a lot more by Alexandra, so she was able to produce a fair meal, even if it all had to come out of the freezer and then the microwave. Jacques sat on the settee and watched her, sipping wine. "What did you think about, when you were hanging?" she asked.

"I didn't think about anything."

"I thought your whole life was supposed to flash by in front of your eyes?"

"Not mine." He gave one of his sighs. "It didn't work."

"Grub up." They sat opposite each other. "How long have you had this problem?" she asked. "It's a heart thing, isn't it?"

"I wouldn't know. I've had it for twelve years, and to my knowledge have never had a heart attack."

"What does your doctor say about it?"

"I wouldn't know."

"You haven't been to a doctor? That's crazy. Why not?"

"My sexual hang-ups are my problem," he said. "Once

131

upon a time I was the greatest stud in Paris. Do you think I want the whole world to know I can no longer make it?"

"You don't suppose you may just have worn him out?"

"No."

He was masticating with great care, and swallowing slowly and carefully. Obviously his throat was still very sore. Cynthia drank some wine while she considered the situation. She genuinely wanted to help this unhappy creature – and she also wanted to find a solution to his problem before he decided to indulge 'in any more bizarre experiments. "Men," she said. "Perhaps you're latently gay and don't know it?"

"I have tried men."

"Recently?"

"Well . . . no. But if it didn't work then, why should it work now?"

"You never can tell. How many women have you had a go at in the last twelve years?"

He shrugged. "Forty or fifty."

"And how many men?"

"Two."

"There you are. Probably neither of the two was the right one. I think you should try some more."

"And have them blackmailing me or going to the papers?"

"Are you that famous?"

"Yes."

"Oh." But she was beginning to get the germ of an idea; it might just be possible for her to get some enjoyment out of this weird assignment. "Let me do it for you. We'll pretend I'm your daughter. No, your niece would be safer. I could be. Take me somewhere I can pick up an attractive young man. I'll bring him back here and make love to him. You can watch us. That might do the

132

trick. But if it doesn't, well, you could have a go at him yourself."

"And end up in a fight, if he's not interested?"

"No, you won't, I'll tell him I'm into threesomes. I mean, you don't really want to go the whole way do you? Will it bother you if he's around, so long as you make it?"

Jacques stroked his chin, and winced. "You're quite a girl."

"Trust me. Just point me in the right direction."

They drove into the village the next morning, to buy some newspapers and see what they could find. By then Cynthia reckoned she had achieved a considerable success. She had been allowed to spend the night in her own bed, making her own plans. And Jacques seemed content to accept her leadership. They studied the papers, and she opted for a professional tennis tournament currently being held in Toulouse. It was not a very important tournament, as there were few big names taking part, but that meant the field would be men who were young and eager, and probably finding it hard to make ends meet, which was an important part of her plan. They drove up there that afternoon, and joined the crowds in the stands, studying form. "That one," Cynthia decided.

"He's not doing very well," Jacques objected. "I think he's about to be knocked out."

"But that's the whole point," Cynthia pointed out. "If he was going to win, we'd have to spend the next three days here while he did it. But isn't he gorgeous? You'd be turned on by him, wouldn't you?"

Jacques merely grunted. But *she* was certainly turned on. For one thing, he was an American. For another, he was a handsome hunk of masculinity, all strong thighs

133

and good calves, broad shoulders and tight buttocks. His face was nothing to swoon about, but his features were regular, and at that moment she was not very interested in that aspect of him. A few minutes later he had been eliminated. "Wish me luck, and I'll see you at the car," Cynthia said.

Jacques caught her hand as she stood up. "You be there."

"Or you'll set Alexandra on to me. Don't worry, I'll be there."

She went to the dressing rooms with a pleasant sense of anticipation. It seemed for all of her adult life she had been the servant of others, doing what they wanted. Now she was doing what she wanted, for a change. The thought of failure never crossed her mind. She had laid her plans with some care, and the programme had presented her with all the background she needed. Her name having been sent in, Tom Lane duly appeared, wearing a blazer and having just showered. "Miss Haslar?"

He had clearly expected a feature writer, and spent the next few moments openly admiring her legs. Cynthia having opted for a short skirt. "Hi," she said. "I know you'll think I'm imposing . . ."

"Oh, no," he protested.

"Let's sit over here," she suggested, leading him to some chairs, and sitting, doing her crossing the legs act. As it happened, she was wearing knickers, but Tom Lane was clearly impressed. "My uncle and I watched your game."

He grimaced. "I can play better than that."

"I know. Let me see. You were at Cannes a fortnight ago, and San Remo before that."

"You mean you were there too?"

"Watching you."

134

He licked his lips. "You'll have to fill me in on this."

"You speak very good French. But I'm sure you'll be more comfortable in English." She switched languages. "My uncle is a very wealthy man. And one of his habits is sponsorship. Do you have a sponsor?"

"Only my Dad."

"Well, then . . ."

"Miss Haslar, you do know I'm not very successful?"

"So far."

"Well . . . I guess so."

"If you're not interested . . ."

"Oh, I am." He was trying not to look at her legs.

"Are you? That's super. Well, as you can imagine, there is quite a lot to discuss . . . when are you due in Folkestone?" Something else she had gleaned from the programme.

"Next Monday."

"Well, then, you have a day or two to spare. Uncle Jacques was thinking you might like to spend them with us, at a farmhouse he has in the Pyrenees. So that you can discuss things."

"Well," he said. "I'm actually checked in to an hotel here until tomorrow . . ."

"We can cancel that, and collect your things at the same time. It'll be much better out at the farm. So quiet."

"Will you be there, Miss Haslar?"

"Oh, yes," Cynthia said. "And do call me Cynthia. After all, it looks as if we are going to be partners in business."

She sat in the back with Tom while Jacques drove. Jacques kept up a flow of conversation in surprisingly good English – he also knew a surprising amount about professional tennis and the circuit – but he was also watching them in the rear view mirror. Not that there was anything to watch; Tom was a perfect gentleman. He was also trying to find his depths, work out what was really happening. But Cynthia wasn't bothered. She knew he had fallen for her. Now it was just a matter of how she played it.

They stopped for coffee and a beer in a village in the foothills. "Do you live here?" Tom asked.

"No, no," Jacques said. "It is a hideaway from the pressure of life in Paris."

"You know," Tom said. "You have no accent at all, Cynthia."

"I went to school in England," Cynthia explained.

They resumed their journey while the evening drew in, and it was almost dark when they reached the farmhouse. "Say, this really is something," Tom commented as he got out of the car. "Talk about seclusion."

"Here we can do what we like," Cynthia told him. "Try this." She threw back her head and uttered a baying scream, which echoed off the hillside and through the trees. "Try doing that anywhere else and not arousing a few neighbours."

"I think we should have champagne," Jacques said, leading them into the house and opening a bottle.

Tom gazed around him in admiration. Cynthia had seen that the place was clean and tidy before they had left. "Some *thing*," he said again.

"You can use this room," Cynthia said, leading him into her room. She had already moved her few belongings upstairs.

"Great." He put his bag on the floor. "I still can't really believe this is happening. I mean, what made your uncle choose me?"

"He didn't," Cynthia told him. "I did."

* * *

136

She left him to freshen up and returned to the living room. "I think you want to leave us alone, just as rapidly as possible," she whispered to Jacques. "And it would be a good idea not to try to muscle in tonight. Tomorrow would be better."

"You are enjoying this," he commented.

"Well, of course. I try to enjoy everything I do."

"Well, just remember that I paid a lot of money to fuck you, not have some itinerant youth do it for me."

"I'm doing the best I can," she pointed out, and smiled at Tom as he appeared. "Uncle Jacques was just wondering if you'd excuse him for an hour before dinner. He's very tired and needs to lie down."

"Oh, surely, sir," Tom said.

Jacques grunted and went up the stairs. "Let me top you up," Cynthia said, as they watched him go out of sight. She brushed her glass against Tom's. "Here's to us."

"Oh. Right." He drank. "Your uncle is all right, is he? Those marks on his neck . . ."

"I know. It is a skin problem. He is older than he looks." She sat on the settee, and Tom sat beside her.

"And you accompany him everywhere?"

"He's my only living relative. So I act as his Girl Friday."

"Heck. But he's a lucky guy, whatever his problems. Having you around, I mean."

"Thank you. But now, you have me as well."

"Eh?" His eyebrows shot up.

"I'm going to look after you as well," she explained. "Now, are you going to have sex with me?"

For a moment he looked so surprised she wondered if she had jumped the gun – or if he was indeed gay. But that would be a terrible waste, and from the way he had been

137

looking at her she was sure he was not. Now he cast an anxious glance at the stairs. "Uncle won't be down for at least an hour," she told him.

"Heck! But . . . are you sure you want to? I mean, we've only just met."

"I want to," she said, and held his hand to lead him back to the downstairs bedroom.

He was decidedly uncertain, at first. Cynthia didn't suppose he was a virgin, but presumably he had spent more time playing tennis than chasing girls. But he was deliciously strong and masculine, and she was quite sure he had never had the run of anyone quite like her before. He was inside her before she really wanted it, but she wasn't going to object; she reckoned he was the first truly straight up screw she had ever had in her life, and it felt so good. "Do you smoke?" she asked, when he lay beside her panting.

"Doesn't go with the game."

"I'm glad of that. I don't either."

He rose on his elbow beside her. "Now more than ever I feel I'm dreaming."

"About what?"

"You. You are just marvellous. I mean . . . wow! We only met a few hours ago, and now . . ."

"You've had me. Do you want me again?"

He kissed her mouth. "I want you, forever, Cynthia."

Oh, Jesus, she thought. "There's no such word, as forever," she protested.

"There is. There can be." She got up and went to the bathroom. He followed her, and she washed him. "You do everything so . . . so perfectly," he said. Because I'm a whore, you silly great lovely man, she thought. "Cynthia," he said, holding her arms. "May I ask you a question?"

138

"As long as I don't have to answer it."

"This man, Jacques, he's not really your uncle, is he?"

"What makes you say that?"

"Well . . . you don't look the least alike. And you don't have an uncle-niece relationship."

"Oh, yes? Well, if he's not my uncle, then what is he?"

"I'd say he's your lover." Jesus Christ, she thought, and I had assumed you were just a hunky body. She went into the living room and refilled their glasses. She needed to think, desperately. He stood in the doorway and watched her. "Aren't we going to get dressed?"

"I wouldn't bother. If Jacques is my lover, then our relationship is even odder, wouldn't you say?" She sat down and crossed her legs. No need for haste this time.

He sat beside her. "Not necessarily. There are lots of older guys with young mistresses who get a kick out of watching them perform."

"You," she said, "know a hell of a lot too much."

"Let's say I'm observant."

"OK, so you've observed." She looked down at him. "It doesn't seem to have turned you off. So you're a bit kinky yourself."

"Cynthia, I have never met a girl like you."

"I'm sure you will."

"I don't want to." He held her hand. "Listen, let's get the hell out of here. You and me."

"Do what?" Her voice rose an octave and she cast an anxious glance at the gallery, but there was neither sound nor movement from up there. Maybe Jacques had lain down and gone to sleep, after all.

"You must at least like me," Tom pointed out. "I mean, the way you went at me . . ." Because I'm a whore, she thought again, and wondered why she just didn't tell him the truth and put him out of his misery? But she did

139

like him, there was the trouble. "I don't have a lot of money," he said. "But I've enough for us. Dad gives me an allowance. OK, so I was keen on the idea of relieving him of that burden, but if that isn't on, what the hell? Cynthia . . ."

She held both his hands, pressed them into her lap. "Thomas," she said. "I cannot, repeat cannot, run away with you."

"Why not? Does he have some kind of hold on you? Or is it the money? You can't be in love with him." Cynthia sucked her lower lip. What on earth was she going to do? Her little scheme for some amusement had backfired in the most ghastly way. Why did men always have to be so awkwardly possessive? "If you're afraid of him," Tom said. "Don't be. I can protect you."

Tell him, she thought. Tell him everything, and watch him run a mile. But this was a chance to escape Alexandra's clutches. Could she? She would need the help of a strong man who adored her. This could be the one. He was going to England, Alexandra would hardly dare touch her in England. Even supposing she could find her. But of course she could find her, because Jacques would tell her where they'd gone; he knew as much about Tom's programme as she did. "If I ran away with you," she said, "you'd have to skip Folkestone."

"Because Jacques would follow us there? Heck, if he doesn't own you, I'll just see him off."

"It's not as simple as you think. He has friends."

"You mean he's a crook?"

"I wouldn't say that, exactly." Cynthia wished she knew, exactly. "But he is a powerful man. It would be best for us to avoid a confrontation. I really wouldn't like anything to happen to you."

"I can look after myself. And you."

140

She kissed him. "I'm sure of it. But I'd like you to stay just the way you are."

"OK, I'll skip Folkestone. I'll send them a wire and tell them I've pulled a muscle or something. They generally require a doctor's certificate for a late cancellation, but I guess we'll be able to pick one up somewhere. But you will come with me?"

Cynthia hesitated a last time. She didn't love this man, but then, she had never loved any man. And she thought she *could* go for Tom Lane, more quickly than anyone she had ever met. So no doubt his entirely physical desire for her would wear off quickly enough, but by then she would be free of Alexandra, while possessing all of Alexandra's training. She didn't doubt for a moment she would do very well for herself. She would be free of Alexandra! She kissed him again. "We'll have to work it out. Now listen to me, very carefully."

Jacques came down fifteen minutes later. By then Cynthia and Tom were fully dressed, and Cynthia was preparing supper. "She cooks like a dream as well," Jacques said, indicating that he knew what they had been doing in his absence.

Tom merely looked embarrassed. "Tom has problems," Cynthia said, as Jacques opened a fresh bottle of champagne. Jacques raised his eyebrows, as if to say, not another one? "He has some unfinished business in Toulouse," Cynthia explained. "We wondered if we could borrow the car tomorrow and drive up there. We could be back for lunch."

"No problem," Jacques said. "I'll drive you up myself."

"There's no need for you to bother . . ."

"No problem," Jacques repeated.

Cynthia dropped the idea. "Then there's the matter

141

of our contract with him . . ." Jacques gave her an old-fashioned look to indicate that he felt she was carrying this farce a bit far. "He feels he should contact his father as quickly as possible," Cynthia went on. "He had thought there'd be a telephone here," she couldn't resist adding.

"He can contact his father from Toulouse, tomorrow," Jacques said. He finished his meal and announced, "I am sure we would all like an early night. Eh, Tom?"

"That sounds great," Tom agreed.

"Well, then, we'll see you in the morning." He stood up, and held out his hand for Cynthia.

Tom looked as if he was about to object, but Cynthia gave a quick shake of her head. She could tell Jacques was aware that there was something going on of which he knew nothing, and she certainly didn't want to make him any more suspicious. She accompanied him up the stairs and into his bedroom. He closed the door on them, and without another word grasped her shoulders and threw her on to the bed, kneeling beside her to throw up her dress and wrench off her knickers, before discarding his own clothing in a series of kicks. To her amazement she saw that he was really hard enough to enter her. She gave a little sigh of relief, and spread her legs, but as he went down on her he softened again, and he was left lying on her, working his body on hers and sucking her neck, while quite ruining her dress. "Bitch," he muttered. "Bitch, bitch, bitch."

"Look," she said. "It's working, You damn near made it then. Rome wasn't built in a day."

He raised his head to look at her. "But you want to go gallivanting off with him tomorrow."

"We are both gallivanting off with him tomorrow," Cynthia pointed out. "I'll bet, when we get back, if you were to look in on us, you'd make it. You may not want

142

to admit it, but it's the *thought* of us together that's turned you on tonight. When you see us actually together, you'll be as horny as hell. Believe me."

At last he rolled off her, and she could breathe again. He lay on his back while she undressed them both. "You're either a genius or a witch," he remarked.

"I would hope to be a bit of both," she told him.

She desperately wanted to go down to Tom in the night, not for sex, particularly, but to reassure him that their plans hadn't changed. But she did not dare in case Jacques were to wake up. She didn't sleep very heavily though; she had too much on her mind. Quite apart from the heady prospect of escaping, there was the more mundane problem that she would be unable to take any of her things with her. Well, she'd just have to manage. And she did have her passport. She stroked her watch, lovingly. At least she had something of value.

She was awake at dawn. Jacques was still fast asleep, snoring slightly. She slipped out of bed, contemplated taking at least a change of knickers downstairs to put with Tom's things, but decided against the risk: the sound of the drawer opening and shutting might just wake him up. She went downstairs as she was, put the kettle on, and opened Tom's door. He was awake, and a moment later she was in his arms, his hands sliding over her still bed-warm naked flesh. "Oh, my dearest girl," he said. "I nearly went mad last night. The thought of you . . ."

"He didn't do anything," she said. "I told you, he's not very well, and a long drive like that exhausts him."

He pulled her down to sit beside him. "You haven't changed your mind?"

"No way."

143

"But . . . if he's coming with us . . . listen, why don't we just take his car now, before he wakes up, and drive like mad?"

"Because car theft is a crime and he'd catch up with us. The one thing we mustn't do is panic. Listen, we'll find a way just to get separated from him in Toulouse, and catch a train. There's nothing illegal about that."

"Oh, my darling." He held her close, kissed her eyes, her hair, her mouth, her nose, then dropped his head to kiss and suck her nipples. "I want you," he muttered. "Now."

"Be patient," she told him. "We can't do anything to risk upsetting him now. You're going to have me, forever."

"Forever," he murmured, reluctantly letting her go as she stood up, but retaining a grip on her hand. "Cynthia! Will you have a child for me?"

Cynthia considered, very briefly. If she did that, with all the palimony suits rushing about . . . that would entirely offset any negative aspects of her being a whore. "If you'd like me to." She found the idea rather attractive.

"I'm going to marry you, of course," he said. "You do understand that?"

He was such an absolute gentleman. It occured to her that she'd never actually met a gentleman before. "Yes," she said. "I do understand that. Now, plans."

It was all absurdly simple. Cynthia whistled cheerfully as she prepared breakfast, just to let the whole world know what she was doing, and sure enough Jacques appeared in the middle of it, looking a lot fitter than yesterday. "How's your throat and neck?" she whispered, giving him a hug.

"Sore, but not that sore." He appeared in a high good humour, his aggravation of last night forgotten, and remained downstairs, engaging Tom in conversation

144

while she showered and dressed. She wore jeans and a shirt, but it was a simple matter to put on an extra pair of knickers, and to roll up a silk dress and cram it into her handbag. In her handbag were her contraception pills. She took them out and flushed them down the toilet. This was the start of a new life for her.

Before Jacques had even appeared, Tom, acting on her instructions, had packed his bag and put it in the boot of the Citroën. They didn't know if they'd be able to get it back out, but she was full of confidence. They left about eight, and reached Toulouse in time for an early lunch. Here, again, everything worked like a dream. On the drive they talked terms, and Jacques, encouraged by Cynthia, offered to sponsor Tom to the sum of five hundred pounds a week. Cynthia's only fear was that that seemed so generous he might want to accept and forego her. Then the only parking space Jacques could find was round the corner from the chosen restaurant. They ate and drank well, then Tom said he would phone his Dad in America and put him in the picture. "It may take a little while to get through," he reminded them as he left the table.

"He really believes in all this," Jacques remarked. "Do you suppose he will turn nasty when he is shown the door?"

"Not if we handle it right," Cynthia assured him. "I need to go to the loo. Back in a moment. Supposing I can find it."

She asked the waiter, in full view of Jacques, and was shown to a door leading to a corridor. Once in the corridor, she found another door at the far end. This led into a storeroom, from which there was a door into the kitchen. The chefs looked at her in amazement but she put her finger on her lips and went out the back door, hurried round the corner, and found Tom

145

waiting for her. He had already extracted his carry-all from the boot of the Citroën, having broken the lock with a wicked-looking Swiss army knife. The street was deserted. "Now what?" he asked, trembling with excitement.

"The railway station?" she said.

She had not supposed life could be so excitingly simple. They opted for a slow stopper, so as further to throw Jacques off their trail. Tom was worried that he would have policemen out looking for them, but Cynthia, certain that Jacques would never risk the publicity, was able to reassure him. She thought he would most likely complain to Alexandra and ask for his money back. Alexandra would certainly be hopping mad, but as she would not have a clue where to start looking, there was nothing she could do about it.

They reached Boulogne, having changed trains twice. At dawn the following morning, they were on a ferry to England. They walked the deck, or sat in the saloon, holding hands and gazing into each other's eyes. Cynthia still didn't know whether or not she loved Tom, but she was certainly having a love affair with him. They landed in Folkestone. Cynthia was nervous, travelling as she was under her own name, but as it was now a year since her disappearance nobody was the least interested in her. "Do we have any money?" she asked.

"Not a lot. But I'll get on the phone to Dad the moment we check in and he'll wire some."

"Check in where? We can't stay in Folkestone. This is the very place they'll look for us."

"They?"

"I meant Jacques and his goons."

"We'll go up to London," he said.

146

"I need some clothes," she told him. "I don't even have a toothbrush."

"We'll get those in London," he assured her. It was all assuming the quality of a dream. They arrived in London early that evening, and Tom checked them in at a quiet hotel he had apparently used before. "It's not very grand," he apologised.

"I think it's super," she said, and her opinion of the place rose when the staff supplied her with a toothbrush.

The next three days were sheer bliss. Tom had to go down to a tennis club to practice for several hours every afternoon, and usually she went with him to watch him. For the rest of the time they ate, slept, did some shopping, explored the city – something she had never been allowed to do with Cuthbert – and made love. Of course she could not stop herself imagining what might happen if they somehow encountered Cuthbert. But obviously such a nightmare was extremely unlikely to happen unless they started going to the kind of clubs he had frequented. Yet try as she might to present to Tom the essence of an essentially innocent young woman, she could not prevent her sexual experience seeping through from time to time, but this seemed to please Tom – who *was* an innocent in bed – as he accepted that she had learned everything from Jacques.

Having been encouraged into oral sex, he naturally soon discovered her butterfly brandmark but, as instructed by Alexandra, she told him it was a birthmark, and he seemed happy with that.

The only discordant note arose because Tom was naturally very anxious to resume the tennis circuit. "They get real shirty with guys who drop out for a while," he explained. "A sprained ankle is one thing, but it can't last forever."

147

But Cynthia was afraid that, even if he wasn't famous, Alexandra would be scrutinising the names appearing on all tennis tournaments looking for his. She couldn't explain this to Tom, who had no idea anyone like Alexandra existed, thus she had to pretend a continuing fear of Jacques himself – which Tom continued to dismiss with disdain. "Listen," he said. "We're going to get married, then that fellow can go take a running jump."

"Oh, Tom." She snuggled against him. "Are you sure you really want to? I mean, I've been another man's mistress, and my background, well . . ."

"You can always tell a person's background by their frontground," he pontificated. "And your frontground is swell. You have better manners than I do." He really was innocent, she thought. But if it was what he wanted . . . "Then I'll take you back to the States, and we'll set up house and have a million kids."

"What about your parents?"

"They'll love you."

The idea was growing on her by the moment. She slept more soundly still that night and awoke to a gentle knock on the door of their room. "Too early for breakfast. I'll get it." Tom rolled out of bed, pulled on his dressing gown, and opened the door.

"You must be Tom Lane," Mayne said.

Chapter Seven

Cynthia says: *"I'd heard of people's hearts being stopped by a sudden shock, but I never expected it to happen to me. Seeing Mayne standing there was the worst moment of my life. So far."*

Cynthia scrambled out of bed, carrying most of the bedclothes with her, as a kind of protective shield. As she did so, she saw that Mayne was accompanied not only by Denise, but by two of the menservants from Eboli, each bigger and more powerfully built than Tom, who was still gaping at the elegant woman standing in front of him. "Can I help you?" he asked.

"You can stand out of my way," Mayne recommended, placing her hand on his chest and pushing.

Tom staggered backwards, and before he could recover, all four of the intruders were in the room, and the door had been closed and locked. Cynthia found herself against the dressing table. Her brain was whirring, but it was mostly sheer panic. "Who the hell are you?" Tom demanded, recovering both his balance and his nerve, and clutching the bath robe more tightly round himself.

"My name is Mayne Mayne," Mayne told him. "And I have come for that creature over there."

"You . . ." Tom turned his head to look at Cynthia,

whose tongue seemed cloven to the roof of her mouth. "Who the hell do you think you are?"

"I have told you," Mayne said. "I happen to own her. And as you have not paid for her, I have come to reclaim my goods."

"Your . . ." Again Tom had to fight for words. But he was still looking at Cynthia. "Just who is this dame, Cyn?" he demanded.

"I am sure you should explain it fully to your lover, Cynthia," Mayne suggested.

Cynthia licked her lips. "I . . ."

"We really do not have all day," Mayne said. "Cynthia is a prostitute who also happens to be a convicted drug smuggler. I rescued her from a Turkish prison. I had to pay to do this, a considerable amount of money. Therefore to all intents and purposes I own her. She understands this, I am sure."

"But . . . the uncle . . .?"

Mayne smiled. "I do not know what she has told you, but the man from whom you extracted her is a client of mine, who paid several thousand pounds for the privilege of enjoying her company for a week. During this week she appears to have concocted some little scheme for escaping him, and me, using you as the fall guy. Jacques is naturally very upset, as am I, as I have had to refund him most of his money. There is also a matter of reputation involved; none of my people has ever behaved so badly before. So you will understand that I also am very upset. Were you proposing to make trouble?"

Tom looked at her, then back at Cynthia. "Tell me none of this is true." Cynthia bit her lips.

"Ask her to raise her right leg," Mayne said. "You will find at the very top of the inside of her thigh, where it joins her groin, a brand, in the form of a butterfly. Perhaps you

150

have already noticed it. Ah, I see from your expression that you have. I put it there." Tom sat in the one chair the room possessed. He looked absolutely shattered. "Kindly get dressed, Cynthia," Mayne said. "There is no need to shower; we can attend to that later."

All manner of ideas flitted through Cynthia's mind. But there was no hope of escaping them, if Tom would not help her. "Are you going to let them take me?" she asked. He raised his head. "Do you have any idea what they are going to do to me?" Cynthia's voice rose an octave.

"I was going to marry you," he muttered.

"You still can!" she shouted.

"You're a whore!"

"That doesn't mean I can't love you, and be good to you," she said, starting to cry. "Oh, God . . ." She found herself sitting on the dressing table.

"Cynthia," Mayne said. "Do please hurry. We haven't got all day. Would you like Denise to help you?"

"Don't touch me," Cynthia said. She picked up her knickers and put them on. Tom gazed at her for a moment, then turned and lay on his face across the bed. She rather thought he might be crying as well, but that wasn't going to help her very much. She finished dressing, picked up her suitcase.

"Leave that stuff," Mayne said. "It's pretty tatty, anyway. Now Cynthia, I do most urgently suggest that you behave yourself. Otherwise you may be hurt, very badly."

"You mean I'm not going to be hurt, very badly, anyway?"

"There are degrees of badly, dear. Behave yourself, and it may be possible for my mother to forgive you. Misbehave, and she has told me that she will not for-give you, and in fact that she will not wish to see

151

you again. I do hope you appreciate what I am saying."

Cynthia looked at Tom's back. "Did you hear that?" she asked. "They're going to kill me."

Mayne smiled. "Silly girl. That is only if you behave badly."

Tom did not raise his head.

"Bastard," Cynthia said. "Why are we hanging about?"

They went down the stairs to where a car was waiting. Mayne tipped the porter – at that hour there was no one else about – and the three women got into the back seat. The two men got into the front, but one of them turned back to look at Cynthia all the time. "I think you were being a little hard on that young man," Mayne remarked. "Jacques tells us you set the whole thing up. Well, that boy is clearly an innocent. How can you blame him for going along with a beautiful girl when she throws herself at him? Or for collapsing completely when he discovered what you really are . . . You have probably ruined his faith in women."

"I'd like to have ruined more than that," Cynthia muttered.

They drove out of London and to a private airfield and boarded an executive jet. To Cynthia's surprise, no one made any attempt to tell her where to sit, or to touch her. She chose a window seat and strapped herself in, turned her head resolutely to the glass as the aircraft taxied and then took off; she was determined to ignore them for as long as possible.

It was not possible for very long. Once they were airborne, Mayne came and sat beside her. "Take off your dress," she said.

152

Cynthia turned her head. "You mean you can't wait until we get back to Eboli?"

"No, I can't. When we get back to Eboli Mummy will wish to punish you. But I wish to punish you too. I had such hopes of you. It was my decision to get you out of that Turkish jail. And now you have let me down with a bump. I am really very angry. Take off your dress."

Cynthia realised that Denise was standing beside her, and that the two men had also taken off their seatbelts. She unfastened her own belt and lifted her dress over her head, mentally bracing herself for whatever was coming next. Mayne took the dress from her hands and threw it on another seat. Instantly Denise dropped a leather band over Cynthia's shoulders, sliding it past her breasts to just above her navel. There it pinned her arms to her sides as it was drawn tight and buckled behind her seatback. Mayne then refastened her seatbelt, pulling it as tight as possible. "There we are," she said. "Now you're strapped in twice. Will you fetch the pepper, please, Denise. Oh, Cynthia, you may scream as loudly as you wish. Up here no one is going to hear you, not even the pilots."

Cynthia had no recollection of returning to Eboli.

The drive there was short and on arrival she was merely pushed out of the car and on to the hot concrete of the front drive. As she was clutching her burning breasts she fell heavily on to her shoulder, and rolled across the heat, adding a new dimension to her pain. "Up girl." Alexandra stood above her.

Sobbing, Cynthia rose to her knees, and then got to her feet. But she immediately started to fall again, and Denise had to catch her and hold her up. Through the haze of pain and tears overcoloured by a red mist of angry outrage, she saw them all; Madeleine and the other girls, including

153

Angela, peering at her. "What are you going to do to me, you awful bitch?" she spat.

Alexandra smiled. "Why, do you know, I have not yet made up my mind. I see you have already been punished to a certain extent. I shall have to consider. Take her to her room. And I wish someone to stay with her at all times."

Cynthia threw herself on her bed, and rolled to and fro. She wished she could escape her body, just for a few hours. She pushed herself up, stared at herself in the mirror. Her breasts were swollen, the nipples hard and red. Her eyes were swollen as well, and red. And she did not doubt her lungs were also swollen. She realised Irina was in the room with her. "You were very foolish," the Russian woman said. "No one escapes the Countess."

"You mean others have tried?"

"Not since I have been here. There was one, once. She disappeared. We never heard of her again."

"My God!" For a moment Cynthia even ignored the pain. "You can just sit there and say that?"

"I am telling you what the others told me."

"And you think I am going to be murdered?" Cynthia hurled herself face down on her bed. She didn't know what to think. She didn't want to think. All manner of chaotic images floated through her mind. When she thought what she had been through . . . her head jerked as the door opened.

It was Madeleine. "I have some cream here, for your tits," Madeleine said. "It will ease the pain." Cynthia crawled up the bed, away from her. "Don't be foolish," Madeleine told her. "I'm not going to hurt you. I'm going to help you." Cynthia turned, staring at her, breath coming in great rasps. "Look," Madeleine said, and held out the jar of cream. "Put it on yourself, if you prefer. Do you think it is another form of torture?" Madeleine lifted her shirt over her head, unscrewed the lid, took some of the cream on her finger, and delicately circled her own nipple. "You see? Come along now."

Cynthia submitted. Nothing had ever felt so good. "What's going to happen to me?" she muttered.

"I really don't know," Madeleine said. "Alexandra is very angry with you. But then, she is also very fond of you. We will have to wait and see."

The cream was certainly soothing. Mentally she still felt as though she had been put through a washing machine and then a tumble dryer. And now it was time to face Alexandra.

Alexandra sat behind her ornate desk in her huge study in the penthouse apartment, flanked as always by Mayne. Cynthia was escorted by Denise and Madeleine. "Well?" Alexandra asked, quietly. "What have you to say for yourself?"

"Does it matter what I say?" Cynthia asked.

"It matters a great deal. Tell me why you did it."

Cynthia shrugged. "I wanted out. I don't want to be a whore. I never wanted to be a whore."

"You *are* a whore, dear. You cannot change that now. You have just tried, and failed."

"Because you would not let me go. I would have been good to Tom."

"After your fashion, no doubt. Why did you abandon Jacques? He did not beat you. He could not have done."

"He made me do . . . ugh! To get it up. And I didn't succeed."

Alexandra nodded. "He is becoming a problem. I may have to drop him from my list. But that still does not

155

excuse what you did. You should have sat it out, and when you returned here, made a full report to me. Then all of this unpleasantness would have been avoided. Now . . . I have had to make a considerable refund, and my reputation for supplying girls of absolute reliability has been tarnished." Cynthia could not help but wonder which mattered the more. "Jacques is of course convinced that you will have told this man Lane all of his unhappy secrets," Alexandra said. "Did you do this?"

"Certainly not. He thinks Jacques was my lover, of whom I was tired."

"Well, I hope I can convince Jacques of that. The question is, what am I to do with you? You could have had a great future, Cynthia. You are young, you are quite absurdly beautiful, you are intelligent . . . but how can I ever trust you again?"

My God, Cynthia thought: she is condemning me to death. But that couldn't happen. So what do I do? Stay alive, no matter what. "I am sorry," she said. "It will not happen again."

Alexandra looked at her for several seconds. "What proof have I of that?"

"My word. I told you, I never wanted to be a whore. I ran away from home and got in with Cuthbert. I never used drugs or smuggled them. Cuthbert set me up. Then you rescued me. Believe me, I'm grateful."

"But you always intended to escape me the moment it became possible," Alexandra said.

"Yes. But now that I know it is not possible I will not try it again," Cynthia lied. "I am asking for another chance."

Alexandra continued to gaze at her for several seconds. Then she said, "Very well. I will give you another chance. But there will be no others. I wish you to understand this, very clearly. When I first got into this business, oh, a very long time ago, I was employed by a pimp who ran a whole stable of girls. If any of them got out of line, he would have his goons slit her cheeks open, pack them with salt, and then throw her out into the street to starve." Cynthia gulped. "I should hate to have to do that to you," Alexandra said. "But if I did, I would not merely throw you out on to a London street. I would have you dumped in somewhere like Calcutta, or Sao Paolo, where you would find survival very difficult. Do I make myself clear?"

Cynthia had to swallow before she could speak. "Yes."

"Very good. Now go back to your room and stay there until the pepper has worn off. I will speak to you again then."

"Has she actually done that to any of her girls?" Cynthia asked Denise, as she was escorted back to her room.

"You will have to ask the Countess," Denise said. "I am not going to lock you in. You are free to do what you wish. You are also excused any training until you are returned to normal. That will be about forty-eight hours, I would say. Have a good rest."

"Denise!" Cynthia caught the Frenchwoman's wrist. "Do you hate me?"

"Certainly I do not," Denise said. "But I think you were very foolish. Did I not tell you, months ago, that the way to be happy was to obey the Countess in all things?"

"Are we happy?" Cynthia asked. "Can we ever be happy?"

"Of course. Happiness is here and now, Cynthia. You cannot plan for happiness. Oh, I know many people do. But it is never as they hoped. Happiness is for the day. So the next time you wake up, and realise that you are in

157

possession of your health, that you are not starving, that you are not going to be beaten or bullied, and that you have nothing unpleasant to anticipate during the coming day, then you are happy. And you should enjoy it."

"And when you do have to anticipate something unpleasant during the day?"

"That is the price we pay for the happy days," Denise pointed out. "It does not only apply to us. We are hired out on an average six times a year, for an average of a week at a time." Cynthia shuddered. "But think," Denise said, "of having to go to work every day, to do a job which may bore you or which you may positively dislike, in the company of people who bore you . . . they have far more cause to be unhappy than us. And they are in the vast majority."

Something to consider, certainly. "Denise," Cynthia said. "Make love to me."

Denise's smile was sad. "No one is to touch you," she said. "Until Alexandra has done so."

Cynthia supposed she was right, about happiness. But perhaps *she* had not been thinking about happiness. There were other factors involved, such as pride, and ambition, and above all, an end! She was owned, like a pet dog or cat. She resented that. And her owner sublet her from time to time. She resented that even more. And where was the end? Alexandra had done very well for herself, but Alexandra was essentially cold-blooded and pragmatic. When it came to personal relationships, she had Madeleine, and Madeleine had her. They had risked much together, endured much together, and eventually triumphed, together. Cynthia did not criticise them for what they had achieved, together. But it was not a relationship she herself would find satisfying.

Mayne appeared content to be her mother's daughter.

158

There was no suggestion of anyone else in her life, male or female, unless Denise filled that role. Oddly, Denise was someone with whom Cynthia felt she could build a meaningful relationship. But Denise was too much entirely Alexandra's woman. Or Mayne's. It came to the same thing.

As for the girls, they had nothing. Oh, they toyed with each other, physically as well as emotionally. But they did not love. Perhaps they never had loved, and no doubt it was in Alexandra's interest to keep them in a permanent state of nonhuman commitment, even as regards themselves, forever content with their luxurious lifestyle, and the fabulous clothes or jewellery they were from time to time permitted to wear. They were, in fact, very beautiful zombies. Cynthia resolved to try and escape again.

It was actually very relaxing to be left entirely alone for a few days. As Denise had suggested, within forty-eight hours her breasts had returned to their normal size and the pain had disappeared. But it was another twenty-four hours before she went down to meals or to swim. The girls were of course eager to hear of her experiences, and she told them what she thought they would find titillating. "You were very lucky," Ingrid said.

But only the next day they were distracted by the return of Carmen, who had a new set of experiences to recount, and then by the arrival of another of Alexandra's 'gentlemen'. Cynthia was not even allowed to be present when he made his selection, so she gathered Alexandra had not yet made up her mind to trust her. This man, an Italian 'count', went off with Rona. It was that night Alexandra sent for her.

"We shall have supper *à deux*," Alexandra told her. "And talk, about things."

159

Cynthia had been required to wear evening dress. For the first part of the evening Alexandra played nothing but the gracious hostess. No doubt it amused her to do so, but Cynthia was given an insight into how well it was possible to live. They ate the best food, drank the best wine – served only by a single manservant in a white shell jacket and wearing white gloves. She also observed, however, that Alexandra ate and drank sparingly, and she got the impression that her mistress was very tired. She wondered if her escapade was responsible for that? But tired or not, Alexandra was as sexually aware as ever, and while she made conversation she smiled at her acolyte, and occasionally touched her hand. Then the meal was finished, and the servant was dismissed. Alexandra held Cynthia's hand to lead her into the bedroom. "It is months since last you and I slept together, and then we were on a ship at sea," she said in her soft voice. "I suspect we were not concentrating upon the matter in hand."

She slipped the straps from Cynthia's shoulders. But Cynthia was not concentrating on the matter in hand now, either: she was too absorbed in looking around her, at the magnificence of Alexandra's bedroom, the pale blue drapes, the pink satin sheets and pillowcases, the indirect lighting . . . "Do you ever entertain men in here?" she asked.

"Not recently," Alexandra said. "I find men so exhausting." She slipped Cynthia's gown past her hips and let it slide to the floor. As instructed, Cynthia was wearing nothing else apart from her shoes. "Now undress me," Alexandra commanded. Cynthia obeyed, and was held close for a long kiss. "You are so beautiful," Alexandra said. "Do please behave yourself in the future, Cynthia. I should hate to have to destroy you. Now come to bed."

* * *

160

Alexandra had claimed that men exhausted her, but Cynthia could not help but wonder if it was not actually the other way around; she was an even more vigorous and indeed violent lover in her own bed than on board the boat. When they had satisfied each other Cynthia quickly slipped into a deep sleep. Happiness, Denise had told her, was a matter of the moment. Well, at this moment, she was happy. As for tomorrow . . .

When she awoke, for a moment she did not know where she was. The drapes were drawn, and the room was dark. Then she inhaled Alexandra's scent, and felt the older woman lying beside her. Alexandra was clearly still fast asleep. What to do? Was she supposed to sidle off and resume her place as just one of the girls? Or would the Countess require another sexual session when she awoke? In any event, Cynthia desperately needed to go to the toilet.

Carefully she eased herself off the bed on to the carpet, and tiptoed into the bathroom. Here again she had to pause and look around her at the pink and ice-blue magnificence, the gold-plated taps – or were they solid gold? – the massed ranks of perfumes, and piles of heavily-scented soaps. Through the window she saw that it was broad daylight outside, although the sun was not yet evident. She switched off the light and stepped back into the bedroom, closed the door softly behind herself, and found she was holding her breath, faced by a sudden chilling and unnatural silence.

Oh, Jesus, she thought, and ran to the bed, careless now of making a noise, and switched on the lights, all of them, turning the bedroom into a glowing cavern. Alexandra lay on her side, facing away from her, arms extended in front of her, sheet half draped across her naked buttocks. But there was no movement of her torso, no

161

sound of breathing. Cynthia licked her lips. "Alexandra," she ventured softly. "Countess!"

She took a deep breath, touched Alexandra's shoulder. It was cold. Gently she eased the Countess onto her back, gazed at those features, pale now, mouth open, suddenly instantly ugly, where last night she had been so beautiful. She was the first dead person Cynthia had ever seen. She slid off the bed and dropped to her knees in horror. Then she leapt up and ran to the door, pulled it wide. "Help!" she screamed. "Help me! Alexandra . . . the Countess! Help!"

Doors opened and people ran to her and past her. Madeleine was first, but Mayne and Denise were close behind. There was further sound as the menservants were aroused; some of them would of course be already up.

Madeleine and Mayne needed only a single look at the Countess to know she was dead. "What happened?" Mayne asked. Her voice was like a rasp of steel.

Madeleine picked up the phone and starting punching numbers.

"I . . . I don't know," Cynthia said. "When I woke up . . . she was just lying there . . ."

Madeleine was speaking to Dr Cardona. "Please come at once," she said.

"What do you think happened?" Mayne asked her mother's oldest friend.

"I think she had a heart attack. There are no external marks. Apart from, well . . ." She looked at Cynthia.

"You made love last night?" Mayne demanded.

"Yes. But . . . she seemed all right."

"Go to your room and stay there," Mayne said.

"I didn't have anything to do with her death," Cynthia protested.

"You were there. Denise!"

162

"Come along, Cynthia." Denise held her arm.

Cynthia allowed herself to be escorted to her room. "She can't hold me responsible, Denise. She can't."

"I am sure she will not, when she has thought about it, and talked to the doctor," Denise said. "But Mayne is more . . . emotionally vehement than was the Countess. You must give her time to come to terms with the situation." She gave a half smile. "We all have to do that."

Cynthia glanced at her. She displayed no sign of shock or grief. "You think things will be different?"

"Very different," Denise said. "At the very least in style."

The change of style was not immediately apparent. Mayne went into the deepest mourning for her mother, and commanded that all her people do the same. The pool area was banned, and the girls were not to appear unless dressed in black; as none of them had any black clothes – except for various pieces of exotic underwear – this meant they could not appear at all until clothes had been bought for them in the nearest town, which took a couple of days.

By then, Dr Cardona had been and examined Alexandra, and agreed that she had died of a heart attack, brought on by physical exertion. Denise told Cynthia this, and she was again very anxious, as it had been lovemaking with her that had finally pushed the old woman over the edge. But Denise assured her that Mayne did not hold it against her. "After all," she pointed out, "it is certainly the way Alexandra would have wanted to go. I suppose it is the way all of us would like to go."

Speak for yourself, Cynthia thought; she had no desire to go at all, for a long time yet. To the other girls she had become even more an object of combined admiration and

163

respect. She had attempted to escape, and survived, and she had seen the old dragon off. But like her, they were concerned with what life under the new dragon might be like.

Alexandra was buried in the castle grounds, as she had wished, beside the body of her husband, who had lain in the ground for fifty years. Every member of the staff was present, and a surprising number of people from the neighbouring towns came to the simple ceremony. They might all have been aware of Alexandra's background, and even perhaps of her current activities, but she was the Countess of Eboli, and she had been a good neighbour to most of them.

But there were also visitors from afar. Captain Olivares came up from Gibraltar, and there were several obviously wealthy men, who Cynthia gathered were clients, who came to pay their last respects.

"Nothing has changed, or will change," Mayne told them all. "My mother is dead, and I have taken her place. That is all."

Life slowly returned to normal, but it was a subdued life compared with when Alexandra had ruled. This was not because Mayne imposed any new restrictions once she had got over her grief; the girls were again allowed to swim, and returned to their usual exercising routines. It was simply that no one felt quite secure in their anticipation of how Mayne was going to behave, and their insecurity grew as Mayne did not appear to be about to change any of her mother's arrangements.

For the first fortnight after Alexandra's death Mayne was far too busy conferring with lawyers, and making sure that she had inherited every last penny. Cynthia actually found herself feeling sorry for Madeleine, who had had no stake in the business apart from her lifelong love affair with Alexandra, and who thus now had no stake in the business at all. She and Mayne were not close, and now the Frenchwoman seemed like a lost spirit, always present but with no part to play, not knowing when she was going to be shown the door.

But Cynthia's ability to feel sorry for others was abruptly terminated on the day, a month after Alexandra's death, when she was summoned from the pool area to the office, to stand before Mayne and the ever-present Denise. Mayne was seated behind her desk, a diary in front of her. "You were due to have your period a week ago," she said. Cynthia raised her eyebrows. So much had happened during the last month or so she had quite forgotten to keep track. "Well?" Mayne demanded.

"I suppose I was so upset by what happened . . ."

"Do not give me any stupid excuses," Mayne said. "Denise has arranged for you to see Dr Cardona. He will test you and then we will know."

"But . . ." Cynthia had been going to say, that's not possible. Instead she bit her lip.

"He will also wish to see your pills," Mayne went on. "You will take them with you."

Cynthia drew a deep breath. "I don't have any pills." Mayne leaned back in her chair. "I threw them away when I went off with Tom Lane," Cynthia explained. "I wanted to be his wife, and have his child."

"God, what a fool I was to get you out of that Turkish jail," Mayne remarked. "Well, I would say that you have succeeded in your ambition. If Cardona confirms that, you will have to have an abortion. That will put you out of action for another few weeks. I should remind you that you are supposed to *earn* me money,

165

not cost me money. So far you have been nothing but an expense."

"I will not have an abortion," Cynthia said.

Mayne snorted. "We do not indulge such fantasies on Eboli."

"It has nothing to do with my fantasy," Cynthia said. "I wish to have a child. My child. It is the right of every woman to have a child, surely."

Mayne frowned. But she knew that was true enough. "I suppose you think this is some way of escaping Eboli," she remarked. "After having promised that you would not attempt to do so again."

"I have no wish to escape Eboli," Cynthia lied. "But I wish to have a child, should I be carrying one." Tom's child, she thought. He had let her down, yet there was no other man she had met she would rather have as the father of her baby.

"I see," Mayne said. "So, in addition to all the other expense you have cost me, I am now required to carry you, without earning, for nine months, at the end of which time you will no doubt announce that you intend to feed the child, and be out of action for another six months. You must take me for a fool."

"All right," Cynthia said. "I know you will be out of pocket. You can take it out of my fees. You said I would receive twenty-five per cent of whatever I earned. Well, keep the twenty-five per cent until I have paid off my debt." She had never yet earned a fee, as the business with Jacques had left everyone out of pocket. But she had faith in the future. And she would have a child, if that is what fate had decreed. Being a mother, being able to love and cherish something of her very own would go a long way towards alleviating the horror of her situation.

Mayne had been studying her. "If I decide that you will

166

have an abortion," she pointed out, "you will have an abortion, even if you have to be tied up. Do you really suppose you can defy me?"

"No," Cynthia said. "But, should I be pregnant and if you force me to abort, so help me God, I will kill myself at the first opportunity. You may be able to have me watched all the time I am on Eboli, but you cannot keep tabs on me when next you hire me out. So you dare not hire me out, as when I go I may well choose to take the client with me."

Mayne's mouth was open; she was quite unused to being spoken to like that. Denise gave a little cough; it was difficult to determine whether she was warning Cynthia or amused by her. Mayne glared at her. "Being a mother often rounds out a woman's character," Denise remarked, again aware that she was quoting the Countess. "Cynthia is very young; she has a long way to go. And besides, having a child about the place might be rather amusing."

Mayne snorted. "There will be no child about the place," she declared. "If I let you have this baby, Cynthia, you must understand that it will be put out for adoption."

Cynthia bit her lip. But she also understood that even to be allowed to have the baby would be a triumph. To attempt to push too hard would be to risk everything; as everyone recognised, Mayne was less stable, and far less pragmatic a character than her mother. "I understand," she said.

Mayne pointed. "I also wish you to understand that if I go along with you on this, I expect in return utter loyalty. A loyalty you never revealed to Mummy."

"I understand," Cynthia said again. "I promise."

Mayne continued to stare at her for several seconds, and Cynthia wondered if she had been too pat with her answers. But at last Mayne nodded. "Very well," she said. "Go away and find out if you are going to be a mother."

167

Denise went outside with her, and hugged her and kissed her. "I am so happy for you," she said.

Cynthia says: *"The next nine months or so were the happiest of my life to that moment. That they were to end in catastrophe is neither here nor there. I was not aware that while I was bearing little Tom, Mayne had my future entirely mapped out to her satisfacion. And besides, it was during those nine months that I first met Miss Gray.*

Cynthia discovered that Mayne was as good as her word. When her test proved positive, she assembled the girls to inform them that Cynthia was being excused exercise, except as she felt like it, and would be excused all hostess duties, during the term of her pregnancy. "I may tell you," Mayne lied, "that Cynthia's condition is one desired by my late mother. It is not one of which I approve. I am going along with it because it was Mummy's wish. Any future cases of pregnancy will be dealt with most severely."

She then went on to forbid any sexual relations between Cynthia and any of the girls; Cynthia did not know whether this was because she somehow thought it might harm the baby or because she was feeling frustrated herself. But she was happy to accept that ruling; when the girls crowded round to discover the truth of the matter, she merely smiled and told them it was a secret between the dead Countess, Mayne, and herself. And Denise, to be sure.

The next few weeks were absolute bliss, as she was allowed to do exactly as she pleased in the near perfect surroundings of Eboli. Her behaviour was to a certain extent monitored by Denise, who prevented her from eating too many chocolates and forbade her any alcohol at all, and who also encouraged her at least to indulge

168

in light exercising . . . "We don't want you to lose that magnificent figure," she chided.

But restrictions apart, she could do anything she wished. Save of course leave Eboli. So she slept late, and would then spend the morning sitting on the terrace looking out across the fields at the mountains, always shaded by a huge umbrella to keep the sun from her pale complexion. Afternoons were much of the same; she fell into the Spanish habit of enjoying a siesta, but when she awoke it was back to the terrace to watch the sun setting over the hills.

She did a great deal of reading, for the castle contained a huge library, and much of it was in English. She'd never read before, except when it had been necessary for school. The castle had a satellite dish and they were thus able to receive English programmes, and in addition there was also a large library of videos, although these comprised either pornography or old movies, to which Alexandra had been fond. But one could not watch television all the time, and reading introduced Cynthia into a whole new world.

It was also enjoyable being an onlooker at the business of the castle, rather than a participant. Even before she began to show, Mayne would not allow her to join the girls for their presentation to visiting clients, but she was allowed to watch the proceedings from behind a tapestry on the minstrel's gallery, always with a feeling of relief that she was not the one about to be parcelled off. She suffered almost no morning sickness, but later in the pregnancy she sought greater solitude or enjoyed the company of either Denise, who seemed to be genuinely fond of her, or Madeleine, who was undoubtedly lonely. Cynthia enjoyed Denise more, because she liked her more, but Madeleine was fascinating, as she would reminisce about the great

169

days in Paris in the Twenties, when Alexandra had just been starting out, and had been recruiting women far and wide.

"She would only accept the very best," Madeleine said. "That has always been Alexandra's motto, only the very best will do. That is why she became so famous and so wealthy. Men knew that when they went to Alexandra's they would never be disappointed."

She indulged in some reminiscing herself, to herself. It was incredible that, as she entered her sixth month of pregnancy, it was now over a year since Cuthbert, and Turkey; at this distance in time she could even look back and smile.

It was in this sixth month of Cynthia's pregnancy that I visited Eboli for the first time. As I have indicated in the foreword to this book, I had met Alexandra some years before, when she was in her heyday as the Countess of Eboli, her active days as a prostitute behind her. She seemed interested in me, I presume because we both hailed originally from British Guiana, now known as Guyana, and we saw something of each other for a while. I was then an aspiring young writer rather than a novelist, and I was totally in awe of this fabulously beautiful, and by account, fabulously wealthy, woman, who was also, again by account, the greatest prostitute in history. But after a while she returned to Spain with her entourage, and we lost touch.

I was thus totally taken aback when, following Alexandra's death, I received an invitation from Mayne to visit Eboli, where I was told that it had been Alexandra's wish that I write her life story. To this end, Mayne told me, she had been commanded in her mother's will to provide me with all possible information, including an enormous pile of notebooks and exercise books, which I

170

*had already received, in which from time to time Alexandra
had recalled, presumably for her own satisfaction, all the
principal events of her life. Obviously, as can be imagined,
I was utterly fascinated by this project, as I was utterly
fascinated by Eboli, and its inhabitants. Wandering about
the place, I found it difficult to devote my time to any of
the girls, on that first visit; my interest was concentrated
on traces of Alexandra, and in this regard I spent most
of my time with Madeleine, who had known the Countess,
and the Countess's experiences, better than most. Even then
I was aware, however, that Cynthia Haslar was the most
beautiful as well as the most intelligent of the girls, and I
was additionally interested in her because she was by then
very obviously pregnant, which seemed singular, and, in
the context of Eboli, unique.*

*However, I was given little opportunity to speak with
her, nor did she appear very interested in speaking with
me. Madeleine merely told me that she was an unusual
young woman, and that her pregnancy was indeed a unique
affair as regards Eboli, but had been condoned by Mayne
because of special circumstances. She did not tell me what
these special circumstances were. When I returned to Eboli
again, more than a year had passed, and Cynthia Haslar
had disappeared.*

Cynthia says: *"The visit of some writer who was going to tell
all about the Countess was very exciting for the girls. Each
of them I think was hoping that they would somehow have
a mention; they seemed unable to grasp that Miss Gray was
intending to write about what might be called Alexandra's
active life, which was well before any of them, or I, had
been born. In any event, as far as I was concerned, her
visit was soon forgotten. I was about to be plunged into a
succession of cataclysmic events."*

171

Chapter Eight

Cynthia says: *"Successfully giving birth is, I suppose, the high spot in a woman's life. I suspect everyone at Eboli, with the possible exception of Mayne herself, was as excited as I, and the last days of my pregnancy solicited a huge outpouring of affection and anticipation. The birth itself was almost an anticlimax, but it was also delightfully easy – and then I had my little Tom. The fact that he was a boy and that he was healthy was all I wanted at that moment."*

"You do realise that Mayne intends to farm the child out?" Madeleine reminded her, sitting beside her bed.

"And that you agreed to it," Denise said, sitting on the other side. "And promised to be a faithful member of the team."

"Yes," Cynthia said, enjoying the tug of the strong little gums on her nipple. They were both anxiously watching her, but they had no reason to, she was sure. She had already accepted the inevitable. She was only seventeen years old, and she knew she could not properly care for little Tom and at the same time continue the profession in which she was for the moment caught up. He would go to a good home – she would make sure of that – and as soon as she was able, she would reclaim him. She had no real knowledge of the legal ramifications that might be involved; she had no doubt that she would succeed in the end. But to do that she needed money, and she was only going to get sufficient money by working very hard, paying off her debt to Mayne, and then accumulating vast tips by being the best bed companion any man could ever desire.

This resolution made her feel she was for the first time in her life working to a plan, and she now had high expectations. But she did suppose she was going to have a few weeks with her baby before she was called into action. One day soon after the birth she was lounging in the pool, little Tom was in his pram at the poolside well shaded by an enormous umbrella, when Denise suddenly appeared. "Cynthia," she said. "Mayne wishes to see you. You too, Carmen." The two women climbed out of the water and dried themselves.

"There is no need to dress," Denise said. "Mayne wishes you to come as you are."

They accompanied Denise in the lift to Mayne's apartment, and were shown into the private office, where Mayne was seated behind her desk. Seated beside her was a man. "Sheikh Abdullah!" Carmen cried. She might have been taken aback by his sexual demands, but she seemed pleased to see him again; he had apparently given her an astronomical tip after the Caribbean trip.

"Carmen, my dear." The sheikh rose to kiss her hand. "You are as beautiful as ever." He released her and looked at Cynthia. "And you are even more beautiful than I remember." Cynthia breasts were still full of milk; that apart, her figure had entirely returned to normal. Now he seized her hand to kiss it as well.

"Sheikh Abdullah would like you both . . . together," Mayne announced.

Carmen and Cynthia looked at each other. "But . . . I am still feeding little Tom," Cynthia protested.

173

Abdullah smiled. "But that is splendid. You can feed me instead." And as he was still standing virtually against her, he gave her left nipple a little flick. "I shall enjoy it."

"No," Cynthia said. She didn't like the sheikh, anyway, and the thought of him sucking at her was repulsive.

"Now, Cynthia," Mayne said. "I do not want any more trouble from you. In fact, I have resolved not to *have* any more trouble from you, ever again. I must inform you . . ." She drew a deep breath. "That I have sold you to the Sheikh." For a moment Cynthia didn't quite understand what she meant. "He wants you to join his harem," Mayne explained. "Oh, you too, Carmen. It seems that he was very pleased with your performance in the Caribbean; now he wishes to enjoy you permanently."

Cynthia and Carmen looked at each other, as the penny slowly dropped. Cynthia was the first to react. "No!" she shouted. "You cannot just sell us, as if we were slaves!"

"Darling," Mayne pointed out. "You *are* slaves. My slaves. And you in particular have been a bad buy. Well, Sheikh Abdullah has offered all that I have spent on you, and doubled it, to have you for himself. I think that is a very good deal, for me. Whether it is a good deal for the Sheikh . . ." She glanced at Abdullah.

He gave an ingratiating smile. "I have no doubt of it," he said.

"Very good. So, if you would both go and pack your things, the Sheikh has his private jet waiting at the airport."

"I absolutely refuse," Cynthia said.

"Cyn," Carmen said warningly.

"You are telling me I must abandon my son, this minute?!"

"We had always agreed you would do that, Cynthia," Mayne said.

174

"After we had chosen the right adoptive parents for him."

"I assure you, I will look after that," Mayne said.

"You can't separate us. Not now!" She turned to Abdullah. "Let me bring my son with me. If you do, I promise I will be a good wife to you."

"You are not going to be my wife," Abdullah explained, as patiently as Mayne. "You are going to be my concubine. And as for children, I have more than sufficient. However, if you wish to be a mother, I will allow you to do so. But the father must be me. I cannot permit the child of another father to enter my harem."

"If you do not let me bring my son," Cynthia said. "I . . . I'll kill myself." And possibly you as well, she thought.

Abdullah merely smiled. "Then you will make life very hard for yourself, Cynthia. But I am sure you will be sensible soon enough." He looked at Mayne. "I do not think she can be trusted on her own, at this moment. If someone else could collect her belongings . . ."

"Of course," Mayne said. "When you have packed for yourself, Carmen, you will pack for Cynthia."

Carmen nodded. She might have been as taken aback as Cynthia by the sudden alteration in her status, but she was more conditioned to accepting whatever fate threw at her. She went to the door, and Cynthia hurled herself forward as well. She had no very clear idea where she was going or what she was hoping to achieve. She just knew she had to do something to escape them; run to her room, gather up little Tom and run to the roof, and if necessary hurl herself off. But Denise caught her before she could reach the door, holding her arm, and when Cynthia swung at her, pinioning her other arm as well and forcing her forward so that she found herself kneeling in a chair, her head hanging over the back.

"Let me go!" she shouted. "For God's sake, Denise . . ."

"I have some attendants waiting downstairs," Abdullah said. "Are they allowed up here?"

"No," Mayne said. "Denise will deliver her." Cynthia made an abortive effort to push herself up, but Denise's grip was too strong. "However," Mayne went on, "once she has been delivered to you, she is your business. I do not wish to see her or hear of her again."

"You will not," Abdullah promised.

Cynthia sucked air into her lungs. "Help me!" she screamed. "Somebody help me!"

Denise was lifting her upright, while retaining the vice-like grip on her arms. "Please don't make a scene," she whispered into Cynthia's ear. "Or I will have to hit you."

Cynthia gave up. She knew that Denise could break both her arms, and probably both her legs as well, with only the slightest effort. "She must have something on," Abdullah said. "My people cannot look upon the body, much less the face, of one of my concubines. Make sure Carmen understands this as well."

Mayne produced a cheesecloth wraparound, which was tucked under Cynthia's arms, and a cheesecloth veil was draped over her head and the corners tied under her chin. She could breathe, and she could see, but her own features were rendered quite indistinct. Thus garbed she was forced into the lift by Denise, Abdullah following. Mayne remained in her apartment. On the ground floor Madeleine waited. Madeleine! Cynthia thought. Madeleine had always been her friend. "Madeleine," she gasped. "Please help me. Madeleine!" But Madeleine never moved. Once Mayne had made a decision, Madeleine was as helpless as any of the women.

176

They reached the outer rooms of the castle. Here the Eboli menservants waited, together with four Arabs. "Take her to the car," Abdullah told Denise.

Cynthia was forced across the entry hall and through the front door on to the concrete of the park. She was not wearing shoes, and her feet burned as much as when she had been brought back from Paris the previous year. Denise understood this and pushed her almost at a run to the big black Mercedes. The door was opened for them, and she thrust Cynthia inside. Cynthia landed on her hands and knees, and found herself gazing at two veiled women. "She is recalcitrant," Abdullah said from behind her.

The women each seized one of Cynthia's arms and pulled her on to the back seat. Her veil came off but now it did not matter, for the car windows were so heavily tinted there was no possibility of anyone seeing in. Equally it was impossible for anyone inside to see out. Cynthia panted while she got her breath back, looking from one to the other of the women. She could see neither their faces nor their figures, but she gained the impression that they were distinctly overweight.

Abdullah got into the car and sat on the seat opposite. "My two senior wives," he explained. "They do not speak English, but they know how to deal with disobedient girls."

Cynthia blew hair out of her face. "You can't get away with this, you know," she said. "When the law finds out . . ."

Abdullah smiled. "The law already knows all about it. In my country, I am the Minister of Justice."

Carmen joined them a few minutes later, and they drove away.

177

The men sat in the front of the car, which was separated from the rear by an opaque partition. Carmen was also veiled, but she took this off in the car and gave Cynthia an anxious look. Cynthia did not respond. For the moment she was too overwhelmed by what had happened to her, was happening to her, and was apparently going to go on happening to her. She had been overwhelmed with horror once before in her life, when she had been incarcerated in the Turkish remand centre. But she now knew she had always supposed that somehow she would be rescued from a life she had got into, somehow, by accident. Now eternity seemed to stretch in front of her. At least it would be shared with Carmen. She thanked God for that.

"Why are you so unhappy?" Abdullah asked, with apparent genuine concern. "Life in the harem is good. You have to do nothing but eat, sleep, play games . . . and make love. Does that not sound attractive? I have said that if you wish it I will give you another child. I will do this. But you must not resist me. If you resist me, I will punish you. You will not enjoy this." Tears dribbled from Cynthia's eyes, and Carmen reached across to squeeze her hand. "That is right," Abdullah said. "You make her understand that I am not a bad man, eh? You make her understand."

They were veiled again to be moved from the car to the private jet waiting at the aeroclub, but as the jet, like the car, was divided into two compartments, and the men occupied the forward one, they were again allowed to take these off once they were airborne. The Arab women also removed their veils. Neither was the least attractive, but because of their seniority even Abdullah treated them with respect; smiled indulgently when they seated themselves opposite the two newcomers and quite literally explored

178

them. "Submit," Carmen warned Cynthia. "Or they will beat you."

Cynthia made herself keep still while they fingered her nipples, giving great shrieks of laughter as milk dribbled out, and then pulled her legs apart to look at her pubic hair, again laughing most heartily. They did the same to Carmen. "They will shave us," Carmen said.

Cynthia looked down in consternation. "Why?"

"It is their way."

But the women were even more fascinated by the butterfly brands which they now uncovered. Abdullah spoke to them in Arabic. Apparently the sight of Cynthia being examined had aroused him, and so his wives now pulled her from her seat and took her to him, making her sit on his lap, while one of them inserted him into her; she hadn't realised he was wearing nothing beneath his jibbah. She was taken quite by surprise, and despite the women's attentions was not ready, while he was enormous – she had not had sex for so long she was out of the habit of being perpetually half aroused. Now she gasped in pain even while registering surprise that he made no attempt to kiss her, or do anything except rise and fall inside her; the women did all the caressing. When they were finished, she felt more thoroughly raped than at any previous time in her life.

They arrived in Karnah only a few hours after leaving Spain. Cynthia's first impression was one of heat. She had quite enjoyed the flight, once Abdullah had been satisfied; as he had been waiting more than a year to get his hands on her, he took some satisfying. But afterwards she had been allowed to sit with Carmen. "He will soon get used to you," Carmen said. She had been a passive spectator. "And you will soon get used to him."

179

"I do not think that is possible," Cynthia muttered.

"Please, don't do anything stupid," Carmen begged. "It is you and me, now. We must both survive, for each other's sake."

That made sense, but in any event, Cynthia had already abandoned her threat to commit suicide. That certainly made no sense, while little Tom lived. Because one day she meant to find him. Which meant escaping the harem. Just how she was going to do that she had no idea. And the idea became more remote once they landed.

Karnah was actually a tiny island, and its oil wealth was mainly just offshore and under the waters of the Persian Gulf. This had done a great deal to diminish the natural beauty of its situation, fronted by several miles of golden beach, which presently gazed sadly upon a vista of drilling rigs. But the ruling family had ploughed a good deal of their enormous wealth back into the welfare of their people, and the city of Karnah was a bustling modern concern, glowing with electric light after dark, flat roofs sheltering beneath a forest of television aerials, above which rose only the minarets. Abdullah, it turned out, was only a distant cousin of the ruling house, who had forced himself up the heirarchy by a combination of underhand political dealings and considerable energy and talent. Now he was perhaps the most powerful man in the country, apart from the emir, and was greeted with full ceremony when his plane came to a halt. There was a guard of honour of black-robed soldiers – they might have stepped straight out of a *Lawrence of Arabia* film but were armed with modern automatic rifles – together with a band, several dignitaries from the Ministry of Justice, and of course, the inevitable fleet of black limousines. But no member of the royal family.

To land, Cynthia and Carmen were required to don

haiks, the voluminous and all-concealing white robes worn by Arab women, as well as yashmaks, the face mask which left only the eyes and forehead exposed. Cynthia's golden hair was carefully tucked out of sight as well so that no onlooker, and most importantly, no Western cameraman who might be around, could have the slightest idea that she was European. She toyed with the idea of making a public break for it, but was dissuaded by Abdullah himself, who sat beside her as the aircraft taxied to a halt. "We are in Karnah now," he said. "This is a Moslem fundamentalist state. You must remember this at all times. Women who oppose their masters are most often dealt with inside the harem. However, any man is quite within his rights to have a recalcitrant woman flogged in public. The minimum allowed in such circumstances is eighty lashes."

Cynthia swallowed. She had never supposed such barbarism still existed anywhere in the world today. "The sentence has of course to be confirmed by the Minister of Justice," Abdullah went on with a smile. "He weighs all the factors very carefully before giving his consent. Once he has done that, there can be no appeal. I should also point out that any woman who publicly humiliates her lord, whether it be by committing adultery or by attempting to escape his harem, is subject to the death penalty. This is carried out by public beheading. These events, and they are not so uncommon, attract vast crowds, perhaps the entire population of Karnah. In the case of one of *my* women, the beheading would follow the public flogging. Should the woman be as beautiful as you, my dearest Cynthia, the crowds would be even vaster."

Cynthia could hear herself inhaling. If he was attempting to terrify her, he was doing a good job. But she was not going to let him know that. "What are you?" she asked. "Some kind of monster?"

181

He smiled. "Merely a possessive man, who has the power to be possessive. But if you behave yourself, why, as I have told you, you will have the most sensually happy of lives."

"He's a madman," Cynthia told Carmen, when they were in one of the limousines, being driven off. "Do you realise he threatens to kill us if we attempt to escape? And apparently can do this?"

"It's the custom in these parts," Carmen agreed.

Cynthia looked at the women who were in the car with them. These were different women to their companions of the plane, but they were equally veiled and black-robed. "Do either of you speak English?" she asked. The women stared at her. "But we are going to try to escape, right?" Cynthia asked, reassured.

"I think we would need to plan that very carefully," Carmen said. "And I also think we should discuss it only when we are alone."

That made sense, but being alone suddenly became very difficult. Their drive ended in the courtyard of the sheikh's palace, where they were surrounded by walls, and the heat was even greater. There was some relief when they were escorted into the harem itself, an entire wing of the palace into which no man save the sheikh was allowed. "I thought these places were guarded by eunuchs?" Cynthia whispered to Carmen, remembering various films she had seen.

These guards were women. But as they wore uniform, were well built, and had pistols on their belts as well as automatic rifles under their arms or slung on their shoulders, it was difficult to suppose they would be any less formidable than eunuchs. Inside the harem, they found

182

themselves surrounded by some twenty women, of whom two were the sheikh's remaining wives, while the rest were his concubines. For both Carmen and Cynthia this was merely an extension of their existence on Eboli, but there were differences to which they had to get used.

In the first place, as Carmen had predicted their pubic hair had to be shaved. This was a distinctly unsettling experience, even for Carmen; while Abdullah had required her to be shaven during their week together in the Caribbean, she had been allowed to do it for herself. In Karnah the women of the harem insisted on performing the intimate task, involving a pair of sheers, and a razor. Lying on her back with her legs pulled apart Cynthia found she was holding her breath as the cut-throat blade, handled by one of the wives, who was clearly thoroughly enjoying herself, coursed over her pale flesh. But even that was not the end, as the entire area was then coated in a toffee-like mixture, which was still hot from the stove on which it had been boiled, and after being ladled on to the flesh and allowed to dry, was then removed by a silken thread drawn over the skin; with it went the very last vestige of hair, leaving Cynthia feeling like a plucked chicken.

As soon as she was bathed she was marched off to the room where Abdullah waited for her, lolling naked on a divan. To her relief Carmen accompanied her, and he played with them both before making Carmen kneel. "Jesus," Cynthia muttered, when they were sent back to the harem. "How often does this happen, do you suppose?"

"I would say every time he wants us," Carmen suggested.

She was absolutely correct, and as he wanted them pretty

regularly during their first couple of weeks in Karnah, they were shaved pretty regularly as well. But after that things settled into a routine. The harem, the two Western women discovered, was a world of its own, governed by its own laws. Not all of the women, and this went more for the four wives than the concubines, were the least attractive, even to Abdullah. Women were included in his harem often for financial or, more importantly, political reasons. As there was no women's lib in Karnah – or indeed in the whole Moslem world, so far as Cynthia could make out – and certainly no women's jobs except in the most menial of tasks, the ultimate disaster for any female was to wind up for good in her parent's home, totally unwanted, just an extra mouth to be fed, an extra body to be clothed. It followed therefore that no young woman was going to refuse an offer of either marriage or concubinage, even if the end result was a totally loveless existence, ignored by her lord and master because she did not appeal to him. Fathers were inclined entirely to overlook small matters such as their daughters' convenience, or even well-being, much less their desires, where they could claim that their offspring was in the harem of a sheikh, and the sheikh who accepted the girl was from then on a valued political ally.

Within the harem, therefore, there were rigid levels of precedence. The wives came first, in order of seniority. Most of these were political alliances as well, but Abdullah was obliged to sleep with them on a fairly organised basis, even if each might only gain her husband's bed a couple of times a year. As regards the concubines, he was under no compulsion ever to touch any of them unless he chose to do so; the fact that they lived under his roof and could be touched by him alone was sufficient to ensure their status. They thus fell into three distinct classes. All concubines began as *iqbals*, whether or not they were ever called to their lord's bed. Most went at least once, and if they failed to arouse him, or interest him sufficiently, they remained, *iqbals*. There were rumours of harems where there were *iqbals* who remained virgins all of their lives, but there were no virgins in Abdullah's harem. Having been to her lord's bed once, if a girl was recalled more than once, she moved up a step, and became known as a *guizde*, which literally meant, in the eye – of her lord, that is. This placed her on a level with the wives, sexually, if not socially.

When the lord decided to take a girl to his bed on a regular basis however, she became an *odalik*, and as such rose above even the wives, in influence, if not socially. Both Cynthia and Carmen, in being summoned to Abdullah's bed almost on a nightly basis during their first two weeks in Karnah, and thereafter at least once a week, immediately became *odaliks*. As such they were superior to the common herd, in that they had the opportunity constantly to whisper in the master's ear. This was satisfying, but did nothing to lift them from the tedium, or the horseplay, of the harem itself. They could not be harmed physically but equally, unless so harmed, they could not complain of their treatment to Abdullah, as at the end of the day – or more properly, the night – they had to return to the harem and the women.

There was one way in which an *odalik*, or any of the other women, could achieve social equality with the wives, and that was to become a mother. But Abdullah was apparently not very successful in fathering children. He had one son, who had already reached puberty and was therefore gone from the harem to be educated by men, and three daughters; one of these was also considered grown up and was already married. The other two, just approaching their teens, awaited marriage. He reminded

185

Cynthia that he had promised to make her a mother, and he certainly did his best, but she did not conceive. This was a great relief to her, a child would make any escape the more difficult. As for rising above the other women, she had no real desire to do that.

Her companions were actually amazingly friendly, in a real sense; like most Arab women they would rather laugh than cry. But they were also sexual slaves, and were aware of their predicament. As they could not form a relationship with Abdullah himself, they found it necessary to form relationships amongst themselves.

Yet life, as Abdullah had promised, was pleasant enough; they indeed had nothing to do but eat, sleep, gossip – their principal occupation – and make love, either with each other or with their lord. There was a swimming pool in the harem, and they were encouraged to make as much use of this as they chose, so that their bodies were always clean and fresh – again as on Eboli – but unlike the regime demanded of them by Alexandra or Mayne, they were not required to take regular exercise, or indeed any exercise at all. Most of them were distinctly plump and some were definitely fat. Cynthia and Carmen did the best they could by means of push-ups and jogging on the spot every morning – activities regarded with contempt by their companions – but even so they found themselves putting on weight.

Indeed, as the next year drifted by, it became insidiously easy to accept their way of life. It *was* too simple to eat, drink, sleep and make love, and do nothing else. If one simply toed the line, one did not have a care in the world; it was the law that a concubine or a wife, as long as she did not misbehave, was the responsibility of her master or lord for the rest of her life. He was bound to feed and

186

clothe and house her, and take care of any of her medical requirements. To the women of Karnah, to be taken into the harem of a rich man was the ultimate achievement.

It did not bother them that they were then turned into cabbages; there was absolutely no intellectual entertainment within the harem, save for backgammon, a game Cynthia did not really understand. There were no books. But she was determined not to vegetate. The memory of little Tom, her determination to regain possession of him, made her as resolute about that as her determination that she would not forever be treated as a slave.

She worried about Carmen, as the West Indian woman began to show signs of becoming too content with her lot. She began to concentrate on discovering as much as possible about what was going on around her, mainly by learning Arabic, so that she could chat, wherever possible, with their guards, who often drifted into the harem itself for a cup of coffee. These women were members of Abdullah's personal bodyguard, and were utterly faithful to him, but they also knew a great deal of what was going on in the country, and Cynthia was intrigued, and somewhat concerned, to learn that all was not well, politically. The emir and his family had never liked their cousin, and were constantly seeking ways of removing Abdullah from office. But Abdullah, if a playboy outside of Karnah, was a hard-working and efficient Minister of Justice when inside his country, while *as* Minister of Justice he controlled many aspects of Karnahaian life, and had a considerable following of his own.

"Still," Cynthia argued, "if he were to be sacked, all of that would end."

"Sacked?" asked the guard.

"Removed from office. Dismissed."

187

The guard laughed. "That can never happen."

"Surely the emir has the right to remove someone from office, if he chooses?"

"Then there would be war," the guard declared. "Civil war. Sheikh Abdullah would never permit it." That was an even more alarming thought. But before Cynthia could discuss the possibility with Carmen, there came catastrophe: one morning Carmen was found to be missing by one of Abdullah's wives.

Instantly the harem was in a turmoil, which was not alleviated by the reappearance of the missing woman an hour later, looking somewhat dishevelled and hot and bothered. "All I did was go for a walk," she claimed. Both Cynthia and Carmen were by now quite fluent in Arabic.

"Ha!" commented Djmilla, the senior wife, and went off to inform the sheikh. For a woman to leave the harem without permission and unaccompanied was a serious offence.

"You will suffer the bastinado for that," warned Aya, one of the concubines who was as close to being a friend of the two foreigners as it was possible.

"Then I will suffer the bastinado," Carmen said angrily.

They had seen the bastinado being administered before, to girls who had annoyed Abdullah. The victim was forced to lie on her back with her legs in the air and secured to a cross bar. She was then caned across the soles of her bare feet by one of the wives. This could be a minor matter, or a business of up to a hundred strokes. If the latter punishment was chosen, the unfortunate woman would be unable to walk for several days, sometimes longer if her skin had been split. But Carmen was a toughie, who

188

had habitually gone barefoot most of her life; her soles were like leather. So presumably she would stand up to the caning better than most, Cynthia reflected, although she remained terribly concerned for her closest friend.

It was the next day the blow fell. The women were breakfasting when Abdullah strode into their communal living room, two of the female guards at his back. As everyone could see by a glance at his face that he was very angry, they all scrambled to their feet. "You!" Abdullah flung out a pointing finger. "You have betrayed me!" Carmen seemed to stiffen. "You have betrayed my bed!" Abdullah shouted. "Admit it." Carmen licked her lips, while Cynthia looked at her in consternation. Could her friend really have taken such a risk? Without confiding it? But she was heartily glad she had not confided it. "You may as well confess," Abdullah told her. "Your paramour has done so."

"Say nothing," Cynthia whispered.

But Carmen ignored her. "Very well," she snapped. "I have betrayed your bed. With a *man*!"

"Ha!" Abdullah sneered. "He is a man no longer."

"You would not dare!" Carmen shouted. "You slimy little bastard!" And she flung herself at him.

Abdullah screamed in fear, and his wives closed on the woman, bringing her to the ground before she could reach him. Cynthia stood absolutely still. She could not believe this was actually happening, and she knew she could not help Carmen in any way. "Guards!" Abdullah was shouting. "Guards!" The black-uniformed women ran into the room, and the wives stood away. Panting, Carmen attempted to reach her feet, and was seized by the guards. "Bring her outside," Abdullah snarled.

The guards pushed the panting, struggling Carmen

189

through the door and into the courtyard. The women hastily donned their veils to follow, chattering amongst themselves as to her likely fate. Cynthia tried to run behind them and was seized by one of the women. "Your veil!" she hissed. "Would you be caned as well?"

Caned! Cynthia thought. My God! But she did not want to be caned herself. She tied on her yashmak, pulled the hood of her haik over her head and joined the others. It was just on noon, and the sun seemed to be directly over the palace courtyard. In the centre of this the guards were tying Carmen's wrists to a pole set in the earth; this pole was slotted, so that when the knots were tied the rope could not slip downwards: Carmen was secured, standing, facing the pole. "A hundred strokes," Abdullah was shouting, "A hundred strokes." Carmen's head seemed to jerk.

"Abdullah!" Cynthia shouted. "My lord!" She ran forward to grasp his arm, and received a backhander which sent her sprawling in the dust.

"Commence!" Abdullah shouted.

One of the guards seized Carmen's haik and tore it down the back, so that it settled to either side. Two more tugs on the material and Carmen was standing naked in the noonday sun. And this was not the harem courtyard, but that of the palace. There were men present, even if at some distance, and not approaching. But they were close enough to see.

Cynthia realised that if Carmen was being so exposed, she was about to witness a tragedy. She rose to her knees and again tugged at Abdullah's jibbah. "My lord!" she cried. "Surely Carmen needs to be tried and convicted before she can be punished?"

"Has she not just confessed, woman?"

"But . . ." Cynthia licked her lips as she tried to

190

think of something to say, some argument she could put forward.

"And as for you, when I find out how you were involved . . ."

"Me?" Cynthia shouted.

Carmen turned her head. "She knew nothing of it," she said.

"Oh, Carmen!" Cynthia cried.

"Commence!" Abdullah commanded again.

One of the women tied Carmen's long black hair on the top of her head, and a guard stepped forward with a long, thin cane, and commenced hitting Carmen on the back and buttocks. Carmen gasped in pain but it was the fifth stroke before she started to scream. Cynthia started to scream herself, scrambling to her feet and trying to get to her friend, but she was restrained by two of the other women. "She is hysterical," said the senior wife. "Shall we take her inside, my lord?"

"No," Abdullah said. "Make her watch. It will do her good." Cynthia panted, and sank to her knees as she watched Carmen's back being reduced to a bloody mess. After twenty-five strokes the cane was passed to a second guard. By then Carmen had fainted, but she was revived with a bucket of water. Now she was incapable of sound, and it occurred to Cynthia that she was actually being beaten to death. Perhaps, she hoped, she was already dead. Certainly, by the time the hundredth stroke had been delivered, Carmen hung motionless from her wrists, while blood dribbled down her thighs to the dust.

Abdullah signalled, and a man came forward, obviously a doctor, as he took Carmen's pulse. "She is alive, my lord."

"Ha," Abdullah commented. "Very good. Send in Kislar."

191

A big Arab came across the courtyard, carrying a scimitar, gleaming in the sunlight. "No," Cynthia muttered. "Oh, my God, no!"

"Strike off her head," Abdullah commanded.

The harem was a sombre place that evening. Few of the women spoke to each other, and none of them spoke to Cynthia. She sat by herself in a corner, knees drawn up and clasped in her arms. It occurred to her that to that moment her life, whatever its disastrous episodes, had been nothing more than a game. Presumably Carmen was guilty of adultery. Once upon a time she would have been branded, and before then she might have been stoned to death. But that was history!

And now she, too, was at the mercy of a madman!

Yet she felt less fear than anger. She wanted to avenge Carmen. She wanted to hurt Abdullah. And then she wanted to kill him too. But the consequences! The thought of being tied naked to that post, and beaten insensible, and then executed . . . every time she closed her eyes she saw Carmen's head spinning away from her shoulders, long black hair uncoiling and trailing behind it. Carmen's eyes had been open, wide, staring . . . but Cynthia was sure she had never felt a thing, had not even known what was happening to her. There was a small blessing. She could not contemplate such a thing happening to her. But at the same time she did not know if she would be able to control herself, when next Abdullah sent for her. As it happened, he did not. Perhaps he could sense her hostility; she could not suppose a man like that felt any remorse for what he had done. Indeed, as the days became a week, and the weeks became a month, she began to wonder if he would ever send for her again; never had she been so long without a summons. But in fact, during that period

192

he never summoned any of his women, and the whisper spread through the harem that he was not actually in the palace very often.

It was one of the guards who finally enlightened them. "The sheik is in trouble," she said. "The emir learned about the execution of the woman, and was very angry. It has even been reported in the foreign press, and there is a good deal of criticism of the sheikh's action. The emir is anxious to remain on good terms with the West, and is upset about this. There is a rumour that the sheikh is to be dismissed from his post."

"But you said he would never accept that," Cynthia reminded her. "That he would start a civil war before he would go."

"That is absolutely true," the guard said. "The sheikh dare not retire from office as he could then be placed on trial for murder."

"Then what is to happen?" Aya asked.

"There will be war," the guard said, darkly.

Cynthia didn't know whether to believe her or not; she had certainly never expected to be caught up in a war. At that moment she didn't want to be caught up in anything; she wanted only to be left alone, to think of Carmen, and remember the good times they had had together, and weep. But only a week later the harem was roused, just before dawn, by the sound of gunfire. There was instant pandemonium, led by the wives. They ran up to the flat roof. The guards were up there, as some of them always were; usually they would not allow the women to join them, in case they were seen from some other roof, but this morning they made no effort to restrain them.

It was still dark, although the eastern sky was lightening. Thus the sudden stabs of light were the more bright,

193

the following rumbles or rat-a-tats the more frightening. "They are attacking the emir's palace," one of the guards explained.

My God, Cynthia thought: if Abdullah wins, and becomes emir . . . but surely if she was ever going to escape, it had to be now, in the turmoil of a civil war. Soon after daybreak the firing died down. Now the women could see smoke rising from the vicinity of the emir's palace, but there was no indication as yet that Abdullah might have gained a victory. "What will happen if he is defeated?" Cynthia asked Aya.

"If he is captured, he will be strangled," Aya said.

"And will we then be set free?" She could hardly believe her ears.

"No," Aya said. "We will probably be strangled too. After being raped."

Once again she considered escape, but the palace was entirely sealed by the black-garbed women. And even if she got out, she was now realising, there was nowhere for her to go. Even if she could make the mainland, and that did not seem possible, she would be a destitute white woman in an Arab country. That did not seem a very happy prospect. But to stay here and be raped and then strangled . . . she actually began to hope Abdullah would win; better the devil one knew.

The firing began again at noon. During the morning the streets had been crowded with people trying to find out what was happening. But by midday they were empty again, the people having decided to take shelter. "It is not good," one of the guards told the women. "Army detachments loyal to the emir are assembling outside the city."

"Where is the sheikh?" demanded Djmilla. "Where is my husband?" As if, Cynthia thought, she was his only wife.

"We do not know," the guard said.

"Then what must we do?"

"We must wait here until the sheikh comes for us, or sends a message," the guard insisted.

"That is madness," Cynthia said, when the woman had withdrawn. "If we stay here, we are merely awaiting execution." It had suddenly occurred to her that her salvation might come from right here, in these frightened women.

They were certainly frightened, all gabbling at once. "We cannot disobey the command of our lord," Djmilla declared.

"Who may now be dead?" Cynthia demanded. That made them think.

"What can we do?" asked Kadija, the second senior wife, who had also been present when Cynthia had been taken from Eboli.

Cynthia's brain had gone into overdrive; she knew she had to appeal to their sense of self-preservation and their sense of loyalty, equally. "It is our duty," she said, "as the sheikh's women, to preserve both our lives and our chastity, for his sake. Now I am sure the guard was right, and Sheikh Abdullah would either come to us or send us orders, if he could. But as he has not yet done so, we must assume he is unable to do so. Thus we must act on our own initiative."

She looked from face to face with a growing sense of despair; apparently these women had no idea what initiative was. "What can we do?" Aya asked, putting their feelings into words.

"I think we should withdraw from this palace, which

195

is well known to belong to the sheikh, and take refuge somewhere else."

"Where?" Kadija demanded.

Cynthia drew a long breath. "The only place where our safety can be guaranteed is the mainland."

There was a moment of scandalised silence. "How may we go to the mainland?" Aya asked.

"How could we get there?" Kadija asked, more practically.

"We can take a boat," Cynthia said.

"Do you know how to manage a boat?"

"Yes," Cynthia said. "Anyway, it is only a couple of miles. We can make that."

"But what would we do when we get there?" Kadija asked. "We would need money, to live."

"There must be money, in the palace," Cynthia said.

The woman looked at each other. "You would steal, from our lord?" Kadija asked.

"You are his wife. Are you not entitled to use his money?"

More glances. Then Djmilla decided it was time she took over. "This is outrageous," she declared. "You would listen to this . . . this creature? She is an alien, to us and our ways. She is not even of the True Faith. Now she would lead you to destruction."

"I am trying to *save* you from destruction," Cynthia shouted desperately.

Djmilla pointed. "I will make a full report to our lord. He will have you caned till you bleed for your disloyalty."

They glared at each other, while the other women stared at them. But Cynthia knew she had lost the day. And then there was a rumbling crash; the entire palace shook, and plaster fell from the ceilings. The sheikh's palace was one of the largest buildings in Karnah, and as such was

196

easily identifiable from outside the city. One of the loyal gunners had had the idea of firing a mortar at it, with great accuracy.

The shell did the trick. The woman ran screaming every which way, while from outside they could hear the guards calling in dismay. "Are you going to stay here and be killed?" Cynthia shouted.

She went to the door, and the women followed her. Djmilla attempted to stand in their way, hand upraised as if she were a policeman. But she was hurled aside. One of the guards had remained on the harem door. "No one has said you can leave," she said, and began taking her rifle from her shoulder. But Cynthia was close enough to be able to use her skill at karate. She grasped the woman by the front of her blouse, ducked her shoulder into her stomach, and threw her. The woman struck the floor heavily, gasped, and rose to her knees, and Cynthia used a chop on her neck which sent her sprawling again.

Cynthia knelt beside her and seized the Kalashnikov. Handling weapons had not been included in her training, but she still felt she could do a lot of damage – and she felt like doing a lot of damage. The other women gaped at her in consternation. They had no concept that one of their sex could do things like that. "Come on," Cynthia bawled, and led them at a run across the hallway leading to the sheikh's quarters. Behind them Djmilla was screaming in a high-pitched voice.

There was a guard on the door of Abdullah's private apartment, and she turned to stop them. "Go back," she shouted. "You have no right to leave the harem." As she spoke, another mortar shell burst in the courtyard behind her, and she fell to her knees, struck in the back by a steel fragment. The women trampled on her as they ran to freedom.

197

Chapter Nine

Cynthia says: "*I believe I was the first woman to start up any kind of female emancipation in the Moslem world. My only regret was that I couldn't punish Abdullah before leaving, but life never works out quite as it should.*"

Having escaped the harem, Abdullah's ladies wished only to escape the palace. Cynthia had to wave the Kalashnikov at them to bring them to order. "Money, remember!" she shouted. "And anything else of value we can find." And my passport, she thought, grimly.

Thus encouraged the women fell to looting the palace most thoroughly. Cynthia went straight to Abdullah's bedroom. One of the guards stood outside his door. "What are you doing here?" the woman demanded. "You have no right to be here. Go back to the harem."

"Fuck off," Cynthia told her.

"Go back, or I'll shoot," the woman commanded. Cynthia shot first. Squeezing the trigger was so delightfully simple, and after all she had gone through, delightfully satisfying as well.

After that, escaping the palace was simple. But escaping Karnah itself was an eerie business. All around the women was the rattle of small arms fire, punctuated by the deeper booms of the mortars and always accompanied by distant

198

shouts and the rumble of collapsing masonry. But these remained distant. The streets were deserted although they had no doubt they were being watched from behind the closed jalousies of innumerable other harems as they made for the docks. Panting, they hurried down to where the dhows and small craft were moored against the various piers. Here several men emerged from shelter to confront them. "Who are you, women?"

"What do you want?"

Cynthia pointed at the mainland, clearly visible. "We want to cross the water."

"How can you do that?"

"By boat."

"You have permission to do that?"

"Here is my permission." Cynthia had hitherto kept the Kalashnikov concealed beneath her haik. Now she produced it and pointed it in their general direction. The man hastily retreated, especially when Kadija produced her rifle as well. "However," Cynthia added, "we will pay one of you to take us across." She signalled Aya, who clinked the bag of coins.

The men exchanged glances. "It will take four of us to manage the boat."

"Four?"

"It has to be a big boat, with so many people," he explained.

Cynthia looked at Kadija. She had her own agenda; as Djmilla had refused to accompany them, Kadija was the natural leader of those who would have to pick up the pieces. "Let us go," Kadija said.

"You're on," Cynthia told the man.

The beach in front of the town situated on the coast opposite Karnah was crowded with spectators, soldiers and policemen, and, as Cynthia had hoped and prayed, with a small army of television reporters and cameramen. The arrival of the first refugees from the stricken emirate had everyone hurrying forward to greet them, with various motives in mind; the soldiers wished to find out what was happening, the police wished to stop them landing, the spectators wished to help them, the journalists wished to hear what they had to say. In the midst of all the hullabaloo, Cynthia sized up the throng and made her decision. He was not as young as she would have liked, or as good-looking; indeed he had a hard-bitten drinker's face. But he was clearly Caucasian, he was using a camcorder, and he appeared to be alone. She gave her rifle to Aya, slipped through the bawling, gesticulating crowd, and reached his side. "How would you like a scoop?" she asked in English.

He turned, for a moment wondering where the voice was coming from. Then he peered at her. She was still wearing both haik and yashmak, and the only part of her that was visible was her eyes and her forehead – but her eyes were unmistakably pale blue. "Holy shitting cows," he remarked. "You one of them?"

"You got it." Cynthia reached under the haik and tugged a few strands of golden hair into view.

"Holy shitting cows," he said again.

"Have you an hotel room?" she asked. "Get me out of here, please!"

He didn't need a second invitation. Leaving the throng was not difficult; half of the mob were veiled women, and Cynthia tucked her hair back out of sight before anyone else could notice. "I'm Cory Blaine," he said, as he hurried her across the street and into an hotel doorway.

"And you're Australian," Cynthia deduced from his accent.

"You got that. This here's my cousin," he explained to the desk clerk. The clerk made no comment, and gave him his key. "They're hot on adultery and fornication here," Cory explained, as they rode up in the lift. "You'd better be worth the risk."

"You'll have to be the judge of that," Cynthia told him, and went into his bedroom. As she did so, she pushed the hood of the haik from her head, and pulled off the yashmak.

"Holy shitting cows!" he said a third time.

"You wouldn't by any chance have a drink?"

"Well . . ."

"I know," she said, "They're hot on that too. That goes for Karnah as well, and it's a long time since I tasted anything stronger than fermented milk."

Cory Blaine opened a drawer, and after sifting through some underclothes, came up with a bottle of scotch. "You know what they do to you in this neck of the woods if they find you with alcohol?"

"You receive a public flogging," Cynthia said. "So what's new?"

His eyes narrowed. "That happen to you?"

Cynthia sipped the whisky and felt her system come alive. She was shaking as the adrenalin of the escape drained; she was close to crying with relief. "How much space do you have on that camcorder?"

"I have spare cartridges."

"Then you sit there, and I'll sit here, and I'll talk."

"You betcha." He took up a position opposite her. "You got a name?"

"Cynthia." She took off the haik and revealed her bolero and pantaloons.

201

"Jesus," he muttered. "OK. Talk."

"There's just one thing," Cynthia said. "The bottom line."

"I figured there would be one," he said.

"I'm worth a lot more than you can afford to pay," she pointed out. "Both to look at, in bed, and storywise. But all I want are some European clothes and a plane ride out of here."

"Well," he said. "That could be tricky."

"There is a European-style shop in the lobby," she said. "I saw it as we came up. Just buy me something to wear. It doesn't have to be haute couture. And I have my passport. Here!" She took it from the pocket of her haik.

"You're a pretty well-organised dame," Cory remarked. "So how come you got yourself involved in Karnah?"

"Just listen," Cynthia suggested.

Cory used three cartridges, while never taking the lens from her face except, occasionally, to drift up and down her body. She told him everything about Abdullah, and the harem, and the execution of Carmen. But she never mentioned Mayne or Eboli or her real business, used the old story of how Carmen and herself had been attracted to the Middle East by an offer to work in a dancing troupe, and then been kidnapped. This put the whole situation firmly in Abdullah's lap, and gave her a bolt hole, which she knew she was going to need. "Holy shitting cows," was Cory's invariable comment. "There was a rumour about that girl being executed . . . you mean she was a friend of yours?"

"Carmen was a friend of mine. My closest friend."

"What a story. You know something, what with television and the book I'm going to write, we're going to earn a fortune."

"Forget it."

"Now, listen, babe . . . ."

"The deal," Cynthia said, "was something to wear and a plane ticket. And say a hundred pounds in spending money. In return I've given you this story, and all the profit you stand to make from it. Don't be greedy. Bugger me about and I'll scream rape. Don't forget a public flogging is nothing new to me, but you might find it a bit awesome."

"Shit," he commented. "You *are* a toughie, aren't you?"

"I'm alive," Cynthia pointed out.

"Yeah. People are going to be clamouring for you, when this story breaks."

"So tell them I've disappeared. That should be a saleable item as well."

"You have other saleable items." They gazed at each other. Cynthia considered, then shrugged, and took off her bolero.

He photographed her from every angle, front, back, above and below. He knew what his market wanted. Cynthia didn't object. She was following that agenda. Then they had sex. Risks or not, he couldn't wait any longer. She didn't object to that either. After Abdullah it was intensely satisfactory to lie on her back and be absolutely orthodox.

Then he went out for food and her dress. When he came back he had news. "Guess what," he said. "The revolt has been put down. The word from Karnah is that this guy Abdullah has been hanged."

"Lucky him. If I'd ever got hold of him he'd have been singing alto first."

"Maybe he was. But it seems the loyalists are already

203

rounding up his followers, and that includes his women. They're being allowed to do that over here."

"Then I would suggest the sooner I get out of here the better."

They left together the next morning, on a flight to Rome. Cynthia was more nervous than she realised, but while the local police and immigration might have been told one of the escaped women was a blonde, they did not know her name, and even if she felt a shiver run down her spine as they examined her passport, the mere fact that she had a passport was in her favour. "This isn't a local airline, is it?" she asked, when they were comfortably seated.

"Air France. Didn't you notice?"

"No," she said. "Then I would like a drink. Champagne."

"At eight o'clock in the morning?"

"I'm setting a new pattern for myself," she explained. "Or maybe turning into an alcoholic."

Cory spent most of the flight trying to persuade her to change her mind. But he was an honest man, and he was at least as interested in getting his story and pictures to his Italian agency – he hadn't dared attempt to file the story while in Arab territory – so that by the time they landed he had accepted the situation. "Where are you going now?" he asked.

"You are going to buy me a plane ticket to Madrid. First-class."

"Do you think I'm made of money?"

"You are going to be, when you sell that story," she pointed out. "And what are you complaining about? Two airplane tickets and a dress? In return for sleeping with

204

me? I charge more than that by the hour." Cynthia was high on a new sense of power.

"And you don't want any share in those profits?"

It was tempting. But Cynthia didn't know just how much profit there would be, and although she was still anxious to make her fortune just as quickly as possible, right then she wanted security as well, and there was only one place in the world she knew of where she would be protected from any friend or relative of Abdullah's – even if Mayne had sold her to Abdullah in the first place. She had her own ideas about how to handle Mayne, now. "Just let's say I'm feeling generous today," she said.

Cory obviously would have liked to follow that up, but time was against him. He bought her the ticket. "The flight doesn't leave for two hours," he said. "You going to be all right?"

"Sure."

"Well . . . I'd like to stay with you, but . . ."

"The megabucks call." She kissed him. "I really am grateful to you. Don't spend it all at once."

He squeezed her hand. "Maybe we'll meet again, some time. Here's my card. If you ever need a big one . . . any kind of big one . . ."

"I'll be in touch."

It was the most splendid feeling, sitting alone in one corner of the departure lounge. It was now four years since she had sat anywhere, quite alone, mentally as well as physically. She had bought herself a magazine, but she didn't read it. She didn't want to do anything, except sit. And *feel*.

She was actually very pleased with herself. There was, of course, the sheer euphoria of being alive, where so many were now dead. Including Carmen! She would

205

have liked to avenge Carmen, personally. But life was never quite that cut and dried, and Carmen had at least *been* avenged. She wondered how Abdullah had behaved when he had been led to the scaffold? Had he remembered the twenty women he must have presumed were dutifully awaiting his return? Or would he have been told by his executioners that his women had fled? That would have been the ultimate humiliation, unless they had castrated him before death. According to the women of the harem, that was often part of the death sentence in Karnah, certainly where treason was involved, much as it had been in England only a couple of hundred years ago. So what was new? She hoped he had been castrated, and had died screaming.

But she was alive, and in her brief life she had triumphed over everything that Fate had thrown at her. She felt she had every reason to be proud of that, because Fate had not been been particularly generous – save in giving her so extraordinary face and figure, such hair and such allure. Or was it those things that had got her into trouble in the first place?

She was proud, too, of the way she had taken command of the women and fought her way out of the palace. She was only nineteen years old, and she had done what had to be done. She had killed! She did not suppose that was something about which any reasonably well-bred girl of nineteen should be proud, but again, it had had to be done, and she had done it. Now she was about to become famous! And the fame would give her freedom, even if she was voluntarily returning to prison. That was necessary, if she was going to regain Tom. But it was also going to be a different sort of prison. She was determined about that.

She was looking forward to it.

* * *

206

The flight was called, and she joined the queue of passengers passing through immigration. Almost everyone paused to stare at the strikingly beautiful platinum blonde woman, not least of all the officials. While they walked across the tarmac to the plane, a man came up beside her. "On your own?" he asked, in Spanish.

"And I intend to remain that way," Cynthia told him. "So bugger off."

She stared out of the windows as they came in over Madrid. How odd, she thought, that I have spent so much time in Spain and never visited Madrid? Something to be done.

She was first out of the customs hall, as she had no luggage. She went to one of the airport banks and changed the francs Cory had given her into pesetas, and then to a restaurant and had lunch before hailing a taxi. "Where do you wish to go, senorita?" asked the driver.

"Eboli." He scratched his head. "You must know where Eboli is," she said. "If you don't, I'll direct you. It's up by Saragossa."

"I know where Eboli is, senorita. It is a long way. It is more than two hundred kilometres."

"So?"

"It will be very expensive."

"Then you should be laughing."

The man shrugged, and opened the door for her, then noticed what was wrong. "You have no luggage."

"Do I need luggage, to ride in your taxi?"

He scratched his head some more, and got in behind the wheel.

The road to the north-east was good, and they raced along. It was now just on three, and Cynthia felt herself nodding

207

off: she had had an exhausting few days, and not a lot of sleep last night, as Cory had been most attentive. She was in fact fast asleep when she was awakened by a series of jerks, and sat up to discover they had left the highway and were bumping down a beaten earth track. She had no watch, but there was a clock on the facia, and it showed just past four. "Something wrong?" she asked.

"I have to pee."

Cynthia made a face, but she couldn't argue with that. The car came to a halt in the shade of some trees, and the driver got out. As he obviously intended to do what he needed to do right there, Cynthia got out of the opposite door and leaned against the hot metal with her back to him, drinking in the sunlight; she had bought herself a pair of dark glasses. "You no want to pee, too?" He was standing beside her, and if he had pulled up his pants, he had left the flies unzipped.

"Listen," Cynthia said. "I hired you to drive me to Eboli. Let's get on with it."

The man gave what he no doubt believed was an ingratiating smile. "Out here," he explained, "there is nobody for miles. There is nobody but you and me."

"Is that supposed to scare me?" Cynthia asked.

"You lean over the bonnet, eh?"

"Listen, amigo," Cynthia said. "If you lay a finger on me, I am going to kick you in the balls."

The man grabbed at her, and a moment later was writhing in the dust, hands grasping his genitals while he moaned. "You have hurt me," he groaned. "You have assaulted me."

"Tell it to the judge," Cynthia suggested. "How soon are you going to be able to drive?" For reply, he made a grab at her ankle, so she delivered a karate chop into his shoulder, where it joined his neck. His face crashed back

208

into the dust. "There goes another half an hour," Cynthia said. "I do wish you'd give this up, senor. I would like to be home by dark."

They made it just on dusk. The castle looked at its most beautiful in the rays of the setting sun, and at its most peaceful too. "How we get in?" asked the driver, surveying the closed gates; he had not spoken very much on the drive, no doubt brooding on what might have been, although she supposed he was also probably still in pain.

"Sound your horn," Cynthia recommended.

He did so, and a few minutes later a scooter came down the drive, ridden by one of the male staff. Cynthia got out of the car. "Good-evening, Salvador."

He peered at her through the bars. "Senorita Cynthia? But . . ."

"Later," she told him. "Open the gates and let us in."

"I must check with the senora . . ."

"Do it," Cynthia said.

A last hesitation, then he pressed the button and the gates swung inwards. Cynthia got back into the car. "You own this place?" the driver asked, as he engaged gear.

"Only in a manner of speaking."

The car pulled up in the forecourt, and Cynthia looked' up at the balcony, where several women had gathered; Salvador would have telephoned from the gate. "Hi," she said. "No red carpet?"

"We thought you were dead," Madeleine said, embracing her warmly. "When we saw the news coming out of Karnah . . ."

"It was lots of fun," Cynthia assured her, and looked at Denise.

"I am so glad you got out," Denise said, "Mayne would like to see you."

The girls had all crowded round. "I'll talk to you later," Cynthia told them. "Oh, Denise, this fellow expects to be paid. Quite a lot, I imagine," She went inside, and up the stairs to the office, knocked, and went in. Mayne sat behind her desk. They gazed at each other, then Cynthia sat down and crossed her knees.

"You look very well on it," Mayne commented.

"A little bit of adrenalin is always good for you."

"Was it very rough?"

"Very."

"Well," Mayne said, "I cannot blame you for escaping, certainly if it is true that Sheikh Abdullah is dead . . . he *is* dead, isn't he?"

"He's dead."

"Hm. I suppose technically you belong to his estate . . ."

"Just listen," Cynthia told her. "You know that creep had Carmen flogged half to death, and then cut off her head?"

"Was that Carmen? I feared as much. That poor girl. He was a monster."

"To whom you sold us."

"I can understand your feeling bitter," Mayne conceded. "If you wish to call it a day, I shall not object."

"You mean, I just walk away, leaving you in possession of everything Abdullah paid you for me."

"You're not suggesting you have any claim on that money?"

"I would say you owe me half," Cynthia said.

"Really? I suppose the sun in Karnah was very hot."

"Listen to me," Cynthia suggested, and told her about Cory Blaine. "That story should break about the middle of next week," she concluded.

"You wretched girl," Mayne declared. "You have broken every rule of client confidentiality to which you swore."

"Uh-uh," Cynthia said. "I swore that to this house. But when you sold me, I ceased to belong to this house. Right?"

Mayne gasped in impotent anger.

"And there is something more," Cynthia said. "I have not betrayed your house. I gave Cory my story. Scans well, doesn't it. Oh, well," she remarked, as Mayne showed no sign of smiling. "Have it your way. The point is, I withheld all the gen on Eboli, and you, and your mother. Cory was keen, but I didn't play. Now that part of my life is written out, and filed in a safe place, with reliable people who have instructions, should I not check with them in person every four weeks, to send it on to him for publication."

Mayne looked ready to explode. "Just what do you want?"

"Now we're talking. I want, first of all, half the money Abdullah paid you for me." She could almost hear Mayne's teeth grinding. "Then, believe it or not, I want to start working for you again." Mayne's eyebrows shot up. "But on my terms," Cynthia said. "Half of everything I earn."

"You have got to be out of your tiny mind."

"This time next week my story is going to be on at least page three of every tabloid in the world. It is going to be accompanied by photos. Cory took lots of photos. The ones he is going to use in the tabloids are only going to convince people how beautiful I am, while as the ex-concubine of Sheikh Abdullah no one is going to be in any doubt that I know how to make a man happy. Right?" Mayne nodded before she could think. "But he took some, shall we say, artistic studies as well, and these he is going to sell to the leading girlie magazines. All of that is going to

211

up my price to something astronomical. Think about it."
Mayne was apparently doing this. "So," Cynthia went on,
"you can afford to pay me half of everything you get, and
still not be out of pocket, in real terms. I'm being very
generous, when you come down to it." Mayne licked her
lips. "There are just two other points I wish to make."

"Oh, yes?"

"Yes. One is, I have the final choice as to who I go with.
I want the entire set-up, up front, and if the price isn't right
for what the client wants, or if he wants something that I
won't accept, it's off."

"And the other?" Mayne asked.

"I want my son."

Cynthia says: "*This last demand, of course, was the
difficult one. Mayne had never liked me. As she had
said more than once, she regretted having bought me
from Colonel Isantsi: I was really just too much for her
to handle. However, she was too good a businesswoman
not to recognise a goldmine when it was presented to her,
and thus she agreed to all my demands. Overnight I became
the highest paid whore in the world.*

"*But no one can be a whore and a mother at the same time
successfully, unless, like Mayne's own mother, she operates
from, and in, her own place. Alexandra had apparently had
Mayne in close proximity all the while she had been feeling
her way into the heart of the business. No doubt she was an
exceptional woman. I prefer to reckon that she was living in
a different age, and certainly in different circumstances.*"

Seeing Tom again was a dream. He was now two years old,
and a strong and healthy child with a happy disposition.
He was also growing up quite contentedly in the care of
a Spanish farmer and his wife. Mayne had put them in

212

the picture, while at the same time warning Cynthia that in her opinion to wrench the little boy out of his secure environment to live at Eboli, where he could not help but soon be aware what his mother was at, would be very bad psychologically.

Cynthia was not really disposed to take Mayne's point of view in anything, but she soon realised that the older woman was right. Juan and Esmeralda Lopez were very nervous when they met, but Tom was so obviously at home with them, and so well cared for, that the barriers soon came down.

Tom of course had no idea who Cynthia was, but she was just content to sit with him on her lap, while he gazed at her with enormous eyes. It was arranged that she could come to see him whenever she wished or had the time, and that the whole situation, together with the question as to whether or not he would be told who she really was and what she did for a living, would be reviewed when he was twelve. That seemed an awfully long way away – but for the time being she knew she was doing the right thing.

Meanwhile the girls, who included a new recruit named Hayley, an American, were delighted to have Cynthia back. They regarded her as something of a heroine, and couldn't hear too much about life in the harem. When Cory's story finally made the papers and magazines they were over the moon.

The headlines he and his various editors chose told it all:

TRAPPED IN A HAREM OF HELL
ENGLISH GIRL BARES ALL
HOW I SHOT MY WAY OUT, BY CYNTHIA
I SAW MY BEST FRIEND BEHEADED
MYSTERIOUS BEAUTY DISAPPEARS

213

"You don't suppose the old emir might take offence at some of this?" Denise wondered.

"I don't see why he should," Cynthia argued. "It blackens the memory of Abdullah, and that's what he's trying to do himself."

"Still, I would say there must be quite a few people in the world anxious to track down this 'mystery woman'," Madeleine said.

"So? I flew from Rome to Madrid. And only Cory actually knows that."

"What about the taxi which brought you out here? The driver had a pretty good look at you, didn't he?"

"Yes, he did," Cynthia agreed. "And I can assure you that he's not going to come too close again, ever!"

It was all really academic, because Mayne introduced Cynthia to her next client as the woman who had escaped from Karnah, and as he had seen the photographs, he didn't need much convincing. But Cynthia didn't like the look of him. "You *are* going to take someone on board?" Mayne demanded. "Some time?"

"Of course," Cynthia said sweetly. "Some time."

In fact, for the first few weeks after regaining Eboli she wanted to do nothing but lie in the sun and lounge in the pool, and soak up security, aided by the thirty thousand pound deposit she was able to place in a Saragossa bank. More money than she had ever had in her life. But she knew it was a long way from what she wanted, and needed, if she was going to set herself up for life. So before too long she accepted one of Mayne's clients, a very wealthy Spaniard, whose desires were entirely orthodox: he just wanted the right to sleep with the famous Cynthia. That was fine, and fifty per cent of his fee – he took her to the Riviera for a week and escorted her in heavy disguise – added another five thousand pounds to her bank account.

214

But she now knew she was looking for something more. She recalled the story of Alexandra. Alexandra had been a famous Parisian madame with whom the Count of Eboli had fallen in love, making everything else possible. She wanted something like that to happen to her. But it would not in this case. She would willingly have married Jose Martinez, had he been in the same class as Pedro d'Eboli. But although wealthy, he was not a millionaire landowner. Perhaps they no longer existed, she thought sadly. Nor did he ask her; he had a wife and family tucked away in Madrid.

Over the next few years, Cynthia was hired out to a variety of men. She was also hired out to a woman, to whom she refers only as Sylvia. Sylvia carried her off to her home in Canada, for a whole month. Cynthia doesn't talk much about this episode, but I would say she enjoyed herself, while perhaps feeling a little bit uneasy at doing so. It is of course almost impossible for a prostitute, even at the very top of the trade, not to be ambivalent in her approach to sex.

Through her various clients, she travelled the world. She was particularly popular with the Japanese, and acquired an apartment building in Osaka, in partnership with Mayne, of course. Payment in kind became quite popular as the Eighties continued on their irregular financial course, and Cynthia also found herself the owner of several cars as well as two race horses and several condominiums, as well as another apartment building – in Istanbul of all places. She was nervous about accepting this, but Mayne persuaded her that there was no longer a risk; Isantsi's various activities had been discovered and he was now an inmate of one of his own prisons. Cynthia wondered how Carol was faring? She learned, to her sorrow, that Natasha had indeed been hanged.

There were other ghosts from her past. She received a letter from Billy, of all people; Miriam apparently could not bring herself to write. They had recognised her picture in the papers, of course; so had a good many other people. Now, she wondered, how on earth had he discovered her address? Only via someone in Turkey who knew that she had been 'bought' by the Maynes. That raised a whole lot of questions, not all of which she wanted answered.

The letter itself was meaningless. Billy wrote that if she ever wanted to come home he and her mother would be delighted. She did not bother to reply. But she kept up with the English news as far as she was able, and was intrigued to read that a Cuthbert Lucas had been shot dead on his own doorstep. The police, it was reported, had told the press it was a drugs related crime. She had nothing going for Cuthbert, but she was saddened that his dog Hannibal had been shot at his side. Poor old Hannibal had never done anything more than obey his master. But then, neither had she, until Cuthbert had abandoned her. She shivered to think that had he not done so, she might have been lying dead beside Hannibal, just for being at his side. But it did seem that the past was dropping out of sight; only the future mattered. This made her desire for security the more important.

The crux for Cynthia seemed to have arrived a year later, when Mayne entertained a particular client. However, for this man the girls were not paraded; instead Cynthia was informed that she was to have dinner with Mayne and her guest. "Me alone?" Cynthia asked Madeleine.

216

"This is a very special guest," Madeleine told her. "He has come here for a specific purpose: you."

Although Cynthia was now twenty-three – it was the summer of 1990 – she felt quite fluttery, and was the more excited when both Madeleine and Denise turned up to help her dress, in a black velvet evening gown which, cunningly wired, appeared as if it was suspended by her nipples and nothing else, and which, of course, showed off her pale hair and colouring to perfection. Her shoulders and cleavage were bare. Her hair was to be worn straight down her back, brushed for an hour to make it even more lustrous. "This guy must be really something," she suggested.

"He is," Denise assured her.

They escorted her to Mayne's apartment, but left her at the door. She hesitated for some seconds before opening it and stepping in. Two of the menservants had been allowed in here for the evening, wearing white tie and white gloves. They knew who she was, of course, but bowed and fussed as if she was a guest who had driven a hundred miles to be present. One of them scurried across the foyer to open the inner double doors to Mayne's drawing room, and announce, "Senorita Cynthia!"

Cynthia entered and paused, while the doors were closed behind her. Both Mayne and her guest were standing, drinking champagne. Mayne was also wearing evening dress, and was at her elegant best, though she paled into insignificance beside Cynthia. But Cynthia had eyes only for the man, who completely took her breath away. He was tall, and dark-haired with attractive little wisps of grey at each temple. Unlike the two women, he was not wearing evening dress, but an open-necked white shirt which revealed masses of black hair on his chest, amidst which there nestled a huge gold St Christopher

217

medallion. The loose shirt and the tight-fitting pants indicated that he had the most splendid body, long legs, slim hips, and powerful torso. But all of these assets were but a showcase for his face, which was the most handsome Cynthia had ever seen. The features were strong without being pronounced, with a strong chin, straight nose, and wide lips. She suspected these could be hard, but at the moment they were parted as they took her in. His eyes were brown, and again, powerful. She felt quite helpless for a moment. But apparently he felt the same way, looking at her. "Cynthia, this is Carlos de Sousa," Mayne said.

Cynthia advanced into the room. "Your photos do not do you justice," Carlos de Sousa said, in English, with just a trace of an accent.

"It is nice of you to say so," Cynthia replied.

"Nor could they possibly convey the sound of your voice," he commented. "Senorita, I am enchanted."

"You'll take a glass of champagne, Cynthia?" Mayne handed her a flute. "Shall we sit down?"

Carlos sat beside Cynthia on the settee; Mayne sat opposite. "Senora Mayne tells me you are English," Carlos remarked. "What part of England do you come from?"

"Surrey. But I lived in London for a while."

"Ah, London. One of the most exciting of cities. Although I must admit it is some time since I have been there."

"What part of Spain do you live in?" Cynthia asked. She was being polite, but she was also interested.

"Sadly, I do not live in Spain at all," Carlos said.

"Senor de Sousa is a cattle rancher, in South America," Mayne said.

"Oh! That sounds exciting." Again, she meant it.

218

"It is boring work, really," Carlos said. "But it is exciting country."

"Which one is it?"

"Bolivia." Cynthia wasn't quite sure where that was. But that made it sound even more exciting. "Would you like to see my ranch?" Carlos asked.

"Oh, yes," Cynthia said.

"Well, perhaps it could be arranged," he said, and looked at Mayne.

"I think we should have dinner," Mayne decided.

Both women made all the small talk they could over dinner, but it was difficult, as Carlos did nothing but stare at Cynthia. Nor was he very talkative about his ranch, although Cynthia did gather that it was huge, and that it was close to the headwaters of the Amazon, which made it sound even more exciting. But at last they reached coffee and liqueurs. "Will you have a cigar?" Mayne asked, beckoning one of her waiters forward.

"He may leave the box," Carlos said. "And now, is it possible to be alone with the senorita?"

"Ah . . ." Mayne looked at Cynthia. Carlos raised his eyebrows. "The decision must be Cynthia's," Mayne explained.

"You run a very democratic business," Carlos conceded. "Well, senorita? Am I good enough for you?"

Cynthia actually felt herself flushing. "Of course, senor. It is merely a formality. And there is another formality, no doubt." Now she looked at Mayne.

"Senor de Sousa has offered to pay one hundred thousand pesetas for the pleasure of your company, for one hour, after dinner," Mayne said. "Should he wish to remain for another hour, the price is doubled."

"Do you always discuss such matters so openly with

219

your people?" Carlos appeared to be more interested than offended.

"Only with Cynthia," Mayne said. "She is very special to me."

"I can understand that," Carlos said. "But I have not been told what this five hundred pounds actually buys me. You are lovely to look at, senorita, and delightful to know, but . . . I cannot remember the rest of the words."

"Your money buys you me, senor," Cynthia said. "From the top of my head to the soles of my feet."

"I am enchanted at the prospect. Senora?"

"I will leave you," Mayne said. "I'll take this, shall I?" She picked up a large attaché case which had been lying on another chair. Cynthia had not noticed it before, but now she remembered that many of Mayne's clients paid this way – although from the obvious weight of the case it had to contain more than a hundred thousand pesetas.

"Of course," Carlos agreed.

Mayne went to the door. "The time is eighteen minutes past ten." The door closed behind her.

"Is she always so strict, with time and money?" Carlos asked.

"She is strict in every way," Cynthia said.

"It is good in business," Carlos acknowledged, "but in affairs of the heart . . ."

"This is business, to Mayne, senor."

"And to you?"

Cynthia made a *moue*. "It is my business to disguise it."

He laughed. "And make me feel I am the only man in the world, when all the time you are thinking to yourself: what a bore; when do I get to bed, alone?" Cynthia bit her lip, and he laughed again. "Oh, I am not offended. I enjoy such frankness. Especially from you. Do you know,

220

I suspect you are quite the most beautiful woman I have ever seen."

She had to join his mood or be entirely submerged beneath his personality. "I would prefer you to think of me as a person rather than a woman, senor."

He smiled. "I adore women. But I understand that they are seldom as they appear. Sit by me." Cynthia sat beside him on the settee. "Now you, for instance," Carlos said. "You possess a quite unearthly beauty. But what does it conceal?"

"Nothing very out of the ordinary, I don't think."

"Were you really in an Arabian harem? Very few women ever escape from such places."

"I shot my way out, Mr de Sousa. Just as it said in the newspapers. Does that make me more, or less, attractive?"

"It makes you perfectly enchanting. Will you take off your gown?" Cynthia reached behind her for her zip, slid it down, and then stood up. The velvet gathered about her ankles. She remained standing, awaiting further instructions, and to her surprise, Carlos leaned forward to pick the gown up, and kiss it. "Now take it right off." She stepped out of it. "Do you never wear underclothes?"

"Only when it is appropriate, or necessary."

"And tonight you knew that whatever you were wearing, I would wish you to take it off."

"I thought you might have that in mind."

"Sit on my lap." She obeyed, and he began to explore her, sliding his hands over her breasts, elongating the nipples between thumb and forefinger, but very gently, raising her arms to kiss the shaven pit, an experience she had never had before, thrusting his fingers up the nape of her neck and deep into her hair. Thus far he had not moved beneath her navel, but she knew he was going to,

221

and felt curiously breathless. As he could tell: He slid his hand down her side and across her thigh, then over it to allow his fingers to sift through her pubic hair and beyond. Cynthia had known several men who enjoyed masturbating women; the trouble was that few of them had any real idea how to go about it, and as she was not as a rule emotionally involved, it was a matter of faking it, which she could do to their entire satisfaction. She had anticipated nothing different tonight, but Carlos de Sousa knew just where to go and what to do when he got there. It was only when she was subsiding that he kissed her. "Do you always make a noise like that?" he asked.

"I'm sorry. Did it annoy you?"

"I found it enchanting. It even suggested it may have been genuine."

"It was." Then she kissed him herself.

"You grow more enchanting by the moment," he said.

Oddly, she thought, he did not ask her to undress him, as so many men liked, nor did he wish her to touch him. He merely made her kneel on the carpet and bend over the settee, while he found his own way, orthodoxly enough. She did not turn her head, as she had not been invited to, but she estimated he was quite big, if not perhaps in Cuthbert's class. While he worked his body against hers his hands slid up and down from her shoulders to her buttocks, and finally came to rest there, as he climaxed. Then he pushed himself up, went to the bar, and refilled their glasses with brandy. He also lit a cigar from the box. "I assume you are protected?"

Now at last she turned, sitting on the carpet. His body was as powerful as it had suggested when he had been dressed. She already knew his penis was powerful. "Only by the pill," she said. "I assume you do not have Aids?"

222

"I am a long-term client of Mayne's," he said, and brought her goblet to her, then sat on the floor beside her, their thighs touching.

"Did you really come all this way for sex?" she asked.

"I came all this way to discover if you are as good in the flesh as you appeared from your pictures."

"And?"

"I thought I had made that clear."

"Then I am flattered." She looked at her watch. "Are you going to be able to fit in another hour? Mayne will be here at eleven-eighteen sharp."

"I don't find that the least intimidating," he assured her. "No, I shall not fit in another hour. I might be able to, but I do not think either of us would enjoy the effort. I would like you to come with me to Bolivia. Will you do that?"

"I should love to, if you can agree a price with Mayne."

"Then call her in."

Cynthia got up and used the cunningly concealed bell, placed to enable her to call for help should it become necessary. Both Mayne and Denise appeared immediately. Mayne took one look at the naked Cynthia, and then the naked Carlos, and realised she did not need assistance. "Thank you, Denise," she said. Denise closed the door. "I imagine you have a proposition, Carlos," Mayne said.

Carlos got up, stubbed out the half-smoked cigar. "I wish to take Cynthia with me."

"For how long?"

Carlos appeared to consider. "Shall we settle on a month?" A whole month, on a Bolivian ranch. It sounded heavenly.

"She is expensive," Mayne pointed out. Carlos shrugged. "Where would you be thinking of taking her?"

"I would like to take her home."

Mayne frowned. "I am not sure I can let you do that."

Cynthia looked from one to the other, understanding that there was something going on of which she knew nothing. "You have but to name your price," Carlos pointed out.

Now Mayne looked at Cynthia, but Carlos put his finger on his lips. "Am I allowed to ask what is the problem?" Cynthia enquired.

"Mayne does not like the interior of South America."

Carlos explained. "She is afraid you will like it so much you will not wish to return to her."

"Who knows?," Cynthia said, teasingly.

"One hundred thousand pounds," Mayne said. Cynthia gasped. Had she gone off her head? Abdullah had only paid sixty thousand, and he had been buying her! Carlos only wanted her for a month. "I should explain," Mayne said, "that by the terms of our arrangement, half of everything she earns belongs to Cynthia."

"But that is very fair," Carlos commented. "Very well. I assume Cynthia trusts you to make the division?"

"Of course." Mayne looked at Cynthia.

"I trust her," Cynthia said.

"Then the matter is settled."

But he was not writing a cheque. Therefore the additional very large sum of money had to have been in the attaché case, which would account for its weight. Cynthia again looked from one to the other. They were carrying on an entire conversation above her level of knowledge. But she felt she was getting the drift. "Very well," Mayne said.

"Good. Where is the bathroom?"

"Through there."

"Will you come with me, Cynthia?"

Cynthia looked at Mayne, who nodded.

They showered together. "You've actually bought me,

224

haven't you?" Cynthia asked. "Because if you have, there is a problem."

He looked down at her, water running from his hair to fall on her face. "I have rented you, for a month."

"For a hundred grand? You must be as rich as Croesus."

He smiled. "The cattle business is thriving, right now."

"But there must be some hidden clauses for that kind of money. Are you going to flog me to death, or have me fricasseed for lunch?"

He kissed her nose. "What an enchanting concept. But I prefer you with your flesh on your bones, and unmarked. You will come and live with me for a month, and at the end of that time, well, we will see. Does that not please you?"

"That pleases me very much."

"So tell me what is the problem?"

"Ah . . . we'll discuss it at the end of the month." She didn't want to take any chances on spoiling their relationship by mentioning Tom, until she had to. As long as she was coming back . . .

The whole idea entranced her. Not even his possessiveness bothered her, and he was certainly possessive. He accompanied her to her room to watch her pack, making sure she included her riding gear – "We spend a lot of time on horseback on the ranch," he explained – and remained at her side when she was saying goodbye to the other girls. For some reason, they, like Mayne, seemed unhappy at the idea of her going off into the jungle. But there was no way she could ask them why in front of Carlos. She did ask Mayne, however, when it was just the three of them, before she got into his limousine. "There's no need to look so bothered, Mayne," she said. "Carlos has promised not to eat me."

225

"As he said, I do not like jungles."

"Wasn't the Countess born in the South American jungle?"

"Maybe that's why I don't like it," Mayne said.

"Well . . . see you in a month."

"Stay out of the sun," Mayne advised.

Chapter Ten

Cynthia says: *"I wouldn't have been human if driving off in a limo to the private airport hadn't brought back memories of the two most unpleasant episodes of my life, after Turkey. In fact, as my return after attempting to elope with Tom Lane, and my removal by Abdullah, had both occurred in the middle of the day, this midnight journey should have been even more sinister.*

"But I was with Carlos, and I could not believe there was anything sinister about so charming a man, even if there obviously was a mystery."

Carlos left the lights on in the back of the car, with the curtains drawn; the smoked-glass partition kept them private from the driver.

There was an ice-bucket and a bottle of champagne too, which he opened with great expertise, handing her a glass and taking one for himself. But the mystery of his having paid so large a sum had to be resolved before she could truly feel at ease. "So tell me what it's all about?" she asked as she sipped. "Mayne isn't really afraid of losing me in the jungle, is she?"

"As a matter of fact, she probably is," he said, seriously. "Bolivia, you see, my dearest Cyn, is one of the last true jungles in the world. Snakes and alligators and mosquitoes and all manner of unpleasantness."

"From which you will protect me, I'm sure," Cynthia said.

"Absolutely. It is also where most of the world's supply of cocaine originates."

Cynthia sat up. "Oh, no! You're not a drug dealer? You told me you you're a cattle rancher!"

"I am."

"But you deal in drugs on the side."

"I do not deal in drugs. Not in the sense that you mean. I grow coca, yes. Acres and acres of it. Actually, my cattle and horse ranches are businesses I run on the side."

"And you sell your cocaine. Doesn't that make you a dealer?"

"Again, not in the sense that you mean. May I ask why my line of business should concern you so greatly?"

"My first lover was a pusher. Although, come to think of it, I doubt he would have accepted that description, either. He smuggled the stuff."

Carlos frowned. "You do not use it yourself, I hope? Both Alexandra and Mayne have always assured me . . ."

"And they were telling the truth. None of us are allowed to touch the stuff."

"But before, with this other lover of yours . . ."

"I never have, Carlos."

He nodded. "You are a very sensible young woman."

"But I know it's wrong. To offer it, I mean."

He regarded her for several seconds. Then he said, "I am sure you are right, in a perfect world. But you see, Cyn, the world is far from perfect. You must understand that for so many people, life is a terribly humdrum business."

"But you're not suggesting that's an excuse for taking drugs?"

"Sadly, nowadays, things like excuses no longer have any credence. Everyone can justify everything."

228

He smiled. "I am not a criminal, Cyn. It is not illegal to grow coca in Bolivia. In fact, coca is one of our staple crops, and has been grown by our people for hundreds of years."

"And sniffed by them, for hundreds of years?"

"They used to chew the fruit, actually. Most of them still do."

"You wouldn't say that is why Bolivia is a very backward part of the world?"

"That depends entirely on your interpretation of the word backward, Cyn. Compared with your urban jungles in Europe and North America, we would regard ourselves as a progressive society."

"As you say, there is an excuse for everything, nowadays."

He squeezed her hand. "Now you are angry with me. I do not wish you to be angry with me."

"And I can't be, can I, because you have just hired me for a month." She was so *disappointed*, because he was so handsome and likeable a man.

"That is not the reason at all," he argued. "I merely wish you to understand. I am a farmer and a rancher. My principal crop is an old and established one. My family has been exporting cocaine for years. That, in recent times, some of the world's governments have banded together to declare the trade illicit and have endeavoured to put some of my oldest customers out of business, concerns me, but is not a reason for me to bankrupt myself, and turn my people out to starve, by abandoning my family business."

"And that these customers may be crooks and murderers doesn't bother you?"

"My dearest girl, I also export horses. All over the world. Are you saying that I should not sell my horses to

229

Libya, which may be involved in international terrorism which causes thousands of deaths?"

She had no answer to that.

"I felt it necesary to explain these things to you, because I am very anxious for you to enjoy your time with me. And if you are to do that, I must have no secrets from you. Say you will be happy, at Rancho Sousa."

Cynthia smiled. He was *such* an attractive man. "I'll be happy," she promised.

Why shouldn't I be, she wondered, as the executive jet climbed into the blue sky. She couldn't bear responsibility for the world. And if the cocaine was going to be grown anyway, why should she have any doubts about being hired out to the man who grew it? Who was also just about the most charming man she had ever met.

Carlos sat beside her; apart from the steward and the pilots, there was no one else on board. "You have flown in a plane like this before?"

"Oh, yes," Cynthia said. "Mayne and her mother use one. And then, I went to Karnah . . ." She bit her lip.

"Ah, yes," Carlos agreed. "That so infamous, or was it really famous, episode in your life. Do you know, my dearest girl, I sincerely regret that Sheikh Abdullah was executed by his own people. I would have liked to do it for them. And that was before I met you."

"You say the sweetest things," Cynthia murmured.

"But there are so many aspects of your life of which I know nothing," Carlos said. "Would you tell me of your life?"

"What, warts and all? It's not terribly edifying."

"Warts and all."

"Well . . . if you'll tell me of yours."

"Mine? Yours may not be edifying, but I am sure it is

230

also not boring. Mine can be summed up in a very few words. I was born into a family which has been very wealthy for generations. I went to an English public school and then to an English university. When I had graduated, I went on a world tour. Then I returned to Bolivia, and have lived there ever since."

"Continuing the family tradition of making lots of money. How come you never married?"

"Oh, I was married. Sadly, my wife died some years ago."

"Oh, I am so terribly sorry. So now you make do with us?"

He kissed her fingers. "Only until I can find a replacement."

Travelling with Carlos was a dream. They flew into Rio, it seemed, thanks to the time difference, only an hour after leaving Spain. By then they had lunched, and watched a film. But they had not had sex again. This was one of the most attractive aspects of his personality, from Cynthia's point of view: unlike almost every other man with whom she had been associated, Carlos did not seem to find it necessary to stretch her repeatedly on her back, or on her front, or make her kneel before him, or even manhandle her. He was content to enjoy her company, and look at her, and occasionally touch her hand. Well, of course he knew he had her for a whole month, but it was nonetheless very pleasant to be treated as a lady.

The Rio stop was merely for refuelling. This was a disappointment, as she would have loved to explore, but Carlos said, "You have seen the best of it, from the air. Rio is one of those places where it does not pay to delve behind the facade." Then they were off again, flying over huge prairies and then, increasingly jungle. Soon there

231

were hills, and then, in the distance, mountains. "The Andes," Carlos told her.

Cynthia had never seen mountains so high. "Do we fly over them?" she asked.

"No, no. My estate is on this side."

More jungle, a blanket of close-packed trees, broken up only by the rivers which, like winding bands of silver, snaked through the green depths. Very occasionally there were roads or tracks, but as they flew on they now began to see the occasional village or town, as the jungle began to thin. Then they were flying over savannah. "Where's the Amazon?" Cynthia asked.

"Many miles away, to the north-east," Carlos explained. "I said I lived on the headwaters. That river down there flows into the Madeira, which in turn joins the Negro just above Manaus to form the Amazon."

They were descending. "When do we see your land?" she asked.

"You are flying over it."

Cynthia peered down, at the green hills and valleys, some wooded, quite heavily, some clear. She could see several hamlets, and one fairly large town as the jet sank ever lower. "All this is yours?"

"A man needs space," Carlos told her. He smiled.

They landed on a modern airstrip, where a helicopter waited for them. There were no formalities, and five minutes later they were again airborne. "It is a two hour drive to the house," Carlos explained. "But fifteen minutes by helicopter."

Below them the road wound between neat rows of large plants, perhaps six feet or more tall, with yellowish-green leaves. "Coca?" she asked.

"Indeed. Coca has grown wild in Bolivia for hundreds,

232

perhaps thousands of years. Disciplining it, if you like, was simply a matter of procedure."

"And you get cocaine from the fruit?"

"Actually, no. There *is* cocaine in the fruit, which is a little red berry, but not in suffcient quantity to be economical. We obtain our product from the leaves." There were people working in the fields, and they looked up to wave. They looked happy. Well, why shouldn't they be? she wondered. It was difficult to imagine anyone feeling unhappy in this warm sunshine. Carlos seemed able to read her thoughts. "It does rain, from time to time," he said. "Sometimes quite heavily."

Then she saw the house.

She had thought Eboli magnificent, but Eboli would have fitted into one corner of this immense white marble palace, rising out of nowhere as the helicopter descended. The main building was shaped like a cross, so much so that Cynthia presumed, had they been flying at any height, she might have supposed she was looking at a cathedral. The difference was that Carlos' home was two-storied.

The helicopter came to rest on the front drive, and was immediately surrounded by people, men, women and children, mostly Indians, and by barking dogs, of several different breeds. They all seemed delighted to receive their patron home again, and Carlos seemed as delighted to see them, greeting several by name, while he assisted Cynthia down from the cabin. She was wearing a dress, and the still rotating blades above her head were causing a considerable updraught, but she had a sudden overwhelming urge to preserve her modesty, and needed both hands to clutch on to her skirt. She was aware, however, that her hair was rising straight from her scalp, and was intensely grateful when she was hurried away from the machine to the

233

foot of the marble steps, and found herself looking at two very handsome young women. Both were tall and slender, with rich black hair and full figures; both wore jodhpurs and riding boots and silk shirts buttoned at the wrist, despite the heat. To her great relief, Cynthia realised that they both looked very like Carlos. "My sisters," Carlos introduced. "Angelina and Sophie."

Cynthia took a deep breath. She had not expected to be sucked into the bosom of his family. "Hi," she said.

"Hello," Angelina said. She was definitely the older of the pair, Cynthia decided. But neither was any older than her, which was surprising.

Carlos as usual seemed able to read her mind. "It is disconcerting, isn't it?" He kissed each of his sisters in turn. "My father married twice. My mother died when I was quite young. Then he fathered Angelina and Sophie by his second wife, before they too died. That left me the elder brother and father-figure to my two half-sisters. So you see, I have brought them up."

"Everyone around here seems to die," Cynthia said. "Oops. I do apologise. I was thinking . . ."

"Of my own dear first wife," Carlos said. "People do die, sadly. In this climate perhaps more quickly than in some others. Something else Mayne was worried about." He smiled at her. "Now you will wish to fly straight back out."

"When I feel it coming on, I'll tell you," she said.

"As I knew you would. This is Yarico." The Indian woman was short and stockily built, but had a pleasant face. "Yarico will be your personal maid," Carlos said. "She speaks English."

"If senorita will come with me?" Yarico invited.

Cynthia glanced at Carlos. "I will see you for cocktails before dinner," he said.

234

"Oh. Right." She glanced at the sisters, who had remained silent spectators since their first comment. Now they both smiled, as if given a cue by their brother. Do they know what I am and why I'm here? Cynthia wondered. But no doubt Carlos would tell her in his own good time.

She followed Yarico up the carpeted marble staircase. Was everything in this house made of marble? Something else to find out. But she could not remember ever reading that marble was found in Bolivia, so all this stuff would have had to be brought in . . . so what, where money obviously had no meaning? At the very least, if she pleased Carlos, her tip was going to be astronomical!

Her bedroom turned out to be a suite of five rooms, which contained two double bedrooms, a lounge, a dining room and a bathroom the size of her parent's entire house. "Do I take my meals in my apartment?" she asked.

"Only if you wish, senorita."

"But . . . there's no kitchen."

"If you want food, you have but to ring for it." Yarico indicated the telephone. There were in fact six telephones in the apartment, one in each room and two in the master bedroom, one on each side of the bed.

But when Cynthia looked more closely at the one Yarico had indicated, she saw that the number pad contained only four buttons, numbered from one to four. "How do I dial out?"

"You cannot dial out, senorita." Ah, Cynthia thought. Even paradise has its restrictions. "We are too far from any exchange," Yarico explained. "If you wish to talk to anyone off the estate, you must use the radio room."

"Ah," Cynthia said aloud. "So who can I dial in the house?"

"The phone has four connections. Number One is connected with the patron, wherever he might be, providing he is on the estate. He wears a bleeper, and usually carries a mobile. Number Two is similarly connected with me. Number Three is connected with the bar. And Number Four is connected with the kitchen. I will attend to any other matters that may arise."

"Very organised," Cynthia remarked, and saw that her suitcase had been placed on a rack in the bedroom.

"Senorita must be very tired after her long journey," Yarico remarked. "Would you like a bath?"

"I think that would be a brilliant idea." Up to that moment she had been in such a state of wonderment at her surroundings that she had been unaware of the time, but as it was now seven o'clock – it was dark outside – it was actually the small hours in the morning in Spain. But how long ago Spain seemed now.

She went into the bathroom. The entire room was walled with mirrors, which faceted her from every angle. Slowly she undressed, admiring the view; she really was a very lovely woman. "It is ready now," Yarico said. "You wish me wash you?"

"Ah . . ." Cynthia had no idea what the form was here, and she didn't want to make a mistake. "I'll manage, thank you." Yarico made a little bow of acquiescence.

Cynthia pinned up her hair and sank into the foamy warmth. To stay here, for the rest of her days, seemed like utter heaven. Had he really suggested that he might want her to? But what would the sisters say to that? "You come out now?" Yarico asked, standing beside the tub.

Cynthia's head jerked; she had almost nodded off. "I guess I'd better." She stood up, and Yarico enveloped her in a huge bathrobe, then returned into the bedroom. When Cynthia joined her, she discovered that her case had

236

been unpacked and her clothes neatly put away or hung up, while spread across the bed was her black velvet evening gown. "I know that's very pretty," Cynthia said. "But I wore it last night . . ." Was it really only last night? "So Senor de Sousa has seen me in it. I think we should try something else."

"There is nothing else," Yarico pointed out.

"Oh, really?" Cynthia opened the wardrobe, chose a cocktail dress. "What's wrong with this?"

"It is not a dinner gown, senorita."

"You mean I have to wear a dinner gown?"

"How else may you eat dinner, senorita?"

There did not seem much point in arguing with such simple logic. But . . . "Then we have a problem," she said, as she allowed herself to be dressed.

"The patron will take care of it," Yarico said. Cynthia surveyed herself in the mirror. "If senorita will sit, I will brush her hair," Yarico suggested.

Cynthia obeyed. This place was obviously going to take some getting used to. "May I ask you a question?"

She was watching Yarico in the mirror, and the maid seemed surprised. "I am your servant, senorita."

"Did you know Senora de Sousa? Before she died?"

"Yes, senorita. I was her maid also."

"Were you? How long ago did it happen? Her death, I mean."

"Four years ago, senorita."

"Oh. What did she die of?"

"You must ask the patron that, senorita."

When Cynthia got downstairs she found the family waiting for her. "Oh, I am sorry," she said. "I nodded off in the bath. If Yarico hadn't rescued me, I would probably have drowned."

237

She looked from face to face, expectantly, but neither of the sisters smiled. Both wore off-the-shoulder gowns, Angelina's in red and Sophie's in dark green, and they looked absolutely stunning. "We are very glad Yarico was there, this time," Carlos said. However casually he might have dressed at Eboli, in his own home he was wearing a dinner jacket, and now he beckoned a waiter forward with a tray of champagne cocktails. "May I say that you look ravishing, as always, Cynthia?"

"Thank you. I'm afraid I only brought one dinner gown."

"My people will make you some clothes tomorrow."

Just as Yarico had prophesied. But Cynthia was still digesting what he had said.

"What did you mean, about Yarico being there, this time?"

"It is simply that my first wife fell asleep and drowned in her bath. But she was alone."

Cynthia gulped. "Oh, I am most terribly sorry."

"It was some time ago."

"Yes, but I shouldn't have brought it up . . ."

"You didn't bring it up," Carlos told her. "Shall we eat?"

Dinner was on a par with everything else in these magnificent surroundings. Cynthia didn't really have much idea of what she was eating, either for the fish course or the meat course, much less the dessert, and felt it would be safer not to ask – she had an uneasy feeling that the chicken-like main course might be monkey – but it was delicious. As for the dessert . . . a fruit shaped rather like a pear, which one broke open with one's fingers to get at the stones inside, each covered with a creamy white flesh which one sucked off before delicately spitting out the stone; Cynthia had to watch the others to see how it was done. "It is a sugar apple," Carlos explained. "Because it is so sweet." It was certainly sweet, even if it bore not the slightest resemblance to an apple.

After the meal they sat in a mosquito-netted porch to drink their coffee and brandy. Here again, Cynthia had never tasted anything quite as strong or as sweet as this coffee. "I don't usually take sugar," she remarked.

"But here you have no choice. We grind our own beans, with sugar, you see. There is never any need to add any."

"Don't tell me you grow coffee as well?"

"Of course. Everyone around here grows coffee."

She wondered who else was 'around here' when his estate encompassed something like a million acres. "Are we going to have a storm?" she asked, pointing to where the eastern sky was suddenly a brilliant crimson.

"That is heat lightning," Carlos explained. "It means nothing more than it is very hot. But the land cools very quickly. You will know when there is going to be a storm. It has been a very long day. Would you like to retire?"

"Oh, yes," she said, and hesitated.

"Then I will wish you good-night." He kissed her fingers. "We both need several hours sleep, I think."

His manners, his whole demeanour, were so perfect, his wealth so obviously immense, Cynthia had to pinch herself to make sure she was not dreaming. She absolutely crashed out, and awoke with a start . . . to find him standing by her bed. She sat up, instinctively clutching the sheet to her throat; she was naked. As was he. "I did not mean to startle you. I wanted to see you in bed, and waking up. You can learn a lot about a woman from the way she sleeps, and awakes."

239

"Oh!" She pushed hair from her eyes. "Then I guess I get a D minus."

"On the contrary. You get an A plus. May I join you?"

"Wouldn't you rather I had a shower first? Or at least washed my face?"

"I am sure you washed your face last night before going to bed?"

"Well . . . yes, I did."

"Besides, I want you warm and tousled, all over."

Well, she reflected, he certainly wanted her, and he believed in tousling. What she found fascinating was the almost clinical interest he took in exploring her. He seemed to examine her pubic hair, very gently, before burying his face in her groin. He made her lie on her face while he stroked her buttocks, kneading and kissing as well as scrutinising. While when he finally began between her legs she started to wonder if he had not at some stage been trained as a doctor. She could not help but be extremely aroused by this attention. "You are utterly delightful," he told her.

"You're not too bad yourself," she gasped, face half buried in the pillow. She knew he was staring at her, although she would not turn her head. She wanted him to want her, more and more and more.

"You have a busy day ahead of you," he said.

Now she did roll over. "Making love?"

He smiled. "I wish it were possible. No, no, duty calls. I have arranged for the seamstresses to come up this morning, as I wish you to wear a new gown tonight."

"Is that possible?"

"Everything is possible, if one has the means and the will. Tonight we are entertaining guests."

Another surprise; all her previous clients had kept her strictly to themselves. "Neighbours?" she asked.

He took her seriously. "Not in this instance."

Cynthia got out of bed. "What will you introduce me as?"

"My current mistress. Do you have a problem with that?"

"Not if you don't," she assured him.

As he had promised, after she had spent the entire morning with a small army of seamstresses, she found herself the possessor of a pale blue evening gown, cut in a deep *décolletage* at both back and front, with just thin shoulder straps. After lunch and a siesta she went riding with the sisters, who seemed disconcerted by her expertise on horseback, and by the fact that she possessed riding gear. "I didn't know women of your . . . occupation ever rode horses," Angelina remarked.

It was the first sour note since her arrival, but Cynthia merely smiled; it was several hours late in coming, by her estimation. "Women of my occupation, Angelina," she said, "are accomplished at everything."

"*Touché*," Sophie laughed. "Now, if you tell Carlos what Gina said, he will probably beat her."

Cynthia's head turned sharply, and Angelina flushed.

There was no opportunity to be alone with Carlos before the guests arrived, brought from the airfield by helicopter; Cynthia gathered they were going to be staying several days. They turned out to be three American men, impeccably dressed and charmingly mannered, who were, as Carlos had intended, suitably impressed by the beautiful young woman introduced to them during pre-dinner cocktails. The dinner conversation was all about New York. "I've never been there," Cynthia confessed.

"Haven't you?" Carlos seemed surprised. "Then I shall take you." She was delighted.

As before, he did not sleep with her, but came to her at dawn. If that was his style, it suited her perfectly.

Once she had grown used to the idea of sex first thing in the morning, it seemed a delightful way to start the day. "I'm afraid I am going to be rather tied up over the next few days," he told her. "These lawyers, you know."

"Are they all lawyers?"

"Two are lawyers. Joe Adams is their client, who wants to do business with me."

"Shipping cocaine?"

He grinned. "Business. It is no concern of yours. But there is a lot of money involved. So you will have to amuse yourself with my sisters."

"I don't think they really like me. Angelina, certainly."

He frowned. "Has she been rude to you?"

"No, no," Cynthia lied. "But I think she would like to be. What would you do if she was?"

"I would be very angry."

"Would you beat her?"

"Probably."

"Carlos, she's a grown woman. I think you should be finding a husband for her."

"Point one: I regard her almost as a daughter, and daughters need to be disciplined every so often. However, if it bothers you, I promise you that I shall not beat her as long as you are on Rancho Sousa."

"Oh, Carlos . . ."

"As for the other, I have given the matter some thought. But it is difficult. To be perfectly frank, there is no young

242

man I have ever met, and who either of my sisters would be prepared to look at twice, who has the wealth to give them a tenth of what they have here. They know this as well as anyone, and so it will have to be a remarkable fellow who could prise them away from the luxury of life here. While from my point of view, I cannot be sure that any man who might marry either of my sisters might not be looking for a share in my wealth. I would never permit that."

"So you'll happily see them turn into old maids."

He kissed her. "There is lots of time yet. Would you really like to go to New York?"

"I should love it."

"Then I shall see what can be done."

"But Carlos . . ." She caught his hand. "There's only just over three weeks left, and with these business people here for a week . . ."

He kissed her again. "I can always apply to Mayne for an extension."

Once again that heavenly suggestion of permanence had been hinted at. She thought it would be the most delicious irony if having begun her adult life as the mistress of a small-time drug smuggler, she wound up the wife of a wholesale cocaine supplier. No doubt she would be damned forever. But if she was going to be damned, Hell was sheer paradise.

She didn't know if Carlos spoke to his sisters or not, but after that initial ride they couldn't have been more pleasant. They were clearly very close, and Cynthia would not have been the woman she was if she did not wonder if they had a relationship over and above the filial. Failing that, she could not imagine what they did for sex; having lived all her life heavily surrounded by the subject, she could not envisage anyone not needing it on a regular basis, and from what she had seen of Carlos she could not imagine either of them risking an indiscretion with any of the men on the estate. They each had their own apartment, of course, but she was never invited into either of them, nor did they accept an invitation back to hers. While when they were out riding one day and came to a bubbling stream and she suggested they strip off and skinny-dip, they were clearly horrified. "Suppose someone came along?" Angelina asked.

"We'd give them the thrill of a lifetime."

"Ohhh!" Sophie shivered. "Anyway, one never knows what sort of fish are in these streams. There could be piranha."

That suggestion quite put Cynthia off the idea.

The girls obviously confided in Carlos. The next morning he remarked, "I see you are trying to corrupt my sisters?"

"Sorry. I'm into sex. It's my business. Are you going to beat me?"

He grinned. "I am not allowed to do that, by the terms of your contract, as you well know, you little minx. Anyway, I think you will do them good. I give you carte blanche to corrupt them as much as you like. Let me know how you are progressing, and who knows, I may come along and join in."

"You mean you have not yet tried incest?"

"Would that shock you?"

"I'm not really too shockable."

"Have you ever tried it?"

"I'm an only child."

"You are adorable. I will make a confession." She waited, eagerly. "I have dreamed of taking my half-sisters to bed almost since they reached puberty. But I have been afraid to do so."

244

"You? Afraid?"

He sat up, hung his legs over the side of the bed. "All men are afraid of something. Unless they have experienced everything. If they have, and have sustained no psychological damage, then they are very enviable creatures, but they are also very rare. So, with Angelina and Sophie . . . they are very close."

"Do you think they're lovers?" she asked.

He shrugged. "It is difficult to say. But they could be, with no one the wiser. They are expected to spend a great deal of time together, and if, shall we say, two sisters decide to share a bath, or even a bed, to exchange intimate thoughts, who is going to think that immoral? But for me . . . You think this is a vast estate. Well, perhaps it is, as estates go. But everyone on it, except you, has lived here all of his or her life. Anyone over the age of thirty knew and remembers my mother and father. Our priest remembers them very well, and everyone on the estate confides in our priest. Talking of which, you must come to church on Sunday."

"Me? I've never been to a church service in my life!"

"The ultimate heathen. But my people would like it if you were to come."

So rich, she thought, so powerful, and yet so totally hidebound by tradition. "Then I shall. But you'll have to show me what to do, and say."

"That will be no problem. Then, once you have met Father Jaime, we can talk about our wedding."

Now it was her turn to sit up with a jerk. "You can't be serious!" Oh, please be serious, she thought.

"I am."

"Oh, Carlos!" She threw both arms round him and bit his ear. "But . . . I'm a whore."

"No one on Rancho Sousa knows that, or would dare

245

say it if they did. As for when we travel, I do not think anyone would dare say it then, either."

"But . . . what will Mayne say?"

"Mayne knows I had this in mind. I bought you, shall we say, on approval." He turned round to take her in his arms. "And . . . I approve."

I should be insulted, she thought. I have been bought and sold again, like some animal. She was going to be the wife of one of the wealthiest men in the world. She was going to be the mistress of all this. "I can't believe it," she said.

"Don't you want to be pulled out of that gang of female harpies?"

"Oh, yes."

"You are a reincarnation of Alexandra, only you are fair where she was dark. She eventually married her prince. Why should you not do the same?"

And from what I've heard, Cynthia thought happily, Alexandra's prince had one foot in the grave when they got married, whereas Carlos . . . she hugged him tightly. "We've travelled a long way from my seducing your sisters so you can bed them."

"But when we're married, you'll be able to do that, and I'll be able to do that as well, without arousing any suspicion," he told her.

She never knew when to take him seriously, but in any event was far too excited to worry about it. She was marrying a man whom most people would regard as a villain, but he was her villain. She was about to enter a life of utter sybaritism. So what if he wanted a little perversion on the side? She wasn't averse to that, and his half-sisters were two extremely pretty girls. She thought of little Tom. Carlos so obviously adored her he would surely agree to having Tom on the estate. Of course he would want children of his own, but until they came along, he would probably be delighted to have a surrogate son. Yet she knew she had to proceed with caution: she was't married yet. "Do you mean," she asked, "that you regret nothing that may have happened in my past?"

"Your past is done," he told her. "Only your future matters." She wasn't sure that was exactly what she had wanted him to say. Tom would have to wait until after they were married.

Even the American businessmen went to church on Sunday morning, although they were departing that afternoon: apparently everyone resident on Rancho Sousa was required to go to mass, and the church was packed to the door. Cynthia felt like a fish out of water during the service, even as Carlos guided her through it. She had been introduced to Father Jaime when they had arrived at the church, but there had been no time for any discussion. After the service, however, Carlos took her into the vestry to speak with the priest. This was difficult, as although Spanish was Jaime's native tongue, it was Bolivian Spanish, and Cynthia understood very little of it. But he seemed delighted at the prospect of marrying her to the patron, and it was arranged that the ceremony should take place the following week.

"Just like that?" Cynthia asked. "What about banns?"

"We will be married by special licence."

"Where can we get that?"

"From the local alcalde."

"And you think he'll go along with the idea?"

"Of course. I am the local alcalde."

Cynthia was not at all sure how legal that was, but there could be no question that she was getting married; once again she found herself surrounded by seamstresses from the town. But they were there mainly to create a trousseau. For the day itself, Yarico produced a white satin gown from one of the wardrobes. "The mistress wore this," she explained.

"The . . . oh, good grief, I can't wear her clothes!" Cynthia protested.

"It will have to be altered," Yarico agreed. "But only a little. You are very like the mistress in height and build, senorita."

Cynthia went to see Carlos. "But it is my wish that you do so," he said.

"Carlos . . . you can't recreate the past. If you're still that much in love with your first wife . . ." She knew she was being a fool. All she had to do was get married and the world was her oyster. But she genuinely liked this man.

He kissed her. "I am creating a new future for myself, my darling. And for you." There could be no argument with that.

The sisters were obviously going to be her bridesmaids, and the seamstresses busily created new dresses for them. The real surprise was on the Friday, the day before the wedding, when the helicopter flew in from the airstrip, and out jumped Mayne and Madeleine, Denise and five of the girls: Hayley was apparently working. "Well," Mayne said, "we couldn't let you get married all on your own, could we?"

"You mean you don't mind?" Cynthia asked, getting her alone.

Mayne gave her a long stare. "It's your decision, darling."

"I want to bring Tom out here."

"Have you discussed this with Carlos?"

"No. He doesn't know about him. But I think he'll go for it. He's . . . well . . ."

"Very much in love? Anyone can see that. However . . . you don't know him very well yet, do you?"

"How well is well?"

"Sex is one thing. But you still do not know the man. Carlos was born rich and has been rich all of his life."

"He has told me this."

"But you do not realise what that means. It means he has never been crossed in anything. That, in fact, he has been utterly spoiled all of his life. Anything he has ever wanted, he has stretched out his hand and taken." Mayne gave one of her cold smiles. "That includes you. Now, he may go for having your son here. Or he may not. I think you need to find out his feelings about that before you raise the subject."

"How do you think I should go about that?"

"Now that you will have to decide for yourself."

"Well, once I'm married," Cynthia said. "And mistress of Rancho Sousa . . ."

Mayne's lips twisted. "I do not think you ever wish to forget that Carlos has been married before," she said.

Now what on earth did she mean by that? Cynthia wondered.

Carlos did not come to her on their wedding morning. She awoke in a hot sweat. This was partly alcohol-induced, as there had been a tremendous party the previous night, with everyone consuming a great deal of champagne. Yet she had taken a good while to get to sleep. And now . . . She opened her eyes. Yarico was standing by the bed. "We start, now, senorita," she said.

Cynthia pushed herself up. "Yarico, what was Mrs de Sousa's first name?"

Yarico frowned. "Janine."

"Oh. She wasn't Bolivian, then?"

"No, senorita. She was American."

"Oh. And how did she die?"

"You know this, senorita. She drowned in her bath."

"Yes, but I mean, people don't just drown in their baths. Do they?"

"I do not know, senorita." Yarico's tone indicated that she would not have fallen asleep. "You must ask the patron this; it was he found the senora. But senorita, today is your wedding day. It is not good to brood on things past on your wedding day. One should be full of joy and happiness."

"Yes," Cynthia agreed. "I shall be. But answer me one more question, Yarico. Was the patron very upset about Janine's death?"

"Upset, senorita? He wept for days. It was feared that he would take his own life."

"Oh," Cynthia said. "Right. I'm ready for my bath, now, Yarico." Of course he could not have been in any way responsible, she told herself.

The wedding was a huge affair. All of Carlos' people attended, forming a huge mass outside the church; there was only room for the senior managers as well as the guests inside who included several dignitaries from the provincial capital flown in for the occasion. The ceremony itself was very simple, and then Cynthia was emerging into the hot sunlight on Carlos' arm, ducking beneath the flower petals which were hurled at her from every direction. The inevitable helicopter was waiting, and a few minutes later they were being flown back to the house. "Gosh!" she said. "I still can't believe this is happening."

"It will grow on you," he assured her.

250

"What happens next?"

"There will be a big party at the house, and a big luncheon, and then I shall take you to bed, and then . . . we leave."

"Leave?"

"We are going to honeymoon in New York. Did I not promise to take you there?"

I have got to be the happiest woman in the world, Cynthia thought, as she stood on the observation platform of the Empire State Building on a cloudless day and looked out over the city.

"It is fabulous, isn't it?" Carlos asked.

"Out of this world."

"And yet, like Rio, one doesn't want to look too closely," he said. "This is possibly the most violent city in the world."

"But not for us," she could not help but remark. Because walking behind them, and standing behind them at all times, were two of Carlos' people, and these weren't Bolivian Indians, but big husky Caucasians of indeterminate nationality, who only spoke when addressed by their employer. "Are they really necessary?" she had asked her husband after the first day.

"I'm afraid they are."

"But . . . you're not a criminal, are you?"

He had laughed. "Of course I am not. But I do have enemies. All very wealthy men have enemies. I would not like anything to happen to you."

"To me?" She had been alarmed.

"Desperate men often try to strike at their enemies through their families," Carlos pointed out. "But there is nothing for you to worry about. My boys can take care of anything."

After that she looked on his 'boys' with a fresh attitude, and by now, after three days, she wouldn't dream of going anywhere without them. And there were so many places to go. They had spent most of their days shopping, while Carlos bought her the most fabulous clothes and jewellery – in that respect he reminded her of Cuthbert, save that Cuthbert had never been remotely near this league. He also took her sightseeing, and they invariably lunched at one of the many really good restaurants in the city. But they usually dined in their room, and Carlos was clearly not interested either in nightclubs or theatre. "We're honeymooning," he reminded her.

She was happy to go along with that, although it did seem rather pointless to load her with necklaces and bracelets and evening gowns, and then not take her out to show them off. But then, they would be returning to New York, she had no doubt. Again and again and again. So she kept reminding herself that she should just sit back and enjoy herself. One perfect afternoon, when they were getting into their waiting limo, she said without thinking, "There it is again."

"There is what again?" Carlos sat beside her, and his 'boys' got into the front half of the car, behind the driver.

"That car. It was behind us this morning, and I'm sure I saw it yesterday as well. There's a slight dent in its front bumper."

"Yes," he agreed.

"You mean you've noticed it too?"

"Oh, sure. They're getting very careless, using an automobile with such a distinguishing feature."

"Who're getting very careless?" she asked.

"The FBI."

She sat bolt upright. "The what? Why are they following us about?"

252

"They're following *me* about, my darling."

"Right. You. What have they got on you?"

"There is the point," he explained. "They have absolutely nothing on me. But it is their great ambition to have something. So they follow me about, hoping that I will make contact with one of their underworld."

"Why should you do that?"

"Exactly."

"But why do they want something on you? How come they even know you are here?"

"Well, of course they know I am here," Carlos said. "My aircraft is well known, and so am I. Wherever I go, because of the nature of my business, police chiefs stir themselves and have people watching me. But as you have pointed it, it is always a complete waste of time and the taxpayer's money. Whatever business I do, I do it on Rancho Sousa."

"But what you do is illegal."

He smiled, and squeezed her hand. "It is not illegal on Rancho Sousa. I have explained this to you. Now stop worrying about it. The fact that our friends are following us everywhere is actually protection."

She had no doubt he was right, yet it was worrying; after her Turkish experiences, the one thing upon which she was utterly determined was never to get involved with anyone remotely resembling a policeman again. It also distracted her from her build-up to approaching Carlos about Tom. Now she felt she should wait until they got back to Bolivia, and she was less tense. But the tension remained, and increased when, the next morning, and they were driving along Fifth Avenue, with, inevitably, the FBI car behind them, he suddenly squeezed her hand. "At the next lights," he told her, "we are going to make a left. We will do this without signalling, and there will be

253

some blowing of horns and, this being New York, a good deal of swearing. As a result we will slow almost to a halt while our driver shouts back. As he does so, I am going to open this door and step out."

"What?" She was aghast.

"It is simply that I have somewhere to go, where I do not wish to be followed by the police. There is nothing for you to worry about. It is a very crowded street, and I will disappear into the crowd long before they can get their act together." He grinned. "And, I may point out, there is nothing illegal in dropping a tail – even a police tail."

"But . . . what am I to do?"

"Continue down to B Altman, do your shopping, and I will join you for lunch."

"Oh," she said. "Right." But she was holding her breath as the driver carried out the manoeuvre exactly as Carlos had said, and amidst a good deal of tooting and shouting he stepped out and disappeared. When they finally got moving again, she looked out of the rear window, and saw that the FBI car had also disappeared in the traffic.

Carlos certainly knew his way about, she reflected, and sat back for the remainder of the drive to the department store. There the drill was as always: the two "boys" got out first, one standing on either side of her door as she descended; she wondered why they were staying with her rather than at least one of them going with Carlos, but it was reassuring to think how highly he regarded her. She smiled at them, walked across the pavement and into the store, began to wander, the boys keeping a discreet distance behind her. She was standing in front of a showcase looking at dresses when she realised there was a man standing beside her. "Hello Cynthia."

She recognised the voice before turning her head to look at him. It was Tom Lane!

Chapter Eleven

Cynthia says: *"Talk about one's past suddenly rising up in front of one! I had never expected to see Tom Lane again, ever."*

Cynthia was so surprised she couldn't say a word. "We have to talk," Tom said, still staring straight in front of himself. "Do you ever get out on your own?"

"Never. Tom . . ."

"Then you'll have to manage it somehow. Here is a phone number. Call me when you've set it up."

His hand drifted across to touch hers, and a slip of paper was thrust between her fingers. She folded it into the palm of her hand without thinking. But who the hell did he think he was, telling her what she should do?

"Make it soon," he told her. "If you don't, you are going to wind up in serious trouble. Or dead."

She turned her head, sharply, but he was gone. Of all the cheek, as if it was she who had let him down rather than the other way round. And threatening her with jail . . . he must have found out about his son. But surely he couldn't do anything about that, in America? On the other hand, she didn't know what kind of laws America had about paternity . . . and he was as attractive as ever.

But how the hell was she to get out by herself?

*   *   *

Her initial worry was whether either of her two minders had seen the exchange, but neither gave any indication of it. As soon as she reasonably could, she went to the toilet, and there unfolded the piece of paper. It contained a phone number and nothing more. Her memory wasn't all that sharp, so she did not dare destroy it. Instead she folded it again and again until it was as small as she could make it, and fitted it into her lipstick.

As arranged, she met Carlos for lunch. "How long are we staying in New York?" she asked.

He raised his eyebrows. "Not enjoying yourself? I thought this was one place you had always wanted to visit?"

"Well, it was. But now I've visited, and as you said, it's not all it's cracked up to be. Frankly, darling, it's not my scene to be followed by minders wherever I go, and to know that if I ever don't have them along, I'm liable to be shot at or kidnapped or something."

"Point taken. As it happens, we're leaving tomorrow."

"Just like that?"

"I thought you'd be pleased. Well, I've completed all of my business here, and there is business calling in Bolivia. I'd have stayed on if you were keen, but as you're not . . ."

"Tomorrow is just fine," she said. Once she was back in Bolivia, Tom Lane could whistle.

"However," Carlos went on, "I am sorry to have to tell you that you will have to spend your last evening in New York alone."

"Where will you be?"

"There is someone I have to meet, tonight. It is very important."

"Oh! Well, I'll spend the evening watching TV."

* * *

Was that fate? she wondered. It was not something she normally believed in. But to have it turn out so fortuitously . . . or was it a trap? But that couldn't be. Anyway, there could be no harm in pretending to play ball with Tom, because there was no possible way they could meet. And by pretending to play ball she could put him right off until she was safely home!

She and Carlos returned to the hotel. He was going out at six. "I'll be back around eleven," he said. "But don't worry if it's later than that. Benito will be on the corridor, and Jose on the fire escape, so you'll be as safe as if we were back at the ranch."

"I hope Jose never peeps through the drapes," Cynthia remarked.

Carlos grinned. "There is absolutely no chance of that, my darling. He knows that if he did, I'd have his balls for breakfast."

Cynthia didn't dress, remained in her négligée. She gave Carlos fifteen minutes, just to make sure, and then dialled the number Tom had given her. The voice at the other end merely repeated the number, but she recognised it. "Hi," she said.

"Good girl," he commented.

She found herself becoming irritated again; he was so patronising. But she really did want to find out what was on his mind. "Well," she said, "I have good news and bad news. The good news is that I have the evening to myself. The bad news is that there is no way I can leave this hotel suite."

"That's not a problem. What's the number of the suite?"

"It's the bridal suite. Didn't you know I'm honey-mooning?"

257

"My heart bleeds for you," he said, and somehow she had a feeling that he wasn't entirely being sarcastic. "Right. What you must do is have dinner in your room."

"I had intended to do that, anyway."

"Right. But not too early. I have to set it up. Order it for eight-thirty. Have you got that?"

She gazed at the phone. "You got something to do with this hotel?"

"That's right. I'll explain it to you when I see you. Eight-thirty, Cynthia. I'll see you then."

The phone went dead, and she replaced her own. What the hell was going on, she wondered? If he could just walk into this hotel and take the place of a floor waiter by snapping his fingers . . . well, at least she was going to find out. She considered dressing, and decided against it. She'd let the poor bastard drool over what he'd abandoned six years ago. But she was aware of a growing sense of combined anticipation and apprehension. There was a bar in the suite, and she poured herself a glass of champagne to steady her nerves, then attempted to watch television, but not very successfully, as she suddenly became filled with fear that Carlos might complete his business early and come home. But that was very unlikely.

At eight-ten she telephoned room service, and ordered a fairly lavish meal, with another bottle of champagne. "I would like that for eight-thirty please," she said.

"No problem, Mrs de Sousa," the woman said. "Eight-thirty it shall be."

Cynthia had another glass of champagne and went back to the video she had been watching. But again what was happening on the screen was meaningless, as she kept looking at the time recorded in the bottom right hand of the picture. How slowly the minutes moved, and yet how quickly. Before she knew it it was twenty-five past.

She switched off the set, got up, took a couple of turns up and down the sitting-room, and listened to a knock on the door. "Room service for you, Senora."

"Let him in, Benito." Benito opened the door, and Tom, wearing a waiter's tuxedo, wheeled the trolley into the room. "Thank you, Benito," Cynthia said.

Benito hesitated. "I have searched him," he said eagerly.

"I was sure you had," Cynthia agreed. "Now you may let him set out the meal." Another hesitation, then Benito withdrew, closing the door. Cynthia said urgently. "If you want to tell me what this is all about, you'd better make it quick." She was able to study him for the first time. But this was a different Tom to the boy she remembered. He was leaner and harder and meaner looking, especially in his face.

Tom opened the flaps, and started laying the table. "So you married de Sousa?" Cynthia showed him her platinum ring.

"A week ago. I told you, we're on our honeymoon."

"I assume there's no love involved? That he bought you from that harpy who employs you?"

Cynthia sat down and crossed her legs. "You have a problem with that?"

"Not personally." But he was flushing. "I'd just like to establish that you're not in love with the bastard."

"Carlos is not, actually, a bastard. He has a pedigree longer than mine. Or yours, I suspect. And as for whether or not I am in love with him, what the fuck has that got to do with you?"

Tom rested both hands on the table, and stared at her. "He is one of the biggest, and nastiest, most vicious crooks in the world. And we are going to get him."

"We?"

259

"The DEA."

"You work for them?"

"That's right."

"How come?"

"I gave up playing tennis and got a proper job."

Cynthia snorted. "Proper job? And you've been keeping tabs on us since we arrived in New York?"

"Someone has, certainly."

"So how did you get involved?"

"De Sousa's photograph, and those of his entourage, which naturally includes his wife, were circulated throughout the agency, as a matter of routine, and I happened to recognise you." Another flush. "Yours is a face one does not easily forget. So, as an old friend, I was appointed to get in touch with you."

Cynthia recrossed her legs, the other way. "Is my face all you remember?"

He came around the table and sat beside her. "I didn't come here to renew old memories, Cynthia. I am trying to help you. I will help you, if I can."

Cynthia tossed her head. "What makes you think I need your help? You may regard Carlos as a crook, just as you regard me as a whore. I am sure there are lots of people who agree with you. However, Carlos is not regarded as a crook in Bolivia, and I am not regarded as a whore there. So I recommend that you keep your nasty little thoughts to yourself. And if it is any interest to you, we are leaving New York, and the United States, tomorrow. I doubt we shall bother to come back."

He stared at her. "Tomorrow?"

"That's right. Are you going to try to stop us?"

Tom got up, walked to the window, and then returned again. "Cynthia, listen to me. We are going to get this fellow. We had hoped to get him here in the States, but if he's leaving tomorrow, then that's out. But we still mean to get him. The plan is already laid. Nothing can stop it. The reason I am here tonight is that I have managed to persuade my bosses that you are not a willing accomplice of this man, but rather an innocent who has got herself caught up, not for the first time, in something she doesn't understand. I'm giving you an out. If you have any sense, you'll run, now. Before he takes you back to Bolivia. We'll offer you protection until the matter is sorted out."

"In response for turning states' evidence against him, is that it?"

"We're not asking that, at this time. It shouldn't really be necessary. OK, maybe it's all too sudden for you. But I'm still offering you an out. If you go back with him, again, I'm advising you to get out, just as quickly as you can. But I'll give you a third option. If you haven't got the nous or the guts to do that, when the balloon goes up, use my name, if you have the time, and you'll survive."

He wants to help me, she thought. And he doesn't know about his son. But she wasn't going to tell him now. Instead she asked, "Why are you offering me all of this?"

For the third time he flushed. "I guess maybe I fell in love with you once, and I'm slow to change."

How she wanted to be loved by this man, to be able to love him back. But could she ever trust him again? And he was talking about betrayal, of the only man who had ever treated her as a woman instead of an object to be mauled, beaten, used, or, in his case, abandoned when the going got rough. "I think that's absolutely sweet of you," she said. "But the fact is, Tom, that I offered myself to you, once, in marriage. And you turned me down. So, I moved up a notch."

"You call marrying a drug dealing, sadistic murderer moving up a notch?"

261

"Oh, really, Tom. Carlos does not deal in drugs. He grows coca. If people want to buy his crop, that is their business. As for describing him as a sadistic murderer . . . he's the sweetest, kindest man I've ever met."

He glared at her, and she heard the latch turn. Immediately she switched on the television. "Get down to it," she snapped.

He dropped to his hands and knees beside the set, just as the door swung in, followed by Benito. "Something wrong, senora?" he enquired.

"With the TV," she said. "This guy's trying to fix it."

"I think that's it, madam," Tom said, standing up and dusting his hands together.

"Why, thank you."

Tom hesitated, then turned and left the room, followed by Benito. Cynthia sat down. Her knees felt weak. She was terribly attracted to him still and it scared her. But he had had his chance. As for threatening Carlos . . . she debated telling him about it. But that would be to open a can of worms. If they were leaving tomorrow anyway, the United States authorities would never be able to touch him.

She was asleep when he came in, actually after midnight, but woke up long enough for a kiss and a cuddle. "What time are we leaving?" she muttered.

"Dawn," he said.

She vaguely registered that that was an unusual hour for departure, then went back to sleep, to awake again to a call from reception. Carlos was already up, showering. She joined him. "What *did* decide you to go home early? Really and truly? I know it wasn't anything to do with me."

"Am I that much of a monster?" She raised her head, sharply, was held by his serene brown eyes. "But you are absolutely right," he said. "There is a bit of a crisis. One

262

has to endure these things from time to time, when one is dealing in megabucks."

"Can the crisis affect your megabucks?"

"It could have, perhaps. But I have sorted it out. However, it does mean I must leave New York, immediately."

"Anyone would suppose," Cynthia said, buttering toast, "that the DEA are after you. Or something."

"Well, of course, the DEA are always after me."

"Eh?" She dropped the toast.

"I told you, my darling, that there are many people in the world, and especially in the United States, who regard me as a criminal. Now, they cannot touch me unless they can prove that I have broken an American law, and they have never been able to do this. But sometimes one of my associates does something very foolish, and the authorities get very close."

"And that is what has happened now?"

"That is what has almost happened now. But it obviously makes sense to leave while the various authorities are in such an excited state, and wait for them to settle down again." He looked at his watch. "We must go."

Cynthia felt like a cat on hot bricks as they were driven to Kennedy. It had been so stupid to tell Tom that they were leaving today. He had said that would mean a change of plan, the original plan obviously having been to detain Carlos in the States until some charge could be brought against him. But suppose Tom could create a reason for stopping them? She kept expecting to hear the wail of a siren. "Why so tense?" Carlos asked, squeezing her hand.

"I'm scared stiff," she replied, with utter truth.

"Because of what I told you at breakfast? My darling, you will have to get used to living with a certain amount of

263

tension if you are to be my wife." He squeezed her hand again. "Of one thing you can be sure: I will always protect you, and mine. No matter what may be involved." She squeezed his hand back.

The executive jet was parked down one of the taxiways, and the limo was able to drive right up to the door. "Everything aboard?" Carlos asked the pilot, waiting by the steps.

"All correct, Senor de Sousa."

"Then let's go."

Cynthia went up the steps, and was admitted by their usual steward. She entered by the forward door, and glanced over the empty seats of the day cabin. Behind that was the dining room, and aft of that another few rows of seats where the staff sat. She observed that there was someone already seated back there, but as the person made no move to greet her she ignored him, and took her own seat by the window. Carlos, Benito and Jose also came on board and the doors were closed. Carlos sat beside her. "I always feel a great sense of relief when I leave America," he said.

"Join the club. Who's our passenger?"

"A business associate of mine."

"Is he coming back to Bolivia with us?"

"No," Carlos said. "We are dropping him off along the way."

The engines roared, and the aircraft taxied out to take its position at the end of the runway. This early in the morning the traffic had not yet started to build, and in only a few minutes they were airborne. Almost immediately the aircraft banked to the left and flew out over the sea. The steward served coffee, and the captain came aft. "When do you wish, senor?" he asked Carlos.

264

"You tell me," Carlos said.

"It would be best after we are south of Miami radar."

"Then we shall wait," Carlos said. "Just let me know when you think it is best." The captain returned to the flight deck.

"What was all that about?" Cynthia asked.

"A manoeuvre we are going to carry out, at some stage on the flight. But as it involves a loss of height, we do not wish to carry it out where some officious air traffic controller may notice it and attempt to interfere. I do promise you it has nothing to do with the safety of the aircraft."

She believed him. Besides, she had too much on her mind. The meeting with Tom had brought the future of her little Tom into the foreground, even more than before. Tom obviously didn't have a clue he was a father, at least by her. But suppose he were to find out? If he was a member of the DEA he might well be able to. And before he could do that, and take any sort of action, little Tom had to be right out of his reach. She could only accomplish that by bringing him to Rancho Sousa. Therefore she would *have* to tackle Carlos about it. But Carlos obviously also had things on his mind. It really would be best to wait until they got home; there was nothing he could do about it, anyway, while airborne.

It was mid-morning, and the steward appeared with champagne cocktails. Shortly afterwards the captain returned. "We are beyond Miami control, senor."

"Then now is the time," Carlos said.

The captain went forward again, and almost immediately the aircraft began a slow descent. Cynthia looked down at the sparkling blue waters of the Caribbean Sea. "Where are we landing?" she asked.

"We're not. We are just making that manoeuvre I

265

mentioned. Now, there may be some turbulence shortly. I want you to fasten your seatbelt, very tightly, and do not under any circumstances release it until I tell you to. Understood?"

"Sure," she said, mystified and just a little apprehensive. "What about you?" she asked, as Carlos released his belt and stood up.

"I shall be all right," he assured her, and went aft.

Cynthia looked out of the window, and swallowed to pop her ears. They were now descending quite steeply, but there was absolutely no sign of land, or even of the lighter shades of blue and then green which might indicate that the water was shoaling. Then she heard a shout. She twisted her body in her seat to look aft, but the curtain had been drawn in front of the dining saloon. But someone was shouting back there, screaming in fact, so loudly that the sound was rising above the noise of the engines.

She released her belt and got up, made her way aft. She parted the curtain, went through the dining room, and parted the curtain at the other end as well, stopped in consternation. Benito and Jose were manhandling the mysterious passenger. She realised that the reason he had not risen to greet her was that he had been tied into his seat, and also gagged. Now they were releasing him, and the gag had slipped, enabling him to shout. But his hands were free, and the two big men were pushing him towards the rear exit door. This was presently shut, but both the minders were wearing harnesses which strapped them to a rod in the aircraft ceiling. Equally, now she realised why the plane had dropped so low – to reduce the pressure when the door was opened.

Carlos was standing behind them also wearing a special harness. The steward was in a seat on the far side of the aisle, strapped in. They all saw Cynthia at the same time.

266

"Senorita!" the man screamed. "Help me! Senorita . . ."
Benito hit him in the stomach, and he bent over, gasping
for breath.

"I told you to stay in your seat, strapped in!" Carlos
snapped.

"I heard this screaming . . . I thought you said he was
a friend of yours?"

"Sit down. Now!" The unexpected rasp in his voice took
her by surprise, and she sat down. Immediately Carlos sat
beside her and strapped her in, then strapped himself in as
well. The aircraft was still descending, but now it levelled
out. Cynthia looked through the window and saw the sea,
deep blue and restless, seeming very close but in reality,
she knew, several thousand feet below them.

"Now!" Carlos snapped. "Now."

Benito pressed a switch, and the rear door slowly slid
back. Instantly the cabin was filled with screaming noise,
while air whipped in and blew Cynthia's hair to a frenzy,
and even though they could not be more than five thousand
feet she felt an enormous tug on her body, against the belt.
Carlos threw both arms round her to make sure she was not
dragged from her seat. "Help me!" the man screamed a
last time, but his words were lost in the wind as Benito and
Jose thrust him forward. He went out, leaving his scream
behind. Jose went with him, but Benito clutched his sleeve
and jerked him back inside, while pressing the button again
to close the door. It had all happened so quickly, and so
tumultuously, that for a moment Cynthia wasn't sure it
had happened at all. Her mouth was dry, but above all,
she felt sick.

The door clicked into place and the cabin was almost
quiet. Carlos released Cynthia and unclipped his harness,
then released his seatbelt, and did the same for her. The
aircraft was now rising again, rapidly. "Drink," Carlos told

267

the steward. He held Cynthia's hand to help her up, and she jerked it away from him. "You weren't supposed to see that," he said. "Curiosity has been the death of many a good woman."

She gulped air. "Are you going to throw me out too?"

"Now what would be the point in that? That man was a traitor, who sought to betray me. And then had the gall to boast that I would never dare touch him, because he had left papers which would incriminate me the moment his body was found. Well, he has no papers now. He has simply disappeared. Even if his body is ever found, in twelve hours it will have been so enjoyed by fish it will not be identifiable. Nor are there any marks of violence on his skin. Even the rope burns will disappear in the water. And he will drown in international waters; the US has no jurisdiction down here."

"Oh, my God," Cynthia whispered. Tom had told her she was married to a sadistic murderer, and she had laughed at him.

"I know," Carlos said, sympathetically. "It is never a pretty sight, to watch a man go to his death while he is begging for mercy. But that is a measure of the man, whether or not he begs. Come forward."

"Don't touch me," Cynthia said.

Carlos hesitated, then shrugged. At the same time, he nodded to Benito and Jose, obviously warning them not to touch her either. But Cynthia knew she had to humour him to a certain extent. On this plane she was absolutely at his mercy. So was she not also at his mercy at Rancho Sousa? She had not a friend on the place. But on dry land she would at least have a chance, to escape. Then she remembered Janine de Sousa. Perhaps she had tried to escape too!

She pushed herself up, went forward, moving from

268

seatback to seatback. This might have been necessary anyway, as the aircraft continued to climb quite steeply back to its original cruising height. But she knew it was mainly because her knees felt too weak to support her. She slumped into a seat, and the steward offered her a champagne cocktail. "Drink it," Carlos said. "It will do you good." She certainly felt like a drink. She gulped at the sparkling liquid. It was as bitter as bile.

"Come along, my darling, wake up," Carlos said. Cynthia blinked at his handsome, smiling face. That had to have been a nightmare, she thought. Oh, God, let it have been a nightmare.

She pushed herself up, and he helped her to her feet. She realised the plane was stopped and the doors were open, and that it was as warm as toast. They were in Bolivia.

"I hope you have had a good sleep," Carlos said, holding her arm to guide her to the steps. She was so drowsy she wasn't quite sure why she should hate and fear him. She allowed herself to be led down the steps and across to the helicopter, where she was again strapped in. Then they were flying over the country she had come to love so much. And now despised, as memory flooded back. "I understand that you are very upset," Carlos said. "What want you to do is relax and simmer down. No one is going to trouble you or interfere with you."

She looked at him. "And suppose I decide to tell someone what happened?"

He shrugged. "Whoever you tell, on Rancho Sousa, will be in my employ, and will know that from time to time I have to do unpleasant things to preserve the integrity of my business."

"The integrity! Does that go for Father Jaime as well?"

"Of course. But that is an idea. Why do you not

269

go to confession? It will make you feel so much better."

"I'm not a Roman Catholic."

"I assure you that Jaime will not mind."

"I would," Cynthia said.

Yet he was as good as his word. Carlos was his usual delightful, well-mannered, gentle self. Had she not seen what had happened on the aircraft, she would never have believed it, just as she had refused to believe even the possibility of it before it had happened. But it *had* happened.

Again, as Carlos had promised, he did not sleep with her that night. Now that she was Mrs de Sousa she had been moved out of her guest apartment into the master bedroom, an enormous expanse of soft pile carpet and gleaming magnolia walls, with magnolia satin sheets on the bed, and an *en suite* bathroom even bigger than Alexandra's. The bed was big enough to accomodate a dozen people without the least crowding, and Cynthia spread her arms and legs as wide as she could while she tried to think through the champagne and sedative which were still dulling her brain.

Her principal emotion was a desire to weep. All of this could be hers, would be hers, for the rest of her life, if she just forgot about the plane, and about Tom. Well, Tom was a distant threat, here in Bolivia, and the man in the plane had almost certainly been a drug dealer and therefore entirely worthy of death . . . but that couldn't alter the fact that she was married to a man who killed whenever he felt it necessary, in totally cold blood. There was no way she could bring little Tom here now. And so there was no way she could stay here, either. Quite apart from being married to a monster, that would mean that she would never see her son again. But how was she to get away?

270

She remembered her time with Cuthbert, it seemed a million light years ago. She had been faced with the same problem there, and had been unable to find a solution. And Cuthbert had had only a dog to keep her in place. She was as free as air, yet she could not leave the ranch, simply because it was so enormous. But yet . . . it couldn't be *that* enormous.

"I hope Senora slept well." Yarico placed the breakfast tray on the bedside table; she revealed no surprise to find her mistress alone on the first night after her honeymoon.

"Yes," Cynthia said. Amazingly, that was the truth; the additional champagne coming on top of the drug had laid her out. But today her brain was clear, and cool. There were things to be done. She sat up. "Now that I am Mrs de Sousa," she said, "I wish to take an interest in the estate."

"I am sure that will please the patron." Yarico poured coffee.

"So, the first thing I want, is a map. A map of all of the patron's land. There is such a thing, isn't there?"

"I would say so, Senora. But I do not know about these things. It would be better for you to ask the patron."

"Very good," Cynthia said, aware that she could not risk going too hard in any one direction. "I will ask the patron. I would like to go for a ride today. Will you have a horse saddled for me, please?"

"Of course, Senora."

"And draw my bath?"

"Of course, Senora."

When Cynthia went downstairs, Carlos had already left on one of his tours of inspection, but Angelina and Sophie were waiting for her, also wearing riding gear. "We had not supposed you would wish to go out this morning," Angelina said.

Cynthia wondered what their half-brother had told them of their trip, if anything. But she had no doubt at all that they had been designated her watchdogs. Or would watchbitches be the better term? she wondered. But now that she was settled on a course of action she was filled with determined vigour. She would tear this family apart, as only she knew how. Besides, Carlos, in his arrogance, had given her carte blanche to do so. "Last night I was tired," she told them. "Today I am totally restored."

They cantered out of the villa grounds. "Where would you like to go?" Angelina asked.

"North, into the woods."

They did not argue. The woods were about three miles north of the house, the earliest beginnings, Cynthia presumed, of the Amazonian forest. It was also where the stream was to be found. "Carlos has never told me," she said, as they rode along the bridle paths, "just how far to the north his land reaches."

"All the way to the Mapiri," Angelina said. "And the Mapiri flows into the Rapirran, which is our northern border with Brazil."

"The Rapirran flows into the Madeira," Sophie explained. "Which is the river that eventually becomes the Amazon."

"It's all so immense," Cynthia said. "Difficult to grasp. So if one crossed the Rapirran, one would be in Brazil?"

"Of course."

"Do you ever go up there?"

"What, through the jungle? It is quite severe, north of the river," Angelina said.

272

"It is severe *south* of the river," Sophie said. "These woods are nothing, compared with the jungle."

"I'd love to go into the jungle," Cynthia said.

"You will have to ask Carlos," Angelina said.

"Does he ever go into the jungle?"

"He has done so. But not every often."

Cynthia listened to the rustle of running water. "The stream," she said. "I do love this place."

"This is as far as we normally come," Angelina reminded her.

"I know." Cynthia dismounted, letting her reins trail; the horse was unlikely to wander off. "I am going to bathe."

"But . . . you can't!" Angelina protested. "You have no suit!"

"I asked Carlos," Cynthia said, sitting down to take off her boots. "And he said he has no objection to my skinny-dipping. He also said it is perfectly safe in this stream. The water flows too fast for there to be any piranha, and it is too shallow for alligators." Her boots off, she stood up again to release her waistband and slide her jodhpurs as well as her knickers down to the ground. The sisters watched her in scandalised consternation, but they had also dismounted. Cynthia took off her silk shirt, carefully laid it on top of the jodhpurs, then, still wearing her flat-brimmed black hat, stepped into the water, slowly sinking to her haunches. It was actually surprisingly cool after the heat of the air, and she gave a little shudder. "This is heavenly," she said. "Aren't you coming in?"

The sisters exchanged glances. Then Sophie undressed, revealing a lithe, strong, surprisingly pale-skinned body. She stepped into the water and gave a little shriek. "It is so cold."

"You'll get used to it." Cynthia watched Angelina, who

273

was altogether more voluptuous than her sister, with breasts almost as big as her own. Angelina moved with a stately grace in everything she did. Therefore, Cynthia decided, she should be her first target. She waited while Angelina slowly lowered her body into the rushing stream, immersing hips and thighs and belly, while keeping her breasts and shoulders clear. Her long back hair trailed in the stream, but she did not seem to notice. "Isn't this great?" Cynthia asked.

"Well . . . different," Angelina agreed.

"Then let's make the most of it," Cynthia cried, and launched herself through the water. Angelina gave a startled scream, but didn't have the time to take evasive action before Cynthia reached her, to throw both arms round her and tumble her off balance; they both went below the surface with a flurry, losing their hats in the process. Cynthia was first up, gasping for breath, wet hair plastered to her neck and shoulders. Angelina came up a moment later, equally dishevelled. "You beast!" she said. But she was laughing.

"Now you!" Cynthia turned to Sophie, who gave a shriek and waded for the bank. But again Cynthia was too quick for her, and this time she threw her arms round Sophie's thighs as they emerged from the water. Sophie shrieked again and fell to her hands and knees, and Cynthia was on top of her, forcing her beneath the surface. This time she did not let go, but rolled on her back, still holding Sophie tightly. Sophie's head came up and she squealed with embarrassed pleasure as she kicked her legs in the air. When Cynthia released her, she sat on the bottom of the stream, which flowed around her shoulders, gasping for breath. Cynthia put her arms round her again, and fondled her breasts while she kissed her on the mouth. Sophie gasped, but did not try to push her away. There

274

was a splash, and Angelina was kneeling on Cynthia's other side. Cynthia put her arm round Angelina's waist and nuzzled her breasts in turn. This is going to be easier than I reckoned, she thought. And far more enjoyable.

"Are you going to tell Carlos?" Angelina asked, as they rode home.

It was more than an hour later, as after playing with each other in the water they had had to go downstream to regain their hats, flitting through the trees naked, stopping every so often to touch and caress and kiss and hug. Cynthia no longer had any doubt that the sisters made love on a regular basis, but they had never allowed their desires to overflow, as it were, and she could not remember ever having known two women so turned on by having the use of her body. She was indeed a prized plaything for the frustrated pair. She had enjoyed herself thoroughly. If she was determined to tear this family apart, she was also going to have fun while doing it. "Of course," she said. "Should a wife not tell her husband everything?"

"Oh, but . . ." Angelina drew rein.

"He'll have to cane you too," Sophie said.

"Why not?" Cynthia asked.

"But . . . it'll be so shameful," Angelina said.

"What's shameful about two people making love?" Cynthia asked. "It doesn't really matter what sex they are."

Angelina had obviously never considered that point of view before.

Carlos was on the front steps as they rode up and dismounted, tossing their reins to the grooms. He knew at once that they had been bathing, as did everyone else; if their clothes had long dried, their hair was still damp. "It was Cynthia's idea," Angelina said. "She said you wouldn't mind."

"Why should I mind?" Carlos asked. "I was merely worried that you were late returning."

"We were making love," Cynthia said. He frowned at her, then gave a quick glance left and right; there were several grooms within earshot. "Now I am going to have a hot shower," Cynthia said, and went up the stairs.

Yarico promptly appeared. "I must take your clothes, Senora," she said. "They are not clean."

Cynthia stripped and left the riding gear lying on the floor to be gathered by the maid. She stepped into the shower, soaking her hair as well as her body in the hot steam, and heard the door open and close. She soaped, and waited, and a few moments later the curtain was drawn back and his hands slid over her body. She turned in his arms for an almost savage kiss, then she was lifted from the bath and carried, dripping water, into the bedroom and thrown on the bed. He was on top of her and inside her before she had stopped bouncing, clutching at her with an almost savage intensity. Perhaps he'll have a heart attack, she thought. But after he had climaxed he rolled off her. "We're going to have to change the mattress," she remarked, sitting up. Bathwater was still running out of her hair.

"Did you do it?" he asked.

"Have they not confessed to you?"

"They would not. But I can tell something has happened."

"Perhaps I told them about the man you threw out of the plane," Cynthia said.

He seized her round the waist and threw her flat again. "They already know about that."

276

"Ah," she said. "Well, yes, I have had them both." She gazed up at him. "So, now it is your turn."

He stared into her eyes. "You mean you want me to?"

"Sex is my business, just as drugs is yours. You knew that when you married me. They are two lovely girls. To share them with you will be a treat."

He sat up. "But incest!"

"You amaze me. You will throw a man out of an aircraft without a second thought, but you regard incest a crime?"

"You do not understand. The first was a business matter. Incest is a moral matter."

"That's semantics," Cynthia said. "Either murder is a moral matter too, or there is nothing moral about incest. It's up to you."

He got up, went to the bathroom, came back. "Will they go for it?"

"Of course they will. If you let me turn them on first."

"How long?"

"Oh, half an hour."

He stood above the bed. "You are corrupting me, you gorgeous little witch."

Cynthia smiled. "I'll take that as a compliment."

That night she went down to dinner, wearing one of her new long gowns, complete with plunging *décolletage* and jewellery. She drank little, while the sisters were almost frenetically vivacious, laughing and talking, and drinking, a great deal. Carlos matched their mood, but he also drank little, and spent most of his time surreptitiously watching Cynthia. He had received his instructions, and did not get up when Cynthia strolled on to the patio after the meal. "Come and look at the heat lightning," she said over her shoulder.

277

Angelina joined her immediately. "Have you told Carlos?" she asked.

"Of course not." Cynthia held her hand and gently walked her out of the light from the doorway. "Have you?"

"God forbid! I can't imagine what he'd say. Or do."

"Well, there is no reason for him ever to find out," Cynthia said. She turned Angelina into her arms and gave her a long, deep kiss, while sliding her hands over her bare shoulders. "Just as there is no reason for us not to spend every siesta together."

"Oh, Cynthia!" Angelina's hands closed on Cynthia's shoulder blades, and then slid round in front to hold her breasts. "What have you done to me?"

"Made you happy, I hope. Angelina, I want you. Now."

Angelina pulled her head back. "But . . . Carlos . . ."

"He is not sleeping with me at the moment. He thinks I am upset about what happened on the plane." She peered into Angelina's eyes. "You know what happened on the plane?"

"Yes. That man Rodrigues was a thug. He was going to betray Carlos to the FBI."

"Then you have no regrets about what Carlos did?"

"Of course not. That is the way he has always dealt with traitors."

Then there is no reason for me ever to regret what I am going to do to you, Cynthia thought. "I agree with you, entirely," she said. "But Carlos thinks I am upset by what happened. Well, I suppose I was. I had never seen anyone killed before," she lied. "Anyway, at the moment he isn't sleeping with me. He wishes me to get over it. So there is no reason why you should not sleep with me instead."

"Oh, I should love to do that," Angelina said. "But . . . are you sure he will not come in?"

278

"Absolutely. He will not come to my room again until he is invited." Cynthia thought that one lie per night was sufficient.

They kissed again, then she led Angelina back into the lounge. "That ride today really tired me out," she said, giving Sophie a meaningful glance. "If you don't mind, Carlos, I shall go to bed early."

He caught her wrist and pulled her down for a gentle kiss. "Sleep well, my darling."

"Good-night, girls," Cynthia said, and went upstairs. Yarico as ever was waiting for her. "That will be all, Yarico," Cynthia said. "I am just going to have a quick shower and then go to bed. You go to bed too." Yarico hesitated. It was her business to see her mistress safely tucked in for the night. "Off you go," Cynthia said.

Yarico went. Cynthia showered, then got into bed. She hadn't been there more than five minutes when her door opened, and Angelina came in. "Wasn't that easy?" Cynthia asked.

"I'm scared stiff."

"Then come here and let me cuddle you."

Angelina draped her clothes over a chair and went into the bathroom. When she came back she was glowing with anticipation. Cynthia sat up to take her in her arms, and the door opened again, to admit Sophie.

"Join us," Cynthia said. "It's a big bed."

Sophie giggled and ran into the bathroom, scattering her clothes behind her as she did so. She was back in five minutes to join them on the bed, but they had barely started to make love when the door opened again. Sophie bounced off the bed and stood up, panting. Angelina rose to her knees, also panting. Cynthia remained lying down. "Why Carlos," she said. "How lovely of you to join us."

* * *

Cynthia says: "*I of course had no moral qualms about what I was doing. I would not have had in any event, after the many things that had been done to me, but in addition I believed Carlos to be the most amoral and vicious person in the world – even Abdullah had only acted viciously when aroused: Carlos did everything in cold blood. My plan was to let nature take its course. I knew the sisters were to a certain extent already jealous of each other. I planned to make that jealousy increase, over both me and their brother, until something snapped, so that they either destroyed each other, which I had no doubt would also destroy Carlos, or one of them would fall so heavily for me that she would help me to escape Rancho Sousa, no doubt coming with me. But that was a problem I felt I could solve, once we were free of Carlos.*

"*Of course, as with so many of my plans, this was a nonstarter, although I did not realise it. I did know it might take some time to come to fruition, and I was quite prepared for that. What I did not understand was that while I laid my puny plans, there was an immense and unstoppable force already determined to deal with Carlos, and this force was coming closer every day. Tom had warned me.*"

The next couple of weeks were the most sexually tumultuous Cynthia had ever known. She realised that Carlos had wanted to get his hands on his half-sisters for a very long time, perhaps ever since he had become their guardian. Now he could not keep his hands *off* them. He came with them on their rides, and enjoyed the delights of bathing in the stream and making love in the water. He slept with the three of them every night, for it was very important, in his estimation, to preserve propriety at all times, and thus Cynthia had always to be present.

Fancy me, she thought, acting the chaperone! But as he

280

was still also desperately in love with her body, she was not neglected. She had no idea what his valet or the girls' maids thought about it all. Certainly she knew Yarico was aware of what was going on, but Yarico had more sense than to say anything.

So, she thought, I have recreated the harem, only a harem where everyone is beautiful and desirable, and where I am the wife and mistress. Now it was just a matter of waiting. And filling in her time. She continued to take an ever increasing interest in the operation of the estate, to Carlos' delight, as he conceived that she had entirely recovered from the shock of Rodriguez' murder. In fact she found little that she could possibly use that was a better bet than the sisters, but she was intrigued one day when she entered the gymnasium, and found Benito and Jose working out together, practising their skills at unarmed combat.

They were old friends now. "I've done a lot of that," she told them.

"You, Senora?" They exchanged glances.

"Would you like to try me?" Cynthia asked. Benito grinned, and she advanced on him, hands held rigid. She grasped his shirt front preparatory for a throw, but found she could not budge him. "Well," she panted. "You're a bit heavier than most."

"Karate is a sport, Senora," Benito pointed out. "It should not be used in real combat."

"I've used it," Cynthia pointed out. "Successfully."

"That is because your opponent did not know any better, Senora."

She bridled. "Oh, yeah? So how would you go about tackling someone with your bare hands?" Benito looked at Jose. "I really would like to know," Cynthia said.

The two men shrugged. She was the patron's wife, and

281

if she really wanted them to mess about with her . . . over the next week they taught her a great many things she had never considered before, such as approaching her opponent from behind and slapping both hands together, as hard as she could, over his or her ears. "That can cause brain haemorrhage," Jose told her.

She was taught how and where to kick. "When you start kicking," Benito told her, "you must not stop until your opponent is unconscious."

"Or dead," Jose added, helpfully.

They also showed her how to use her hands, and not for conventional karate chops. She learned how to drive her fingers, held rigid, at an opponent's eyes, or to swing the edge against his throat, aiming at the Adam's Apple. "That puts him out of action for a long time," Benito assured her.

Never had she felt so in control of herself. Which increased the temptation to forget about both Rodriguez and Janine, and be the wife that Carlos wanted – and as she was being at that moment. But to do that would also be to forget about little Tom, and that she was determined never to do.

As for his father . . . well, he *had* to be forgotten. If that were possible. But she knew it was not the morning she awoke suddenly. They were, as usual, all in her bed, and Carlos sat up . . .

"What the devil . . ."

Cynthia sat up too, and switched on the light. "Sounds like a helicopter!"

"At this hour? It is not yet daylight. And . . . my God, it is several helicopters."

As he spoke, Cynthia heard the familiar sound of automatic rifle fire.

Chapter Twelve

The dogs were barking wildly. Carlos leapt out of bed and ran for the door. Cynthia also scrambled out of bed, but was checked by the screams of the sisters. "What's happening?" Angelina shouted.

Carlos banged the door behind him as he left. "Turn off the light," Cynthia snapped. Sophie switched off the light. Cynthia moved to the window, hoping to see what was going on, but before she got there the glass shattered and she instinctively dropped to her hands and knees, while the sisters renewed their screams as bullets smashed against the walls and ceiling.

"Oh, my God!" Angelina shrieked. "Oh, my God!"

"Shut up," Cynthia shouted. "Get under the bed, and stay there." She listened to the thumps as the girls obeyed her, but by now the noise of the gunfire was very loud, from both inside and outside the building. When Tom had said they would get Carlos, he had meant it. But surely this was an act of war?

She crawled across the floor to the door, reached up and released the handle, pulled it in. The house was still in darkness, but there was a lot of movement, some stealthy, some loud, and the shooting continued, all around her. There was no way of telling where Carlos was, or who was winning the battle which continued to rage.

She slid back into the room and closed the door again,

crawled to the wardrobe, opened it, and clawed down a pair of jeans and a shirt. "What's happening?" Angelina asked again. "Where's Carlos?"

"Who's attacking us?" Sophie asked. "Who would dare?"

"Listen," Cynthia said. "Get dressed."

"We don't know where our clothes are," Angelina complained.

"We don't *have* any clothes in here," Sophie pointed out.

Which was absolutely true. They had become so blatant in their habits that they had started coming to her room naked. "Well, wear something of mine," Cynthia suggested. "Don't get up," she snapped, as the girls crawled out from under the bed. There had been no more firing into the room since the light had gone out, but she didn't know if they could be seen or not. Angelina crawled across the floor towards her, followed by Sophie . . . and the door burst open.

The three women were bathed in the glare of a powerful flashlight; it was impossible to tell who was holding it. "Don't shoot!" Cynthia shouted, rising to her knees and holding her hands above her head.

Angelina and Sophie followed her example, and as all three women were naked they obviously had an effect on the intruders.

"Stand up," someone commanded.

"With your hands up," added someone else.

Slowly Cynthia rose to her feet, hands still held above her head. Angelina and Sophia did likewise. "Shit!" remarked the first voice. "You reckon they were all at it, together?

"Have you no clothes?" asked the second voice.

"We were getting dressed," Cynthia told him.

"Then do it," he said. Angelina and Sophie used whatever of Cynthia's clothes they could reach, regardless of fit. Cynthia pulled on the jeans and shirt. "We're looking for Mrs de Sousa," the man said.

"I am Mrs de Sousa," Cynthia said. Now accustomed to the growing light, she watched the man's figure-trigger flicker. "I was told to say the name Tom Lane," Cynthia said.

They were taken downstairs by their captors. Carlos lay at the foot of the main staircase, naked in a pool of blood, his body riddled with bullets. Benito and Jose lay close by, fully dressed but also dead. Just like faithful old Hannibal, Cynthia thought. At the sight of their brother, both Angelina and Sophia uttered cries of horror and threw themselves on the bloodstained corpse, having to be dragged off him. "Seems they loved him more than you did, Mrs de Sousa," said Cynthia's captor.

"He was a thug," Cynthia said.

"But you were his wife, right?"

"Mistakenly," Cynthia told him.

Everywhere there were dead bodies, shattered glass, torn drapes, broken furniture, utter destruction; nearly all the dead were Carlos' people. Several of the dogs had been killed in the crossfire. Now it was broad daylight, the full extent of the annilihistic nature of the raid could be discerned. There were even bodies floating in the swimming pool. The survivors, mainly women and children, were herded into the inside courtyard, where they stared at each other with enormous, terrified eyes. Cynthia was relieved to see Yarico amongst them. It was the only thing she had to be relieved about.

285

Now too they could add up the immense force which had been launched against Carlos: there were a dozen unmarked helicopters on the ground, and several more were arriving every moment. The members of the attack force commenced to embark, while the members of the second-wave assault force were still disembarking.

Cynthia went forward. "Stop right there, lady," one of the men guarding them said. "Nobody leaves this compound."

"You mean to keep us here?"

"Where is Tom Lane?" she said.

The man to whom she had said the name earlier had disappeared; she did not know if he was amongst those who had already left. This man merely stared at her. But then a voice behind her said, "Come here, Cynthia."

"Tom!" she shouted, turning to run to him. The guard looked as if he might stop her, then changed his mind. Tom had just come in. Although he wore the same bush uniform and slouch hat as the others, and carried a gun, he looked fresh and clean, so she guessed he had just arrived by one of the incoming helicopters. "Thank God!" she said.

"For what?"

"Well . . . what is going to happen to these people?"

"That is up to them."

"You think killing Carlos is going to end the coca business?"

"Come." Tom led her through the door and out of the shattered building. In the wing the flames still burned brightly; no effort was being made to put them out. He led her out of the front door, and pointed, to more smoke clouds, immense brown waves, sweeping away to the south west. "They'll be starting from scratch in this neck of the woods."

"Jesus," she muttered, only now beginning to realise the scale of the operation.

"We haven't touched the cattle and horses, or the farm," Tom said. "These people will survive. If they have the guts. You could be their leader, if you wished."

Cynthia shuddered. "Not me."

"You're Mrs de Sousa, aren't you?"

"We were married three weeks! And I wasn't given too much choice."

"You expect me to believe that?"

"OK, so I didn't believe you in New York. That was before I watched Carlos throw that man Rodriguez out of the plane over the Caribbean."

"So that's what happened to him. We've been looking everywhere. So you decided to leave. But you're still here." He was forcing himself to be hostile.

"Leaving Rancho Sousa isn't exactly easy, without Carlos' say so." She glanced at him. "It doesn't look any easier now, unless I can get a ride out."

"To go where?"

Cynthia drew a long breath. "To go and find my son. Our son, Tom."

Tom stared at her for several seconds. "You expect me to believe *that*?"

"Yes. Because it's true."

"Because you had a child nine months after being with me? You were with me for less than a week, and you had just been living with that thug Jacques."

"Jacques and I never had full intercourse, Tom. He was impotent. He hired me with the idea I might be able to cure him, but I couldn't do it." She shrugged. "Something else you'll have to believe."

Another long stare. "What did you call him?"

287

"His name is Tom. That seemed natural."

"And where is he?"

"He was farmed out to a Spanish couple, not far from Eboli."

"So you propose to go there and pick him up, is that it? Have you the money to do that?"

"I don't have a cent at the moment."

"But you reckon you can always earn some, right?"

"Listen," she said. "Fuck the morality trip. I'm a whore, right? As you endlessly remind me. So I'll earn my money by whoring. If you'll just get me out of here."

"You'd have to leave, now. We all have to be out of here today, before the Bolivian government can react."

"Where are you going?"

"Back to the base from which we took off. It's not far."

"In Brazil?"

"Let's say in a neighbouring country which is as opposed to the drugs business as we are. There we'll pick up transports back to the States. Getting you a place on those will be no big deal, certainly if you agree to turn states' evidence when you get there."

"Against Carlos?"

"Against everyone and anyone you can think of. But Carlos definitely. What we've done here had to be done. But it still needs to be justified. Your evidence about the murder of Rodriguez will be useful in that."

"And in the meantime, my name is plastered all over the media?"

"Oh, don't get frightened on me. We have a huge Witness Protection Programme in the States. No outraged drug baron is going to be able to get at you."

"I wasn't thinking of any drug baron. I don't know the names of any of them. I was thinking of Mayne."

288

"She won't be able to touch you either."

"She'll certainly be able to touch little Tom."

"Why would she do that?"

"Because she'll reckon I've let her down again. She hates me, in any event. If I wasn't such a marketable commodity, she'd not have wasted her energy on me. Listen, I'll turn states' evidence, but I'll have to get Tom first."

He walked away from her, and then came back to her. "And you reckon you can give him a better life than these Spanish people? While continuing your . . . career?"

"Don't you think I'd like to give up my career, Tom?"

"But you don't have any other talents."

"I'll be a good mother to Tom. Heck, Alexandra was a good mother to Mayne."

"And look how she turned out? Sorry, Cynthia, but I don't think I can go along with you. You'll have to come back to the States and do your stuff, and in the meanwhile I'll see what can be done about Tom."

Cynthia frowned. "You mean you'll take him for yourself?"

"No, I did not mean that. I said I'd see what can be done about him."

Cynthia said bitterly. "Our son, Tom. Our son."

"So you say. Come along, we have to make a move. You have two choices: stay here and try to pick up the pieces, or come with me and try to pick up your life. But you have to decide now."

Cynthia bit her lip. And remembered, so many things. She didn't really want to take Mayne on, certainly not if it might harm the girls, several of whom she remained quite fond of. But if it was the only way to regain possession of Tom . . . "Aren't you interested in where Carlos invested his wealth?" she asked. "Apart from here, of course," Cynthia added.

Tom checked, and turned back to her. "You know that?"

"Yes. And not only Carlos."

"I can see why you'd be scared. But you'll have to tell us about it."

Cynthia tossed her head. "I will, if you'll help me get Tom before I have to give evidence."

"Cynthia, wake up. You can't bargain with Uncle Sam. You're Carlos' widow. To most people that means you're tarred with the same brush. We can take you back to the States and lock you up for the rest of your life. Or we can leave you here to see how you get on with these people without Carlos to protect you. Sure we'd like to hear what you have to say. Sure we'd like to find out where he has been laundering his money, especially if others have been using the same route. But we're not going to let you dictate terms to us."

"All I am asking is possession of my son," Cynthia said, and added, "our son. The two are connected."

Tom frowned at her. "Mayne's outfit? Holy Jesus!"

"Nothing could be easier. Alexandra set it up. She inherited a packet from her count, so when she shifted big sums about no one took any special notice. So, people like Carlos visited her, looking for girls. Everyone knew that. Only at least one of their suitcases was stuffed with money. They left that money with Alexandra. She deducted their fees for whichever girls they hired, and, in the course of time, moved the money through her own accounts to its ultimate destination."

"Which was? Or is?"

"I have no idea."

He took another turn up and down. "What proof have you got of this?"

290

"I've seen the transactions taking place. Without actually understanding what was going on, at the time."

"That won't stand up in a court of law."

"Then you'll have to get hold of Mayne, as well."

"If this is some scheme of yours to get even with her, I'll send you up for a million years."

"It's there, Tom. But it won't be if I am splashed all over the media as having turned states' evidence."

"You realise we can't mount an operation like this against Eboli. Spain, Europe, isn't South America."

"I understand that. But you and I could do it."

"Do you really think I was born yesterday?"

"I won't let you down, Tom. I can't afford to, can I? I can get you in. What you do when you're in is up to you. But you'll come out with enough evidence to cut off quite a few sources of income, as well as enough evidence to present to the Spanish government to have Mayne put right out of business."

"And your son, to be sure."

"Our son, Tom."

"And of course, I, or the United States Government, will pick up the tab for the entire trip."

"God, you are a bastard. I'd say you are getting a bargain. But you don't have to spend a penny. I'll fund it."

"I thought you said you were broke?"

"I am, here. But I have something like a hundred grand, pounds, not dollars, invested through Mayne myself. And I have property investments in various places. All you have to do is let me get at them."

"If this deal comes off, that money will be frozen until the whole mess is sorted out."

Cynthia grinned. "I'll take my share from the cash I know she always has lying about the place. Do we have a deal?"

"I'll have to set it up with my boss. But Cynthia, I'm going to say it again, for the last time. Any funny business, and I am going to drop the whole world on your head, brick by brick."

It was necessary to say goodbye to the sisters and Yarico. "Why are they taking you?" Angelina asked. "Are you under arrest?"

"Sort of," Cynthia said. "Listen, you own all of this now."

"All of what?" Angelina asked.

The house fire had just about burned itself out, but more than half of the magnificent building had been destroyed, and most of the rest was pock-marked with bullet holes, while there was not an unbroken pane of glass. And behind the house the great clouds of black smoke still rose to the skies from the burning fields. "You'll have to put it back together," Cynthia said.

"It'll take years!"

"But wait a minute," Sophie said. "Carlos was a billionaire. All we have to do is get hold of his money. You don't think he's left it all to you, do you, Cynthia?"

"I am sure he has not," Cynthia agreed. "And even if he has, I give it all to you. But . . . there may not be as much as you think."

"Cynthia!" Angelina wailed. "You are coming back to us?"

"I wouldn't hold your breath," Cynthia recommended.

She would have liked to say goodbye to Yarico, but the maid regarded her with hostility. "It is your coming that has caused this catastrophe," she said.

Cynthia didn't suppose she could really argue with that.

* * *

292

From the point of view of any observer, and that included the assault troops, Cynthia really was under arrest, even if she was not handcuffed. Her bedroom having escaped the blaze, she was allowed to pack some clothes, pick up her passport and one or two items of jewellery, then she was flown in a helicopter filled with armed men, but not Tom, across the jungle to their secret base, and was there transferred to a troop carrier for the flight to the States, still without any sign of Tom. She was fed, and given beer to drink, but while the men spent most of the journey staring at her, no one attempted to speak with her – and most of the stares were hostile.

They landed at an airbase in Miami, and two women officers were waiting for her. They were in plainclothes, but exuded authority. "Where are you taking me?" she asked.

"Somewhere safe, Mrs de Sousa."

She wished they'd stop calling her that.

Somewhere safe was a not very salubrious hotel. "One of us will be with you all the time," one of the women told her. "I am Kelly, by the way, and this is Holly."

"I'm Cynthia," Cynthia said.

"You're Mrs de Sousa," Holly reminded her.

Apparently they considered it necessary to keep things in perspective.

The room was small, the bathroom smaller. There was a TV, but Cynthia wasn't interested in TV once she had ascertained that nothing about the raid on Rancho Sousa had reached the media as yet. "Where is Mr Lane?" she asked.

"Around," Kelly told her.

* * *

293

Cynthia spent most of the next twenty-four hours in bed. There wasn't anything else to do, and having got to bed, she discovered how exhausted she was and had been, perhaps ever since that return flight from New York. Security had ended with that flight, now it was back, however uncertain the future, and she felt she could sleep for a week, even if she estimated that she did not have a friend in the world. She couldn't even be sure of Tom. Actually, she realised, she could be sure: he might still have a yen for her, but he regarded her as a criminal as much as anyone. Fuck him, she thought, and awoke with a start to find him standing beside her bed. "Get up, and get dressed," he said.

"Don't you like me the way I am?"

"Get dressed," he said again.

She figured he did. She got up, had a shower, and dressed. When she came out of the bathroom Holly was waiting with a cup of coffee. "What time is it?"

"Breakfast is on its way, Mrs de Sousa."

"Would you wait outside, Sergeant?" Tom requested.

Holly raised her eyebrows.

"I need to speak with her in private." Holly shrugged, and left, noisily seating herself in the corridor. "I've managed to get clearance," Tom said.

"Is that what you've been doing? I thought you'd run out on me."

"However," Tom went on, "the operation has not only to be top secret, but also clandestine. That means we're on our own. If something goes wrong, we could all end up in a Spanish jail, for a very long time."

"So what's new? I seem to have been in some kind of a jail all of my adult life. Mind you, some have been better than others. This dump ranks near the bottom."

"Shut up and concentrate," he told her. "This is the

294

deal, and you must accept all of it, or it's off. We will accompany you to Spain. You will get us in to Eboli, we will do what we have to do there, and then leave. We will then see if we can pick up your son, and get out of the country. Arrangements are being made to facilitate our departure. Right?"

"Wrong," Cynthia said.

"What the hell . . ."

"You have things in reverse order. We pick up Tom first. *Then* I'll get you into Eboli."

He glared at her. "How the hell are we supposed to carry out any kind of operation with a baby in tow?"

"Tom is not a baby. He is five years old. And he's my responsibility. But that's the way it has to be, or there's no deal."

Another glare. Then he said, "Have it your way. But if your son gets hurt, don't blame me."

"Thank you. But I think you meant, our son. Now, you said we. Just how many of us are there going to be?"

"Just three. You, me, and Agent Garcia."

"Garcia?"

"Isn't it the most common of all Spanish surnames? She'll provide additional cover, both as regards the language and the people."

"Meaning you don't trust me."

"Well, would you?"

"Did you say, she?"

"It's a female establishment, isn't it? Full of beautiful women, as I understand it. She'll fit in well, and she's not likely to succumb."

"There are a few men about as well," Cynthia murmured.

Lucia Garcia turned out to be brunette, predictably, and an absolute knock-out, which, Cynthia reflected, was also probably predictable. Lucia was tall, had long, wavy black hair, softly attractive features, and a figure which just about matched Cynthia's own for length of leg and size of bust. Her movements and voice were somewhat languid, but her eyes were not, and Cynthia estimated she knew her business. "Do you sleep with him?" she asked, with apparent innocence.

"Of course I do not," Lucia said indignantly. "He is my boss."

That didn't make sense to Cynthia. "Well, then," she said, "are you going to sleep with me?"

"Of course not," Lucia said more indignantly yet. "On this job we are fellow agents." But she had not said she wouldn't when the job was done, Cynthia reflected. Which suggested that Tom might know more about what went on inside Eboli than she had suspected.

They flew Iberia from Miami International to Madrid, travelling independently. Tom had given Cynthia instructions before leaving the hotel, and when they landed, at eight o'clock local time the following morning, she collected her single bag, refused the help of a porter in obtaining a taxi, and walked round the corner outside the airport complex. There weren't many people about and although everyone who *was* about found her straw hat, golden hair, dark glasses, short skirt and very long legs – made even longer by her high heels – worth a second look, no one attempted to chat her up, and only fifteen minutes later the hired car stopped beside her. "Where's Lucia?" she asked.

"She knows Madrid well. We'll pick her up just out of town."

Lucia had apparently taken a taxi to a predetermined destination, and having dismissed it, was sitting on a bench in front of an apartment building, her bag tucked under her arm. "Thought you guys were never coming," she remarked, languidly.

As Cynthia well remembered, it was a drive of several hours from Madrid to Eboli, and as she had not slept well on the aircraft, she soon dosed off, only properly awakening when they stopped for lunch at a bar-restaurant outside Saragossa. Tom spread a map on the table while they drank their rioja. "Show me the village where your son is living."

"*Our* son is living there." Cynthia prodded the map.

"All on the way. We'll be there in an hour. You'd better stay awake. But we need to make a stop before then."

Cynthia had every intention of staying awake, and she was glad she did when Tom turned off the main road and bumped down a lane. Shades of that taxi-driver four years ago! Only this time there was a car waiting for them, and two men. Tom stopped some distance away, got out, and went towards the men. "Meetings like this make me nervous," Cynthia remarked. "Tell me what's going on."

"It is not possible for us to travel internationally with weapons," Lucia explained. "Unless we have a prior arrangement with the airline. In this case, as we are supposed to be acting entirely on our own, there could be no prior arrangement. So we had to make contact with our local people. They will not know what we are doing either, but Tom has the credentials for receiving weapons."

Cynthia watched Tom walking back towards them, carrying an attaché case. The two men were already driving away. "What have we got?" Lucia asked as Tom got into the car.

He flipped open the lid. "Two Magnums, loaded, twenty-four spare cartridges." He gave her one of the guns and two boxes of bullets, which she stored in her handbag. "Are there more than thirty-six people on Eboli, Cynthia?"

"Not at my last count. But surely you don't mean to shoot everyone there? I didn't bargain for that."

"I hope we do not have to shoot anyone there. I just need to know we have enough fire power to do the job, in case they try to shoot us."

"And you figure one shot a head, right?"

"Well," Tom said, modestly, "we're professionals."

Cynthia looked at Lucia, who winked. "And what about me?" Cynthia asked. "Suppose someone decides to shoot at me?"

"Do you know how to handle a pistol?"

"Well . . . it can't be very different to a Kalashnikov. I was quite good with a Kalashnikov."

"Anybody can be good with a Kalashnikov," Tom pointed out. "That is why they're so popular. We'll protect you." He started the engine.

Cynthia supposed she would have to be content with that, and she remembered that guns hadn't been much in evidence on Eboli, although she did not doubt they were there. In any event, she was more concerned with little Tom, and an hour later they were in familiar territory. Her heart was pounding as she directed Tom down the side street of the little village. If it was only just over a month since last she had seen their son, it seemed like an eternity. "There's the house!" she cried.

The car drew to a halt, and Cynthia got out. Tom and Lucia got out as well, but remained standing by the car, while Cynthia knocked on the door. "Senora Lopez?" she said. "I've come for Tom."

"But, senorita," Senora Lopez said. "He is not here."

"Not here? What do you mean?"

"Senora Mayne, she came down here, oh, four weeks ago, and took him away. She said that you were not coming back to Spain, senorita, and that she needed to make other arrangements for the boy. I was heart-broken, senorita, but what could I do?"

Four weeks ago? Cynthia thought. That was just after she had left for Bolivia with Carlos. Mayne had known even then she wasn't coming back, one way or the other. The two-faced bitch, coming to her wedding as if she had been taken entirely by surprise, discussing the possibility of having little Tom out there . . . but of course, Mayne was so close to Carlos she would have known all about the murder of Janine. The bitch! She wondered if Carlos had known about little Tom, all along?

But even before then, she had . . . Cynthia stared at the embarrassed woman. "But how could Senora Mayne take Tom away? He is your legal son."

"No, no, senorita. The papers were never completed. Senora Mayne merely told me that I must keep Tom until she decided what to do with him."

While all the time leaving *her* believing that her son had been legally adopted! Cynthia felt her blood beginning to boil. But she kept her voice even. "Well, thanks for everything, Senora Lopez. I assume you have been well paid?"

"Oh, yes, senorita."

Cynthia returned to the car. "Are you sure you don't have another gun?" she asked Tom.

"How exactly are you going to get us in?" Tom asked.

"By ringing the bell." They both turned their heads to stare at her. "The news of what happened in Bolivia hasn't been released yet, right?" she asked.

299

"It won't be long delayed now. We smashed all their radios, and their planes, but people will have seen the fires and started to investigate."

"It's now we're talking about. I am returning, bringing with me a prospective recruit." She smiled at Lucia, who gulped. "That we have a driver will seem natural."

"Wait a moment," Tom said. "Both Mayne and the woman she had with her have seen me."

"Denise," Cynthia said. "She's dangerous. That's why you'll have to go into action the moment you're in. But Tom . . ." she rested her hand on his arm. "I wouldn't like any of the girls to be killed. Or Madeleine and Denise?"

"What about Mayne?"

"Be my guest. But only after we've got Tom."

It was late afternoon when they began the drive up to the castle. "Some spread," Lucia remarked.

By then Tom had elicited from Cynthia all the information he thought he might need regarding the internal arrangements at the castle, and had worked out how he intended to handle it. The two women had also received their instructions. Now he braked before the huge gates, and Cynthia got out and rang the bell. "Who is there?" It was her old friend Miguel.

"Cynthia."

"Cynthia? Senorita? But you are in South America!"

"If I am, this must be thought transference. Listen, tell Senora Mayne that I have come home, and that I have someone very interesting with me."

There was a brief silence. "Is this going to work?" Tom asked.

"Guaranteed."

"Senorita," Miguel said, having referred to higher

300

authority. "Bring your companion and stand before the camera."

As Cynthia had calculated, no reference was made to the driver. She beckoned Lucia, who got out of the car and joined her before the closed-circuit televison camera. "What are you doing here, Cynthia?" Mayne asked.

"It's a long story."

"And who is that?"

"Her name is Lucia, and she's a recruit."

There was another silence, while Mayne was obviously studying the TV picture. Then she said, "You'd better come up. Miguel is on his way."

Cynthia and Lucia got back into the car, and a few minutes later they heard the sound of Miguel's scooter. Then the gates swung in, and Tom drove through. "Straight up to the castle," Cynthia said.

Tom drove up the winding drive, and the castle emerged before them. "Some *spread*!" Lucia said again.

Tom braked before the front doors, where the girls had gathered, as when Cynthia had returned from Karnah. With them were Madeleine and Denise, but again as before, not Mayne. There were also three of the menservants present, which Cynthia knew was only about a quarter of the staff available, with Miguel no doubt coming up the drive behind them on his scooter. But at this moment, only Denise mattered: it was essential for her to reach Mayne, and get little Tom, before big Tom went into action.

She was first out of the car, hugging and kissing them all in turn. She kept Denise to the last. Lucia also got out, standing with apparent shyness by the car. "Cynthia," Madeleine said. "You do the most amazing things." Madeleine was nervous. But then, she had to know about little Tom, so Cynthia could understand that.

301

"What's amazing about it?" she asked. "That thug de Sousa threw me out, so I came home."

"But . . ." Madeleine was puzzled. "You're his wife!"

"He still threw me out. Listen, I have to speak to Mayne about this. And introduce her to Lucia. Come here, Lucia." Lucia advanced, hesitantly.

"How much do you owe the driver?" Denise asked, taking Cynthia in her arms to hold her close.

"I've paid him. But I have some bags, and so does Lucia. Is it all right if he goes round to the servants' entrance?"

"Of course. Fernando, show the driver where to unload the bags."

Cynthia gave Tom his instructions in Spanish, a phrase she had had him rehearse, and he replied, "Si, senorita," and waited for Fernando to get in beside him. The other girls were making Lucia's acquaintance.

"Where did you find her, Cynthia?" Madeleine asked.

"In South America," Cynthia said. "Is Mayne around?" They were running out of time.

"She's waiting for you." Both Madeleine and Denise accompanied Cynthia and Lucia into the women's quarters, Lucia continuing to be audibly impressed by her surroundings, but to Cynthia's great relief, only Madeleine accompanied them up in the elevator to Mayne's apartment. "I don't know what she is going to say, at your so unexpected return," Madeleine confessed. "We had supposed that you were settled for life."

"So had I," Cynthia said, not entirely untruthfully.

They reached the penthouse floor, and Madeleine led them across the lobby to knock on the door. This she then opened, and showed them into Mayne's office. Mayne was seated behind her desk, having been watching what had been happening downstairs on her television monitor.

"Why, Cynthia," she remarked coolly. "What on earth are you doing here?"

"I'm a widow," Cynthia told her.

Madeleine gasped, and Mayne frowned, then both their heads turned to Lucia, who had drawn her huge revolver from her handbag, and was pointing it at them, holding it in both hands. "Just don't over-react," she recommended quietly.

"Are you out of your tiny mind?" Mayne enquired, not specifying which of them she was speaking to, but moving her right hand, very quickly, to slide it beneath the desk.

Lucia saw the movement, and fired. It sounded like a cannon going off in the confined space, and the top of the desk seemed to explode as laminated wood flew in every direction. Mayne gave a shriek, and hurled herself backwards with such vigour that she overbalanced in her chair and went sprawling on the floor. Madeleine also shrieked and stood against the wall as if plastered to it. "Jesus," Cynthia muttered.

Lucia moved forward to check the underside of the desk. "Just a panic button," she said. "Who would she have been trying to summon?"

"Everyone?" Cynthia suggested.

Mayne was sitting up now, drawing up her legs to propel herself against the wall. "Do you think you can get away with this?" she demanded.

The door opened, and Tom stepped inside. "Always ride to the sound of the guns," he remarked.

"You!" Mayne spat at him.

Tom ignored her to look right and left. "Where's the boy?"

"That I am about to find out." Cynthia knelt beside Mayne. "I want Tom."

303

"You'll never get him," Mayne said. "Denise . . ." she bit her lip.

Cynthia stood up. "She's all yours."

"You ungrateful little bitch!" Mayne snarled. "You . . ."

Tom knelt beside her in turn, while Lucia kept her gun pointing at Madeleine. "We want to look inside your safe," he said. "Are you going to show us where it is, and then open it for us? Or are we going to tear this place apart to find it?

"You bastard," Mayne said.

Cynthia left them at it, went outside, and used the stairs rather than the elevator to reach Denise's apartment. As she went down she heard the lift going up, but she didn't doubt Tom and Lucia could deal with the help; they were, as Tom had boasted, professionals.

She reached the next floor, ran along the corridor, and tried Denise's door. It was actually open; Denise had equally presumed that Mayne could deal with anything *she* might try.

She pushed the door away from her, and stepped inside. Denise sat on the sofa, watching little Tom, who sat in front of the television playing an action game. She looked up, and he looked round, at the interruption. "It's that nice pretty lady," Tom remarked.

Denise stood up. "All I want is the boy," Cynthia said. "So help me pack up his things, and we'll be away."

"I'm sorry, Cyn," Denise said. "I'm under instructions from Mayne to kill him before I let you take him."

"Why?"

Denise shrugged. "I think she knows how much you hate her, and she regards him as her insurance policy."

"Well, I can tell you that she is now out of business," Cynthia said. "So you can forget her instructions."

304

"I'm sorry," Denise said again, and stood up. "I'll have to hear that from her."

"Denise," Cynthia said earnestly, "I don't want to have to hurt you."

Denise laughed. "Hurt *me*? Cyn, I taught you everything you know."

"Correction," Cynthia said. "You taught me everything *you* know."

Denise frowned, and then moved forward at full speed, hands held rigid as she sought to deliver the first blow. Cynthia jumped to one side, turning as she did so, moving up behind her old friend before Denise could react and slapping her hands together with all her strength over Denise's ears. Denise gave a scream of the purest agony, and fell to her knees. Little Tom also gave a scream, and scrambled out of his chair to stand against the wall.

Cynthia stood above Denise and kicked her in the kidneys. Denise gasped and fell over, and Cynthia kicked her in the stomach. Denise gasped again and her body arched. Cynthia grasped her by the collar of her blouse and dragged her up to a kneeling position. Vainly Denise struck behind her; the flat of the hand scythed into Cynthia's calf but there was not sufficient power in the blow – blood was dribbling from Denise's nose. Cynthia held her hair and jerked her head backwards, brought her own hand down in a hard edge into Denise's throat. Denise collapsed at her feet.

Little Tom stared at the woman. "Is she dead?" he asked.

Cynthia knelt beside her, heard Denise reaching for breath. "No," she said. She was glad about that, because when she had actually been fighting she had wanted to kill her. "But she'll have a pain. Or two."

"She was my friend," Tom said.

305

"I know, darling. I'm sorry. But I am your mother," Cynthia told him. "Let's go pack."

Cynthia had no idea what was happening in the rest of the house, but she knew she had to hurry. She crammed the more important of Tom's clothes into a bag; he didn't want to leave his video games, but she promised to replace them, when they got to . . . wherever they were going; she actually had no idea. By now there were odd sounds coming from all over the castle, including some firing, as well as a good deal of shouting. Cynthia reckoned she could do with some help, and hunted through Denise's drawers and bureaux. By now Denise was showing some signs of life, groaning and gasping as she regained consciousness, but Cynthia didn't reckon she would be a threat again for a considerable time. And soon she found what she was looking for, a small Walther automatic pistol, with a clip of five bullets. There was another clip in the drawer, and this Cynthia put in her pocket. Tom watched her with enormous eyes. "Are you going to shoot someone?" he asked.

"If I have to." She picked up his carryall. "Hang on to this at all times," she told him. Then she stood above Denise. "You'll need to rest for a few hours," she said. "I truly am sorry, Denise. You backed the wrong horse."

She stepped into the corridor, wondered where Tom and Lucia were, and saw them, a moment later, coming towards her from the stairwell. Tom carried a large valise. "Got what you wanted?" Cynthia asked.

"Enough. And I see you got what you wanted."

"You could say hello to him," Cynthia suggested. "Tom, this is your daddy."

There was a moment's silence, Tom knelt beside his son. "Hi."

"Have you been shooting people?" Tom asked.

"Ah . . . we'll talk about it later. When we get out of here." But to Cynthia's delight, he scooped the boy from the floor and held him in his arms.

"What exactly are we facing?" she asked.

"You tell us," Lucia said. "A couple of guys came up in the lift, blasting away, so we had to take care of them."

Cynthia swallowed. "Just like that?"

"Shit, Cyn, we're not here for our health."

"What happened to Mayne? And Madeleine?"

"We tied them up."

"Thank God for that." She really would have hated Madeleine to be hurt.

Lucia was looking into Denise's apartment, at Denise. "She don't look dead to me." Denise was trying to get up; blood still trickled from her nostrils.

"She needs a doctor," Cynthia said. "But we'll have to organise that later. Right. How many men did you deal with on the way up, Tom?"

"Two."

"That leaves a possible eight, and the girls. But the girls won't cause trouble."

"You sure about that?"

"Yes. Where's the car?"

"Outside the back."

"Then let's get down there." They looked at each other. "You keep Tom," she said. "I'll carry your case."

She took it from his hand, humped little Tom's carryall over her shoulder, and held the pistol in her right hand. Then she went for the stairs, the others following her. They were surrounded by noise, shouts and screams, and the sound of the elevator going up and down. Obviously it

307

would be clear to everyone they were not in the elevator. The question facing the opposition was where on the stairs to attempt to stop them. If they were going to attempt to do so at all. But by now presumably Mayne and Madeleine were being released, and ready to take charge of their pursuit.

They reached the ground level, panting. "We're going to be exposed as we cross the pool area," Cynthia told them. "So we have to move it, right?"

"One at a time," Tom said.

"Right. You go first."

"No," Tom said. "Lucia, you go first, and give us covering fire."

Lucia nodded, took a deep breath, and sprinted across the patio beside the pool. As she reached the other side, the door in the front part of the house opened, and one of the servants stepped out. He carried a gun but was unprepared for Lucia, who shot him while she was still moving. He hit the floor without a sound. But the noise of the shot echoed into the night. Windows opened above them, shrill voices shouted, and there were shouts from inside the house as well. "Go, man, go," Cynthia snapped.

She was more concerned about her son than Tom. But Tom obeyed her, running to where Lucia was standing in the doorway, looking both ways, and firing again, at someone inside the front building. "There they are!" Mayne shouted from above them. "Stop them."

There came the crack of another shot, this time from above them; there was a man still on the roof. The bullet smashed into the patio only inches from where Tom and the child had been a few moments before. Now it was Cynthia's turn to take a deep breath and race across the exposed space. She never heard the shots fired at her, but

308

she did hear the crump of the bullets hitting the patio, and her legs were stung by the flying concrete splinters. But now Lucia was returning fire, pausing only to reload her weapon.

Her earlier shots had driven the remaining menservants to shelter, but they were going to have to be further discouraged if they were going to reach the car. "I'd better lead this time," Tom decided. "Give me back the suitcase, and you take little Tom."

Cynthia nodded, and took the terrified child into her arms. And was then checked by a shout. "Cynthia!"

She turned. "Ignore it," Tom recommended.

"But that was Madeleine," she said. "What is it?" she called.

"It is over," Madeleine shouted. "We surrender."

"Eh?" Tom asked.

"It has to be a trap," Lucia said.

"Listen," Madeleine shouted. "Mayne is dead." The three of them looked at each other in consternation. "She's had a heart attack," Madeleine called. "Just like her mother."

"Does she expect us to believe that?" Tom asked.

"All right," Cynthia shouted. "If it's genuine, call your servants to come out and surrender."

"I'll use the phone," Madeleine said.

"What do we do?" Tom asked.

"Wait."

"I still think it's a trick," Lucia said.

"Not if Mayne is dead."

They heard sounds in the front house, and levelled their pistols. But a moment later the male staff filed past them, unarmed, while the man on the roof came down. "Out there on the patio," Cynthia said. "Where we can see you."

309

"And shoot you, if we feel like it," Lucia reminded them. The men obeyed, lined up by the pool.

"You come down, Madeleine," Cynthia called. "And bring the girls."

They emerged a few minutes later. "Where is Denise?" Madeleine asked.

"In her room. After we leave, you get a doctor to her, and she'll probably be all right."

"What is going to happen to us?" Rona asked.

"That's up to you. But if I were you, I'd make tracks; we have enough evidence of money-laundering here to make the Spanish government very interested in Eboli. Madeleine, you come down with us to the car. You're our safe conduct." Cynthia looked at the other girls. "I'll say goodbye, it's been fun. Just remember, if anyone attempts to stop us getting out of here, Madeleine gets it. And then we'll come back up and deal with the rest of you." They went to the car.

"When Mayne extracted you from the Turkish prison, she started something she couldn't finish," Madeleine said.

"I'm sorry, for you."

Tom drove down the hill to the gates, and Cynthia told him the light signal to open them. "You can get out here," she told Madeleine.

Madeleine got out. "Don't be sorry for me," she said. "I wouldn't have missed a moment of it. Any of it."

Cynthia got out of the car and kissed the old woman. "Take care," she said. "There's enough left for you to survive, someplace else."

Tom turned north. "There's a plane waiting for us, at a private strip close to here," he said.

"I know it well," Cynthia said. "Where is this plane going to take us?"

"Back to the States. You're still our star witness."

"Will I be able to keep Tom with me?"

"Well, yes, of course." He glanced at her and the little boy seated on her lap, his hands still covering his small face. "I reckon he needs a lot of rehabilitating."

"I know," she agreed. "Wouldn't you say it's a job for two people?"